VIA FOLIOS 113

Visits

Visits

Helen Barolini

BORDIGHERA PRESS

Library of Congress Control Number: 2015937925

COVER ART: Mario Micossi
"SHADY LANE FARM" (1962)

Printed in the United States.

Published by
BORDIGHERA PRESS
John D. Calandra Italian American Institute
25 West 43rd Street, 17th Floor
New York, NY 10036

VIA FOLIOS 113
ISBN 978-1-59954-092-4

For

My Grandchildren

TABLE OF CONTENTS

VISITS

Just before the visit to my mother on her seventy-ninth birthday, I dreamt in a different way of the house where I had lived with my husband and our three daughters. Dreaming of my house had always been soothing, like the somnolent replay of an old favorite movie. This time it was a nightmare.

The house had been a barn. It had originally been lived in by an illustrious composer. My husband was Marco, a poet. He died. The summer of my mother's seventy-ninth birthday I was about to marry Max, a businessman.

I loved my house. The clean lines of the barn it had once been were the essential me: stripped to bare form, without adornment and claptrap. The structure itself was a giant box where all was safely contained. Living there, in that golden period with Marco and the three girls, I thought I would eventually come to see and know my own outline as well as I knew the pure shape of the house. I would shed the critical style and the embittering judgments I had grown up with in my parents' house. I would form a new House, new lineage. I would be ennobled.

It wasn't so easy. The simple look of the house was deceiving; inside it some wildness of the composer's dissonant notes was embedded in the wood paneled walls, in the colossal ceiling beams, in the too-dramatic space and height of the great room; he had put something unruly within the very order and form of the barn-box. And it was all there in the way the house shivered and creaked when the wind blew hard, like a ship tossed on turbulent waves.

Nonetheless, in my usual dream the house was reassuring: so foursquare, elemental, basic, and linear, yet imbued with something different and rare. It was all I had ever wanted. It was the container that promised everything.

And I was never so safe as when I lived there.

In my nightmare, I see the white frame house on its height, shaded by trees and garlanded with an ancient wisteria that twined over the porch. I am walking up the country lane towards home, and I can glimpse it through leaves, now more now less, as my walk progresses and I get different sightings. The leafy branches of the grand copper beech at the end of the drive provide a discontinuous but lovely frame to the house. Yet as I get closer I hear moaning and the eerie sound gives me gooseflesh. I feel chilled and uneasy. It is not the wind. There is no wind. It is a summer day, but something disturbing is in the house and, apprehensive, I hear it moan.

Suddenly from the walls spectres and writhing monsters burst forth, and they shriek around me, pulling me towards the house. We are your past, they shriek. I am terrified. We play a different tune! they clamor raucously. No more sweetness and light! No more have your cake, and eat it too! And in their gyrations and shadows I see my dissatisfactions, my reserve towards Marco, the children. I see a distortion of Marco at his desk while the demons flock around him, belaboring him and he screams, let me have my work! And I am nearby, pregnant, wringing my hands and crying, I want my life! Mamma, papà, do you love us? scream the children, hopping and jumping anxiously, darting around us to get our attention. And we set at each other, not at the demons. We pull and pummel and separate each other. The house gets bloated and contorts, its plain lines are gone. It is no longer a pure container, but a mishappen mass of bulges and protuberances, heaving and growing like yeast dough run amuck and unable to be punched back in place.

The house is against us, I scream. It's gone crazy! I look wildly at Marco, at Chessie and Dee and Winnie – have we done this? As in the tale of the wicked sisters whose utterances came out as toads and lizards and repulsive things from their mouths, I saw my ugly kept-down thoughts issuing forth: I resented Marco, resented our daughters. They look accusingly at me, I at them. We are at each other's mercy.

That incubus woke me with my heart beating in great heaves.

It was frightening. It reminded me of my father's anger at us when he'd lash out, "If it weren't for the goddam bunch of you, I'd be in California now!" Knowing how terrified I had been as a child seeing my mother weep at his fury, why would I do the same towards Marco and the children? I tossed restlessly unable to sleep and finally got up to take a sleeping pill. I overslept the next morning, past when we were to leave, and it was late when, with my youngest daughter, Winnie, I set out for my mother's in Ferryville. In the car I told Winnie about my nightmare.

"I have nightmeers, too, Mom," she said.

And that unconscious and endearing use of her baby word solaced me.

CHAPTER ONE

I was glad, that late-summer day, to have more reason than my mother's birthday to drive from Boston to Ferryville, a river town on the Hudson some fifteen miles from New York. What salvaged the trip was dropping off Winnie's things at the freshman dorm of her nearby college. Not that I didn't have a very special gift for my mother. I had bought her an antique Chinese pin at Gump's in San Francisco when I was there with Max in the spring; and I had the news, although I didn't yet know how to say it, that I was going to marry Max.

"Aschermann? Max Aschermann? What's that, Jewish?" she asked during her weekly call when I first mentioned I was seeing him. Oh Christ, I thought. I had somehow trusted she'd skip the comment, so glad would she be for me. No matter. It was not Max's Jewishness that might be trouble, but his drinking and that not even my prescient mother could discover by long distance.

While I drove, Winnie was embroidering a flamboyant, multi-colored bird onto a tee-shirt as a gift for her grandmother. My mother was still an active golfer and in excellent health.

"Watch out," I told Max Aschermann. "I come from a line of women who are not only good looking but also very long-lived — the persistent peasant kind."

"I can handle it," he replied.

He could. I am the one who has trouble handling things, like home visits. My uneasiness with my Sturzo family seems to collide head-on with my everlasting longing still to be part of it. It's as if I carry with me, each time I go, all the stuff of unresolved issues and old grievances, like baggage that's never unpacked but that's full and at the ready, if ever I'm asked to take out my things and stay awhile. Then what pleasant, fair-weather outfits I'd put on! But the prevailing chill never changes for the better; I never unpack.

It was August. Between helping Winnie get ready for college, and spending time with Max on the Cape, I saw the summer slip by. The short trip to Ferryville would be the last interruption of my work; it was also a respite from Max, from his daily calls and discussion of our plans, our future, our "relationship" — his term, and one I didn't like.

I had forgotten the amount of time the draw and pull of attraction between a man and woman could absorb. Since Marco's death the two older girls, Chessie and Dee, had settled into their own lives and I had become used to my life with Winnie. I had my work. Then, with Max, whole blocks of time were suddenly fragmented into particles which I tried futilely to snatch at and put back together for myself while he demanded more and more. It was a problem.

Max was very different from Marco. What do you see in him? everyone asked, amused at the pair of us. But I knew how to reel off our accomplishments: we play tennis, bike, go to the Cape, eat and dance, make love, travel; we're the same age and we look and feel good together. Why did they ask? *They* had partners. Why did they wonder that I wanted one, too.

Winnie groaned, threw the tee-shirt on the dashboard and clenched her fists. "I hate these trips," she said vehemently. "Why do we have to go to Ferryville? We were just there."

"That was Easter."

"Whatever! These trips are a drag. I'm carsick."

Each time we made the trip, Winnie fussed, prey to her conflicted feelings. Even though she scoffed at the solidity and sameness of all the Sturzos in Ferryville, once in her grandparents' home, she glowed with well-being in the familiar, roomy house where her aunts and uncles and cousins came and went and there was always good food and a third floor room and bath of her own with television. This is Disneyland North, she hooted, loving it. Winnie's home dissolved when her father died and I sold our house. I knew (because it was the same for me) that Winnie's resistance to Ferryville was that it made too clear the precariousness of our own lives.

"Mo—o—other! This is such a fucking drag!" Winnie was pounding her fists on the dashboard. "Why the fuck couldn't you drive down with your boyfriend?" She startled me and I didn't like what I heard. I gripped the wheel hard, not wanting to react to her.

"How can you stand to leave him?" Winnie taunted. "He's just trying to buy you, anyway," she muttered.

Great! she had said when I told her Max and I were thinking of getting married. Marry him! Then I won't have to worry about you anymore! You'll have someone else to smother and I'll be out of your life for good when I start college.

I wanted to say, No, Honey, I need you too, not just Max, but I couldn't.

That was going through my mind as I drove some miles in silence. Then I turned towards Winnie to say, "Don't talk that way about Max." And when I looked at her, I felt such a pang of tenderness at her beautiful young face which combines both me and Marco in something fresh and new so that while resembling us both, she is neither, that I laughed aloud, and she did, too. Like me, Winnie's skin is fair and her eyes grey-green; she has Marco's wonderful Italian hair though not as dark nor as curling; she has his expressive face and his ease with humankind.

I could understand Winnie's tremors at being replaced by the new presence of Max Aschermann in our lives. "Don't worry," I told her, "it will turn out all right."

Driving through the wooded corridor of the Merritt Parkway I watched for the different art deco designs on each of the overpass bridges, while Winnie turned the radio on to a rock music station and took up the embroidery again. I was a child of that art deco era. I thought, what is it that cleaves people from one another? Why are we not as simple as the countryside? As fixed and recurring as art deco landmarks? I had not felt alone in the years after Marco's death, because of Winnie. And then Winnie started drawing away and I felt alone. Now there was Max in my life, and Winnie felt left out.

So let her talk, I thought. Talking was better than not talking. At her age I seldom spoke. I can still feel the silence of the dinner table where we sat each night with our taciturn father setting the mood, wrapped in apprehension over whether he'd like the food or would explode at mother. There was no conversation. He liked to eat in peace, he said.

At most he would admonish us to do as he did, to tear out the soft part of the loaf of Italian bread that was on our table each night, and eat only the crust, saying, That soft stuff's no good. I'd ask why. Because I say so, came the answer.

If my father's manner was curt, his cold eye cast silently and searingly on any of us was worse. It meant, I wither you with my contempt; I shrivel you to nothing, I expunge you. His silence seemed to me to be wishing us away, off his back, so that he could be free to take off for California.

He told a strange story: how the old *comari* said his birthday on Christmas was bad luck because he was taking the Saviour's place of honor. But he only laughed and said the bad luck was that he got one gift instead of two, and he was lucky if he got even that. "Those were bad times," he said shaking his head. And he mocked the old people. He wasn't like them, he was for progress. But in my childhood that story worried me. Wonder if he were born under a curse? — would we get it, too? I thought again of my nightmare.

Maybe it was to keep my father's look from me that I was so silent, and kept my thoughts hidden. What good training it was for becoming Marco's translator! Being not the voice itself, but the invisible sounding box letting Marco be heard while I was literally lost in the translation. And now I am an editor, the enabler of others' words, not mine.

With Marco I kept a different table. We always talked at dinner, and the girls were able to speak of anything, to hold their own views, to agree or not. Chessie, the eldest, was impassioned and outspoken, determined to be right and skilled at overpowering us with torrents of words. She's now married to Jules who is equally skilled in the same way. A middle child, Dee was slyer and more selective; if she held strong opinions, she held them close to her until she took them and herself to Italy (in search of her lost father, I've always thought), where she married. Winnie was just beginning to find her words.

In their different ways, they have turned their words on me, the surviving parent and I can't always answer the daughters I taught to speak.

As ye sow, so shall ye reap: that's my father's saying for what he calls his philosophy of life. He used to aim it at my mother as if she alone were responsible for us, and that bitter phrase hung over our childhood, marking me, my brother and sister, as blighted, failed seeds.

Time puts everything right, was my mother's saying. She could have been Mrs. Mollify: the part she played was never to stand up to issues but to play them down, appease, side-step, smile, cry, dissemble, duck, deny, complain, criticize. She was always giving in and crying. At some point I realized how appropriately her name Addolorata, for the Virgin of Sorrows, fitted one side of her nature just as Dolly, her nickname, fitted the perennial child side.

Names are important, Marco always said. Our three girls were named traditionally for family women: Chessie is Francesca after my grandmother for whom I was called Frances; Dee is short for Dolores, an acceptable variant of the too Southern Italian (for Marco) Addolorata; and Winnie is Lavinia, in memory of Marco's mother. You sure go in for wop names, my brother Gussie told me once. He is Augustine, Jr. after our father, who was named for his mother Agostina.

As ye sow, so shall ye reap.

Closer to the New York area, the Merritt Parkway funneled into the Cross County Expressway. The scene accelerated into one of highway interchanges and the industrial parks near White Plains. The trees and space I remembered from childhood were transformed; a few blanched, grasping limbs of dead elms stood out ominously. Those ghosts matched the sadness I always felt in going home. I loved the idea of welcoming family, but it was only an abstraction never a fact.

"If this country valued trees and life as much as it does business, we wouldn't have pollution and the diminished ozone-layer we have today," I said aloud, suddenly furious.

"Really," Winnie responded absently, tapping her fingers on the dashboard to the rhythm of the rock.

When I pulled into the driveway of the fieldstone Normandy house, my mother came out the front door waving and smiling. She was wearing a pink skirt, a floral blouse tied in a big bow at the neckline, and bold button earrings. She looked amiable and well groomed, younger than her age, her white hair well cut, her skin good.

The house, too, flanked by flower beds and with urns of geraniums on the front terrace, looked as trim and cheerful as Dolly Sturzo, and yet, like my mother's smile, there was something wrong in the setting. Falseness lurked there. My father had moved us to that house on the hill when I was around twelve and Gussie a year and a half younger. Adele was born after the move and I associate my sister with the Normandy house. We have never been close. My father made money in his contracting business during the war years, and my mother, always dissatisfied to be so near the in-laws and people she called backward, said it was time to leave lower Main Street for a better neighborhood.

But I had loved my old home in the Building where my early life mingled with my cousins' lives and that of the other children on the street, where there was the library to walk to at the upper end of Main, and the river nearby, and in between all the shops and street life that fed my imagination.

The swells of Ferryville lived up on the hill, apart from the village center. Our Norman house, with its casement windows, peaked chateau towers, slate roof, and ivied archways, was my mother's idea of both progress and romance. She must have imagined that moving up the hill to live in such a house could change us all. Dolly Sturzo as Willy Loman: we must be fine people, we live in a fine house.

Each house on the hill was separated from others by its protective ruff of shrubs and trees. There were no sidewalks, no strollers, no children playing hopscotch or jump rope. No one called from windows to the street below; no one sat out near the roadway. The only walkers on the hill were yard-men, silent as shadows, who kept hedges trimmed, lawns mowed, and plantings seasonal.

"How are you honey girl!" my mother, coming down the front steps and opening her arms, was calling to Winnie. She hugged Winnie to her tightly, then stood back. "Let me see you!"

"Hiya, Nonna," Winnie beamed, delighted to be in her grandmother's embrace, soaking up the warmth of that generous nature, the comfortable girth of her grandmother's roundness. I stood by, waiting to be noticed, watching my mother and daughter together. Winnie is social, like Marco and the Briciola family on my mother's side. I'm of the dour, undemonstrative Sicilian Sturzos — quiet, brooding, misunderstood except in their power. (I said this to Max once and he didn't know what I was talking about.) I had begun both to envy my mother and to mistrust her. She had stayed accessible and in touch with Chessie and Dee who both had once scorned her materialism and reactionary politics, but now seemed to have more to relate to her than to me. I was amazed at my mother's ability to create warm feelings and bad all at once. She projected warmth, whether she meant it or not, and under that cover secured loyalty in almost everyone. I remained skeptical. She was coming between Chessie and me.

"You don't look so good," my mother said, scanning me over Winnie's head. "There are lines under your eyes."

"I didn't sleep well last night — I even had a nightmare." I laughed, trying to dismiss it.

"What have you done to your hair? Are you wearing that outfit tonight?" Then turning back to Winnie and smiling, she coaxed, "Come on in, honey, I have cookies and iced tea for you."

"Nonna, I knew you would," Winnie laughed. "That's why I came — and to get some of your 1920's dresses in the attic for my college wardrobe."

"*Faccia tostella!*" my mother squawked in mock outrage, actually delighted as she tweaked Winnie's cheek. "You rascal! — are you trying to make me seem dated?"

"That's easy, nonna, I always remember your age."

Squealing with pretended horror, she turned from Winnie and kissed me quickly on the cheek. "I didn't know what time you'd get here." she said.

I frowned, annoyed already at the familiar misstating. "I'm here when I said I'd be," I began.

But she was not listening. "I thought," she went on, "I'd go to the market and get the corn before you arrived. But when I was hurrying out to the car, I fell in the driveway and scraped myself. So I took that as a sign to stay put. We can drive to the market together after you get your things in the house."

As she spoke, she raised her arm and revealed a bruised and bloodied underside. Her age showed in flesh that hung in loose wattles and was crepey with thin lines. I was shocked at the thought of her falling on the level, paved driveway for no reason. It made her finally seem aged and vulnerable. Yet I knew she had taken over the care of her old friend Ethel Schotter and was exercising power of attorney for Ethel. She had even taken over much of the household management from my father, thus totally reversing my childhood images of them. And though she was now turning into the stronger one of the two, it gave me a feeling of how uncertain everything was as I stared at her bruised arm. It filled me with feelings I wished I could express.

"I have a gift for you," I said.

"Now you know I don't have birthdays!" she chided. Leading us in from the terrace to the breakfast room, she busied herself around the table, putting out plates, a pitcher of ice tea, and a tray of cookies, lemon and sugar, until I said, "Mother, please sit down."

Winnie, holding the embroidered bird tee-shirt up to her own chest went, "Ta-dah! Here you are, Nonna, burn up the golf-course!"

"For me?" she laughed, pleased, "Winnie, *you* did this gorgeous embroidery? all by hand?"

"I have something special, too." I handed her the Gump's box.

"My goodness," she said as she opened it, adding flatly, "Oh, a pin. I'll have to give you something for it."

I frowned. "Now what does *that* mean?"

"It's bad luck," my mother told me matter-of-factly, "to get anything with a sharp point — like a knife or a brooch — unless you take the bad luck off by giving something in return."

"Hey, Nonna, that's cool," said Winnie, "just like the gypsies or something."

I was too astonished to speak. With anyone else I might have been intrigued by this old-world superstition and found it charming rather than taking it personally; but there's too long a history of my gifts being rejected by her. I watched her get up to find her purse. "Here," she said, giving me a coin. I looked at the nickel in my hand. Bad luck, that beautiful pin? Max had said, She's got to love this.

Nothing satisfied her. Certainly I didn't. Why can't you be more into things the way Yvonne Schotter is instead of always going off with your nose in a book? came the echo of her voice from long ago.

And I hadn't known then that the answer was because I was Fran and not Yvonne. I hadn't yet figured out that what my mother was voicing was her own most compelling wish — not to be who she and my father were, but otherwise; to rub out their despised origins and advance into America and something better.

In the new house I had made the attic my place. It was dim and carelessly crammed with the leftovers of our lives. A barrel under the eaves held business records, school papers, report cards, and photograph albums. The cedar closet was filled with my mother's outdated wardrobe while a trunk held layers of old-fashioned Italian trousseau linens. Propped in a corner was the oval gilt-framed picture of Agostina Sturzo, the dark-visaged Sicilian with the strong square face who was my father's mother and who had died young. Except for my father, none of us had ever known her. Near her were other family pictures including my baby one: round eyes agog in a round face. I'm looking out at the world from inside myself as if I'm in some other dimension. It's still that way.

As my old world of lower Main Street receded and adolescence filled me with worry so that the question of who I really was became ever more tenuous, I found some answer in the attic: I am that baby wondering. I am the melancholy Sicilian. I could not imagine my strong-faced grandmother crying, or placating a husband as my mother did. Agostina looked imperious, stern, a look I have seen in my daughter Chessie. Agostina seemed by her presence at the top of the house to be some kind of divinity presiding over all our lives as she had my father's.

An old cabinet radio, left over from the old place on Lower Main Street and not good enough, now, for downstairs, kept me company in the attic. I listened to "Invitation to Learning" and Texaco's broadcasts of the Saturday matinee from the Metropolitan

Opera House in New York. I loved the names I heard — Aristotle, Bacon, Mascagni, Dante, Nietzsche, Verdi, Mozart, Thucydides. I heard Mr. Lyman Bryson and his guests discuss great ideas; I listened to Milton Cross summarize the operas. When I wasn't listening to the radio, I was reading.

Now and then I would look up from a book and see the brooding face of my Sturzo grandmother. She was handsome but her look was dark, archaic: some bitter knowledge filled it, tied it to a different world from ours, a world in which lives were set in place before people were even born. The look said, Despite their Country Club and Rotary Club, Gus and Dolly Sturzo still go by the old way. That's what they mean when they say, you children owe us respect. It was in the attic, with opera libretti and phonograph records, that I taught myself Italian — a language not offered in the Ferryville schools and not considered important in my family. In college I went on to major in Italian and discovered the work of the contemporary poet Marco Beniferro. I wrote to him in Italy in my careful Italian. We met when he came to the states on a reading tour; I was a recent college graduate, he was forty. We married. We went to live first in Italy, then in Medwood in our barn-house when Marco was called to Harvard. Marco went on being a poet wherever we were; I became his translator and the mother of what Marco, delighted with his life, called *le tre Grazie*.

When my mother and I returned with the corn, my father was home from playing cards at the Club. He was sitting in his chair, reading the paper while the TV blared at the empty, dim room. The old chair he sat in was set to face the television and alongside it was a console table holding *National Geographics*; decades of copies embodied his youthful yearning for California and everyplace else. At eighteen he had bought himself a motorcycle, but got only a broken collar-bone out of it. Above the table was a panoply of gold-leaf frames enshrining photos of all the grandchildren. On the far wall, like a memory prompter, hung an oil painting of Gus Sturzo in his prime, copied from a photograph when he was a handsome man in his forties with a full face and clipped moustache who looked straight out, unflinching and unfooled. He wore a Rotary pin in his lapel; his look said, I've made it and it wasn't easy, but now I'm boss.

"Where's Winnie? Why aren't you talking to Winnie?" my mother shouted at him in the exasperated tone she now boldly used, explaining to my quizzical look that she had to raise her voice because he was too stubborn to turn on his hearing aid.

My father was eighty-three and had become quiet and compliant; he looked up, startled, uncomprehending as she questioned him. He was frequently confused; he didn't remember; he was no longer in charge. He struggled to his feet and laughed in a bemused, embarrassed way as I came to greet him. Age had humbled him. He was a small figure in too-large clothes. I kissed him and said, "Hello, Pop."

"Winnie? Now where is she," my mother was muttering, going off towards the kitchen.

"Well, how are your finances, Fran?" My father peered at me blandly through his glasses as he sank back down into his chair. To speak of money was reassuring to him, it put him in command since that was still something he undoubtedly had, while I just as undoubtedly did not. His mouth seemed full of loose teeth.

Shouting above the television, I answered, "Finances? So, so, Pop. It's a squeeze but Winnie and I manage. She's got a student loan — she starts college in a couple of weeks. And she'll be working, too."

"Is Winnie going to be taking something sensible in college so that she can get a job and not waste four years of her life?"

"Sure," I said. My father was having an interval of being his old self, probing and sarcastic, and his remark was aimed at what was considered my own failure. I had a degree in Italian and, the Sturzos said among themselves, nothing to show for it when Marco died leaving me to make my own living and support our children. "Can't you get into real estate?" was my mother's first thought. "Those women do it in their spare time and make so much money." Or Amway products, Gussie suggested. It was Adele, who was married to a financier and lived in New York, who had the idea of my returning to Ferryville to work at the Ferryville Heights School for Girls.

"Now what about this Max Aschermann? What does he do?" My father had forgotten that we had already had this conversation several times before. His focus was already drifting.

"He's a businessman, Pop."

"What?"

"A businessman — just as you were before you retired," I shouted over the television. But Max didn't deal in basic everyday construction as my father had. Max, I teased him, was a purveyor of schlock. He represented any product that came along if, as he put it, he could make a buck. He handled things like Gizmos, perfumed fluffs that hung in cars as deodorizers; or pressed shrimp — dozens of little ones pressed and squashed together and shaped like one large one and called Whale of a Shrimp — institutions and schools were the big customers for those. He was also considering Mind Control cassettes that people could pop into their car tape-decks and learn as they drove how to project themselves positively. He wondered endlessly about getting into deals like the Grease-and-Go quick hub franchise. Why, I asked him, don't you use your intelligence and selling skills for something worthwhile? You're always criticizing, he would reply, hurt.

Having to shout back and forth with my father depressed me. I went over to turn off the television, if we were going to talk, but he had already picked up his paper. It had never been easy for him to talk with me.

"Fran," my mother said as she came into the room, "don't slouch — that's why your stomach protrudes. You should be doing isometrics, while you sit there." She poked at the paper in front of his face, ""Pop," she said in a loud voice, "did you see in the paper your cousin Tony Parise died?"

He lowered the paper, startled. "Who's that?"

"Anthony Paris. You know. Isn't he your cousin?"

"Oh, yes. His mother was my father's sister."

"Are you going to the wake?"

"No."

"You're not at all close to your relatives," she scolded.

"No, we didn't stick together. We went our own ways."

"That's what I mean!" she tossed over her shoulder as she went off, belligerent, reproving.

I shook my head at the absurdity of my mother, who had herself distanced herself from "those people" of lower Main Street, chastizing my father for not being close to relatives. The close, warm Italian family I've always heard of had never really existed for us but lately my mother seemed to be re-inventing it. "Italian families are strong — they stay together, one for all and all for one. Not like the Americans!" she was heard to say.

It started, I think, with my sister's being courted by Meade McGraw. My mother would ruefully observe to me that she couldn't

18

get to first base with Adele's boyfriend. He never mentions his family! she would exclaim. Would you believe he's never so much as brought a bottle of wine after all the times I've had him to dinner ... and your sister's getting just like he is!

I admired Meade in that respect. Restrained and temperate to the point of flatness, he was, however, grandly impervious to being plied with food in order to be made to feel grateful and in Dolly Sturzo's debt for it. He never got embroiled in her trap of putting people at cross purposes so that, like some genial godmother, she could then resolve everything by good-heartedly calling them all to her table and stuffing great platters of her food past their tightly pursed lips and stopped gullets into their knotted stomachs. How she would beam and smile at all of us from the head of the table! She was pretending we all loved each other. Meade simply paid no attention.

I took the second section of the newspaper from my father's knee. An ad about summer theatre at the Heights School caught my eye. I thought of the unhappy year Winnie and I spent at the school following Marco's death. You've got to be practical, the family told me, backing Adele's idea that I get a job there. You'll have rent-free quarters, free meals, and free schooling for Winnie. Then you can use the proceeds from the sale of your house to meet her coming college expenses.

As children, my cousin Feeney and I had been star-struck by the uniformed girls from the Heights School who used to come in twos and threes into the village center to buy bake goods or magazines. The thought that I might be giving Winnie some great advantage to put her among them made me waver from my first impulse when I said, "I'd like to keep my house in Medwood and get a job in Boston."

It was only Chessie, then, who supported me. She had become closest to me after Marco's death; it was with her I had what I once had with him — the conversations, the dazzling insights, the generous warmth. "You love your house, Mom!" she pleaded. "It's a big mistake to sell it. Why don't you rent out part of it, then you wouldn't have to uproot Winnie — she's got enough problems!"

But I hadn't the confidence, I felt lost and my father's retort still reverberated in my ears: "The year you can earn a thousand dollars hell will freeze over!"

Convinced that I couldn't earn a living translating, and under their pressure to return to Ferryville where they could all help me and give Winnie a family, I sold the barn-house and most of our furniture. I shipped Marco's papers to an archive in Italy, and moved into a dormitory apartment at the school with Winnie, grateful, I tried to tell myself, to have managed it all.

Too late, my bridges burnt, I found myself a poor relation, as constrained as if I had been in Sing Sing itself, just a few miles up the river from Ferryville. The School, like prison, was its own strange and estranging society. In that school for girls staffed mainly by women, an authoritarian headmaster openly showed his jovial contempt for all of us. He wore, at times, a green tie sprinkled with little pink pigs. Yes, he laughed, he was a male chauvinist pig. And so?

It soon became clear to me that many of the women who taught at the Heights School were themselves on the skids: divorced or widowed, they had come down in the world. A few were alcoholics who liked the seclusion a girls' boarding school offered; and some were old grads, still single, who returned to live an extension of their preppy girlhood.

The school was retrenching from the effects of the sixties' era of protest by the time I got there. Enrollment had dropped. The Senior English teacher said, "This will be the last graduating class that looks anything at all like a Heights class." She meant the old Wasp look. The school had started taking whoever could pay; it took Jews and Italians and Blacks; it was taking the too-young who were dumped there from broken marriages and the emotionally disturbed who were problems at home.

In my forties, no other prospect in sight, I found myself living in a girls' dorm, eating with girls in the dining room, working with them all day in the library, and then in the evening, as dorm mother, answering calls for them and repeating that it was study hour and students were not allowed to come to the phone. At night I patrolled the floors making sure there were no smokers in the toilets, or lights on after hours; and in between rounds I sat under my eaves and read poetry: "*Women have no wilderness in them,*" came the voice of Louise Bogan,/"*They are provident instead,/Content in the tight hot cell of their hearts/to eat dusty bread.*" I began to write poetry.

Out of my suitcase of silence came the words. I tried to remember who said, Every woman who writes is a survivor.

Those were the times I dreamt of my Medwood house as a blessed state of being. I saw it all as *cinema verité*: my life had gone from being the young wife of Marco Beniferro, well-known Italian poet and teacher at Harvard, to that of a tired woman in a spotty plaid bathrobe painfully becoming aware that she has made a pact to eat dusty bread.

I had fallen among the Goths. At Thanksgiving dinner in the Normandy house, when Gussie's son Freddy came in stoned, no one seemed to notice it; nor did anyone at the table know Italian, or poetry, or what pesto was. They thought I was weird for thinking

21

any of it important. It was at that time that my brother Gussie turned on me from some ancient hurt I no longer was cognizant of and asked me how much longer I was going to be an atheist. How much more disaster do you want to draw on yourself and your children? he demanded.

Almost crazed with how low my life had come, I began to hallucinate that if I wrote to the editors of magazines who had published my translations of Marco's work, one of them would hire me, that I'd move out of the Heights School and Ferryville and recover my life. I wrote to Henry Levine who had been Marco's book editor and still worked in publishing in Boston. I wrote to a woman named Edith Fisher, a stranger, whose work I had read in a journal and admired. She wrote back on a post-card, If you're in Boston, get in touch. It was enough for me.

That I, the penurious widow, and Winnie the learning disabled daughter, sheltered and off the streets and a burden to no one, should have counted our blessings to be at the Heights School was something my family could agree on. We should also be grateful to have Mom and Pop's nice house on the hill to go to for those Sunday or holiday dinners when I was not on dorm duty. But Winnie and I did not count our blessings, we were not grateful. Loathing it all, we left like parolees at the end of the school year and headed back to Boston, both mother and daughter in an exhilarating oneness of spirit, congratulating ourselves on our flight.

With that awful year at the Heights School recalled to me, I threw down my father's evening paper, exclaiming disgustedly, "This place!" indicting him and his home along with the school.

Then I was ashamed because he was what he was, and what did it matter anymore. Once it had. Gus Sturzo had always asked the questions. He never gave answers. I always wanted to ask: Why are you so mean to your own father? Why don't I know my own grand-father? Why is he allowed in this house only once a year, on the feast day of Sant'Agostino, to give you a box of cigars? Now I could figure it out for myself. I looked at my shrinking father. Like the headmaster at the Heights School, he was no longer a boss in my life.

From upstairs came the sound of my mother's loud, triumphant voice as she found Winnie: "There you are! Hiding on me!"

CHAPTER TWO

"Fran," my mother asked, "don't you miss a kitchen?"

Yes. In the four-square dream of my Medwood house there is a family kitchen: I am standing in my kitchen looking out the double window over the sink. The view is to the hills, to the West and it is large and filled with colors in the afterglow of sunset: orange against the purple mountain rims. I think: it is perfect. In the yard I see Dee's favorite apple tree and beyond it the deck built around a large, leafy maple where we eat under its cool shade in the summer. In the great room Chessie is playing Schumann's Romantic Horseman in the dramatic pounding chords she loves. Baby Win-win is in her crib in the little room next to the kitchen. Soon Marco will be driving home up Shady Brook Farm road and we will all sit together at the kitchen table and eat and talk and he will tell delicious stories of his classes at Harvard, of his boyhood in Italy, of anything — he is a story-teller — and we all wait for him to complete our day.

My mother's back was turned to me as she stood at the sink. I was rolling dough on a counter out of her way, making pastry bowknots and slipping them into hot oil in an electric frying pan. I watched the dough sizzle, swell, slide into shape, puff and bloat as I considered: What was she really asking? Was she implying that if I had not married Marco I could be married to someone else and still have a kitchen? That I wouldn't be living in a Boston apartment with an efficiency area? Kitchen stood for everything else. She might as well have said, Don't you miss a husband? a home? love? Chessie and Dee?

"Who needs a kitchen?" Defending myself my tone was sharp, scornful as my father used to be. "I'm not like you. I have other things to do than just cook."

24

Silence. Her sink is fronted by a window ledge where her pots of herbs are lined; along the window frame were other totems: a string of raffia garlic, a bunch of wax grapes, ceramics of miniature eggplant, peppers, onions, carrots.

"All you think about is food," I kept on. Her back was still turned. As the frying oil crackled, so the kitchen with tension. Nothing was innocent. Comments were buckshot wounds — random, unfocused, but always hurting. Conversation was not the aim; our lunatic words ricocheted capriciously off walls papered disarmingly (as if we were in Paradise) with fruits and flowers.

Wily Winnie had simply disappeared up into the third floor room to watch television and avoid us. I was the hostage in my mother's domain, the overlarge, modernized kitchen she both ruled and resented. Scornfully she had pointed out the magnetic disk on the refrigerator which read "World's Best Cooking Grandmother." It was given to her that morning by her grandson Freddy. "Wouldn't you think he'd have better taste?" she asked me.

No, I could have said but kept quiet.

For years, like a victim against her wishes, her eyes wild and smoldering with the frustration of ideas not listened to, she flung out her arms and cried: "Look! These cabinets! Out of reach! How am I supposed to get at anything? Look at the counters so far from the sink! Pop tells me to re-do the kitchen and then hires someone who won't listen to me, and then listens to him! I could never get my ideas across! Did the guy who did the job have to cook here afterwards? NO! I'm the one who's stuck."

In fact, the kitchen was inefficient, unpleasant; too many white cupboards, too many cold steel counters, too many appliances, a monument to *de trop*. I disapproved of the electric can opener, the electric carving knife, the growling garbage disposal unit in the sink.

But it was still her stronghold. In the old kitchen of my childhood, she had badgered me into eating a concoction of peppers and eggs which I loathed by promising to tell Gussie and me the true story of Ferryville's only kidnapped child. To hear the story, I ate the stuff. I ate things too salty, too oily, too mushy, too burned. I ate to please my mother, to collect rewards, to butter my bread, to be loved. I had always eaten. I ate my heart out. Until I stopped eating.

That happened after I went to her, frightened, because there was blood on my bed sheet and I didn't know what had happened. She was embarrassed. I had been tactless. "Oh, it's something that will happen every month. The nurse in school can explain it. Just don't go swimming." But my friends told me it was the curse and I thought of the *malocchio*. Who was getting even with me? For what? No, no, my friends said, it's what happens to all girls so they can have babies.

Staring at the frying pastries, I saw an amazing scene: I was running up some stone steps at Boldt's Castle one summer in the Thousand Islands with some kids from camp and I lost the Kotex pad I had stuck in my shorts. It simply fell out and I kept going, not caring. Coming back down the steps I saw it there, soiled, and heard a passerby say, How disgusting some people are, like savages. Yes! I felt detached from the disgusting pad, I felt free, free of Kotex, free of becoming a woman, free as a disgusting savage.

I stopped eating. Every morning I drank lemon juice and hot water to shrink my stomach. No one noticed. From a chubby, compliant girl I turned skinny and nervous until I turned off the flow.

When a teacher sent a note home about how poorly I was doing and how tired and run down I seemed, embarrassed again, my mother took me to a doctor who found that my periods had stopped and that I was malnourished and anemic. I began to have liver shots twice a week.

"What's eating that goddam kid?" my father growled, to which my mother tearfully rejoined, "Am I responsible for everything?" She must have thought I was deliberately putting her on the spot. I was a day student at Concordia Convent School then. With the crackle of the frying oil, I hear the sound of the post-communion hymn *Panis Angelicum*, bread of the angels. Bread to the crumb. For my mother's family name is Briciola, crumb. I see myself: I am one of the uniformed students at school with the Irish nuns and we are on spring retreat. The chant has a clean ascetic modal line purged of all emotional content. It sounds modern, atonal. It is free of embel-lishment, It is pure. Like real bread. We, the penitent students, are all crumbs, *briciole* of the bread of angels, but I, an Italian Briciola, more than they, the Irish and Germans. That long, crusty loaf of Italian bread my father brings home each night from the Columbus Bakery, I now know, is the male part his thing, his power. He *is* the staff of life, he endows life, he rules it. All my classmates have gone to the altar to receive the bread of the angels but I do not. The Irish nuns frown at me. But I do not admit the Host between my lips; I do not eat. I stand alone. The real crumb, the denier, the spoiler. I do not want that angel bread. I will live and die on air. I want to be pure. In my rarified state I imagine I can cause statues to weep, holy pictures to nod, barren trees to bear, myself to bloom to a bloodless womanhood.

Christ fasted in the desert forty days. People fast to atone, to be purified. I wanted that. I want to be lifted out of my unhappy fat into pure spirit from which another me would emerge — not my mother's creature, stuffed with peppers and eggs and Sunday din-ners, but a self-made slimmed down new me. A me of sang-froid. I loved the coolness of that phrase. It meant no shouting or crying, no hot-blooded Italian feelings, no blood. I will spurn the food my mother has spent hours shopping for, preparing, cooking, serving; I will not be enticed into my own bondage – to being convinced that by being fed I am cared about.

Italy, when I married and got there with Marco, was another story: *zampone, calzone, ossibuchi, manicotti, saltimbocca, pastasciutta, pinzimonio, gorgonzola, minestrone, melanzane, panpettata*. With Marco my appetite was restored, I learned to eat. He fed me exquisite *zabaglione* and splits of Asti Spumante during my trying pregnancies; he left me sweet notes on the fridge telling me what to have; he taught me his cooking and to know wines.

The body was everywhere evident in Italy the years we lived there: sharply defined buttocks under tight pants was the fashion for both men and women. Seeing the churning dynamos of buttocks under leotards or jerseys, watching them gyrate lasciviously in parks, on grand ceremonial stairways, in piazzas and everywhere in the Borghese Gardens, I thought of Marco's writer friend who called the behind a *mappamondo*, a globe … great rotating globes of flesh straining and surging in mighty swipes through pants that do not contain but simply and visibly outline them. Men's parts bulged in front, no cod-piece required to define the package. It was the decade of the *culo*; cracks and crotches were precisely drawn. I adjusted to my new life. Sang-froid was out.

In Italy I heard the jeer, *morto di fame* and was struck by the cruelty of being insulted as "a starved to death." Abundance is well-being; hunger is degrading. I billowed out in my pregnancies, becoming enormous in indulgence and then, after each birth, eased back to a normal figure. Pregnant, I thought of myself as a Mater Matuta figure – powerful, big and squat, the Good Mother of the

Morning; I saw those female votive statues in the Etruscan museum, and their elementary ampleness, like Gertrude Stein seated with her legs apart, spoke to me of what strength really was. The maters were redoubtable figures, solid, steady, permanent, expansive and pervasive as the morning itself. They sat mightily on throne-like chairs, knees spread, babes nursing at their multiple breasts which were stacked like loaves of bread across their chests. They reminded me of the large real figure of Grandma Briciola, and of my own pleasure in nursing my babies and being a mother. I loved my babes.

I became acquainted with Marco's cousin Lietta, an old woman with beautiful skin who had flaming orange hair and a lover decades younger. Each year for two weeks in the fall Lietta disintoxicated herself with a regime based on the special white grapes of the Veneto region — those and those only were the sacred food of her lasting beauty and femininity, she said. I would have stayed in Italy forever to learn everything, to be as elegant and long-lasting as Lietta but Marco was offered a chair at Harvard and we returned, settling in Medwood at Shady Brook Farm.

In the states I heard of women getting tummy tucks, or having part of their small intestine cut out, and plastic bubbles inserted near the stomach in order to inhibit eating: "It's a Godsend," said one obese woman on a late afternoon television show. I was revolted. As I was saddened by the wave of missing children all over America. America was harsh to its children.

In the supermarket my food was packed in brown grocery bags printed with the photos and vital statistics of missing children. One in particular touched me deeply: smiling from the brown bag was a girl whose oval face, wreathed in dark wavy hair, reminded me of little Chessie. The missing girl was identified as Marilena Alba. Marilyn Dawn. I cut the image from the grocery bag and for a long time kept it on my refrigerator door, seeing Marilena Alba each time I put in or took out food. Who was feeding Marilena, child of daybreak? Had that child with the beautiful name run away, been lost, stolen or strayed? Where was Marilena now? At the infamous bus terminal building in Manhattan where pimps hung out waiting for the arriving children? Working 42nd Street? It was Italy seduced by the sordid streets of America ... the dawn turned to dark.

And who would get the grocery bags stamped with the likeness of Marilena Alba? Women like my mother who had shopping and feeding as the organizing principle of their lives and spent part of each day lugging home stuffed bags from the supermarket. If they didn't feed their families what did these women do? Who were they? what good? I knew the story of Connie Mancuso's mother who died on the kitchen floor, the eggplant parmigiana she was making not yet put into the oven. She had a stroke and tried to telephone for help. When she was found, she was babbling in Italian and calling mamma. Connie's Irish sister-in-law wanted to throw out the eggplant but Connie said, "Are you kidding? — this is Mom's!" and they ate it after the funeral, a memorial service to the woman who cooked.

I started at my mother's voice. Still at the kitchen sink, she was saying, "There's nothing nice about being old."

"What do you mean?" My words flew like beebee shot. "You're well! Your husband's alive! Your children are all going to be with you tonight, and most of your grandchildren. What's not nice?"

"What good is it all with your father as obstinate as he is!" I knew her lines so well, knew she would never reach contentment, much less serenity. "We haven't been anyplace in years," she continued. "He's happy to just sit here and let me take care of him. His tie has to be tied, his hearing aid put in, his feet soaked, his ice cream handed to him because he says he can't find it for himself in the freezer. Then he starts choking on it and calls for water. Night after night! All I do is wait on him."

I laughed. "Well, you've been too good to him. But you set it up — you've always told us how on your wedding day when he said he couldn't eat what everyone else was having, you left the bridal table and had a special order made just for him."

"You see what I mean! He's *always* had me to cater to him!"

As Chessie once remarked, her grandmother would go down in history as the greatest appeaser since Neville Chamberlain.

Then, over the sound of running water my mother tried a new tack, asking, "You really think this Max is the right man for you?"

"That's a funny thing to say! Before I met Max you were praying every night that I'd meet someone!"

"Well, I don't know. You never seem to get the right man."

Silently I agreed. And yet my marriage had worked. I had even been ahead of the times, for it was I alone who gave myself in marriage — there was no family consensus, no father of the bride handing me over to Marco. I wanted Marco and alone I married him. Marco had been too old, too much engaged in his own work, too formed by his own culture to be really suitable for me. And yet we were lucky together and I had loved him. Even my mother can't deny me that: You always seem to land on your feet, she says begrudgingly. For she works hard at her gloomy predictions and it must seem unfair that some things turn out right for me despite my not going to church and my being so impulsive.

"I'm surprised you go for a business man, that's all," she went on. "I thought you'd do better. With all your education."

"That's funny to hear, mother. You didn't do better. You could have been a lawyer's wife, you keep telling us. Instead you chose a businessman. Maybe you were my model."

"That's not very logical."

"Maybe not. Anyway, I don't want to talk anymore about Max."

She picked up a dishcloth, wiped her hands, and came over to where I was working. "You're rolling too thick ... too much flour, I knew it! You're creating confusion — why did you have to start this now?"

"What confusion?"

"Just like when you were a girl! You never listen — so headstrong. You always have to do things your way." She pushed me away. "Let me get at this — you'll be here all night! Oh, dear — get me the spatula. You have to roll like this. You're so rough — as if you have no patience. You have to have a feel for the dough. There!"

"Let me try." I kneaded the dough as she had done.

In a quieter tone she said, "Aren't you sorry you don't live nearer so that we could do this together more often?"

I looked up to see if I could read irony in her face. But no, she meant it. I rolled out more dough and said nothing.

"Each year I have to do my Christmas baking with a different helper," she went on, "after you left, there was Adele. Then Susan, when she was going with Gussie and wanted to impress him, would come over — it drove me crazy! She'd take all night shelling the nuts, then she'd be so dainty putting the filling in and pressing the dough together that I'd have to go over each one again. Each year a different helper — once Chessie, once Dee. Then Stella and Ann. And not one of them came back the next year!"

Thinking of Winnie at her ease up on the third floor, I said, "This year you'll have Winnie nearby."

"I hope she's more organized than you are. Look what you're doing — there are things all over."

"Please! Mother! You don't even have to be in the kitchen with me. I'm making these for your birthday. Here, try one." I took some bow-knots from the paper where they were draining and shook them in a bag with powdered sugar, then extended the bag to her.

She took one and bit. "I told you too much flour. I told you they wouldn't be good. Too thick."

I laughed. "Give me a break! Everyone else loves these!"

"Do you want me to lie? They're doughy. Anyway that's enough for now — go talk to Pop. I want to clean up."

"Can't you sit down and relax for a minute on your birthday?"

"I like to have everything ready and then sit down. You go ahead — go talk to Pop. Now you know how hard it is for me to be here alone with him. He doesn't say twenty words all day. Have some compassion!"

I did feel sorry for her. All that cooking and preparing — she must have told herself long ago that it was the way she could keep us all coming to her. And she had been doing it so long she couldn't stop. If she stopped, everything else would. She hadn't the quietude and patience of women like Aunt Josie who seem to retain some strength inside them that their men respect, that their men need and would never run the risk of losing through disapproval. It was the difference between the strength of the Sicilian grandmother in the attic and the kind of holding on my mother did — frightened, dependent, ready either to concede or to quarrel. I would have liked to disappear, to go to my room for a few minutes. It was the constant noise in that house that wearied me — upstairs and down, tele-

33

vision was always on so that voices sounded everyplace. My mother's talk was at the level of shout; doors were always slammed, Pop was always banging shut the windows we opened. It was his fetish, Mom explained; his way of feeling secure, closed in, protected. Against what, I wondered. Age? Death? What window was there against them?

I made drinks of scotch and water on the rocks, and gave one to my father.

"Do you get the National Geographic I subscribe to for you, Fran?" he asked.

"Yes, for years now. Trouble is, I have no place to keep all the issues."

"Can't you keep them in the basement the way I do?"

"Oh, Pop, I have no basement! No real kitchen, no attic. The house is gone — I live in an apartment now."

"Oh you do," he said, looking genuinely surprised. "I didn't know that." He had forgotten much of my recent life.

We had little to say to each other, but I felt a moment of sweetness with him, like the time he had come back from a business trip with a wonderful book of Fairy Tales for me. I see it still — oversize with a deep blue cover, and full-page, colored drawings on glossy, expensive paper. It was the book of the Twelve Dancing Princesses, of Rapunzel, of the Goose Girl. I treasured it but when I wanted to reclaim it for my own daughters, my mother had already given it away.

While we sat, my brother Gussie came in and I went over to greet him. He towered above me, but he was on his guard as if we were still children and I might try something on him. His hair was thinning, he wore glasses but still had some of those dark good looks he had surprisingly blossomed into after a frail boyhood.

34

"Where's everybody," I asked, "where's your family?"

"Oh, I'm just stopping by to see if Mom needs anything. I do every night. We'll all be along in a little while. How was your trip down?"

"Good. Pop asked me whose car that was in his driveway and I told him mine and he looked surprised. He said, Well, where's mine, if that's yours?"

Gussie laughed sardonically. "He gets worse each day."

I watched my brother treat our father with easy-going insolence, no longer the feared parent now but an object of ridicule. "Hey, Pop," he shouted, "watccha doing?" In Gussie's laugh, I could hear my father's old ridiculing one.

He was staring at the television screen, oblivious of our talking about him. "Is he worse?" I asked.

"He can't drive anymore. I've taken the car away from him and given it to Freddy."

"He's forgetful but he seems okay," I mused. "I mean, he still bowls and plays golf. Today he played cards."

"That's by force of habit. Golf and bowling are safe areas where he's got the pattern down pat. And he's got the lingo — Good shot! Right down the middle. You'll make a birdie on that. You hooked on that. You looked up. Got to keep your head down.

That's golf for him. That's why I can't stand it — always the same, repetitious round. It goes on and on, the game and the lingo always the same. Then in bowling Pop mastered the groove and stayed there, consistent, never varying an inch. With cards, his old cronies love to play with him because they win whatever he's got in his wallet. They wipe him out! And he doesn't care — it's just a way for him to have company. When he's home with nothing to do, he drives Mom berserk. His routine is to do nothing, think nothing

35

until some friend like Howie or Lee or Morris comes to the door to pick him up. If something interferes with that, he goes crazy — starts calling them up and driving everyone nuts. Mom will tell him, Lee's not coming today! and he'll go to the phone every twenty minutes to call him."

"You talking about me?" Mother burst into the room. "Oh, there you are," she said in a distracted way to Gussie who laughed and shook his head at her. She turned to the figure in the chair,

"Pop," she shouted to get his attention, "go change your socks! You've been wearing those same ones for three days and you know we're having people tonight." She looked like one of the Furies, her face taut and drawn down. She was wiping her hands on her apron.

Pop looked up. He glanced from me to Gussie to mother, as if trying to figure out what was going on. "Well," he shrugged, "if you say so."

"And get a better tie!"

"Poor Pop," I said to my brother.

"Boy, I don't ever want to get like that!" Gussie shook his head, warding off what, in fact, might have already begun in him.

When Adele and Meade arrived, late as usual, everything was calmer. Mother had changed and was relaxed. She greeted them effusively, "Well, here you are! Was there a lot of traffic in the city? — I was wondering when you'd get here so that everything isn't overdone."

Adele is mother's favorite. Adele is darker than I, and taller but, aside from her complexion, she resembles the Briciolas only in certain physical and temperamental ways. My mother's family is emotional, outspoken and fiery; not only do they spill out the beans without the least reticence, but, after being injudicious, they bear grudges forever.

Nothing Adele does wrong, like snubbing the Sturzo relatives, really ever disturbs mother because of the important thing my sister did right in marrying a man of means with a background provided by his mother who, born a Meade of the old Hartford line, had only briefly been married to a McGraw. Even the fact that Adele didn't have children (by choice) was, my mother said, just as well since she and Meade liked to have their freedom. I can see our mother gazing at Adele as if she were seeing herself: young and stylish with a doting, undemanding husband. Adele dresses fashionably, Adele brings the air of the city and smart people with her. Adele is a buyer for a top department store and gets mother discounts on designer label clothes. Adele is arrogant, haughty and selfish — all qualities my mother respects but has never dared be. Adele, my mother always says with a smile, did all right for herself, and Meade is not Irish, he's Presbyterian.

My sister did look well, or maybe vivid is the word. Her olive complexion was toned down to a pale green with face powder and the streaks in her dark hair seemed the color of honeydew melon. But then why shouldn't she, in her expression, make a statement? She lives well, has no cares, and has always realistically accepted Meade as he is — big and stolid; what she saw in him was a stout base that would never waver, a reasonableness and blandness quite different from the swirling emotion that engulfed the Sturzos; she saw the kind of reticence and reserve that draws precise boundaries — no intrusions in another's life in the name of possession by bloodline.

Adele had very easily passed over into being what Winnie called a "Wisp," which was the wasping of a Wop.

Smiling broadly at the birthday bouquet they had given her, mother said, "How is your diet coming, Meade? Why look at that," she marveled, staring down and drawing our eyes to his shoes, "I believe your feet are thinner, your shoes look big on you!"

Winnie giggled at the sight of us studying Meade McGraw's feet in his Maine Bass moccasins.

"Well, have to start somewhere, Dolly," he replied, his equanimity holding. I, onetime aspirer of sang-froid, admired his coolness.

Adele, trim in a fuschia linen dress (which almost matched her thick, turbid lips that I always associated with the purple plumes of phragmites grass on Cape Cod), her hair cut in a geometric Vidal Sassoon bob, said smoothly, "I've always thought Meade should have been born in the century when men wore knee breeches — he'd be just perfect, he's got such wonderful calves."

"Well, anyway," mother commanded, "you can suspend your diet for one night, Meade, I've made all your favorite things!"

"What is this, Mother, it's not Meade's birthday, it's yours!"

"Well, never you mind, Adele — I'm just afraid he doesn't get any home cooking at all with you being a career woman. I've got to pamper him a little bit!"

How perfectly my mother gets away with all her effusion and making people feel catered to, I thought. And then, when they've gone, she'll launch the poison barbs. I could just hear her, the minute Adele and Meade left: "Did you see that? Once again no wine!"

With Gussie's and Susan's five children all home, we were thirteen at the table. All of their children are good looking. And all of them, as Dee once noted, boring. That's because they've been brought up right, I told her.

It was a familiar scene in the crimson papered dining room where a copy of Sebastiano Ricci's Adoration of the Magi hangs. My eyes always go to that print for it brings Marco's presence gently into the room; and I thought how, for all his amiableness, he had railed against the Italians in America. A good people gone wrong, he used to say. They've got the work ethic and Calvinist materialism, but they haven't yet caught on to Yankee self-governing. They're like basic dough — good stuff — that hasn't risen.

But there were things Marco hadn't considered: like the chronic indigestion of people like the Sturzos and the Briciolas from having to gulp down America too fast, from being force-fed. They had to shed who they were before there was the leisure to become something else. And no matter the money they made, they would never be, say, the Meades of Hartford. The old ways, suspicious of the new, still hobbled them. No wonder our heads and stomachs and souls were always upset.

At the table the place settings were something new — ornate, heavy silverware unlike the old pattern I was familiar with. "Where did this come from?" I asked.

"Oh you know I've been taking care of Ethel Schotter," my mother replied as if the connection were obvious.

"Aren't you aware, Fran, of what mother gets out of being the Good Samaritan?" Adele said. "Just look around the house — the side chairs, sterling silver, vases, paintings, lace collars — all things of Ethel's."

"You would put it that way, Adele! Ethel wants me to have them."

"Tell me about Ethel," I said. I liked to hear what my mother was doing for her old friend. It was a part of my mother I could genuinely admire.

"She's not the same person anymore — you remember how jolly Ethel used to be. Now she takes up all my time. You know how old people are, wanting attention."

My mother stopped and giggled at herself. "There I go calling *them* old!"

"You'll never be old, Gram," said Freddy, smiling vaguely, his eyes seemingly without focus. He looked high.

"This is what Ethel gave me when I told her my birthday was coming up," mother said holding out her hand and showing a dinner ring of diamonds set in elaborate filigreed platinum that extended to her first knuckle. "I try to keep her morale up — the last time I visited her in the hospital I fed her my home-made ricotta cheese cake and brought her a pretty powder-blue bed jacket to put over her shoulders — old people get cold, you know, even in summer. And I told her how pretty she looked and that made her feel good. She kept telling me, Dolly, take anything — anything you want from the apartment. And I kept thinking how she let all the good things go with her house when she sold it before she got in touch with me. Just think of all the beautiful antiques that were in that house that I would have loved!"

"Oh, come on, mother. Where would you put more stuff? You've got a house full as it is." As soon as mother sounds like herself, I become Cato the Censor.

"It's no picnic, being at Ethel's beck and call, let me tell you!" she retorted.

"You're a real friend to Ethel, she's lucky to have you, now that she doesn't have Yvonne." I regretted the mention of my old childhood friend, long estranged from Ethel. It gave my sister-in-law her cue to ask about my daughters.

"Fran, what do you hear from Chessie and Dee?" Susan asked quietly, her lips barely parted.

I considered bland Susan across the table. Her hair looked the same as it did in her high school picture; she wore no make-up but pink lipstick. She was thick in the hips, soft-spoken and controlled; she still wore dickies. She was as unremarkable in appearance, as she was tenacious and unyielding in her beliefs. In her Irish Catholicism, practiced relentlessly, there was no place for queers, troublemakers, deviants or searchers. Her children were devoted to her.

I was slow to reply because I was sure that, through my mother, Susan probably knew more about them at that moment than I did.

"I have a new photo of Dee's little boy," I said smiling proudly, eye to eye. "I'll have to show you later."

A Pollyanna was how my mother described Susan. "She never sees anything she doesn't want to. She refuses to see any wrong in Gussie or in any of her children. She's always defending them!"

Therefore, I reflected, every family needed someone like me and my children to disapprove of, to use as the material from which to draw a cautionary moral.

"Hey, Pop!" Winnie nudged her grandfather, who was quietly absorbed in his food, not following what any of us said. "You're so quiet, why don't you say something."

"What's there to say," he asked, laughing in his old way. As his bridge slipped and moved in his mouth, he said to Winnie, "These aren't my teeth, you know."

"They aren't mine either, Pop," she said, patting his hand and making him laugh.

"He loves to have people around," mother noted. "He doesn't say much, but he loves to pour the wine for everyone, and just see them."

"He ate a whole artichoke," Susan said as if she were talking of someone absent. "I've never seen him do that before."

"Yes, that's because there are people around — if it's just the two of us, he barely eats. I made the stuffed mushrooms just for Freddy because he loves them, and the artichokes for Stella. There's more of everything. Eat up. There's plenty in the oven so you can take some home."

"Food's wonderful, mother," Gussie complimented her, "just great."

He had an ulcer and at home ate Susan's plain cooking but when he came to the Norman house, he ate everything his mother cooked. "These are good, Fran," he said of the bow-knot pastries.

I was surprised and pleased. I looked at my mother and said, "See that!"

"In my day," my father said unexpectedly, catching our attention, "we used to have polenta on the feast day of Santa Lucia. That was the custom then. And boy," he shook his head ruefully and started to chuckle, "I didn't like that polenta! The day I started bringing money home, I told my mother I didn't want to see the stuff again. From then on I could dictate what I wanted to eat."

"Money talks, right, Pop," boomed Gussie who was making plenty.

"Honey, say something," Adele urged the taciturn Meade. "You know all about money and making it. Or tell them what you said about Mayor Koch that was so funny."

"I think Pop's right," Meade said with his studied air, "whoever brings home the bacon gets to eat it."

"Withdraw, McGraw!" giggled Adele.

"Isn't that what life's all about," Pop asked, "chasing the Almighty dollar?"

"No, I don't think that's what life is all about," I answered. But no one seemed to hear me.

Pop was having a spell of sounding lucid. And if money was (as it was in his world) everything, then he was telling us once and for all his truth, the sum and substance of what he was about. In his terms, he was successful.

"Come on, Pop," Winnie was urging him, "now tell us the story of how you almost went to California to make your fortune."

"Oh that," he laughed, again shaking his head as if to dismiss it but letting his voice take on the recitative tone he used for telling and re-telling the key stories of his life. "That goes back a long time to when my mother died. I was nineteen, the oldest one. I had always worked since I was a kid and helped out in the family. But she got very sick and I realized she wouldn't be there much longer, so I figured there was no reason for me to stay around with her gone — I'd go to California. I always wanted to go there. But you see, when she knew she was dying, she called me to her and she said, Agostino, you've been a good boy, now I want you to promise me that when I'm gone you'll take care of your brothers and your sister Josie. Promise me. So I did promise her and that's why I never got out of this town and went to California."

I had heard this story many times. Sometimes it had the variant of the doctor telling young Gus that his mother would not last much longer and calling him in to her deathbed. I used to wonder why my grandfather was never present in those scenes.

Why hadn't the doctor spoken to the dying woman's husband rather than to her son? But the legend was firmly fixed; in my father's telling, his mother had chosen him rather than her husband. She had addressed her last words and wishes to her first son.

It always seemed to me unlikely and untrue that my grandfather had not been present at the deathbed. That would not be the kind of father Aunt Josie remembered and referred to so warmly. I began to feel that the dying woman set up her son to usurp the father's role. Had Pop ever wondered what lay behind that touching story of his mother's devotion to him? He had eliminated his father from the story of his mother's life and death just as, in real life, he kept the old man from all our family occasions.

La Siciliana's legacy still goes on, rippling out in ever wider circles from that initial intervention in her son's life. It made me wonder how and when it would all be played out. The ripples still lapped at all our lives. That was what Dee meant when she went off saying she didn't want to be trapped in the family; that she was removing herself from the contagion. I pictured my grandmother's strong Sicilian face and her unrelenting gaze up in the attic. She was of a people who had never heard of Freud or Oedipus or complexes. And yet their dramas were classic stuff.

Still carried forward on the benevolence of the evening, Pop recited his favorite maxim:

> Questo è il mondo,
> chi sa navigare
> e chi va al fondo.
> Chi navigare non sa,
> presto a fondo va.

"This is the world," Winnie translated in sing-song, "who knows how to sail and who sinks to the bottom. Who can't sail his ship soon to the bottom goes."

My father laughed, pleased with himself. Clearly he thought he was still navigating, not sinking. He who had not taught the rest of us to steer our way, maintaining that we had simply to stay on his ship, said his maxim with the relish of a captain to those who, but for him, would sink out of sight.

By the end of the meal he was silent again, withdrawn. He poured coffee into his saucer, then back into his cup several times, each time poising the saucer over the cup and waiting, watching, until the last drop fell from the saucer's rim into the cup. Nothing else at the table had so engaged his attention. After having his coffee he left the table. I could hear his footsteps trudging up the stairs.

That night before going to her room on the third floor, Winnie stopped at my room. "I can't stand Aunt Adele," she said strongly. "She's so phony! And did you see Freddy? — he was stoned silly and nobody there could even tell the difference. Everyone pretending everything's OK because Pop ate an artichoke! Actually I can't stand anything about this family. I'm going to have an ulcer, like Uncle Gussie, by the time I'm thirty."

"Why do you want to?"

"For the same reason you got yourself anorexic."

"Eat slower, Winnie, you gobble your food down."

"No matter what you say, I won't do it. I don't listen to you — I do the opposite."

"Why are you so belligerent? I'm just passing on what I know." I looked at her quizzically. It was bound to happen: now here was Winnie declaring herself. Why had Marco called them the three graces? Not one of them had gone her way with grace. I thought of Dee who had gone the farthest.

Dee, the middle child, idealistic and sensitive; she had dropped out of college to differentiate herself from Chessie's brilliant graduate career and now kept herself removed from us all. "I don't need a degree-label to know who I am," Dee boasted. She had been a fruit-picker in Florida, followed a guru to India, and then finally settled in Italy where she married Leone and wrote home to Winnie and me, "Sweethearts, when are you coming for a visit?" She loved us from afar. She had not withdrawn her affection as Chessie had.

"You have nothing to teach me," Winnie concluded defiantly.

"All families pass down wisdom," I said.

"Not this family. It pisses poison."

Late in the night I was awakened by strange thumps and sounds filtering into my sleep. It was my father. He was up, trying to wake mother who slept by herself in Adele's old room, next to mine. "Well, are you going to get up?" he was saying, over and over.

"Pop, it's only two in the morning." Her voice was thick and muffled with sleep. "You went to bed too early!"

"Well, I'm up, I might as well get breakfast ready." At retirement, he had given himself the routine of setting the breakfast table and fixing the grapefruit. "You going to get up?"

"Go back to bed! It's still night! Let me sleep!"

But he didn't go back to bed. I squeezed my eyes tight, hoping and praying he wouldn't barge into the room, open and shut the window, turn on the light, or stumble around and knock over things. He had always been inconsiderate towards all of us in his compulsive habit of checking things out. Accustomed to getting up early and going to work in the dark, he was also used to trespassing on our sleep and privacy. He would routinely come into our rooms without knocking, turning radiators off or on according to his fancy, banging down icicles from the windows in the winter, or checking the screens in the summer, but always ignoring our sleep. We were like prisoners at the mercy of our keeper.

Thankfully, that night, he did not come into my room. He clomped heavily downstairs and I could make out his distant bumping into things. I felt sad at the thought of my father groping through the dark. He no longer knew his way, and his loneliness in the dark merged with mine as I lay awake.

It wasn't just dark, it was Sicilian dark, the dark Sicilian nature with its deep underbed of melancholy: sad, moody, secretive, guarded, skeptical. It was the mark of a people brooding on the *terribilità* of life; never able to be happy without detesting the happiness because it can be seen for what it is, a momentary illusion. That grandmother, stored in the attic, knew it all.

Thinking, remembering, I felt Chessie's defection from my life. (That's only cause she's a coward, Mom, Winnie had tried to reassure me. She really loves you, but she's afraid of you and so she keeps away. And Dee? Well, you know it's really Chessie that Dee had to get away from.) And what about you Winnie, why are you always screaming that I never loved you? What does it mean, all this endless groping in the dark?

I lay there thinking of Max and missing him next to me, the warmth of his body, his protectiveness. I knew why I wanted him as I lay sleepness in the night hearing the remote thumps of the lost creature who was my parent. But no more lost than any of us. The protective shell of family which Marco and I had created had cracked and let in the storm. Accept the hard truth, Mom, Winnie snapped at me. don't go on pretending that Max can fix things for you.

Winnie was probably right — there was no more family, no more home; there were only visits to be paid once in a while to this one, or that.

Sad, sad.... the word made a muffled sound inside my head like the tocsin beat on a wrapped drum in slow procession to the gallows; it mingled with my father's befuddled presence in the distant dark as I began to doze off again. And in that ebb of consciousness, before it went, came this consolation: not by Pop's bread alone do we live....

CHAPTER THREE

The story of Ethel Schotter, currently the biggest thing in my mother's life, was told to me on our way to Ethel's apartment.

"I never got anywhere trying to find Yvonne through Ethel's minister or her relatives. The Schotters disowned Yvonne. She's gone without a trace," my mother related.

Owning and disowning, I thought; that's how families are set up, with parents assuming children are theirs, like property, like money in the bank. "How sad!" I said, "and Yvonne Ethel's only child." I was moved by my childhood friend's fall from grace and exile from her family. It was the story of original sin and the expulsion from paradise. "Now Ethel's all alone. Why didn't she make up with Yvonne?"

"Oh, pride, I suppose." My mother's attitude was brusque, not at all sentimental. Striding purposefully, she marched us into an apartment building where two old people, looking stranded, sat in the forlorn lobby and watched us. There was a sour smell in the elevator. It was a far cry from the Schotters' home on Broad Street. "Albert Schotter was a pillar of the Lutheran church and in those days what Yvonne did was a real disgrace."

"Well, Aunt Josie didn't disown Rose when she got pregnant before she was married."

"Josie had more sense than Ethel."

Every so often my mother surprises me with a remark like that. It made me think of how she had first met Ethel by standing up for Gussie and me when we were kids.

We had been playing along the aqueduct pathway, a grass corridor over the underground viaduct that runs through all the river villages from Croton-on-Hudson to Kingsbridge in the Bronx. In

Ferryville it separates the backyards of the single family houses on Broad Street from the multiple family dwellings and stores on Main Street. It was more than a natural bound; it was, when I lived there, the frontier between two different realms. No Italians lived on Broad Street. We didn't count the Smiths, a swarthy family who had come from the Bronx, as Italian. Their changed name alienated them from the Italians of lower Main Street while their foreign looks kept them from being accepted by their neighbors on Broad. None of us played with the dark, skinny Smith kids. *Cafoni*, my father would spit out contemptuously at the mention of their name. I never knew whether he meant traitor, or if it was defensive on his part because Mr. Smith was a lawyer. My father often mocked people with education, just as he had no love for the Irish.

The aqueduct cut between my life in the old Italian neighborhood and the new definition of us my father created when he moved us up the hill to the Norman house. It was a green swath separating two warring factions of myself: on the one hand an abiding longing for the old self I was shedding, and on the other a swelling urge to be someone new. The aqueduct was no bridge between Italian and American, but division made visible. It was choice: one side or the other. And no matter the choice, there was loss.

That day with Gussie I knew for the first time the shame of being despised. I can still feel the shock that froze our play as the thin woman in dark clothes, staring hard and mean looking, called to us, "You noisy wops! Go back to your own street!" Her greying hair was pulled so tightly back into a knob on her neck that it seemed to push her sharp nose forward in a menacing way. She stood, broom in hand, on the back porch of the Schotter house where she had been sweeping. Gussie's face started to crinkle up. I grabbed his hand and we ran.

Usually a waverer, this time my mother grimly heard us out, changed from her housedress and walked up the block to the Schotter front door on Broad Street. It was Ethel, ample and benevolent, not the thin woman, who came to the door. She said, "I'm sorry, Mrs. Sturzo, that the children got frightened. That was my sister-in-law who's visiting. She's not married and sometimes the sound of children gets on her nerves. It won't happen again." And it never did. My mother was a hero and that same evening two pints of hand-dipped ice cream, fresh strawberry and French vanilla, packed in dry ice from Schotter's Ice Cream Parlor on upper Main Street arrived at our door. That was the start of mother's friendship with Ethel, and out of theirs came mine with Yvonne.

Later I was invited to sleep over at the Schotter house which I remember as something like the movies, really American. Ethel Schotter cooked wonderful pot roasts and sauerbratens, biscuits and potato pancakes with thick applesauce, food such as never appeared on our table. There were warm muffins in the morning and apple crunch with whipped cream at lunch for dessert. Mr. Schotter spoke kindly and helped with the dishes; Ethel was always wearing a flowery bib apron and laughing heartily. The house was full of interesting scenes from the Bible framed in mahogany. There was a Grandfather's clock on the stair landing that played a tune — dah, dah, dah, dum ... dum, dum, dum, dah — and then chimed the strokes of the hour. It was better than the movies.

It was Yvonne who made up the new game called going to the doctor. We mostly played upstairs in Yvonne's room. But when Mrs. Schotter called up to tell us to go outdoors and get some fresh air, we continued our game on side steps that were out of view. We took off our panties and explored each other and I was entranced at the whiteness and pinks of Yvonne's flesh, and how the veins

51

twined vivid blue pathways over it. We were caught and told never again to be so wicked. I was sent to confession to relate my impure acts, and though I got forgiveness through penance from the priest, I don't think I ever did from my mother. I began to gnash and grind my teeth in my sleep. This I still do — both Marco and Max have told me.

In Ethel's apartment, my mother, with her uncanny ability to nail my thoughts, said, "Do you remember when you took Yvonne's baby doll?" This raking up of old sins is her specialty. Nothing is ever over and done with in her memory bank. She has the retention of a giant computer. She's the veritable motherboard, the true matrix of all our jumbled feelings: a network of intricate circuitry meant to retain and keep forever in her unrelenting random access memory whatever gets entered.

I prickled with apprehension and said, "Why bring that up?" I remembered all too well when I had coveted, then stolen, the doll with the exquisite china face.

"With all the dolls you had at home!" My mother shook her head at the stupidity of my ancient crime.

Useless to explain to her, as I had tried when a child, that my dolls were strange ones in foreign costumes which she herself collected for me, saying it could be my hobby. The doll I wanted and asked for but never got was a baby doll. I stole Yvonne's and had it only a few days before I was made to give it back. To have something of Yvonne's was almost to be Yvonne. To be blonde and pink. To be doted upon and praised. Her father owned the Ice Cream Parlor and I can still sense the pleasure of going with her through the door into the delicious vanilla smell, relishing the cool and immaculate interior where we sat at little marble-top tables and had ice-cream sodas. Everyone always wanted to go to Yvonne's birthday parties because of the molded ice-cream forms of flowers and animals in all flavors that Mr. Schotter made up special.

Yvonne, my mother used to say admiringly, over and over, was like a little Dresden doll. Yvonne was the perfect princess with glossy, much brushed and curling-ironed curls, like thick blonde sausages. All of her tended and primped and primed like milk-fed veal — the luxury kind, pale and bloodless, that we had for *scallopine* on great occasions. Yvonne was choice. Her big blue protuberant eyes were empty and doll-like. I never tired of looking at her. The blankness of her face, its utter *plume de veau* vacancy was wonderful: I could imagine all and everything there. I could imagine who I was not.

Years and years later, reading *Luxe, calme et volupté*, it was not Baudelaire's creole mistress I saw but Yvonne.

Yvonne wore hand-made dresses with smocking and lace edgings and was always clean. No one else at school dressed like Yvonne in shimmering materials with wonderful names — velvet, crepe de chine, georgette, taffeta, Brussels lace. Costly, beautiful, they seemed to me the materials of courts and castles. Even her dance costumes, which Ethel also made, were exquisite tufts of tulle and silk-satin bodices while the rest of us wore store-bought outfits. Yvonne's sumptuousness fitted Loew's movie house in Yonkers where our mothers sometimes took us to a Saturday matinee. We were Yvonne's retinue — I, the awkward girlfriend in waiting, and the two dressed up women, like courtiers. She shone for all of us.

Now I know that to have had a childhood friend like Yvonne was both beguiling and deleterious; it was to beget and nourish in me all the psychic sins without hope of remitting them as Saturday confession did the mortal and venial ones.

I had often told Chessie about my childhood with Yvonne. On one of Chessie's visits, when Winnie and I were living at the River-view Heights School, I took her walking on the aqueduct pathway, pointing out the back of the Schotter house where my old friend Yvonne had lived. With Chessie, I could ransack my memories and, indulging, recollect it all to her. She listened, absorbed, as if I were still reading her a bedtime story. What then?, she would urge me on in the telling.

"What ever happened to your friend Yvonne, Mom?" she said, taking long strides and listening intently. She was tall and lean, her narrow face wreathed with beautiful waving dark hair; she wore jeans and an open shirt. In whatever she did she had a high-strung intensity about her, her sensibilities fully engaged and her mind always absorbing. She was a stunning young woman.

"Well, incredibly, she stopped being a princess and turned into a frog. When we were about eleven or twelve, Yvonne started to wear glasses and her lips got thick — even her teeth! — her whole face thickened. She was a different person. After we moved up the hill, I changed schools to Concordia and Yvonne and I just lost touch. I went away to college, and Yvonne got a job as a secretary after high school and still lived at home. It was some friend of Ethel's who ran into my mother and told her about Yvonne's being pregnant. The Schotters were humiliated — they put her out of the house. According to the story, Yvonne added insult to injury by marrying her boyfriend in his Catholic church. None of her family would attend the wedding. And when Mr. Schotter died, Yvonne wasn't to be seen at his funeral."

"That's a real old-fashioned story!"

"That's how things were in those days. We lived in a small, closed world and everyone knew each other. Our world went over to the aqueduct, down to old Memorial Park, up Main Street to the library and Schotter's Ice Cream Parlor. Sometimes in the summer we'd go to the intersection of lower Main and Hudson and put up a stand to sell lemonade to the commuters coming from the station. Living in the Building made me feel so safe, so protected. Just going to school, or staying over at Yvonne's, was a big adventure!"

Chessie nodded, her expression thoughtful. "It's as if you've always been taken in by images that weren't real — *your* image of the Building, *your* image of Yvonne. It's all so different from the glamorous life you had with papà. *This* is such a backwater!"

Chessie had begun to assume an instructive attitude towards me and I, liking her attention, never challenged it. I seemed to know from always that she was bent on usurping my place to become the teacher, I the pupil. As a little girl, she had poutingly asked why I got the biggest room and why I had the biggest bed. Conversely, perhaps now I coveted her place. Didn't I see in Chessie the fulfillment of what I would have liked to have been?

"Who'd have thought I'd end up at the Heights School as a dorm mother!"

"Well, mom, that's because you didn't take my advice and hold onto your house." Chessie spoke briskly. She liked to be right, and that went back to when she used to boss Dee. "Still," she said more kindly, "it's just circumstances that have brought you low. You evolved from lower Main Street long ago, and now you're romanticizing it. The people who live there now have plastic awnings on their houses and they've never merged with the life around them — they'd never think of being on a school board!"

"Let me show you the other side," I said, pointing out to Chessie the little yards which backed up onto the aqueduct, the lush reverse of the austere house fronts.

I have always loved that sight of those cultivated backyards with their arbors and bowers, the beautifully tended rows of vegetables, the fig trees made to bear in a hostile climate, the occasional shrine to St. Francis, or Mary, the Virgin standing in what looks like an upturned bathtub. These are the Priapus and Proserpine totems of the classical world, transmuted but still alive, still beacons of a fantasy that understands human life as one with natural life.

The land slopes down from the Aqueduct to Main Street and so there are terraces in the back which are worked and planted and run through with little pathways that lead to well-ordered areas — the compost heap, a little shed, a table set out under grape vines. The beauty of the interlacing vines is combined with the forethought of providing shade at the table.

"Look, Chessie," I said. "You can see how all is practical in a frugal, peasant way, but all is beautiful, too. Don't you see? — their aesthetic is in the land! That is their true culture. These are people who were, just a generation or two ago, peasants. They have retained their lost world in their land here."

"Mom, don't tell me the obvious. I can see. I can honor their traditions and their hard work without liking their lifestyle. The problem is they haven't progressed from the old mentality as your family did. It's easy for you to romanticize about the past because you're so beyond it!"

I was thinking that Chessie had some of my own romanticism herself in the way she venerated my father. For her it didn't matter that Gus Sturzo had no notion of democratic principles, had been a despot with his wife and children. What Chessie saw was a basically decent man who had worked hard, made money, and protected his family. The Godfather. Chessie chose not to see how over-protectiveness was part of the despotism; how he had weakened his wife into dependency and his children into false notions of what family was. Oh yes, hadn't I read of destructive families … hadn't I always known that fascism begins in the power relations established in families? Because of him I distrusted authority as Chessie did not; because of him I would always be on my own, not wanting to.

We kept walking and then, with a great welling up of pleasure, I said, "Chessie, there's the Building! — the back of it, and Uncle Dominic's garden."

She said exactly what she must have known would please me: "What was it like, Mom, living there?"

"Wonderful! We had a front apartment and my teeny, tiny bedroom had a window that looked out over the river; in the winter, in bed with the lights out, I could look out through the frosted window and see the stars, see the bare Palisades on the other side of the Hudson. I'd feel something so powerful and mysterious I couldn't put it into words in my diary. I could never tell anyone." But I knew what I had felt: it was some existential homesickness. Even as I was safe at home on a winter's night, I had a child's precocious knowledge that home as a place is elusive and we can get sick with longing for it.

"What else, Mom?" Chessie urged.

"We used to play on the aqueduct. Gussie and I and my cousins Vince and Feeney and the other kids used to play Red Light, Green Light. To choose who was it, we'd go:

My mother and your mother
hanging out clothes,
my mother gave your mother
a punch in the nose.
Out goes Y -O -U!"

I was pleased that Chessie wanted to be such a precise and passionate historian of my past, so I went on. "There were a few times — well, maybe only once or twice — when instead of walking home from school, I had to take the school bus across town for some reason. Then I'd feel so strange! I'd be standing in the bus line with my classmates and I'd hear them chant "The bus, the bus, the B-U-S bus." I'd be so shy! I'd mouth the words so I wouldn't stand out, but I wasn't really joining in. I felt out of place because I was going to a different neighborhood."

"That hardly sounds like you, Mom. You go everyplace."

"You never know who's the real me," I laughed.

At that time Chessie's emotional life still centered on us.

We were her supports. She was a graduate student living frugally, glad, when to she came to us, to ransack my closet and wear my clothes, enthuse over the food I made for her and pack some to take back with her. Basking in good feelings in my quarters in the dorm, she enjoyed the rest from her hard routine and from the reclusiveness her studies demanded. I can still hear her saying, "Do you remember our good times at the Medwood house? Do you remember when we'd make popcorn and watch Mary Tyler Moore on television and maybe there'd be a fire going in the fireplace and snow outside? It just had a nice feeling. Do you remember?" Of course, I remembered.

Inside Ethel's apartment, my mother was brisk and organized, "Fran, look over the place and see if there's anything here you want before I dispose of it all in a tag sale. I'll be putting Ethel in a nursing home right from the hospital." She had never shown such decisiveness with her own life, but now power of attorney was literally empowering her.

I shook my head as I looked around. Two spindly Chiavari chairs with rush seats and lavender frames, completely out of scale with Ethel's girth, stood in the hallway; the living room was randomly filled with odd chairs and little tables which stood about like awkward guests not mingling well at a party. A rocker, with plastic seat-pads, faced a television set topped by a picture of Jesus.

Opening a closet and recoiling from its rancid smell, I found a wedding picture of Yvonne face down on a shelf. A buxom Yvonne, in a blue satin gown and picture hat, was grinning like a sturdy Eastern European peasant at a fair. On the top shelf, was Yvonne's old violin case.

"Can you believe that Ethel sold her house and practically everything in it for $16,000 and that's all the money she has left in the world," my mother commented. "She bought herself a French provincial bedroom set with twin beds — as if she were going to have company!"

I was quiet. Why was she so disapproving of Ethel? What would she have done in Ethel's place? What do women do when they're alone? They go to pieces, or they have a Max.

"Here, come and take a look at the kitchen, Fran," my mother called.

Ethel's kitchen, which at Broad Street, had been large and light-filled with a built-in breakfast nook that I loved, was, like those of all apartments, a windowless, mean space which reminded me of my own in Boston.

Throwing open the door of the refrigerator and disclosing an empty bottle of sherry, and a bowl of decaying fruit, mother cried out indignantly, "That's the fruit I brought her weeks ago!" Busily opening cupboards, she disclosed sets of odd dishes, chipped and of varying patterns, among which six perfect shrimp cocktail goblets struck a bizarre note of fashionable entertaining. There was a jar of peanut butter. A box of cereal.

"And she was such a great cook," I said, my words sounding her epitaph.

"You see why I have to commit her! — she won't eat and I can't be here all the time to see that she does. She needs people around her — it's the only thing I can do."

"You're doing your best, mother," I said.

"Well," she concluded, looking around once more, "that's all for now. "I told your Aunt Josie we'd stop by. She's another one! A chronic complainer.. I've been going to see her since she broke her ankle, and of course I always bring something. So each time I'm there I tell her how much I like her blue violet plant. I'd love it for my collection. Now wouldn't you think she'd give me that plant?" My mother turned her question to me with the guileless look of someone who can't understand being denied what she wants. I thought of myself wanting Yvonne's baby doll, wanting to be Yvonne. I had no answer.

Huffy with resentment, she said, "Your father's family has always been like that."

The park off lower Main Street, in my girlhood, had been a neglected dusty lot with a few swings, a rickety table for crafts, and a rusty old shower head under which we gathered for a meager sprinkling on a hot summer day. Once ignored by the village, it had lately been spruced up with a bocce court and benches. Yet the old neighborhood was still much as I remembered it.

There was the proud stone palazzo at #37 Lower Main Street which Mr. Comiso had my father build for him with huge blocks of stone, an arched loggia, and his name carved on the entrance pillars in open tribute to what he remembered from his native town of Benevento. All along the street Victorian clapboard houses had been encased in stucco, porches swallowed, and front yards cemented over. House fronts were still unrevealing; most life was in the rear where people cultivated their gardens, built their grape arbors, hung their clotheslines, and sat out to contemplate the world and greet each other.

At the corner of Main and Elm I spotted the old Sunoco station whose original frame building had long ago been plastered over and painted in tones of burnt Siena and umber. In Italy I recognized it again in Tuscan farmhouses, just as I recognized much of my old neighborhood in Italian hill villages.

It was the same, and yet everything was different. Doc Rivoli's pharmacy where old-world remedies were once concocted for people who needed the assurance they gave, was now transformed into something else and Doc was long gone. But seeing its location reminded me of the scandal when Doc became a Methodist. Father Marchi had gone to reclaim him, but Doc had told the priest politely, In the old country there was no choice about religion, there was only one thing you could be. Now I'm American, I can choose the one I want.

But where, on that summer day as we drove to Aunt Josie's, were the bands of playing children, the clatter of roller-skates, the huddles over jacks on Mrs. Colella's doorstep? The street was quiet. For years now the wheel-barrow man with his long broom and paper-pick had ceased to push his metal barrow along in quiet dignity, seemingly sunk in thought as he cleaned. There was no more fruit peddler's cart attracting women to call out orders from their windows; nor was there Mr. Persico, the Friday fish man who took special orders for eels for Christmas Eve. The name of the knife sharpener escaped me — he was always referred to as *l'affilare*, a word that passed swiftly from house to house as people came out with their kitchen knives for sharpening, or umbrellas to repair. The sidewalks had been busy then. Now they were empty.

The Building was the same — a three-story edifice, featureless enough to be taken for a warehouse, but still housing six families in its apartments. Plain as it was, my heart beat faster at the sight of it and I thought, How beautiful to be back. And instantly my next thought was, No, I am pretending.

Long ago I had known what it was to be foreign. In grade school I had known the difference between us from Main Street and the children from the Hill. It was a fact — we were known as Italian and there was a different attitude towards us in school. We were not supposed to be college material. The teachers told us, Don't bother with Latin, take something useful like typing. They mispronounced our names or contorted their faces when saying them as if something disagreeable had entered their mouths. We weren't welcome at St. John's, the Irish church; we had our own more modest church, Our Lady of Pompei on Hudson Street, with an Italian priest.

By the time I went to the Concordia Convent School I was pulled both ways — forward to pride in our house on the hill and my new mostly Irish friends, back to remembrance of the past. It is the forward thrust that usually carries one with it. Yet in some way I have stayed a true resident of lower Main Street.

Climbing the worn and narrow marble steps inside the Building with my mother, I could sense her disdain for the place she had never liked. But for me the place resonated, down stairways and halls, with the long ago clamor of childhood's rainy-day games. The second floor rear apartment where Aunt Josie and Uncle Dominic and Feeney live has a back porch overlooking the plot of land that my uncle still tends. There is his vegetable patch, his grape arbor, and the squared off flower beds bordered by low privet and connected by little gravel pathways in the formal Italian fashion. Uncle Dominic was from the old country and used to work as a gardener on the estates around Ferryville. He speaks with a thick accent and still makes his own wine. I remembered him in his younger years as a tall, lean man with thick black hair and a roguish smile. He was a simple, gentle man who would tease me about how I had cried as a baby, and how he would pick me up and rock me despite my mother's frowns and her modern belief of not giving in to babies.

Come in, come in, Feeney tittered self-consciously in the doorway. She is a trim and pretty woman in her late fifties, never called Josephine but only by her childhood name. We went through the parlor which had been re-done with wood paneling, a Danish modern couch, and thick carpeting over the old linoleum. "Look what Vince did for Aunt Josie," my mother pointed out. (Josie's children are so good to her, she's always sighing, as if she were being overlooked in some cosmic give-away program.) We all went out onto the back balcony where Aunt Josie, leaning on a cane, seemed as tiny and grey as a mouse, her resemblance to my father grown more marked with age. Uncle Dominic smiled a toothless welcome. Between buildings clotheslines were strung and festooned with the proud laundry of hand-worked bed linen from old dowry chests.

The talk was of Vince and his cancer and we wanted to believe that his condition was stabilized, that his remission gave hope for recovery. Aunt Josie was very bitter about God taking a person who had been good all his life. "Now Josie," my mother admonished, "You mustn't always think you're being singled out." But Vince, a successful accountant, had himself asked Why me? He seemed to be thinking in business terms that life gave back value received and that being a dutiful Catholic son really counted in some divine bookkeeping system. For me the fact that Vince's goodness was not requited was no more senseless than anything else, and in this conviction Max and I differed completely, he feeling that if there were no God in charge to keep people in line and accountable, and to whom one could petition against irregularities, then life was an unbearable mess.

"We're all praying, Fran," Feeny said. I wondered who was praying for Feeny, the oldest daughter in a traditional Italian family, expendable as a person and born to assume the care of others — first her younger sister and brothers, then her parents. Feeney's round face, framed by thick black wavy hair only slightly threaded with grey, was still unlined. She, like her father, was always smiling. She's graceful in figure, she dresses well, she speaks quietly. But at a time when I was in Italy Feeney was said to have gone a little berserk, become moody and difficult; it was change of life, they said, and Feeney was given electric shock therapy to make her nice again. This is something that seemed easily done to women. Brief stirrings of discontent are arrested, turned off as easily as one presses a light switch.

"Come visit me in Boston, Feeney," I said to her.

"I'd love to Fran, sometime when I can get away. I can't leave mother yet with her foot like that and Vince so bad." She smiled apologetically, as if not wanting to hurt my feelings. She had Uncle Dominic's sweet patience.

"It's so good to see you Fran," said Aunt Josie warmly, holding my face between her hands and looking into my eyes.

She meant it. Aunt Josie had never minded having Gussie and me around as children, unlike my mother who always wanted to get us out to the park, to the movies, to summer camp.

"This is Rose's new child, Aunt Dolly," Feeney said, handing around a photo of a very obese baby who was sitting on a blacktop drive next to a radio, looking into the distance with his hands up. "He's very musical," said Aunt Josie proudly.

"Isn't he gorgeous!" my mother exclaimed.

But as we were leaving the Building, she grumbled, "Wouldn't you think Rose would know better than to have such a fat baby? And that child's father is a lawyer." Wondering if I could ever learn my mother's art of dissembling, I knew I couldn't when she suddenly asked, "When are you and Max getting married?" and I couldn't avoid the answer.

"September 3rd," I said.

"You mean *this* September 3rd?"

"Yes, two weeks from Friday. At the Cape."

"You're getting married on a Friday?"

I could have taken that as another of her old-world superstitions, in keeping with the exchange of a coin for the Chinese pin. Friday, in her rules, was a bad luck day on which to start out on a trip or any venture. But I realized that my mother was upset and the words were coming out wrong. It wasn't Friday that mattered, but not being included in the plans.

"Who's going to be there?"

"No one — just Max and I."

"What are you going to wear?"

"Nothing special. Just something I have."

Outraged and wronged, she burst out, "This is the second time you've done this to me! First you get married in Italy to someone we don't even know, and now you're going off to the Cape like an elopement to get married again with no one there. I've never had the pleasure at being at your wedding!"

I looked at her forming a wordless question: Do you want to disown me as the Schotters did Yvonne?

"You're so impulsive!" she shook her head in her endless review of what had gone wrong. "You've always been different."

"Isn't it an answer to your prayers?" I tried to seem light-hearted, spirited. "For years you've been praying to St. Rocco that I re-marry."

"I just hope he's the right one!"

"Why else would I bother?"

"Most women in your shoes would."

"It's not just to be married — I happen to like being with Max."

"There are women who love their freedom as widows."

There flashed to mind the certainty that she would be such a widow. "Aren't you a little inconsistent? Maybe some women didn't like being married in the first place, but I like to be with a man."

"Well," she went on, "what about Winnie?"

"She'll be at school. Max's kids won't be there either. It will be just the two of us. Instead of going on about it being a Friday and what am I going to wear, for God's sake, you might wish me well."

"Well, that goes without saying."

"No, I think it should be said."

"Of course I wish you happiness — you know I've always been concerned about your happiness ever since Marco died. I just hope you won't go overboard now and forget your own daughters."

"What a thing to say!" Wasn't it typical of her to make it seem like my defection and to state things as the reverse of what they actually were — it was *they*, Chessie and Dee, who had left *me*! They seemed to think that when their father died, the family had, too. At first Winnie and I had clung together like the survivors of a shipwreck. Now Winnie was pulling away, too.

The birthday visit over, Winnie and I got our things together in the front hall as my father called goodbye from his chair near the television set. "Keep your chin up, Fran," he chuckled. "Have confidence!"

"What does that mean?" Winnie asked. "Weird!"

"He means well. He's getting old, that's all."

My mother, who had gotten up early to make us a good breakfast and pack food for us to have when we got home, had a headache and a dry, wracking cough. She felt weak and listless, she said. I recognized a pattern of psychic deflation that had developed in her over the last year or so: during the visit we engage in endless activities, my mother's energy never flagging, but then, as the visit comes to an end, she starts not feeling well. She has a low-grade fever, her bowels won't work, she gets a cough. Chessie has noted it, too, and says it's as if the end of all the bustle and talk gives her grandmother a glimpse into her own mortality and the final cessation of all activity.

"Are you all right, mother?" I asked as I kissed her goodbye, thinking, she's not as strong as she seems, she's one of the old people, too.

"Old age is no fun," she laughed ruefully, putting her hand to her throat. She was standing in the doorway, still in a housecoat, her face not made up. She looked her age. Her voice was low and raspy as she said, "Be sure to call when you get there."

"So long, Nonna, I'll come see you from college," Winnie called.

My mother smiled wanly and waved.

Starting the long drive home, I thought how each time you reach some milestone — graduating, marrying, birthing, visiting, whatever — there was the let-down of it being done and over. But people never could be done and over. People persisted in not being fixed to some permanent understanding. They sank or rose like the tides, veered like the wind, shifted like sand. Never anything to steer by.

Meade's family sailed and once he had explained to me how one plotted a course and got a fix on the navigation chart which then determined a position precisely.

"And you can rely on it?" I had asked. "Even in fog, or heavy seas?"

"Absolutely. As you believe in God and country."

That was Meade McGraw, Wasp and Yale. I still had my doubts. I wondered if work could be a fix. No child, no lover, no family seemed to be.

I marveled at the bravado that welled in me and made me think that despite the impedimenta of our long, separate, packed histories Max and I could start fresh again.

In the car I said to Winnie, "I keep thinking about all those women in Ferryville, how their lives were set by their being women, by their bearing or not bearing children. Ethel Schotter disowned her daughter because Yvonne became pregnant two months too early; Feeney cracked when she got to the age of menopause, still a virgin, her body unused for what it was meant for. On the other hand, my cousin Rose used her body cleverly to get herself out of Aunt

Josie's house. I keep thinking of all these women — what is the meaning?"

"Hey, Mom! That's deep," said Winnie cheerfully. "Good old Mom," she beamed with her beautiful smile. "Always digging for the meaning. Don't worry, Mom, it will work out."

What does she know, I thought. Aloud I said, "Maybe, if you're lucky. Max says, it's better to be lucky than smart."

It was a fine August day, clear and sunny and the fields along the highway were vivid with spikes of purple loosestrife and goldenrod. Glimpses of Long Island Sound from the Connecticut turnpike sparkled with light. Summer still held despite the presentiment of change. Driving past one of the service station stops along Route 95 I caught sight of a parked moving truck with G.O.D. plastered boldly and large across its side; underneath, in smaller lettering, Guaranteed Overnight Delivery. Exactly! I thought, just what God should do in a pinch — guarantee overnight delivery from all harm or fear. I turned to say to Winnie, Look at that prophetic truck, overnight I got delivered from Ferryville! but good sense stopped me. I already knew her answer: Mom, you're such a pain in the ass about your family.

I turned to look at her with affection. Taking my hand from the wheel I gave her a pat on the thigh. "Good old Winnie-the-Pooh," I said. "Did you have a good time?"

"Yah, Mom. Pop gave me a going-away check."

"Pop!" I laughed. "He still knows how to make friends and influence people." Then, after awhile, musing aloud, and as if speaking to something in the placid view unreeling beyond the windshield, I said, "Maybe that's what did the women in — not having that same kind of power. Or was it fear of being alone? Maybe it's the same thing."

Within myself I felt deep and thrilling elation at the thought of getting back to Max. It always happened after a few days of separation. First the constancy of him, always there, always demanding my presence, my devotion, my complete absorption in him, rattled me and made me anxious to get away. But then the fact of his love always won me back. I missed him.

Winnie turned on the car radio. "Time af....ter time," she sang in tune with Cyndi Lauper, matching the beat with the thump of her fingers on the dashboard.

CHAPTER FOUR

I did not marry Max. Was that what my nightmare forecast? — that I could not have a husband (home) again, that it would all crash around me? I sank into a tired apathy. It was weeks before I thought of something else to do. Rather, it was my mother who thought of it. She said, you need vitamins ... see a doctor.

So there I was, standing nude, arms outstretched at shoulder level, in front of Dr. Feldspar, a specialist in nutrition and diet, in his examining room. We chatted as if at a cocktail party. I smiled, he ranged around me in his white jacket and wide, outlandish tie painted with palm trees, testing my reflexes and telling me how everyone was a con artist, but no one could fool Mother Nature. He himself had been a junk food addict until he woke up. Now look at him. Indeed. He was a good looking man, tall and lean and very fit.

Before being admitted to Dr. Feldspar, an Indian aide had done my blood count and taken care of my specimen in a numbered vial, lining it up with other numbered vials, all various shadings from pale straw color and true yellow through amber to tannish. I filled in the medical history forms which another aide gave me, emptying the bag for Dr. Feldspar: fatigue, short breath, burning eyes, shoulder aches, bloatedness, depressed moods, memory failure, tired blood, lack of concentration, rattling bones, dry skin, wrinkles, hard stools, flatulence. What I didn't list was the main problem: ambivalence towards men. Do I or do I not want to connect with one? *Vorrei e non vorrei....* I like my freedom, but not being alone. (You've had a marriage, Chessie chides, why can't you just be a dignified widow and get on with your work?)

As I sat in the waiting room, it seemed to me that I was making a mistake to be there: the room was poorly lit and was full of fake plants and jars of feathers. And *he's* a natural foods man? I asked myself. Sitting on a plastic settee that encircled a tank of tropical fish, and that I kept sliding forward on, I stared morosely at photocopied nutrition articles tacked on the orange walls and the varnished plaque which read, We Take Bancamericard. It was tawdry. What kind of wife would have had a hand in such decor? The other waiting patients, straining their eyes to read in that dim light, looked weird. How long did it take him to make people look healthy? Another notice advised that the window should not be raised — anyone wanting fresh air should see the receptionist. The water cooler in the entry was empty. I waited almost an hour before Dr. Feldspar could see me.

He was ensconced behind a huge semi-circular desk on which a skeletal hand held a clutch of pens and pencils. He closed a book, and craning I read the title: *Blind Ambition*, by John Dean. Behind him, with all his diplomas, was a photo of his receiving an award; he was wearing a dark suit and a light turtleneck and smiling handsomely.

He regarded me steadily from behind his aviator-style glasses.

I said, "Dr. Feldspar?"

He said, "Who else do you think I could be?"

I stiffened. He glanced at the medical history I had filled out and tried saying my name. I said it for him. "Italian?" he asked, looking up.

"What else do you think it could be?"

He grinned. Making notes on the form, he continued to question me.

"One hundred and twenty years is a natural lifespan," he said, leaning back, when I answered at what age Marco had died. "If your husband had been my patient, he'd still be here."

72

But would I? Feldspar was like a dizzy dame, chatting on non-stop about himself as if the two of us were on a trans-continental train and his waiting room weren't full of backed up appointments. Following his divorce, he said, at age fifty-three he had set about to be a runner. He would soon be doing his first Boston Marathon. "I'll be looking for you," I told him.

He was, I knew from the start, an operator. Like Max. But an educated one. I could not forgive Max for not being what I expected in a Jewish man, for not being someone I could learn from and ad-mire as Chessie with Jules. ("In all the world how did I get a Jew who drinks too much and doesn't read?" I had exclaimed to Chessie who answered drily, "You must have been looking for him.") The doctor was what I had wanted Max to be; he read, he discussed, he jogged. During the physical he told me he had once been interested in an Italian girl from the old neighborhood in Mt. Vernon where he grew up but her father had discouraged him. Was this a come-on, I wondered, *che gioco giochiamo?* He was interested that I was in pub-lishing because, he said, he had a book in him. They all have books in them.

Although his front office was full of personnel, in the examining room, as on a date, we were alone. Tapping me here, probing there, watching me stretch, flex, bend, he said appreciatively, "You're in good condition. Wonderful legs. A good looking woman." Stretched out then, on the table, as he put his fingers in and up, I held back a contraction. I need something, I told him, for my bouts of apathy, my low energy, my always feeling tired and generally depleted.

"Hypoglycemic!" he chortled, "eighty percent of the world is. I get them all — it's either me or a shrink, and people would rather think it was their diet, not their soul, that's off."

After the physical, I dressed and went back to his desk where the consultation continued. It was $150 for the initial visit. I then had to be scheduled for a 6-hour session for glucose tolerance testing which was extra; each weekly vitamin shot would be $25.

"You cost more than a shrink," I said.

"But I make you look better."

The Vitamin Doctor as the new medicine-man, the magus in an age of megavitamins, health foods, organic gardening, air and water reform, aerobics. Now there was to be lecithin granules and brown rice in my life, de-caf coffee and soy bean snacks. NO SWEETS! he declaimed. No dried prunes — mysteriously he said dried fruit doesn't go with the Italian temperament. No onions, no tomatoes. No wine.

I balked: with all the deprivation I already have in my life, I'm going to add more? How can I fit in to my overloaded schedule that list of nine vitamin and mineral supplements? "We still have to do our best," said emphatically as he scribbled the memo and tossed it to me. "Just this morning my girlfriend said to me at breakfast she heard on the radio that a person would need over a hundred supplements to reach ideal requirements."

Girlfriend? I was impassive as I replied, "What I heard on the radio is that for only $35 I can have my place in the cosmos by sending a check to the Star Registry so they can register a star in my name." I took the diet sheets he gave me and knew I wouldn't return.

More than vitamins and what Chessie called dignity, I wanted a replacement for Max in my life. And for God's sake, no dogs! Fine thing for Chessie to preach — let her be stalwart down there in New Orleans. She had a husband to fly back to every so often.

I had been sure I would marry Max. And yet the very night of my return to Boston, after leaving Winnie off with the luggage and parking the car, as I walked back to my apartment building and considered the clear night sky, I felt my heart tighten with sadness. *M'illumino/ d'immenso.* Ungaretti's poem was in my mind: limitless expanse in just seven syllables. I considered the word consider; my convent school Latin extended the meaning: to see the stars together until the pattern is clear. As I looked at the stars' beauty and distance above me, I was moved by the long journey they foretold. There was so much about me that Max couldn't understand, wouldn't think important. Why was it so hard? One could be close to someone and still be misunderstood; there was no greater emptiness. As a girl I had looked at the night sky and wondered what I was all about. Should I give it up now and live as Max did, not being illumined by the immense, but simply accepting the little things of life day by day? Was that enough?

My thoughts led me to my lost house, to Shady Brook Farm.

It was a place I had loved from the day a real estate agent had driven me through the stone pillared entrance onto a country road flanked by giant maples. It was early fall and the trees were tinged with their coming colors, the air still warm with the afterglow of summer. Marco and I had decided it would be good to be in the country with land around us where the children could play, and we could take walks or plant vegetables and see the sky. Marco would write, I would translate. We had wanted a place for getting our work done, for our children to grow up and come back to, for the rest of our lives.

After we moved into the barn-house, it seemed to me I could feel the genius of Charles Burr, the composer who had lived there, in the very walls. I laughed at friends who stood in the two-story room, furrowing their brows as they looked up at lighting in the beams and asked, But how will you change a light bulb? Not for me their practical worries and timid concerns.

That home framed some ideal Marco and I shared — the devotion to art and to work, to children, nature, love, and trust in the future. And our last child, Lavinia, my Winnie, was born after we moved there.

But nothing lasts.

Especially during the winters, in my Boston apartment, I would think of Marco and Shady Brook Farm; I would remember sleeping close to him and how the old barn-house would seem to shiver and shake in the wind; it would creak like an old ship sailing a wide sea but it was a comfortable feeling and I had felt safe and protected next to Marco, as if the ship would carry me safely to wherever I — no, he — was going. I thought of the grand piano in the same spot where Charles Burr's had been, and Chessie and Dee at their music lessons in the great room; I thought of Burr's whimsical divider, a half-wall with slanted and spaced uprights like a musical staff, which had created a bit of separate space for Marco — but not much, and at times, when we were all in the great room at once and he was trying to concentrate, he'd call out in frustration, "*Ma, questa non è una casa, è un teatro!*"

And yes, it was a theater. At holidays we and our friends the professors, designers, editors would come to play charades in the huge space, to eat and drink at the Italian refectory table, to hear our laughter ascend to the rafters and beams.

I thought of the Italian journalist who had come, years before, to interview Marco at home in Medwood. "*Magnifico,*" he had exclaimed, standing in the great room. "*Stupendo,*" he continued from the top of the hill where his gaze swept the valley, and on to the blue and purple mountain ridges. But then in the interview he asked how Marco, so urbane, so wedded to the Italian language and so much a part of Italian literary life could live so removed from all that in the country. Didn't he suffer from his isolation, his virtual exile? And I had bridled, thinking to myself, but Marco has everything! — a wife-housekeeper and translator; children, friends, colleagues and students at Harvard, esteem, travel, his books, his work, his fame. Marco's solitude was restorative, not the affliction most of us know.

That night in Boston under the stars I asked myself what it meant to be always returning, circling anxiously over my lived life and wanting to regain it, to have it as before. It meant, I feared, some eternal childhood, some failure of the fibre, some willful blindness. I kept seeking home, as if it were *that* very structure, *that* very man.

It was the call from Henry Levine's secretary saying that Henry's wife Flora had died that called off the marriage. The Memorial service was scheduled for the day Max and I were to leave for the Cape to be married.

Henry Levine, senior editor at a fine publishing house and a specialist in European authors, had introduced Marco's work in the states and had been his editor. A tall, thin, austere man of cultivated tastes, I often met with Henry when I was translating Marco's work. I would leave the house in Medwood, dressed to go to the city for our editing talks, with the feeling I had joined the world of purposeful people. I was put off at first by Henry's saying that my fee as translator was pretentious — or was it presumptuous? Whatever it was, he had mentioned it in a disapproving tone. I was, after all, he noted, Marco's wife. And I had wondered if he thought that, as was the custom with everything else wifely, I shouldn't be paid at all.

Marco and I became friendly with the Levines and I was fond of Flora Levine (née Ryan), a pretty woman who was devoted to Henry and had severed with her own offended Catholic family to marry him. Saddened by the news of Flora's death, I called Max immediately: "Sweetheart," I said, "can we leave the following day instead? After all, it's not a real wedding with guests, it's just the two of us and that part-time minister. He won't mind."

There was a pause. "Everyone else seems to come first," Max said.

I was shocked. "Max, I'm talking about the death of a friend! She didn't die on purpose to spoil our plans!"

"I planned to leave Thursday. You know, I gave up appointments with people I could have seen that day. How close to her were you, anyway?"

I felt my face harden and my stomach knot, but I kept my voice level. I could feel him at the other end of the line waiting to be triggered. He had done this before. Whatever frustration he couldn't tolerate became his excuse to drink. ("You are destroying me!" he'd exclaim. "You know what will happen now!" And I would be more frightened by the need he had to find something outside of himself to be responsible for his drinking, than by the drinking itself. But I'd stay calm and say: "You need help Max, and you know where to get it. You can't make me responsible for your life.") "Max, it will be bad luck," I told him quietly over the phone, "I really don't want to be married on the day of Flora's memorial."

"Well, Fran, you always do what you want, don't you?"

His tone was sarcastic. It had the familiar edge of my father's way of talking. But as I surmised, the thought of bad luck did persuade Max to postpone our wedding day.

At the Memorial Service, I remembered the last time I was with Flora. It was just before I met Max. The Levines had invited me to lunch. Flora was still having chemotherapy following a mastectomy, but was so attractive and confident that I could not but think that her danger was past, that she had won.

I kept being aware of how Henry loved and delighted in her. Flora was warm, teasing, and flirtatious with him. She made him playful and tender. It was a revelation to me of how close married people could be, and I kept drinking them up with my eyes. Henry's austerity simply melted away with Flora's charm. They held hands. They called each other pet names. He wore a striped tie she had knit him from the fur of their Russian wolfhound. It was a picture that made me feel in the way, all the more since every so often one or the other made an effort to include me, as when Henry asked politely how I was doing. I was wary. In what sense, I wondered. But he meant financially — did I have work? I told them how hard it was to find well-paying translation work.

"Well, you have Marco's pension, you're not starving, at least," Henry had summed up with a certain severity.

"There are all kinds of starvation." My words lept out, propelled by my new loneliness. At least you're not starving: his words pierced me. Henry, lean and elegant, seemed no other than the fat curé who had responded to Emma Bovary's need in the same way. Neither fat man nor lean knew what starvation was. ("Be natural," the vitamin doctor would later cajole, promising me health, vigor, renewed mental alertness, a heightened social life and longevity on a diet of natural foods and vitamin supplements, telling me to forget Italian cooking.) But I was starved for the company and conversations of Marco. Whole days now went by with no one seen, nothing said except the routine things between Winnie and me.

After lunch, we went to the Levines' nearby apartment for coffee. Once there, Flora began to look wan, with a far-away look in her eyes, her gaiety gone. What did she see? I suddenly wondered if Flora were lost and I shuddered, afraid to be near her.

Recovering, Flora took me around to show me the new decorating in their place, and I thought, if she's re-decorating, everything must be all right. At home in the evening Henry bound books, and she played the flute. They had a place in the country; they went to Venice each year and stayed in the same room in the same *pensione* (Ruskin's) on the Zattere; they had two splendid sons. And yet I felt a presentiment of something terrible in that tasteful apartment. I began to wonder why I was there. Was Flora trying me out in the home setting with Henry as a possible replacement? But that was unthinkable! I was morbid from being too much alone. I kissed Flora goodbye and said, "You look wonderful — I'm so glad everything's going right. Stay well! "

Now Flora was dead. She was just my age, I kept thinking at the service, and now she's gone. Henry looked stricken. But he spoke beautifully, devotedly, of Flora. Edith and some others from Pricer were there, too. I left, wondering what Henry would do with his life.

Max called, belligerent and drunk and asked mockingly how I enjoyed the funeral. I sickened at his words. That night I dreamt I was digging my own grave next to Flora's.

The following day I told Max that it was a mistake, I didn't really want to be married at all; in fact, I really didn't want to see him again. I told him too much: that we were finished; that I had always had doubts which I kept repressed but couldn't any longer; that I couldn't make the impossible work; that I had always wanted someone who would listen to me, take me seriously, and understand me as a person because my family never had, and Marco, though he loved me, was too immersed in himself to give me the sense that I existed totally in his life.

At his best what Max gave me was that sense of my existence because he literally "took me in," visually and tactilely. It was his very possessiveness that made me know how much I did exist for him. And that was the quandary — if he gave me existence, he then claimed it entirely for himself.

I, instead, saw him as my backdrop: my wish was for Max to be the compliant blank in my life which I would fill in when and how I wanted to; he would always be there — he would not grow up and leave me, as my children were doing (filled with my mandate to be on their own and to be independent); he would stay and serve by just being dependably there.

His bluster and boldness had been briefly exciting. Yes, he was the piper of that old Convent School refrain warning us to stay pure: Who pays the piper? — The girl pays. And yes, I was the one who wanted to be led a song and dance and then have to pay the piper, no questions asked. But that was only one part of me; the other part deeply desired my own life and still looked to the immense.

I had accepted this split by reasoning that I needed a grasp on "real life." Max was material, very physical, very insistent on quick results and immediate satisfactions. There were no hard goals to be won first, as with Chessie and Jules; no temporizing as was Meade's style with Adele; with Max it was one fast scheme after another —

let's own a lobster farm on the Vineyard, go around the world by slow boat, collect fine prints for investment, retire and go into real estate, buy a house in Italy to be near Dee. With such allures he had filled my life from day to day. I smiled wryly at the thought of Max engaging in some absorbing, quiet, patient hobby such as Henry's book-binding.

No, I had always known we were incompatible, I told him, and had always put the knowledge aside; I would not any longer. *No*, it couldn't be.

I called my mother and told her what had happened.

"Oh my God, not when I've told everyone you're getting married!" she cried out.

When she calmed down, and after a long interrogation of my motives, she said, "Maybe there was a reason for Max. The good Lord must have sent him to prepare you to live alone. Do you think you're mature enough to be on your own now?" To that I had no answer. The question hung in the air, enveloping me as if I were in that thin misty air that sometimes rose up from the river at Ferryville and that Marco used to call *foschia*, damning its sly presence and slipperiness.

I was impressed that my mother could even have framed the question. Was the answer my work?

I had been too disheartened, too shy, when I got to Boston to be in touch with Edith Fisher who might have helped me right from the start. First I struggled along with translating, then I got into publishing through a career agency, which placed me as an assistant editor for the special imprint, Dual Visions. It was the paradox that struck me: as if I weren't conflicted enough ... as if my ambivalence, my inability to choose one way over another, to drive on one side of the dividing line or another, weren't already precisely and permanently enough established. The agency must have sized me up at first glance as material for Dual Visions.

"Dual Visions? It sounds out of focus," I had quipped, smiling at the agency woman who was briefing me.

The woman raised her eyebrows, looked several seconds appraisingly at me, and went back to scanning her work sheet. "It's a good publishing company. What they need is someone to work on their series for classroom use. It's on issues, sells well. It's an important line."

Abashed, I became very thoughtful and asked, "What kind of issues?"

The woman consulted a sheet and said, "It's humanities and social studies oriented — offering both sides of questions for school debate and discussion purposes. Issues like Environment, Euthanasia, The Welfare State, The Death Penalty, Genetic Engineering. That will give you an idea."

"Yes," I nodded, while the woman continued to survey me beneath her arched eyebrows. I began to feel at ease. Here's where being indecisive, seeing value to both sides of an argument and not being able to decide between two positions might at last be an asset. Where was it said that bread cast upon the waters comes back one hundredfold? My daily bread had been miserable stuff at the Riverview Heights School; now it could be substance. I would be employed to examine alternatives. And what was happiness, if not having an alternative in life?

It was at a Book Fair where I represented Dual Visions, that my eye was caught by the very finely printed and elegant offerings of a small Boston publishing house still family owned. I knew the line and had several books from their distinguished Poetry series in my own library.

I have always loved a well-made book — not only the ideas embodied in a deft flow of language, but the distinctive typeface, the feel of special paper, the heft and look of the volume in my hand. From childhood I have loved books. Every Saturday in Ferryville, after confession at the church on Hudson Street, I went to the public library on upper Main and returned home with my arms full. I piled the books on top of the bureau in my bedroom, glad of their company, of having the names of those wonderful authors there with me.

At the fair I picked up and scanned a handsome paperback book called *The Stalker's Guide to Gourmet Wild Foods* and thought how Dee would love it. Dee with her spring lust for wild shoots and her summer pursuit of berries and nuts. Dee loved the land, accepting all its fruits and foods, storing the summer bounty for their winters. And I thought Dee's artist-husband, Leone, would appreciate the illustrations — perhaps they'd be inspired to do a book together. I bought the copy for them.

Pleased, I told the woman at the booth, "It's for my daughter and son-in-law in Italy. He's a painter and she's a peasant with gourmet tastes."

"Charming," she laughed. She was an attractive woman, of a certain age, and her fingers were laden with all kinds of rings. She wore the bright red lipstick of another time and her blue eyes were deeply shadowed with more blue. She was wearing a stunning wool tunic over expensive, rust-colored suede pants. And even though she was so well groomed, there was an edge of zaniness to her and a cheerfulness in her talk that saved her from being conventionally smart. As we talked I learned that she was Edith Fisher, Editorial Director of Pricer Books.

"No! I'm Frances Beniferro — I wrote you. I was going to get in touch with you."

"Frances Beniferro! — I know your husband's work. I recognized your name when you wrote me from that girls' school and I've been wondering when you'd show up in Boston. I'm delighted, absolutely delighted, that we've met."

We found that we knew Henry Levine in common and when I said I had hoped that Henry might have known of a job for me in publishing that would have used my Italian to send me to the Bologna Book Fair since my daughter Dee lived not far from there, Edith said Pricer sent books to the Bologna fair, and if I ever wanted to switch jobs, to let her know.

"How can I be so lucky?" I wondered.

"We were bound to meet sooner or later, it was going to happen," she said confidently.

Out of Dual Visions and into the clear, I told myself. I went to work for Pricer Books and began to love my work. I loved the beautiful books that Pricer produced. Edith suggested that I collect, order, translate and annotate Marco's unpublished work for the Pricer Poetry Series. I hesitated. Then came my boldest stroke. Rather than being once more the silent handmaiden to a husband's glory, I offered a different idea. How about, I asked, something that hadn't ever been done, a collection of work by Italian American women writers. Edith said yes to my proposal for an anthology with my Introduction. It would be, she said, an important, original contribution. And then in her own irreverent way she added, "Have you noticed? — Women are striding these days while men have a mincing walk?"

In my new career I thought of Chessie — now there was someone to emulate! Compared with Chessie's steadiness, in the past I

85

had been unsubstantial, *sfumata*, like a photo in soft focus, smoke rings that would drift away into nothing. It was as if I could filter into anything — married life, translating, motherhood, teaching, editing — but not be there fully. Just the opposite of Chessie who might be narrow, but who knew her work in life and was anchored as securely to that as she was to Jules.

Was it her absorption in her work that had estranged her? Or was it her fear that I might jeopardize her relationship with Jules? If so, how fragile was the relationship? Right from the beginning, before I ever met him, she had set the wrong tone. "I don't know how I can have him meet you and Winnie in your tacky little place," she had said. That astounding denial of us, her family, was the beginning of strain between us. Betraying a reliance on outside props that I had not suspected, Chessie saw me as no longer the mistress of the Medwood house and no longer the wife of a Harvard professor. Thus, I must be nobody Jules would want to know. The first seeds of diffidence between Jules and me were sown in Chessie's mind by Chessie herself.

It worsened when she called with such a tale of grief between her and Jules that I had said in joking exasperation (but, who knows?, perhaps with an edge of conviction that her super-sensitivity caught and clung to), "Well, you could always leave him!" I had made mistakes before. Would time ever diminish them? Or would I compound them, as had happened with the weeds in my Medwood garden. There I had devised a weed-deterrent for the flower-beds by laying plastic mulch on the ground. But it was the wrong plastic — clear, not black — and the weeds had grown thick, robust and profuse under that hothouse treatment. A simple error, but fundamental.

So my error with Chessie. I can imagine the startled look that must have come over her face at my silly words — her silent gasp, her brow furrowing in dismay, even a quick knock on wood to neutralize the sound of what I had said. She must have been horrified at the casualness with which I implied that Jules could be cast off like last year's fashion; it must have sobered her like a splash of cold water. I imagine her making then and there the estimate that her very closeness to me presented a hazard. I can hear her mind clicking shut as she decides she has to be independent in the most drastic way possible: Jules or me. Thinking of me, she must have feared becoming like me and decided she wanted what Jules promised: security and stability. She wasn't resilient or adept enough to have us both.

The distance she created when my spirit was at such low ebb was crushing to me, like a second death following Marco's.

CHAPTER FIVE

A chance to visit Chessie in New Orleans came when the American Booksellers Association convention was scheduled to meet there and I was to represent Pricer Books. I called her.

It's disconcerting to start a telephone conversation with Chessie. She answers with a gulped and furtive Hello as if speaking from a hide-out. There is nothing welcoming about the half-mouthed sound, muffled with a touch of annoyance as if an intruder has jostled her, that she makes into the receiver.

"Chessie, how are you? This is Mom."

"I know."

I always leave a pause after my opening, each time waiting for Chessie to respond with a greeting, or ask how I am. Each time the pause is left hanging, emphatic in its isolation. It was like her occasional bare-bones postcards — no 'Dear Mom' at the beginning, no 'Love' at the end, just a niggardly 'Best Wishes from Chessie and Jules in Virginia' sort of message, the minimum due me. And if I said anything, she'd stop sending even that.

"I'm coming to New Orleans, Chessie for the ABA. I'd love to see you. How about my staying with you?"

"You'd have to sleep on the couch," she said quickly, "I'm not giving up my room. When are you coming? How long? Don't all you convention people stay in a hotel?"

Chessie's questions were quick, probing, non-stop. My mother always said she should have been a courtroom lawyer. I get the feeling of Chessie backing me into a corner and picking my brains, digging out information or retaining off-the-cuff remarks that aren't meant for anything beyond the moment, but that later might be used against me. She gives little of herself, and that begrudgingly.

When I ask about her work, or what friends she's made in New Orleans, or how a long-distance marriage felt, she simply said it was nothing she wanted to discuss. Communication isn't a one-way street, I tell her, hoping still to be friends but willing to settle for basic politeness. I'm not interested in communication, she answers.

"I'd rather stay with you than at a hotel," I said laughing in embarrassment at her telephone resistance. "It seems like ages, Chessie. How I miss those times we used to go to the opera together when you were at Barnard and I'd come down."

Chessie warmed a bit. "Yes, that was nice."

"Do you remember "The Dialogues of the Carmelites?"

"Oh, yes! The Salve Regina — so heavenly. I'll never forget those sad, majestic voices of nuns in chorus that fade away as each goes off, one by one, to be guillotined. What a hymn for the daughters of Eve — from women to a woman. I keep thinking of that prayer: 'Hail, Holy Queen, Mother of Mercy; our life, our sweetness, and our hope.... To thee we cry, poor banished children of Eve....."

"Reminds me of my Concordia days," I said, grateful that, despite the recent years of strain, she would occasionally soften and be the old Chessie.

Abruptly she asked, "Do you miss Max, Mom?"

Caught unawares with this reference to another of my mistakes, I bluffed: "At my age, I guess, it's better to be wise than wrong."

"What the fuck does that mean?" she said crossly.

"I guess it means that the only pay-off to being right, as I was to break off with Max, is being wise."

Chessie said, "I really feel sorry for Max." Taking his side in her analysis of why things between us had not worked out, allowed her to vent herself to the point where she could finally say, "It's not terribly convenient, but I guess you can stay here. I'll meet you at the airport, Mom."

A few days after that telephone conversation, I received a post-card from her, so unexpectedly full that it made me hopeful about the coming visit. "Tonight I'm happy," Chessie wrote, "because it's Saturday and one more week is behind me. If that sounds like a terrible attitude, it's just that my schedule is so grueling because I'm still teaching. Yet the other night I caught myself being happy, all by myself, in my apartment, happy because I'm doing what I love best and people actually listen to me. See you soon."

Chessie was like Marco in that she could totally immerse herself in her work and not pine excessively for home life, friendships, all the social activity that took so much time. She was not as sociable as Marco, though she was just as self-centered in her work. Once Chessie's direction was set, she did not look back with regret. She wanted both marriage to Jules and her career and if that meant an initial period of their being apart, then she would do it. Her commitment was absolute: she could not be distracted. She was considered promising, outstanding, and she was determined to be so.

As a little girl Chessie would hang on my stories, pleading, "Mommie, tell me another one!" She had found her way from the stories to literature, and from there to the psyche. "Homer said it best," she explained, " 'A dream, too, is from Zeus.'" And for Chessie, who had learned the language, he had said it in Greek.

Chessie's was a modern, career-tending marriage carried on by expensive long distance nightly calls to Jules in New York and frequent trips for both of them, sometimes to some romantic week-end place between their two cities. They had married while she was still in graduate school and he had stayed in New York while she returned south to finish her degree and teaching commitment.

They had met three years earlier when Chessie had come up to spend Christmas with Winnie and me at my parents' home in Ferryville. From there, one afternoon, she had taken the commuter train into the city to attend a lecture on alchemy and literature. She was a comparative literature scholar and an intellectual, and the academic world gave her the order she craved. Winnie says Chessie has always been in need of law and order, but I remember her freer, more imaginative. In college Chessie was a war protester and aspiring writer for just the right amount of time — one eye remained focused, always, in her career direction. She made no apology about being an elitist.

From when I first read to her and then taught her to read, she has been a passionate reader. What grips her is people's stories and why they act as they do. I still marvel at the leaps of insight she is capable of, and the elegance of her literary analysis. Even before meeting Jules, who is a theorist of cognitive psychology, Chessie was absorbed by the analytical process.

I told her once that I thought her becoming a psychoanalyst was not only due to her love of unraveling stories, but also to her Italian family background with its deeply felt responses to life. "You like to make things so simple!" she retorted.

Yet she had met Jules in the simplest of ways — she had simply been drawn into his magnetic field: at the lecture, which he had also attended, he had stared at her (wearing my fur toque over her long hair and looking like a Baltic princess) until her eyes had been drawn to him.

She later related the story quite matter-of-factly, but I remember her first telling how uncomfortable she was when she became aware

91

of his stare. She had returned his look, then immediately looked away. And when it persisted, she had darted him another look, wrinkling her brow in perplexity to make sure he understood her annoyance. Such invasiveness! Talk of the zipless fuck! All the more distracting because he was so attractive.

Jules is a bearded man, and his beard and very slightly thinning hair are between a gingery color and amber. His eyes are a cool blue, his look very steady and penetrative. He was certainly not to be deterred by a stunning young woman wrinkling her brow at him. In fact, after the lecture, as Chessie told it, he went up to her and with a self-introduction began his courtship by commenting on the lecture. She would have walked away, she said, but the fact was that he was cool and his remarks so very cogent that she was snared into replying, and her own response carried them forth on the current of some deep mutual interest in things of the mind that became, as they strolled out into the dusk of a winter afternoon, also very physically compelling. They began seeing each other.

Jules was impressed by Chessie's publications and it was he who suggested she start training as an analyst even while she was still doing comp lit at Tulane. Through his recommendations and influence, and because she was so able, she managed it. They had a traditional wedding, a long and expensive honeymoon in Europe, and then went their separate ways until their careers would allow them to be together in one place.

They were admirable; everyone said what a handsome and gifted couple. And it's true. But it's as if everything about them comes from some control box in the brain, not the heart.

As a cognitive psychologist, Jules seems to have placed all his bets on logic — to have, in his rationalist zeal, rejected the kinds of knowledge given the poet and story-teller, whereas Chessie has never abandoned them. Nevertheless, little by little, but noticeably over the three years of her marriage to Jules, she has deferred to him as the superior manager of their lives because of his logical argumentation; his mind worked computer-like whereas hers, she felt, was still too swayed by emotion. As well it should be! I continued to think, skeptical of anyone (like Jules) who distrusted life as it's really lived, not as it's computed. I had lived with a poet; Marco had known life to the core. Jules could be filled to the brim with IQ and reason, but it was at the expense of mystery and wonder and that, to me, was too impoverishing. Why didn't Chessie see it?

In any case, Jules adores Chessie and she adores his adulation which she returns with unqualified acceptance of his views on how their life should go. Winnie gets furious with me when I say this, but I sometimes think Chessie is like those old people who deliberately impoverish themselves in one way so that they are taken care of in another, like giving up their assets so they'll be eligible for a nursing home. I keep feeling that Chessie is giving up her old ties to insure herself with Jules.

Before they were married, when Chessie moved in with Jules, I was his champion. I had found him charming and attractive when we met and I liked the idea that Chessie had a male companion who was so clearly her intellectual equal. And I said so when my mother and the rest of the Ferryville family disapproved and said it wasn't decent for her to be staying with him. I supported Chessie against her grandparents' criticism and then found that it was I, in the end, whom Chessie turned against.

I think it started when I called her once at Jules' place. He is like my parents in that he likes the appearance of propriety. Chessie later told me that Jules thought it highly inappropriate of me to call her there.

I was amazed. "Why is that? I'm the one who accepts your choice to be where you are."

"He feels you're too intrusive."

"He should be glad that I feel able to call you at his place. Why is he so defensive?"

At first Chessie had agreed with me.

But a strain had set in. I began to distrust Jules. So unlike Marco! so hard to be at ease with. Jules' humor is biting and is always about others, never about himself.

As Jules and Chessie withdrew from me, they surprisingly reinforced ties with the Ferryville relatives and became close to my sister Adele and her husband in New York. Calling her regularly, Chessie must have sensed a natural ally in her grandmother, for my mother understands deference towards men as I do not. And they're both pragmatists, always on the side of the stronger. This pleases Jules; he's made my family his which is convenient since he doesn't get on with his own.

I tried discussing this with Chessie. "Jules is an empiricist," she said sharply, her eyes flashing; "he likes the facts and he likes people who get them right!"

"Jules is a rational prig!" I retorted too quickly, not thinking.

When I called Chessie in New Orleans, it was with a real longing to get us past the barriers that were piling up.

Why do you care so much about Chessie? Winnie would chide, jealous perhaps of the attention I was giving to the muddle. Friends told me, Back off — when she's ready she'll be back. Always on the fence, my mother said to me what she'd never say to Chessie: it's not right for a daughter to walk out of a mother's life. (But it happens, I thought; hadn't Yvonne walked out on Ethel Schotter?) No one could understand what I felt. With first Dee gone then Chessie, the whole thing tumbled — my world was gone. More than the loss of Marco (which I couldn't do anything about — death was death!), or the loss of the house (sold was sold!), Chessie's change of heart toward me marked the end of my life as I had known it. I could foresee myself alone.

Sometimes I blamed myself — how could I have let things go so wrong? Other times I felt humiliated ... stigmatized ... as if I wore a big, bright A on my chest, not for Adultery, but for something far worse — Abandoned.

Then there was anger: how dare she! Or I'd feel helpless, spiritually assaulted by something I couldn't understand.

It's a hard pill to swallow. I know it doesn't have to be this way — I've read of, heard of, know of daughters who grow into friendly and tolerant women, chums of their mums. Why is Chessie frozen into the warrior pose, straining forever to attack, devastate, annihilate me? No answer. Just like life. There is no answer, no explanation for random and unjustified affliction. No rhyme or reason, no why or wherefore. It just happens.

Hadn't I always proudly espoused my skepticism of rewards and punishments saying there was no heavenly system of equity, that nothing made sense. Now here was Chessie to prove me right in the cruelest way. That's life, Mom, I hear her crow, bursting into a chorus from Pinafore (recollected from all the performances of Gilbert & Sullivan I took her and Dee to, and that she adored): *Never mind the why and wherefore....*

And me, foolish as Lear in my grief, to rail and rant *But why?*

Deep inside I kept thinking it was Jules; like all old-fashioned shrinks he was still blaming mothers for everything; he hated his, Chessie's, all of them. But Winnie swears it was Chessie herself who turned Jules against me. She wanted to be free of me, a Pallas Athena sprung full-born from the head of her esteemed father without connection to an earthly mother who had come on hard times.

I thought back to my own mistakes, my own crossed intentions. I intended to be a good mother. Hell, Madam, is paved with good intentions! — Dr. Johnson, of course. And what did he know of child-rearing?

I knew of the hell of intentions not being understood.

I'm back in Italy, with Marco, on a hot hazy day outside of Naples. Some country place off a narrow road. We're tramping through the countryside with a guide, a dark-haired man with a cigarette in the side of his grinning mouth who's thinking we're crazy, on such a hot afternoon to be doing this. But Marco wants to see the miraculous fresco of the Madonna painted on an archway somewhere in these surroundings. I am more interested in the guide — in his quips and good-natured cynicism, his lounging, tempting good looks. When we get to the sanctuary, Marco studies the painting of Madonna and Child wrapped in a cloud, and our guide relates stories of miracles associated with the fresco. Marco is a believer, I a scoffer, the guide a realist who's there for a fee and to earn it he is entertaining us.

Long ago, he says, even centuries, a man who had been playing nearby had unluckily hit the face of the Madonna with his ball and blood had issued from the painting. The people of the nearby hamlet were aroused with fear and fell upon the unfortunate man. He was lynched and the tree from which he was hung soon withered and died. Another long time went by, during which the Madonna was greatly venerated and pilgrims came from afar to honor her. It happened that one of these visitors was a rich woman from Spain who came with the noble intention of giving thanks to the Madonna for a great favor received. When she got out of her carriage at the archway in order to gaze upon the painting of the Madonna, this Spanish lady happened to step upon a wax replica of an eyeball, a votive offering which had accidentally fallen from its place on the arch.

It was learned that not long after her visit to the Madonna, the Spanish woman's feet had to be amputated. They were then encased in a glass box and sent to the sanctuary to be shown near the arch as a kind of cautionary exhibit. The glass box is no longer there, but the story is still told. It's bad luck, the guide says shaking his head and smiling ironically, but the lady had to pay.

I'm furious, Marco entranced. The guide dangles his cigarette and shrugs his shoulders pragmatically: one never knows with the powers. One has to be careful. Conspicuously he extends his index and small fingers in a sign to ward off any malevolent spirit that might be lingering nearby.

Good intentions are not good enough, I'm thinking, my mind churning furiously. One must have not only the noblest heart and worthiest motives, but another more powerful intercession – the benevolence of providence, charms, spells, amulets, formulas to propitiate the cosmos and to be succored against all the resentments of all one's fellows cumulating for all time in all the space around us. No one is free of lived time. No matter how well intentioned I am, I have to be lucky, too.

Many years after that visit to the Madonna dell'Arco, Winnie was saying to me, "There's so much evil, Ma — so much we don't even know about." Yes, I agreed. Life is full of traps and bad happenings between people despite the best intentions. Everywhere and with everyone we are vulnerable.

Chessie denied even my intentions. Still, in New Orleans, without Jules, she might be receptive. Her card raised hopes.

Keats. Every so often I think of him in Rome. Dead at twenty-five. Served rotten food in that little room above the Spanish Steps. "Severn, I die!" he cried. Lovelorn. Wasted. Winnie in profile reminds me of John Keats. Also in sadness. I wish I could assuage that sadness in Winnie, but when I try I'm met with disgust, insults, rejection. *Nil desperandum* — not to worry, I tell myself. Time will tell. Time will heal. In time my daughters will know me.

On the plane to New Orleans my seat was next to a portly man. As one does, we exchanged conversation and I learned he was an author going to the booksellers' conference in New Orleans to promote his latest mystery novel. We talked about books, exchanged business cards (his name was Houston Kelly) and delivered the noncommittal histories of ourselves which strangers do on travels. He was wearing what I believe is called a lounge suit — it did not have the structure of a business suit. It was grey with dark stitching on the lapels and pockets, softly tailored and befitting him, who was also soft. At first he appeared to have no shirt or tie on, just a black sweater, but then as he moved around I could see that his fat neck and chin had covered his shirt collar and knot of a black knit tie.

A zany scene from a play called "The Dancing Bear" came to my mind. It was about a man who was not only portly, but bald as well. And very sexy. He was courting a young attractive woman who patted his huge pot belly and said, What about that? It disappears in bed, he answered.

Houston Kelly's eyes were grey, his face puffy and pale, but I had no way of knowing if he were a dancing bear. He had been born in upstate New York, he said, had been a high school math teacher for some years but when his first books were successful, and when he and his wife of many years divorced, he decided to give it up and be a full-time writer. He said that in his marriage he hadn't wanted children because of the problems they represent but that now he was close to his only child and, as a matter of fact, the boy had never been a problem, never given trouble, never asked for money.

"You were lucky," I said. "I have three girls. Three sets of problems."

"I'll tell you one thing," he said affably, "I'd never marry another Pisces. I'm Taurus and Nadine — my ex-wife — and I are good friends, and we agreed on everything with the split, did it neatly, both of us contributing equally to our son's education, everything in order, right down the middle. Best of friends! But no more fish in my life."

I laughed. "Fish is good for you — better than Scorpions, anyway."

He regarded me intently with his clear blue eyes. "You're not one of those are you?"

"Would you change your seat?"

"You bettcha! — they're bad news, with their horns and stingers."

He had two whiskeys as we chatted, and I white wine. Usually I read on planes, but he was determined to talk and I didn't really mind.

"Maybe we can meet for a drink on Bourbon Street," he said when the plane was descending for landing.

"Boston's better," I told him. "I'll be visiting my daughter here in what time I have left over from the ABA."

"Visits are difficult," he said shaking his head. "I know from when I've gone to see my kid. You're not on your own home-base anymore, you're in their home, their territory and you have to tread carefully."

"I know! It's a mine-field!"

"I've seen it happen," he went on. "I go to visit Bick, a grown-up person, and somehow, no matter how careful I am, he reverts back to being the child — and then resents *me*! It's trouble."

"I'm relieved that you have some problem with your paragon son — why should you get off easy?" I silently hoped that Chessie, with all her psychological know-how, would have figured out our truce ahead of time.

That wasn't, for the moment, what bothered me. It was the feeling that, little by little, despite my efforts to hold on, the fabric and texture of my life was unraveling, becoming worn thin; that I couldn't count on anyone to last — look at Max, Flora, the vitamin doctor, Chessie. I seemed to be stalled in one gigantic, paralyzing grid-lock, a chilling image of stasis: I couldn't go forward and get on with things, I wouldn't go into reverse.

I was marking time. But as my mother says, sometimes you have to give time to time (and then she sounds like Gertrude Stein saying History takes time).

"Good luck on your visit," Houston Kelly told me as we said goodbye. "How about my giving you a call in Boston?"

"How about that?" I replied cheerily.

CHAPTER SIX

Chessie was waiting for me at the airport, her lips tight. She must have told Jules about my visit. I imagined him saying to her, You're so compliant to your mother. That would set her off.

You don't have to tell a partner everything, I once told her. I have no one else to talk to, she replied. I wished she had at least one close woman friend, or had stayed in touch with her sisters. Instead, everything spilled over to Jules, like flood waters over the reservoir. Keep some of you in reserve, I counseled. Some things have to be kept in one's still center until time lets us separate truth from the chaff.

Smiling and waving, I walked out the gate towards Chessie, hoping for the best. As our looks meshed, she nodded her head, turned abruptly, and walked away. She was wearing a long sweeping skirt and elegant high-heeled boots; her hair was done up in a twist with loose wisps curling around her ears.

I hurried to keep up with her fast pace, carrying a raincoat over my arm, a suitcase in one hand and my briefcase in the other. My shoulder bag kept slipping down causing me to pause as I hitched it back up. Without a backward look, Chessie strode into a restroom. I put down my bag to wait outside. She popped her head half-way out the door and in the way of a parent to a lagging child, said, "Mom? Wait for me. Don't move."

Maybe, I told myself, she acted like this because she was uncomfortable waiting so long to go to the bathroom; maybe it was silly of me to think she resented my being there. And another airport scene came to me from years back: I'm picking up Chessie and Dee when they're little girls returning on the New York-Boston shuttle after a visit to their grandparents. I'm standing at the gate watching for them. I see them come down the gangway and watch them follow the other passengers to the terminal. Then Chessie spies me and sprints ahead, leaving little Dee behind. This annoys me. It's so typical of Chessie, wanting always to be first before her sister. She's running and as she hurtles herself at me, I fend off the impact by raising my arm. Instead of ending in my embrace, Chessie is sent sprawling to the ground. "Oh, Chessie, honey, I'm sorry, are you all right?" I exclaim, extending my hand to her, embarrassed before onlookers. Then I hug little Dee who has just joined us. It's a scene still vivid to me and maybe to Chessie, too.

In the cab to Chessie's place I pulled from my briefcase a little packet wrapped in lavender tissue and tied with a pink string bow — Chessie's colors. "Here, Chessie," I said, handing it to her, "I have something for you."

Opening the paper, Chessie took out and studied a little tin plaque embossed with a butterfly. "What is it?" Her tone was flat as my mother's when I gave her the Chinese pin.

I laughed in embarrassment. "Well, of all people I thought you'd know! It's an Italian votive offering I found in an import store. The butterfly is Psyche, the soul — I thought it was just right for you. You can hang it above your desk."

"You know I'm not like you with all your hangings and mementoes. I hate clutter at my desk." Chessie continued, expressionless, to handle the tin plaque, weighing it in the palm of her hand. It was very light. Now it looked flimsy and foolish to me.

She used to love my surprises. I said, "I thought of you the minute I saw it because of the symbolism. You know, the soul is often seen in paintings as a butterfly. I thought you'd love it."

"Thanks Mom," she said putting it in her bag.

I felt as if I had made a social blunder. I should have remembered the clues of how Chessie has changed. She likes labeled things now that have big price tags and one doesn't have to guess about — a Coach bag, a Hermes scarf, a Tiffany jewel. Jules' first gift to her was a Mark Cross pen.

All experience is so variously seen, I mused looking out the cab window at the lights of the city. *Experientia docet/* experience doesn't. How strange it is that all the things we lived through together as a family I see one way, my daughters another, like an endless variorum with each of us a differing editor of the same text. What are we but anxious psyches ... a hovering of butterflies, each fluttering its own way ... ephemera.

I felt isolated in the cab, felt the quiet edginess in Chessie next to me, as if she were tensed to spring, verbally, if I uttered another word. There was so much to say, yet I said nothing, just looked from the window at the city unfold. Speaking was fraught with danger and misunderstanding, with wrong interpretations. We should by now all be struck silent, left to signing and gesturing.

Chessie is brilliant with others. In company she shines with wit and intelligent conversation. As a couple, Jules is the social heavyweight and she makes the impression. Yet Chessie defers to him, considering his silence the mark of a mind at work. She accepts his opinions and assumptions; no decision is made individually, she consults him about everything. Again I thought it must have been her deciding to let me stay with her before first talking it over with him, that now accounted for her mood.

When Jules had disapproved of Max, Chessie revised her original acceptance of him. "I used to think of you as a goddess, who could do no wrong, including Max, and because of that I would sometimes be in conflict with Jules," she told me in the tense aftermath of a family occasion with Max, "but now you've gone too far. Now I see your flaws and I resent having my own identity compromised by someone like Max in your life."

That staggered me; if Chessie could see that I was flawed, could she not understand that Jules, now promoted to god, would inevitably be, too? And poor Max! He was what he was, but certainly not responsible for Chessie's identity.

"She has no mind of her own!" I told Winnie in exasperation. In my turmoil I thought of Chessie as another Dorothea Brooke subsuming her treasures on an empty and finicky Casaubon.

"Let her go, Mom, she's a bitch. She's jealous of your having had Papà, and the house, and everything because in comparison Jules is such a cold fish."

"Oh, Winnie! What are you saying? What's going on? We're a family!" I would utter helplessly, not knowing how to stem the tide that was swamping us.

In the cab I took a different tack and said, "Chessie, how did Jules like the book I sent him?" Jules dabbled in book collecting and I had started sending him an occasional Pricer volume signed by the author. He never thanked me directly nor ever mentioned reading them; I always had to ask Chessie if they'd arrived. Each time I wondered how they who loved protocol, ceremony, exact procedures, and proper ways could so easily brush aside common courtesy.

"Oh, fine, Mom," she said now, obtuse to my real meaning. "He always likes what you send."

The cab pulled up to a yellowed building, not yet drab, but with signs of incipient peeling and lack of attention. Chessie had told me how lucky she was to get an apartment in a good area for a reasonable rent.

"What a fare!" I exclaimed as I read $38 on the meter. "Let me get it."

"Well, you should. You are staying free in my place," Chessie said.

Her apartment, one bedroom and a living room, was sparsely furnished, but the three closets were jammed with her clothes. She indulged, she admitted, but said she had to have some pleasures in life and with the hermit's existence she lived between Jules' visits, she felt she could treat herself to a wardrobe. I admired Chessie's ability to please herself. Everything else was spartan: her bathroom shelves spare with a few necessities, her room and desk were unadorned. No clutter, no disorder, no distractions. Indeed, where would the little tin votive offering fit in?

Chessie pointed out the couch, with a pillow and blanket already laid out on it, where I'd sleep.

"There's Marco's old desk!" I exclaimed. "How good to see it again — reminds me of home." I gazed affectionately at the one nice piece in the room, the elegant Italian writing table originally from the old Verona law office of Marco's long deceased uncle, which I had given Chessie along with Italian silver and china. The desk had been in Marco's alcove of the great room. There he had written his lectures, and poems to each of us in his life.

"You know, Chessie, sometimes I dream of our old house. I miss it so much! How beautiful it was with all that tall fox-grass rippling on the hillside. How snug we felt when the snow came up to the windows and we built a fire and had tea. I loved that old barn! How I miss it!"

"We all loved that house, Mom, but I always think of it as your house because you made it so much yours." Chessie appeared to be taking a milder tone, but then she added crisply, "That's just another of your mistakes — Jules says you should never have sold it."

"Sometimes, Chessie, we do things we don't want to do."

"Not you. You always do what you want. You're completely self-centered."

"Did Jules say that, too?"

"I'm not going to discuss Jules."

No, of course not, I thought. For if ever there was a plan of mutual self-exculpation it was in those two.

The wonder is that anyone survives being a mother. Children are like a litter of piglets that are darling, wee things but hungry, too — rooting, snuffling, struggling amongst themselves, each one trying to displace the other, vying for a place at the sow's teats to suck off her. It is, they say, the natural order of things; the young must consume and displace the parent in order for life to go on. But what of the male parent? He's never in that picture, being drained by the onslaught — he's out of range, living high off the hog, hogging time for himself, his higher art.

I had the woman's job, which is life. And all I wanted was that my daughters not be my enemies.

I stood looking around Chessie's place — a television set, an armchair, a low table in front of the couch. No curtains, no pictures, no concession towards making a home. Chessie's clear strategy was one of resistance towards getting comfortable and settled in New Orleans.

"It looks so temporary," I said.

"I'm not like you," Chessie boasted, "always having to make a nest wherever you are."

No, she was tougher, not impulsive; she could wait out the short run for the long.

Off the living room was her kitchen, small, neat, with a round table and two chairs at the window. There was no fruit bowl on the table. The counters were bare. Tacked on the wall near the sink was a paper placemat giving eight maxims of life: Take time to WORK ... it's the price of Success/ Take time to THINK.... It's the source of power/ Take time to DREAM ... it's hitching your wagon to a star..., and so on. I recognized the paper mat from my father's favorite diner in Ferryville. He had sent me one, too, with the notation, 'Fran, here's good solid advice and common sense for you, it will give you peace of mind, longer life and keep you happy at all times.' Well, it hadn't. I had thrown away the garish, tacky piece of paper, offended at its cheapness.

"Chessie, why would you have this thing, this pop psych on your wall?"

"Because I love Pop, not pop psych. That's something you wouldn't understand."

She was wrong. I could both understand and explain my father, a man unschooled and unformed but groping towards some sense in existence. He had wanted a philosophy of life, hadn't known how to think it out and form it in his own words, then had found it on that placemat from a diner. But that didn't mean he could make it mine. I would find my own.

I went over and opened the refrigerator. It was barer than Ethel Schotter's. Die of starvation, it said to me, I will not feed you.

"What are you looking for?" Chessie frowned.

"Don't you eat? I was hoping you'd have some fruit — you're in the South, after all! I get hungry, you know, my low blood sugar. Hypoglycemia."

"Now I've got to have a person with special needs to think about! I knew this would happen. It's not a visit, it's a visitation! I hate having my whole apartment occupied."

"Well, what about when Jules comes? Or your colleagues from New York? Didn't you tell me you just had someone here? Was your fridge empty then? Did you give her the couch?"

"That's different," said Chessie. "Of course I didn't give her the couch — but she didn't stay long, either."

My visit seemed to be a mistake. Chessie once told me I had been a great team leader for them when they were children, but that I didn't know how, gracefully, to deal with my grown-up offspring. To which I replied that my own parents hadn't exactly given me models of graceful behavior. At least, Chessie had replied, they're consistent in who they are — you're flakey, volatile. Nobody knows who you are!

As I stood in Chessie's unwelcoming kitchen, I felt like a child, away at camp for the first time, and homesick. The unbidden words leapt from my mouth: "I miss Max."

"That's typical of you," Chessie said tartly. She had taken a sponge from the sink and was passing it over her spotless counters as she lectured me. "Having bad judgment in the first place and then never sticking to things and making them work. A real relationship has a dialectic in which, at times, one partner is more dependent than the other and then the balance switches. But the important thing is that they balance each other and stay committed. Actually, I didn't like him, but I always felt sorry for Max."

Chessie, obviously, was handling her life more efficiently. "Enough, Chessie. Let's think about eating."

In a cupboard I found some dried porcini which I soaked in tepid water. I opened a jar of artichoke hearts, added the drained mushrooms, and combined them with a few eggs for our meal. Fortunately there was a bottle of wine, and after a glass or two, Chessie relaxed and became friendly. Her hair fell in long waves upon her shoulders and though she looked wan she was still very girlish.

"How is your teaching, Chessie?"

"Wonderful! That's what makes it all worth while. My lectures have become famous — my students give me fame."

"That's really fine. That must make up for your being down here and not in New York — why don't you look at it that way."

"Yes, Mom, it helps. But now everyone in the department is trying to persuade me that I'd be selling out if I gave up my position here. They want me to stay. They make it seem like I'm anti-feminist to want to be with Jules."

"There's something to what they say, after all you're on tenure track here, you've published in your field, your career is going well. It's a big step to move out of it and start psychoanalytic training."

"Yes, I know all that. Jules and I have discussed this endlessly. He thinks I can make a big contribution in psychology and I am definitely interested — it's a great challenge. But the main thing is it will get me back to New York, and we'll have our work in common."

"Then don't worry what the people in your department say. They're not in your shoes. You have to go with your own feelings."

"That's what I'd like to do, Mom." Chessie was warming up now. She liked being affirmed in her own judgments. "I want to have my marriage."

"But how did you arrive at the decision that it was you who had to move to where he was?"

"It's not just a question of career. I have my family in the north, too. I've lived up there and have friends, and all that counts. Still, everyone here makes me feel like a defector. As if I'm giving up everything for a man!"

"Are you?"

"Of course not! When I go back to New York, it will be on terms that satisfy me, too, and not just for Jules. But he is part of my decision."

"I don't see anything wrong with that," I told her as if I were some sage imparting a blessing. And yet I did. As much as the idea of Chessie being geographically closer appealed to me, I sensed that she wouldn't, in fact, be closer. Jules would be even more in charge.

Cheered, Chessie became affable. "I really appreciate your saying that, Mom. It's good to have someone to talk things out with who's not taking some ideological stand! Do you feel better, now that you've eaten? Tomorrow we'll do some food shopping. I don't have much in the place because I eat out a lot."

As she spoke, Chessie got up from the table, took the sponge and wiped crumbs from the table. She was a compulsive wiper. It touched me to see her wipe, wipe, wipe as she talked, as if she were wiping the slate clean between us to give us a fresh start.

She put on rubber gloves to do the dishes, and said as she did so, "I have super dry hands — something like eczema."

"Is it nerves?"

"What do you mean?" Chessie frowned.

"I never remember your having dry skin before. But dryness is an interesting thought — the Latin *siccus*, like the Italian *secco* which means dry, gives us our word sick. To be sick is really a drying up, not having the vital juices flowing. It's interesting."

It's a sign, I told myself; her human feelings are drying up. Alarmed, I plunged on, "Anyway, to get back to food shopping, don't worry about me. I have people to see and will be out a lot myself. But maybe we can have Sunday dinner together."

"Sure, Mom," said Chessie, "and if you can fit it in, you can come to my class on Friday."

"Good Friday," I laughed. "I'd love to." I loved my beautiful daughter, the first child of my house. I was proud of her, and had always seen in her what was missing in me. Was that what she felt and acted against? Was it too much a burden of idealization I put on her?

Chessie's lecture was worth having to re-arrange my appointments for. Chessie, as Dr. Francesca Beniferro was superb, more a star in that role than she was as Mrs. Jules Mann.

I sat in the back of the room as she began the session with announcements. She was dressed in a bold blue suit, blue stockings, low taupe boots, and a bowed blouse. She had very carefully put on her make-up that morning, outlining and shadowing her eyes. Her eyes are small (the sign of a neurotic I once read somewhere) and she likes to enhance them. Her hands darted to her hair which was left loose and curling to her shoulders. From her ring finger gleamed the large gold band studded with diamonds and topped by an engagement ring of a solitaire that impressed my mother and made her proclaim that Chessie, at least, had made a good marriage. The rings looked heavy on Chessie's delicate, tapered hand. As she warmed into her material, she took off her jacket, sat on the desk, and crossed her blue-stockinged legs. She was extraordinarily attractive.

I thought of Chessie at seven or eight years old, a darling girl with long curls, who had even then an intense need to be right, of knowing something for certain.

For some lesson on health or hygiene, her grade school teacher is asking,
"Which would you choose, if you had a cold, a handkerchief or a paper tis-
sue?" And Chessie's hand shoots up and she says assuredly, "Handkerchief."
In her family there are hundreds of them: large monogrammed ones for
Marco, embroidered, linen ones for me, small ones with the names or initials
of Chessie and Dee in garlands and curlicues, exquisite old Venetian heir-
looms from Marco's family. All colors and sizes, some of fine white cambric
bordered in lace, others that were patterned and plainer for everyday – the
girls choosing a different one each day to match what they were wearing.
The hankies came from all over – Italian convents, Switzerland, China, the
Philippines and at Christmas I always put some fresh new ones into their
stockings.

"Handkerchief," says Chessie boldly, secure in a proud tradition.

"No," answers the teacher. "They can spread germs. Paper tissues, like
Kleenex, are only used once, and then can be thrown away so they're prefer-
able." Chessie will forever remember being told publically she was wrong,
and, as the upholder of beautiful things, being put down in the name of
something utilitarian and throw-away. Smarting over the matter, Chessie
comes home to ask me what I would choose. The handkerchief, I say. That
reassures her for she believes me utterly, my word prevails over the teacher's.
But that was long ago.

In her class, Chessie quickly got past her announcements and
some comments on the assignment and went into the substance of
the session. She was lecturing on the psychic journey, paralleling the
exploits of heroes to that of the searching soul; she made the analogy with Dante's Divine Comedy, the necessary descent into the In-
ferno and the confrontation there with all the horrors of human-
ness, the purging, and then the emergence. As she spoke, Chessie,
with her sense of drama, got up from the desk and strode in front of
the class, gesturing. Ending the lecture she said, "The only creature

who has the power to err is the human one with his or her free will, but remember, though the journey is through hell, the final goal is to come out again, to see the stars — *E quindi uscimmo a riveder le stelle*."

The students clapped and I did, too. *Bravissima*, I said and gave her a kiss. Chessie had found her place. I recognized her as a learned person, an emerging authority. Easily, without rancor, I coveted the professionalism Chessie had earned through years of self-directedness in her graduate work.

Chessie showed me her office. It was not as bare as her apartment and I understood that it was here that her real life took place. There were prints and posters on the walls, plants on the windowsill brightening up the little space and offsetting the institutional grey desk and chair and file cabinets. The two photos on Chessie's desk were of Jules, tanned and handsome in his hiking boots and knapsack, and Marco as a young man lounging lengthwise in a beached *sandalo* on the Venetian Lido. He was a lithe, bronzed Adonis, slim and muscular, with a sly-fox smile of provocation at a time I was a child of two or three on lower Main Street, far away who must have dreamt him.

One wall of Chessie's office was lined with books, other books were piled on a long table in the center of the room which held Marco's bust of Dante crowned with a laurel wreath. Marco's books were there. His presence was in the room. Mine was nowhere. I began to feel let down, tired.

"How about lunch now, Chessie, I'm famished."

"I knew this would happen," she glowered, quite different now from her professional self. "I know all about your low blood sugar, but it just feels as if you're clinging to me like a leech."

"Well, really, Chessie, it's just this once," I said, offended in turn, "I'm at the convention every other day."

We went to the campus cafeteria and were able to sit out on a patio in the sunshine. I gazed about contentedly at the warm day filled with colorful students coming and going on the walks. Nearby a jazz trio of piano, saxophone and flute was playing and asking for donations for some cause.

Chessie said, "Why don't you ever go stay in Italy with Dee?"

"Stay? You mean live there? What an idea! I have to make my living here, and what about Winnie, she still needs me."

"I suppose. But maybe eventually. Wouldn't you like that? You would have family again with Dee and her child. You'd like that. Then you wouldn't be alone."

"That's not realistic. Italy is fine to visit, but what would I do living there?"

"Didn't you always want to write? You started writing poetry when you were at that girls' school."

"Yes, and I still do. I can do that here. But no matter where I am I'll always miss a companion in my life, someone to talk to. Like we used to, you and I, after your father died."

We ate in silence as I considered this strange new proposal of Chessie's that I remove myself to Italy. Was that what she needed to make her future work? But she already had everything in her favor! I gave words to my thoughts: "You really have an enviable place in life right now. You have your work, the esteem of your colleagues, Jules, youth, beauty, income, independence...."

"You'd really like to think that, wouldn't you," Chessie flung back, enflamed. "That's what you'd like to think! — that everything's easy for me. You want to make it seem as if *you* came from nothing and became an achiever while I had everything given to me! Well,

I'm telling you you're wrong — I'm just as insecure and vulnerable as you are, probably more. It's catching in our kind of family! I don't have papà, the one person with unconditional love and support I could turn to! And there's all the pressure now of combining two fields and seeing how I can make a significant contribution, get published, perform at peak."

"Exactly what you've always wanted to do," I murmured. I marveled: it happened every time. Chessie had to come out first even in hardships. Even if she had to deny her very gifts, her happy childhood. As a child she'd withdraw from any game she was not winning. I'm not playing! she'd say and walk away. And she'd write in the books that I bought for both of them, Dee keep out this is mine.

She was so far removed from reality that I should have realized that one can't evaluate another's woes; even illusions hurt. My mistake was always to respond to her. "I gave you the chance to express yourself Chessie, to be yourself."

"You only did what every enlightened parent should do."

"But what you forget is that I hadn't found my own freedom before showing my children theirs."

"What does that mean?"

"That I will be alone in life, unprepared. I am not a Wasp from a long tradition of outspoken, cantankerous, eccentric, independent women. I am not part of a community network like Jules' mother and other Jewish women, or even Black women. I am simply trying to form myself without the cultural or family tradition that could help me. I'm starting late...."

Chessie raised her head haughtily. "You made your choice — you could have married Max."

We sat silently watching the students pass before us as I thought with despair and pain how words, which had been such envoys of pleasure between us, were now our enemies. Perhaps reading my thoughts, Chessie said in a milder tone, "I wish I could help you, Mom, but I can't." It must have cost her something to admit she couldn't control everything. I was grateful for her words.

"Let's hear about your work," she went on. "Seriously, Mom, why are you doing this Italian American anthology, isn't it a bit much?"

Hesitant and shy before her implied criticism, I could not answer what I felt. I gave my editorial explanation: "Well, as you know, there's a great interest now in ethnicity and also in women's writing. I put the two together and came up with a group, Italian American women, which has never been perceived as having literary writers. These are women who are truly missing. It will be a discovering volume, something for the historic record."

My real answer lay in my heart: I have been a silenced woman, like these other women. I have been someone else's voice and nourisher ... now I want to be me. This book is for all of the women, but also for me.

It was something I could not now say to Chessie, so I said lightly, "We have to be accounted for before we're all something else — I mean, if you have children, they'll have Jules' name, while Shirley Temple's grandchild has an Italian name."

"That's beside the point. What you're doing may have some historical significance, but I can't see that it's literature."

"Yes, literature," I replied firmly.

"Well, if it's a whole group that's been overlooked, it must be because there really wasn't anything so wonderful about their work in the first place."

"That's what was said about women as a group once, too. Now we know better. You sound like your grandmother — neither of you think much of women because you overvalue men."

"You always go too far, Mom!"

"There's far to go to recover these women. We're doomed by birth and by history to be the eternal mother to our men and children. But what of our needs? what of our never heard selves? what of denied women who project their own deprivation onto their children?"

"I'm not going to listen to this," Chessie said firmly, getting up to leave. "I have other things to do. I'll see you back at the apartment."

I smiled and said, "*Ciao, cara,*" feeling better than I had since the visit started.

On my way back to the apartment, I passed a sidewalk flower vendor from whom I bought Chessie a bunch of anemones, gorgeous in shades of pink and orange and purple. Chessie came back, relaxed from having time to herself, and pulled from her book bag a sweet bread for our breakfast and two Perugina Baci. She was in good humor which was a relief since I was cluttering the small space with papers, hand-outs, publicity posters and books. The undoing of Chessie's ordered and ascetic life was totally visible.

She put the bunch of anemones in a drinking glass on the little round kitchen table where they made a jubilant blaze. I gazed out the window at a neighboring backyard where a woman was hanging out clothes. Her yard was a flowering bower of calla lilies, fuchsia, primula, geraniums, flowering broom, roses, wisteria, daisies, nasturtium. "*Che bello!*" I exclaimed.

"You made the flowers bloom, Mom," said Chessie cheerily.

"A nice thought. What are you doing this afternoon? Would you like to come over to the convention and visit the book exhibits?"

"No. Today I'm going to take care of my errands. You can be on your own."

When Chessie left I went to her room to get the phone with its long cord to use from the table with my papers. On Chessie's desk, always so bare, lay a scattered heap of correspondence — as if she had gotten packets of it out of drawers to look over. Those piles of letters strewn about her usually neat desk weren't accidentally there. What's put out is meant to be seen. Freud says there are no accidents; Aristotle, on the other hand, says there is a place for the accidental, the unforeseen, in life. That's what luck is. Hesitantly, as if they would crumble to my touch, I picked up the envelopes. They bore the address label of Mrs. Augustine Sturzo, Ferryville. Years of letters from my mother to Chessie. All the years that Chessie said she hadn't time to call or write me, she had been writing regularly to my mother and running up hundreds of dollars in telephone bills to Jules. My eye fell on a page of a letter in my mother's handwriting: *Your mother has always been strong-willed, but your disapproval of her can have a bad effect on you, and it's you I'm thinking about. Leave her to herself, she lost her way a long time ago and I hope and pray she will find it back to God. P.S. Please let me know about a sweater. I would love to make one for you.*

These were the years my mother had told me she had arthritis in her fingers and could no longer knit. I was not surprised that she offered to do so for Chessie. But I was angry, and felt betrayed by their hidden alliance.

In Ferryville, I had asked my mother how she could always take Chessie's side no matter how badly she acted with me. She had an-

118

swered simply with probably the only sincere words of her life: Chessie makes me feel good. Higher values did not enter into her scheme of things. She was engaged in her own version of triage by weighing who made her feel good against who didn't and could be most easily jettisoned. Apparently, it was I who would go overboard.

That night I said to Chessie, "That's quite a bunch of letters from your grandmother all over your desk."

"Yes, I was wondering about whether I should keep them. I really don't have the room. On the other hand, it doesn't seem right to throw them out."

"There's nothing worth keeping of what my mother writes," I said harshly. "I know from her letters to me: all platitudes. Nothing real. Just like the diary of her honeymoon trip to Italy which she gave me to read! — there was nothing but travelogue talk as if she were writing lines memorized from a brochure. She's never said what she really feels, only what she thinks is the approved line."

I was surprised at the vehemence of my remarks and recognized the cause — I couldn't stand to be left out, to be excluded from my daughter's life as I had been from my mother's.

"You should have more humility," Chessie said curtly.

"I'm not buying that crap anymore!" I exploded, enraged. "Your grandparents would love to stuff that humility and self-denial crap down my throat, but I'm surprised at you! — I let you and your sisters grow up to be and do what you wanted. All my parents ever did was criticize and knock self-confidence out of me."

"I wish you'd stop about your family," said Chessie. "I really don't want to hear it...."

Of course, I thought, this is just another game Chessie doesn't want to play unless it's clear she can win. The thought of Chessie's bare and stingy fridge incensed me — suddenly, when I was there,

Chessie didn't shop or eat? Were only mothers supposed to prepare food? I supposed that Chessie disliked seeing me with my briefcase going about my business as an editor. It was all right for her to be a professional, but her mother, no! If I had stayed in and baked bread instead of going to the convention that would have suited her fine. Now she had latched onto her grandmother, who would never be any competition for her.

"...knocking self-confidence out of you!" Chessie scoffed, "just imagine...." As she began, eyes narrowed and her voice rising to lash back at me, the telephone rang. She picked it up quickly from the low table in front of the couch where I had put it, and took it on its cord to her room, closing the door.

It must be Jules, I thought, sinking down, saved, onto the sofa, to catch my breath and still my pounding heart.

Sunday was pleasant. Driving out into the country for dinner, we passed members of a wedding coming out of church. One young woman was sheathed in form-fitting black which outlined her rear and ended in a flounce of tulle below her knees. She was wearing ornately patterned black stockings and outrageously high red spike heels.

"At a wedding!" I gasped at the sight.

"It's OK, Mom."

I turned in my seat to stare at the woman who was in the road-way near a parked car, imperturbably re-arranging her face. Her blondish hair was caught up in a frizzy spout on top her head and long dangle earrings brushed her shoulders.

"So outlandish," I went on. "She doesn't even care she's stand-ing in the road with traffic going by — it's as if she's only concerned with her self!"

"And she probably is."

"So inappropriate, so vulgar...."

"And so of our times. Everyone is making a personal statement these days."

"That's it! You know I don't care for the new Pope, he's retrograde and anti-woman. But I do think he has a point when he condemns the extreme individuality of our times. It's bizarre. The Greeks knew, Aristotle knew — people have to connect to other people, not just do their personal thing."

"Aristotle? You keep mentioning him."

"Yes. I'm taking a philosophy course at night. That's what I do now instead of be with Max."

"Well, Mom, maybe there's still hope for you."

"Don't write me off yet. You know, Chessie," I confided as in our old times, "I think everything of importance goes back to the Greeks. They faced all the great problems head on — I don't mean abstractions, I mean truly what it is to be human involved with other humans. I think I want to go to Greece."

"Good, Mom, good."

North of the city we stopped at a restaurant where we ate outdoors on a terrace. A male colleague from Chessie's department stopped by to chat and we were relaxed, conversing well and enjoying ourselves.

"A beautiful day," I said, "thank you, Chessie, for a beautiful day." And thank God, I thought, for this time with her alone without the presence of Jules hanging over us like a dark cloud.

"Thank *you*, Mom," she said, as I picked up the check.

That evening as we were watching television, Chessie took the glass of anemones from the kitchen table and put it on top of the

TV set so that we could continue to see them. "Aren't they wonderful," she kept saying and I was glad.

"Well," I said happily, "some good came from this visit after all."

"In fact, I'm going to miss you," said Chessie.

"Thank you, sweetie, for saying that. I was beginning to feel I was in the way with all my clutter and hunger pangs."

"You're just lucky I love you," Chessie said.

"That's what they all say," I laughed. But I wondered what she meant. I wondered if, after I left, that love would continue or be all grabbed back by Jules.

CHAPTER SEVEN

Henry Levine and I spent a Saturday at the Boston Museum of Fine Arts. We had passed through a room of classical funerary objects where I pointed out a cylindrical marble urn with a removable cover that was shaped and sculpted like a wicker beehive. The legend identified it as a late First Century A.D. urn holding the ashes of Eurysaces the baker's wife. We admired it.

I said, "You know, Henry, there was an author at the ABA in New Orleans promoting her biography of Rose Kennedy. She said that when Rose was asked what she most regretted in her life, the answer was not being allowed to go to Wellesley. Can you imagine, Henry? There's a woman who lost a son in the war, then a daughter, Jack was assassinated, and Bobby, and Rosemary's been put away — and she mentions that after being accepted at Wellesley, her father consulted with the archbishop who advised against it and she was sent to a convent school, and that's what she most regrets."

"Of course I understand that!" Henry exploded. "Rose Kennedy's life could have been another one if she had done what she wanted. Instead of going to some Catholic institution which put her on track to be a mother-of-sorrows figure and a compliant wife to a philandering husband, Wellesley might have opened her mind. Her life could have been better or worse, but at least it would have been her own. What she was regretting was that her decision had been taken from her — she was totally honest in mourning her lost life. You, Fran, are such a mother, you can't imagine being anything else." His grey eyes cold as steel behind his unrimmed glasses, he turned to me in front of Eurysaces' urn and repeated, "You're such a mother! Can't you ever get past that?"

The accusatory word hung in the air like a slur. It was a revelation. I had never thought I appeared to people as just "mother." It clashed in my head with other, contradictory, echoes: Chessie saying, you weren't like a mother — you were like another of papà's daughters; and Dee: Who are you? there seems to be no one there; and Winnie: you've never loved us like papà did!

I suddenly realized that with Henry all I seemed to speak of were my worries about my children.

Abashed, I looked away thinking, it's too soon after Flora's death to be looking at funerary urns — it's upset him. Henry was still mourning Flora the woman, his wife; what did he care that she was the mother of his sons? It was as if he saw me as some squat, black-clothed, backward Italian peasant woman, widowed and hanging on to her children. A throw-back to a whole tribe of wailing, clutching mamma-mias. I echoed Dee's question: who in fact was I? I wasn't that squat figure, I wasn't Flora, nor Dolly Sturzo, nor Chessie.

My thoughts went to a poet I had heard read in Cambridge who introduced each of her poems with a little snippet from her life. Her life was better than her poetry. She had everything. What, I thought, if I had a husband like the one she alluded to in her remarks, an astrophysicist about to take her to Florence for a year where he'd engage in thought and she would write, or not write, as she pleased. What if I, too, were Jewish and bold and sassy, thin and chic? What if five or six of my books of poetry were all published, reviewed, acclaimed? If I were in addition to being a poet, a respected critic, the recent author of a theoretical work on women's writing, a winner of awards, a teacher in college, a mother of daughters but also of a son? What more could I then want? That fortunate, but not great, woman poet had both life and art without having to choose. She could dwell on the pure line of her poetry, her mind shielded from having

124

to grapple with making a living, keep the car running, doing the tax returns, supporting Winnie through the world's most expensive college. Yes, her children and her marriage might occasionally impinge on her, but she would have the physicist with whom to share her concerns. She was not alone in the universe of her own work, but on a lead-line that drew her safely back into the spaceship with her loved ones when that universe grew rarefied and chilly.

Henry's remark was like a slap awake.

The next day I went into Edith's cluttered office, threading a path between book piles on the floor and looking for a place to sit. There was none. Books and papers were everyplace; cards, messages, and cartoons littered every surface. "This," I said, extending my arm to take in the whole space, "is what Marco would have called a total poem."

Looking up from her littered desk, Edith questioned me with her lifted eyebrows.

"Henry Levine, on a date," I said, "is impossible."

"I could have told you that, but now you know for yourself."

When Houston Kelly telephoned, he sounded, in contrast to Henry, very warm very easy. He invited me for dinner at his place. "I make a mean stuffed pepper," he said.

I thought that was interesting. Winnie had taken a summer waitressing job at Cap's Place on Cape Cod, and the apartment, after awhile, was morose without her there. I would enjoy eating a stuffed pepper with Houston and hearing talk.

I brought him early lettuce and some pansies from my window-box garden and a bottle of Pinot Grigio.

"Role-switching, eh! I'm here cooking and you're bringing the wine and flowers."

I laughed. "Does that bother you?"

"Hey, lady, you don't know who you're talking to! I'm a convinced feminist. You could even support me while I stay home writing and it wouldn't threaten me a bit. "

Houston's round dining table was laid with brown earthenware dinner plates that said, emphatically, man-stuff. I arranged the pansies in a bowl and put them on the table as a centerpiece. Nearby, on an end table, were an array of pipes in a holder. Looking around, with my appraising eye, I saw Family Circle decor for a bachelor: Browns, woods, plaids. I'm being an editor, I told myself; I'm being my mother — too critical.

"The house drink is whiskey sours," Houston said affably, handing me one.

"Good, I love them. But why is it pink?"

"A little juice from the cherries."

"Oh, Houston, how could you? Haven't you heard of red dye in maraschino cherries? No one has anything to do with them anymore."

"You're not a health freak as well as a Scorpion are you?"

"Well, about some things, yes. Why gussy up good whiskey and make it pink? You know me — or, I guess you don't — but classic and good is my style."

"I like that for a title — Classic and Good."

"Feel free, it's yours."

He was boyish, bouncy, attentive, and flattering: "You're such a pretty lady!" he said as we toasted and drank. And he made me feel good, just as Chessie did my mother. I recognized a truth — appropriate men, like Henry Levine, made me feel terrible. We exchanged information about our past. Houston said Nadine, his ex-wife, was a good woman but hadn't been able to handle his success as a writer; she had wanted him to remain in the security of a teaching career with long summers off for travel. "She just couldn't grow with me. Too bad, but that's how it was."

"Yes, I know what you mean. Max was like that."

"We understand each other," Houston said amiably, patting my hand. As I regarded him, I thought him unhealthily flabby, and maybe not sexy. Did that matter? No. If I had to choose, it would be for the company. But I wondered about his contradictions: if he and Nadine were best of friends, why had he been so vehement on the plane about never getting involved with another Pisces; why did he put himself on the side of change but value predictability in his son?

He showed me a photo of Bick, a nondescript young man, and then he read me an excerpt from Bick's most recent letter. It was completely trite and I wondered at a writer like Houston reading that stuff with ringing accents as if it were sensational. I compared the letter to the flavor and bite of the merest postcard from Dee — she of the non-degree, the complications, the rebellions and demands. Bick, the good child who gave no problems, was a bore.

Houston showed me around. I wondered about the narrow single bed in his room where he showed me his wood-working equipment. When I admired a box he had made and adorned with decoupage, he said "I'll make you a jewelry box for Christmas."

I felt as if we were rehearsing the script of Life can be Good in a Second Marriage. He was being homey, and he served a good dinner. Then we played backgammon, each move laced with small talk and the innuendo of sexual parrying. He told me he lived alone but had had a girl friend, Vicki, for the past couple of years. But what he really was interested in was settling down with someone, making a home, not occasional visits from a sex athlete.

"You attract me, Fran, in every way. There's something to you — not like Vicki, she's a kid, good for a romp, but nothing to her. With you there's substance, I can feel it! You've had a whole life. And I'll tell you something, I can sense you want someone in your life. I feel our meeting has been fated, that we can help each other along the way."

"Jesus, Houston, keep it light! We've just met!" But as he talked, I liked his saying what no one else had — that I had substance. He was a writer, he saw into me, maybe he did know who I was.

"How did you and Vicki manage in that skinny little bed of yours, Houston?"

"Is that what you're worried about?" He got up quickly, went to the sofa and with a rapid movement opened it to a fully made queen-size bed. "Voilà, Madame!"

"Oh, quit it," I laughed "I wasn't fishing."

"All you have to do is say when."

I felt the intimations of the evening hanging over us gently like a hint of rain on a spring day; it was promising, but nothing more.

"You are such a pretty lady!" he repeated. "I want to kiss you and hug you, to put my arms around you and to make love to you."

"Isn't Vicki still in your life?"

"Oh, honey, I got rid of her months ago. I can't handle a crazy kid — she was fooling around with drugs and that's not for me. She's called and I've told her it's no good. I haven't heard from her since before I went to New Orleans."

"Do you like to get away for weekends, go to the Cape?"

"You call it. What can you lose?"

Much, I thought. I have always lost in the feelings arena.

128

Physical danger was less frightening to me than people encounters. Yet I wanted closeness with someone — a best friend, a daughter, a lover. *Vorrei e non vorrei....*

I left at about 1:30 AM but couldn't get to sleep until after three. Still enveloped in the overtones of the evening, I threw the I Ching and got signs for the Creative and the Joyous, with the image of the Gently Penetrating.

It was my suggestion to Houston that we visit Winnie in Provincetown and then spend the rest of the week-end elsewhere on the Cape, his choice. Houston had become a warm and generous lover, one who understood my work commitment, my need to be alone as well as together. For the moment it was perfect — we visited each other's apartments. We hadn't yet spent whole time together. We were together and separate. As Chessie once said, reprovingly, you want your privacy, your work, your solitude, and then, when you're finished, you want to open the door and have someone there ready for you. Of course, I answered, recognizing Chessie's own pattern in the description, doesn't everyone?

Houston told me he thought of me all the time. I do too, I said. It was the familiar feeling of buoyancy and hope. He made all the arrangements for us, and I was glad not to have to be, for once, the team leader, deciding everything, that I had had to be with Max, and before him with Marco.

In a dream I rehearsed the coming week-end with Houston. He appeared as someone thinner, svelter, better dressed. And there was Chessie, in a white doctor's coat and stethoscope, saying, "You're so undignified, Mom. Why don't you quit over-indulging yourself and toughen up?"

129

I was fretful at work the day before Houston and I were to leave. At noon I went out shopping to buy a new nightgown. All the time I'm thinking, tomorrow I'll wake up and go to the mirror to see what I'll look like, getting up in the morning with Houston there. I will not look good. My eyes will be small and slitty and the lids wrinkled; my face will be drawn and thin, making my nose prominent. My hair? thin — needs shaping, needs to be young. Before I gave birth I had hair. I gave my thick and healthy hair, my bones and my teeth, to my daughters. My belly protrudes; it will never go down from the pregnancies, no matter how much I exercise. Who knew then about keeping in shape? Women weren't supposed to think of being desirable after they were mothers. They had done their biological duty, and could rest on their laurels. Houston says I'm such a pretty lady. I say he's fat and flaccid and doesn't turn me on, but I need someone on my side, which he clearly is, now that everyone's gone. I need someone to love me, which he's willing to do. I think I am catching a cold. I have a headachy feeling in my right temple and my eyes look bleary. In the morning, instead of putting jelly on my English muffin, I'll do my Sicilian thing and put minced garlic on two big chunks of Italian bread and drizzle it with oil for breakfast to ward off a cold. I'll drink my orange juice and, for once, take my vitamins. But I'm not with it; I feel down, apprehensive. Sex is boring, being too much with someone is boring. By our going away for a week-end do I open a can of worms? open the door to his hints about our living together? I'm different from Vicki who was top-drawer sex. Don't worry, love, he says to me, we're going to make it. But I can't be Vicki. Are her eyes bleary and squinty, her belly flabby? I'm quality, I'm class; Houston says he's proud to be seen with me. He feels protective towards me. I'm a real lady. He wants me to meet his mother; he wants to flaunt me before Nadine.

I look around me — all the flotsam and jetsam of my past life, when I was a signora with a distinguished husband living in a beautiful house, is piled around me: on chairs and chests, on the sofa and tables. My family idols, the totems of who I always wanted to be: someone married with a family. Safe at home. Lowell: "as if in the end,/in the marriage with nothingness,/we could ever escape/being absolutely safe." I am not able to remove any kind of accumulation, especially the past. I need it all ... it pads me, it insulates me against the cold. Yet I Ching reads, Cast off the past. And Houston says we'll make it. He wants a real life together, not what he calls conjugal visits. What blocks me? I am hopeless. How can I love Houston? — I only need him. Graffiti scrawled on a billboard in the subway station: "Love hurts...." So it does. "Want it all?" blares another poster showing a suburban house. Of course. I want my hands to look nice, but I am getting brown spots. He likes my legs. So did the vitamin doctor, and Max. They all liked me. I am late for everything. Lowell: "We are poor passing facts....All's misalliance.."

Houston chose for our stay a nineteenth century Inn, owned by generations of the same Cape family, which he said would provide exactly the background he needed for his next mystery. Arriving there with him was to experience the same convergence of sexual morbidness and repression that had infused my days at Concordia Convent School. I had been twenty years a wife and four a widow with lovers, and yet it was like being, again, an adolescent. The sign on the drive read, "Slowly and Quietly, Please." Gazebos dotted the place like Stations of the Cross on the convent grounds. The Inn loomed up like a vast, wood version of Concordia's red brick Motherhouse and school. Inside I recognized the dark, threadbare rugs;

the wide, oak stairways, the genteel sitting areas of wicker and plush, the bracketed wall light fixtures, the faded wallpaper, and the reproductions of Raphael's Madonnas. Silent, clandestine couples (such as Houston and I), legitimate honeymooners, or single, elderly ladies and older gentlemen hovered in the shadows of the ill-lit sitting rooms where bridge tables stood vacant and shelves were filled with the brown volumes of long ago. A sign at one sitting room (bare and irreproachable in its lack of seductive comfort) read, "Keep the Door Open Please." I was transported back to the convent with its "God Sees You" reminders everyplace.

The main parlor had an upright piano where a little boy was dragging his fingers up and down the keyboard playing an idiosyncratic scale. One summer, at a family Inn on the Cape, I had seen Chessie and Dee at just such a piano. Chessie, self-consciously striving for effect in front of the Inn guests, had sat at the piano in the parlor and played, with loud emphasis, excerpts of half-remembered Chopin and Beethoven from her music lessons. She meant to awe, to get attention and admiration, but she was stiff and choppy and when it became apparent that she was in trouble and couldn't remember the rest of Liebenstraum, she stopped in a huff as if the piano itself were to blame. Chubby, easy-going Dee went over, then, and played "For he's going to marry Yum-Yum" in a way which melted all the elderly ladies in the parlor who clapped and said, "Oh, Gilbert and Sullivan! Very well done, dear." The accolade to Dee angered Chessie who remarked at dinner how stupid and rude the people were in this place.

That evening at the Inn I scanned the dining room and my eye was caught by a couple who were sitting side by side and I thought, how odd that they don't sit facing each other. The man was a replica of Max except that he was wearing glasses and Max only put them on to read a menu. He was good-looking, his nose prominent, his hair still dark and wavy. He had big square hands and wore a gold wedding band, as Max had when I first met him.

After my break-up with Max, Adele had telephoned and said, "Meade and I always wondered about such a match — you two just weren't suited. What was it between you — the sex?" I could hear Adele chewing on food as she talked to me and it annoyed me that she was always eating when she called, as if conversation alone weren't enough.

Should I tell her I wanted to do something for Max, open his mind and let him reach his potential? But my sister's remark was an easier, quicker explanation; it would be understandable to Adele, who had a terrible sex life with Meade, that I had been hooked on sex. So let her believe it. It would save me from having to admit the truth, my seeming dependency on a man, any man, with or without sex.

Wasn't that the explanation for Jean Harris, whose story was in all the papers, when she shot her lover, a doctor who lived and practiced not far from Ferryville? She wanted to hang onto him, with or without sex, while he womanized around the county.

"I can understand Mrs. Harris finally being provoked to the point of wanting to kill the creep," I said to Houston over stuffed quahogs, "but what I can't understand is her hanging onto him all those years and swallowing the humility he dished out to her."

"Now there's a story," Houston heartily concurred. "The genteel Wasp headmistress who lets herself be used and demeaned and dangled for years by the social-climbing Jewish doctor who specialized in loving and leaving the shiksas he probably hated through and through."

"A real back-street woman," I said disgustedly. "He sleeps around and she sleeps alone at the girls' school." I was thinking of myself at the Riverview Heights School.

"Look, honey, the perks, if not the pricks, were good. He takes her around the world, takes her to the country club dances, has elegant dinners for famous people with her the hostess, makes her feel she's finally living."

"She was a fool."

All that spring and summer as the story of the murder unfolded, I sat in judgment not of the despicable doctor, but of the woman who had let herself be humiliated. Why had she put up with his belittlements? Was her life so nothing without him? Didn't her sons, her work, her sense of self make up anything? I disliked Mrs. Harris intensely, because I *was* Mrs. Harris — almost the same age, same education, same pretensions, same fear, sole support of children without a father, paying my own way, wanting morality for others but not big on it for myself.

"I can't stand Mrs. Harris," I told Houston while my eyes darted to the man who looked like Max. "So superior! Her sins are both arrogance and naïveté. Two sides of the same coin. Even Galileo couldn't get away with that combination. He thought he could tell the Church a truth it didn't want to hear. They got him, and they'll get Jean Harris unless she gets smart."

I will not be so naïve, I decided. I will know what I'm doing with Houston. And I won't buy a gun.

Houston was more interesting than Max; I didn't love Houston, but, as in literature, one often didn't in life. One made arrangements, one played by the Etiquette book — one thought of heroines like Margaret Schlegel, and Isabel Archer, and Nina Leeds. Houston was a good writer of mysteries and he was very good with Winnie. After our visit to her in Provincetown, she had waved goodbye and called out, "*Ciao*, parents!," making me giggle with embarrassment. On our last day Houston and I bicycled from the resounding ocean beach on the narrow neck of the Cape over to the Bay side. We stopped at an old cemetery identified with a marker as having been used by the early settlers up to the Civil War period. On the stone of one Alfred S. Martling, and wife Martha, were three entwined circles with the letters F L T, one in each circle.

Beneath the circles were the words Friendship, Love, Trust.

"I guess that's what Alfred and Martha stood for," I said. "It says it all, doesn't it."

"Gottcha, babe," said Houston.

He *was* quick. Agile as a dancing bear. Quick on his feet, good on a bike, able to catch meanings: The best marriage was friendship.

Leaving our bikes leaning against the cemetery fence, we walked to the bay shore and came to a jut of land overlooking, in the near distance, the marshes and then, in the next distance, Cape Cod Bay, with, in the furthest distance the barely perceived shoreline of Provincetown and its Pilgrim's Tower. It was just before sundown, in a moment of shifting, brilliant colors over the water. We were hand in hand.

"Houston, how beautiful! We could buy a piece of land and move my old house — the barn — here." I spoke the words before I even thought them, like revelation.

"Gorgeous," he said, "beautiful. I've always wanted to live in a barn. Let's do it."

Looking at the incredible sky, the water, feeling my hand in Houston's firm grip, I was taken by the nobility and boldness of my vision. My house, my beloved home, to rise again in this beautiful place, to be restored to me. The house would call back my daughters, re-establish the old family. It would be a House in the grand sense, and I would be the head and everyone would come to visit. And I would do it with Houston whom I would surely come to love because his help would make it possible.

"What a magnificent dream," Houston went on exuberantly. "We could retire here. We could work from here."

His words cut into my thoughts and my brow furrowed at their sound, what they meant.

"Are you still seeing that man?" I could hear water running as my mother spoke and could picture her standing at the sink as she made her weekly telephone call to me.

"Houston? You know his name, why do you call him that man?"

"Well, I don't know. Maybe you're seeing someone else. How would I know?"

"Yes, I see Houston. That's about all that came out of my trip to New Orleans. I never hear from Chessie. I saw her in the spring and here it's fall and no word from her. She and Jules have been to see you, haven't they?"

"I didn't ask them," she answered quickly, "they invite themselves. What am I supposed to do, not let my own granddaughter come see me?" Her voice got hurried and excited as she tried to get on a different track, "Oh, that Chessie's so intelligent! You should be so proud of her!"

"What I am is disappointed. She and Jules act as if I don't exist."

"He's so good to her. He gives her anything she wants."

"There's a price tag on everything."

"Well, what should she do? Leave him?"

The worst, most fearful thing my mother could imagine was for a woman to leave her man — to be on her own in the world without any male protection. By putting that fate into words she was asking me how I could want that for my daughter.

"Of course she doesn't have to leave him, mother! What an idea. But she doesn't have to leave me, either."

"Listen, Fran, she's really crazy about him. She feels you're interfering. She feels you don't like him. Maybe that's why she stays away from you."

"I'm the one who stood up for him! I'm a person of principle — if I had objections to Jules, on principle I wouldn't have given them the costly wedding I did. For years I've been trying to build connections, not interfere! But they're just for themselves."

"Well, just be glad she's doing so well in her career and that she has a husband she loves."

"Let's drop the subject, mother. Let's just say that it's nice that you and Chessie get on so well. She's got a real mother in you and you've encouraged it."

"Now wait a minute!" her voice got harsh and angry. "I don't like that kind of talk! But maybe it's because I'm nice to Jules and butter him up. What you have to do is play up to him, make him feel important. Don't be so disapproving. If you get on his good side, he'd be nicer to you."

"And if you, instead, showed you don't like the way they treat me, they'd change their behavior. You keep welcoming them! They wouldn't dare act that way if Pop were in his right mind — he'd see right through them and shrivel them just with a look!"

I hated these conversations that circled, like donkeys with blinders around a grindstone, over and over the same ground. I knew in advance of each phone call how we'd end up compulsively repeating the same phrases. Wearied, annoyed with myself for the futility of it all, I cut her off with a pretense: "The doorbell's ringing, mother, I have to go. Good-bye."

"Oh boy!" her voice trailed off disapprovingly as I hung up. It occurred to me that she was as frustrated by me as I was by Chessie.

One night Houston took me to Maxl's.

Maxl's on a Friday evening was a friendly sing-along German Rathskeller where a pretty girl in a drindle and white stockings was perched on a high stool playing an accordion, accompanied by a pianist in a setting that was the replica of a Bavarian cottage. It was hearts and flowers and good feelings all the way to match the stylized heart cut-outs on the cottage shutters. Checkered curtains in the windows, a cuckoo clock, a window box of blooms, coziness.

I saw the Germans as they saw themselves: chummy, fun-loving, beer-loving, and music-loving. They sing sentimental songs, they tell mildly dirty jokes about traveling salesmen and the farmers' daughters, they yodel. But gradually I was over-powered by the Germanness of it and what it brought to mind.

I sat there, in my latinness, across from Houston, the Scotch-Irish ex-GI from World War II. How did he feel? He was enjoying himself. Obviously he didn't equate being in a Rathskeller with the

Holocaust as I did. For I had begun to realize that something complex was going on, an interplay of good-evil themes. The Holocaust made vivid and real all the hidden crannies of one's own vindictive and revengeful nature, unmasking the fear and hate we harbor for the weak, the vulnerable, the submissive, the different, the "other" — who is really us.

I was riveted by the Holocaust and the evil of the human soul, had always been. It is part of my unrelenting judgmental character, that I will not forgive Germans, I will not visit their country. Yet Marco, who had been a partisan during the war and had eight friends of his exterminated at Matthausen, forgave them. Maybe he could do so because he was truly secure within himself, was truly great-souled.

As Houston marked time on the table with his stein, I made myself join the fun and try to enjoy the performance, even the sing-along with its refrain in pidgin German and English. It makes us all comrades, I thought: Teutons, Wops, Micks and Jews.

But the thoughts wouldn't let go of me — there was the German film "Homeland" in which the Germans are made out to be the victims of the historic conditions entailed in getting their beautiful land rid of its Jews. The Jews made them suffer; the Americans were gross materialists. If only they could have had their homeland to themselves, all that mess of World War II would not have happened and they would have been spared being seen as criminals by the world. (As Marco had said mildly when I had expressed my indignation at "Homeland" to him, Of course they're going to distort history — they have guilt as wide as the ocean.)

But I could relate that distortion to myself: the revisionists have to revise what happened to make themselves seem victimized, otherwise how can they live with themselves; they are the larger I — I have to sublimate my own harshness and mistakes with my children, with men, and see myself as all benevolent and well meaning, a gentle and kind homeland to them all; if I saw that I let my history (my father) dictate in me as cruel and harsh a conduct as I had experienced as a child, where would progress and growth be? Would I be other than what my father is? I am obsessed with the Holocaust because I see the German in me: I am both the sentimental, homeland German and the harsh German. I despise the submissive Jew (my mother?) and I want to be allied with power (my father, Il Duce). I want to wipe out all differences from myself (my children who are becoming different from me, who act out their differences against me) — I want a homogeneous and fair race of obedient descendants who will love their homeland (me) without making any demands on it. I want to wrap it all up by going home, literally, to my old house and with a man named Houston!

Yet such control is obscenity — an obscenity manifested in the technical perfection of the extermination.

The singing in the Rathskeller swirled around us. Good hearted people sang and relaxed. Houston sang. I sang. So we can sit here in Maxl's and order a meal and sing with our dark side; and I can look at the pretty girl in the dirndl and see death.

Maxl's haus, rein und raus, everyone sang vigorously, ending up in a loud finale with applause and laughter and good feelings for all.

CHAPTER EIGHT

Winnie was in her second year at college. Dee wrote fitfully from Italy sometimes testy, sometimes lyrical depending on how things were going in her own life. Chessie had left Tulane and permanently joined Jules in New York.

I learned they had bought and moved into an apartment on the upper East side during a call from my mother. She told me how impressed Gussie's daughter Stella was when she and her boyfriend stopped by Chessie's for drinks. "Will you be spending Thanksgiving with Chessie and Jules at their new place?" my mother asked. "Adele and Stella and everyone say it's spectacular — has a river view. They've invited me to come when I want, but I haven't gotten into the city yet."

"Mother! I don't even know their address!"

"They probably think you're too busy to come down."

"What an excuse," I exclaimed excitedly, hurt and angry, at how Chessie could move and not let me know where she was in the world. What was going on? Why? Was this new silence about Houston? My mother still called Houston That Man; she did not refer to him by name, burned, I suppose, by believing in a Max who had never materialized for her. I always spent week-ends with Houston, though sometimes also during the week we'd cook dinner together — his place or mine. We started playing tennis at an indoor court where I found he was surprisingly good for an overweight man with a paunch, and consistently beat me. "My dancing bear," I called him affectionately, hugging him to me, glad to feel him close. In the early fall we drove to the country for fresh farm vegetables and then came back and cooked everything up: the freshly picked corn, the peppers which I made into peperonata with tomatoes and onions, the ripe peaches which Houston threw into the blender and mixed with gin to make us Ruggieros. I had told him about Ruggiero the bartender at Harry's Bar in Venice, where Hemingway and everyone hung out. "That's what I love about you, Beniferro," he said, "you're so literary, even in the kitchen." Being with Houston had its satisfying moments.

Others were less so, for he surprised me with how demanding he was not only of my company, but my very thoughts. Very unusual for a writer, I thought, remembering Marco. Most writers were so wrapped up in their own thoughts they had no need to get into those of others. Then I began to discover that to himself Houston was a failed writer; he was not the literary writer he wanted to be; his talent, he laughingly but deprecatingly said, was in the pulps. "I have to make a living and Coleridge got it right, Never pursue literature as a trade. So I write what will sell."

"So be a good mystery writer," I told him. Though he agreed, he wanted more for himself.

Once, frustrated, he turned on me, saying, "I'm not for you! I can see the writing on the wall — you're impressed by the literary lights, you'd like some guy like Marco you can show off at your office parties. We're just wasting time. What I am is an escort — someone for the week-ends. You don't want anything permanent with me."

I reminded him of our vision of moving my old barn-house to the Cape where we would be together. But the impetus of that vision seemed to have vanished after Labor Day in the frantic schedule of our day to day work. Yes, the barn was a beautiful dream, but actually neither he nor I had the time to sit down and figure out the move and translate the scheme into action. Houston was busy writing another mystery: "I've got to keep going, honey," he said. "I can't just daydream about a dream house."

In early October we went to the country to pick the last of second-blooming raspberries. Driving back, I told Houston how to get to Medwood so that I could show him Shady Brook Farm, my old house.

After its sale, I had returned only once, when Winnie wanted to see it and that visit had dejected us both. The barn-house, along with adjoining houses and land, had been acquired by the Vested Brands corporation, and stood empty.

V-B, as we called the company, had once been an inconspicuous neighbor over the hill from Shady Brook Farm, where it maintained a headquarters for management training. Though the corporation had greatly expanded since the fifties and its emphasis had shifted from manufacturing household goods to making critical components for nuclear weapons systems so that it was known as a hub of the nuclear weapons industry, I assumed that its management institute would have remained the same. But power is corrupting, and nuclear power infinitely so. I read in the new York Times of V-B's sweetheart defense contracts with the Pentagon, of V-B's billions in profits on which no taxes were paid.

Already at the old entrance Winnie and I noticed change — the old stone pillars had been removed to enlarge the once country road; the giant maples were gone. Other trees in the old orchard had been chopped down to open an area that was now a helicopter pad for visiting V-B execs. An exit ramp from a circle road had been opened as a feeder to the corporate headquarters. It was a preview of the vaster waste and destruction V-B was dealing in.

From their original site in the old Buchard mansion, V-B's expanded headquarters now formed a complex of power-exuding buildings spilling down to Shady Brook Farm road. Once the view from our house had been of the donkey meadow and orchards where the children used to play. But when Winnie and I looked across the pond we saw a new copper-roofed building that looked like some sinister, futuristic abbey.

We encountered pickets and a roadblock at the fork where the wide paved road went up to the Vested Brands office buildings. The pickets faced my car and yelled, "Stop V-B! stop nuclear weapons!" Their signs read, Boycott V.B.!.... Tell V.B. with your pocketbook to go back to peacetime production!.... From coast to coast V-B leaves a trail of radioactive waste!

One of the pickets came over and handed Winnie through the window a bumper label that read, Boycott V-B, Stop Nuclear Weapons. "We agree," Winnie said. The picket waved us up the road. It was embittering and ironic to me that this place of great peace was now the focus of picketers and protest. Was it then, that the seed had been planted in my mind of rescuing my old house, of taking it out of the V-B domain?

When I drove there with Houston, it was autumn, but V-B's felling of trees had eliminated much of the foliage that, before, had showered the place with golden light at this season.

I had Houston park the car on the shoulder of the narrow road along the stone wall and I led him on a path through underbrush, arriving at the hillside where my old house stood alone and quiet. We walked up some stone steps to a wall-enclosed patio. It was now filled with debris, which Houston kicked aside. The doors were locked, the ancient wisteria that had curled around the entrance porch seemed to have been hacked away, the paint was peeling and a fallen tree lay across part of the backyard. The apple tree that Dee had made her own, climbing up to nest in it for long periods of time, was reduced to a chopped stump. Gone was the wood deck built around a maple tree at the far end of the grounds. Looking through window panes in the back door, I could see that everything in the kitchen had been torn out, revealing a crazy patchwork of different layers of paints and wallpapers. But when we moved on and peered through the tall picture window, the great room looked as it always had, encompassing its superb space.

I thought back to the time when I had entered the wide barn door of the front entrance for the first time and caught my breath in the two-story room, wood-paneled and beamed. A huge window framed a view of ruddy fox-grass on a back hillside bounded by a stone wall. Beyond a large fieldstone fireplace, at other end of the room, a stairway went up to a balcony, off which were the bedrooms. I imagined first Chessie, then Dee, and last Winnie, coming onto the balcony and down the stairway to be married in the great room. I imagined their children climbing the trees in the yard as I watched from the kitchen window making them an apple pie.

"You know, Fran," Houston broke into my thoughts, "I think I'm past the time for houses and all the responsibility that goes with them. Look what happened to this place — gone to ruin. What makes sense for us is a condo situation — with a pool and a tennis court and no upkeep. We just lock the door and go when we feel like it, free to travel when we want, no break-ins to worry about, nothing tying us down."

"This is a creative place. I would think as a writer you could see yourself in such a setting."

"Honey, I'm also practical. Like those V-B guys across the way."

I said nothing more about the house, knowing that Houston's mood swings were like Winnie's. I was learning the other side to this cheerful, affable guy from what he disclosed from time to time.

He had a dominant mother; his father had been a weakling whose only role was to bring his wife tribute in the form of a weekly paycheck. He was dead, she lived. Houston spoke glowingly of her and kept saying he wanted me to meet her — everyone loved her; she was cheerful, she played the piano and sang old tunes, she was still going strong. What Houston didn't say out loud was understood: she had killed off the weakling father. And this knowledge, buried deep, made Houston who he was.

I tried to picture Houston in the great room, in the space where Marco used to write. He was the wrong shape, the wrong kind of writer. Maybe it was a wrong idea to begin with.

Looking around the empty room, taking in the V-B expansion across the roadway as I peered from a window I felt remorse. "I get so depressed, Hous, when I think of how everything's wasted, how wrong thinking can take over the world and make it a ruin. How even something so basic as farming has become technological and now depends on the oil industry; how there are no more steel mills in America, and American cars are going the way of buggies. And those chief executives of the automobile industries vote themselves million dollar bonuses while they tell the workers they have to tighten their belts, and tell the rest of us we're un-American if we buy a better car, a Japanese one. Oh, Hous, everything is so temporary! This country's already on the skids. We're all so temporary ... my father got on the phone during my mother's last call. He asked if the check he sent me was in clubs or spades. He didn't send a check, but I went along with him and said, dollars, Pop. Then he got mad and yelled, I said, was it clubs or spades! That made me so sad."

"That's why we have to make the most of today, babe."

"Today's temporary, too. The Italian poet Quasimodo said it perfectly:

146

Ognuno sta solo sul cuor della terra
trafitto da un raggio di sole:
ed è subito sera.

"Translate," he said.

"Each of us is alone on the earth's heart, pierced by a ray of sunlight, and it's suddenly evening.... Three lines, that's the whole poem. They're so great these Italian poets — epigraphic, like the Greeks. Come on, Houston, let me take you to the view."

We went around the back of the house and then uphill, past rock outcroppings that were like Leonardo's setting for The Virgin with St. Anne. Through an old farm gate, the path led to the hilltop where an even more magnificent sweep of the countryside opened before us. Years ago I had felt as if the secrets of creation would unfold in that special place if only I were patient and attentive and there to listen.

Chessie and Jules were not joining the family for Christmas in Ferryville. They wanted to be alone. They were going to Guadeloupe for the holidays to rest.

Before their departure I sent Chessie one of three identical Christmas gifts I made for each daughter: a beautifully bound blank book in which I had written out my new poems in a careful hand with a different color ink and dedication for each one. In return, by Express Mail, I received a copy of Chessie's own book, based on her dissertation and long in the works, entitled *Small, Sweet Courtesies: The Psychology of Courtly Love*. The dedication read: To the Memory of My Father.

For years I had been hearing about Chessie's book as she worked on it, then while it was being passed on by readers. Now I was as stunned to see it published, as when I heard of her newly bought apartment. My mother had received her copy three months earlier.

"How could she send you a copy of her book and I don't even know it's out?" I demanded sharply.

"Oh we didn't ask for it," my mother answered quickly, establishing her innocent bystander role. "Adele got one — we just assumed you did, too."

Chessie's book dedicated to a memory!... and sent to me only as a quid pro quo Christmas gift.

"Maybe she's envious," said Edith, with whom I had become close enough to fill her in on my turbulence with Chessie. "You had Marco in the flesh. So now she's got him back, between the covers of her book, as a memory, the ghost to whom her book is offered."

"I don't understand, Edith. It was always Chessie and I who shared our great readings. Marco was so closeted in on himself. And now she dedicates it to him as if I didn't count!"

Edith lit a cigarette and said, "There may be something wrong, Fran. I remember during my marriage I went through such a traumatic time trying to stay married that I displaced all my anger onto my mother. I had been close to her, but I avoided her during all that period while I was angry at myself. And then she died before I could reconcile with her. That is something I still haven't got over."

I tried to imagine Edith married, or even angry. She had such equanimity. It's as if she had left the world of everyday cares and entered some privileged territory of which only she knew the language. She had married young and then after a few years divorced her husband, she told me in a dismissive way, because of his irritating and repetitive phrase, Anything you want dearie, it's okeydokey with me. Once she got rid of him, she said, even her allergies cleared up. Edith had had a former career as an analyst and author. Her great love had been a Belgian philologist who died before they could decide to marry. Now she was unattached, happily settled into her work at Pricer.

"No, Edith. Chessie really loves Jules. She is crazy about him, and he about her. I mean, they probably have the usual disagreements — but nothing is rocking their marriage. They're rock solid."

"Just the same, keep the door open for her. Happy wives are happy daughters. There may be some subtle pressure you don't know about."

I asked Winnie about that as we were driving back from Ferryville after Christmas. Winnie was a will-o-the-wisp, veering in her tirades from Why don't you stop trying to smother Chessie?, to Why don't *you* call Chessie, *you're* the mother — why are you always abandoning your children?, but still I asked her to explain her sister.

"She has to separate, Mom, that's all."

"I thought she did that years ago when she went off to college. Does she have to kill me off completely?"

"I don't want to talk about it, I'm on vacation."

"Now you sound like Chessie! — don't tell me I'm going to have another one like her."

"I'll never be like her," Winnie said vehemently. Her hair was long and straggly and she looked, I thought, over-tired. She had lost her pugnacious, cocky John Keats look. "I can't stand her. I called her before she left and told her exactly what I thought of her. And all she could say — and she said it in this bored tone of voice — was that I was a spoiled brat and a pain in the ass, and that she was sick of my moodiness."

Chessie had a point. Winnie was certainly hard to be with at times. She seemed to fade in and out of reality, to be either totally acute in her perceptions or totally off-target.

"Well it seems to matter to you what she thinks about you."

"I can't really care about her except in some distant way. Chessie's like a vase or a plant that one's got used to having around. But Dee is different! — I can get really passionate about her, like a wonderful record I'm listening to, or a great meal I've had. Chessie would make the perfect brain-washer; she doesn't respect other people thinks they should all be re-made. With Chessie you have to be businesslike — be snobby and walk with your knees together, especially you, Mom. Then she'll respect you, too. Right now she's obsessed by you — that's all she talks about. Is Mom getting the message, she asks me. Then she tells me she prefers Nonna to you. What an ass!"

Shaking my head, I said, "She's my child — but what accounts for her?"

Winnie who hadn't wanted to talk at all a few minutes ago, kept going: "Nonna's just the kind of woman I can't stand — she should have nipped it in the bud when Chessie started dumping on you. Then Chessie would have come round. I sure would like Nonna better if she had stood up for you, her own daughter."

I reached out and patted Winnie's thighs, "The ham that am! Thank you, Sweetie, for saying that."

"Nonna's so empty inside. She needs all that garbage from Chessie like, How nice you look, Nonna! Jules loves your cooking, Nonna! Jules just loves to come to your house in Ferryville! That's what she lives for. She's basically frigid inside that smile of hers."

I wondered if Winnie were right. I had always seen my mother as warm and friendly, popular, and giving. But the pearls she gave me at graduation had turned out to be paste; a gold chain, plate. And just as specious, it dawned on me, was all her advice.

"And I'll tell you something, Mom. The reason your mother is always rejecting the gifts you give her is because she's sexually repressed. She's never had a love life."

"Oh, Winnie, what are you saying?" I laughed in embarrassment.

"See! — you're repressed, too! What I'm saying is that, of course she doesn't like what you give her. She's telling you, 'You can't give me pleasure, I won't let you.' And it's because she's never had sex she enjoyed. Why do you suppose she's always reading those trashy novels you criticize her for? It's this curiosity about the sex she's never had."

"Jesus, Winnie, I can't believe you're saying this. We never talked that way when I was growing up — not even in college did we discuss our grandmother's sex life! I don't think we should."

"I don't agree with you 100%," Winnie said.

"That's okay, Pooh-face, that's what you're being educated for."

At the half-way point, I stopped at a station to fill up with gas and to change places and let Winnie drive. A middle-aged woman in a grey coat with a lapel pin that had a cross in the design, came over to us and said through the window, "I haven't seen the words *Festina Lente* since I was in eighth grade and my teacher wrote it on my papers — Make haste slowly."

"Oh," I laughed, "You mean my bumper sticker — it's great, isn't it?. And it's even greater to find someone who knows what it means. Where did you go to school?"

"St. Rose of Lima in Brooklyn!" said the woman quickly.

She was middle-aged, wore glasses, and spoke in a hurried, clipped way. As she was turning away, she held up a gray cloth she was carrying in her hand. "This is my veil. I'm a nun."

"That's why you know Latin!" I called after her. "But why did your teacher keep writing that on your papers?"

"I was always too much in a hurry," the woman called, dashing away with a big smile. From her car, she waved a hand as she sped away.

I laughed and said to Winnie, "That was great!"

Winnie was grinning. "Weird," she said happily. I knew that Winnie loved me to talk to strangers, to have these exchanges, to prove I wasn't just a shy, sad-sack Sicilian, but what Winnie called a full-fledged human being.

"I'm glad we met up with the nun," I told her, "but it's too bad she ran off so fast. You could have told her about that hearse you saw with all the kids in it and the bumper sticker that said The Grateful Dead."

"Let's look for bumper stickers, Ma, it will make the trip go faster."

"When I was young we used to collect cows. But who sees cows now?"

I liked these trips. Driving to Ferryville was worthwhile just for the occasion it gave me to spend time with Winnie. As she drove, she chatted on and on about college, her courses, her friends. She mimicked her professors. She was reading the Hobbit books, she said, because it was an in-thing and she had missed it before. She spoke of the Orks, the Ents (who were not hasty — not like that nun, she laughed), and Glimly the son of Guile and all the other creatures of middle-earth.

"You must be an Ent and I'm a Hobbit," I told her, "because you're slow and deliberate, and I'm hasty and impulsive. Maybe I should be a nun."

"You got it, Ma!" Winnie laughed.

It felt good to be with her.

"I'm worried about Pop, Winnie."

"Poor Pop," she said, "It's sad."

His condition had seemed much worse to me this Christmas than the year before. I could still see him in the sunroom: Fran! Fran! he was calling. He was standing at the window in the sunroom gazing out into the growing dusk. I had gone to him. "What the hell are those shirts doing on the tree there?"

"Pop, those are just a few of the last leaves left on the tree."

"Whatta talking about?" he had answered gruffly, turning on me irritably. "Christ Almighty! I know what leaves are! — those are shirts."

"Well, why don't you go pick them off the tree?" I had been irritable, too. It was catching in that house, everyone irritable with each other, exasperated, fed up, impatient.

"You go pick them! Whatta you think, I don't know what I see? A bunch of goddam rummies, all of you, that's all I've ever been surrounded with."

"See that!" my mother had exclaimed, coming into the room. "He's a Jekyll and Hyde — nice to his friends and rotten to his family. Always been like that."

That night, I had heard him again in the dark of my room as he went to my mother's room and woke her, asking like a lost child, "Where's mother?"

"I'm mother," she said groggily.

"Get up, I've lost my wallet. How can I buy the bread?"

153

"Go back to bed," came my mother's muffled words. "It's night. We'll find the wallet in the morning."

"Where can it be?"

"Did you have it when you went to lunch with Susan?"

"What lunch with Susan? What are you talking about?"

"Yesterday — when I had my Women's Club meeting, Susan came and took you to lunch."

"I don't know what you're talking about," his voice sounded pathetic, searching, befuddled. "What lunch? What Women's Club? Where's mother?"

"I'm mother! Go to bed! It's still dark."

"Go to bed? You mean under the covers?"

"Under or over — I don't care! It's still night, turn that light off and let me sleep. Go back to bed!"

"Shall I take off my clothes?"

"I don't care what you do! Just go lie down!"

He had retreated after that. The next thing I heard was the rattle of dresser drawers being open and shut. He must have been looking for his wallet. Then there was the heavy-footed thump of him going downstairs. From the living room came the distant, eerie sounds of things falling, then again the heavy thump of feet on the stairway as he climbed back up. Back to my mother's room, but no longer the little boy searching the dark, this time the tyrant.

"Jesus Christ! Are you going to get up? You sleep all night and all day! I told you there's no bread — now how are we going to have breakfast?"

"Turn off that light! It's three o'clock in the morning. It's not time for breakfast! Go to bed."

"Christ Almighty, I'm awake! I think that woman took my wallet."

"The cleaning woman? — she did not! She was here on Monday and you've had it since then."

"Give her a call. I've got to get the bread."

"I will not! — go back to bed. Let me sleep, you son of a bitch!"

"That's right, sleep your life away!"

I turned on the small lamp next to the bed. The picture on the table was of my mother with her two sisters, Catherine and Frances. Aunt Ernestine was missing, just as she was always missing at family parties and weddings. Why isn't Aunt Ernestine in the picture? I would ask, knowing, however, that the real answer would never be given. Ernestine had married beneath her, she was poor, she had been deserted. She embarrassed the family; her shame made her unwanted. She was a woman alone.

On the far wall my baby picture that used to be in the attic looked down at me. The look was solemn. Beyond the picture an archway led to a walk-in closet. On either side of the archway book shelves were recessed in niches. Outside an archway covered with ivy led down steps to a terraced patio with pear trees on either side. There was symmetry everywhere. The house was stuffed with my mother's furnishings and *objets* but the arches lightened the whole. I love a house with archways. Because they point upward to the sky? Yes, maybe.

I regarded the solemn baby looking at me from the wall. Was I Aunt Ernestine? No.

In his eighties, my father had gotten up in the night searching for his mother, that ideal mother who never existed while he berated real women in the person of his wife. And the real woman who swore back at him had been swearing at herself because she hadn't been brave enough to swear earlier when it mattered.

155

From these parents I had come, passing it all on. The family style. The message had been early received — it is risky to be who one is, the safe way is to be who they want you to be, or abandonment comes. But abandonment can be beautiful, too! — there is the abandon one feels in love and in sex, the abandon of feeling that can be realized in poetry and art. Satisfied with that, I had turned out the light and slept.

The next morning we had found books thrown in the middle of the living room, china from a bric-a-brac stand in the corner smashed around it, a jar of rose petals strewn over bunched-up scatter rugs, and wall pictures askew as if they had been clutched at for support. My father stood there looking bewildered as mother pointed out the scene he had created; he shook his head, he couldn't remember anything.

"You see," she said triumphantly, turning to me, "he denies!"

The last night of that visit I had been awakened by a large terrible thud, which I could not ignore as I had the lesser thumps and mutterings in the night which accompanied Pop's sleeplessness. I had jumped out of bed and gone to the hall where I turned on the light at the same time as mother came from her room, her face grimacing in the brightness and wrinkled with sleep and apprehension. "Now what? now what?" she kept saying.

There at the foot of the stairs, near the two-step landing which led from the living room through another small hallway to the kitchen, was the figure of my father in long white underwear and dark socks groping around in the dark. When we turned on the downstairs hall light, we could see his face — bewildered, bloodied, terrible. He must have fallen in the dark on the steps of the landing.

"Pop! Pop!" mother had shrieked, "What did you do?"

"I set the table for breakfast." His answer was surreal. My father, in retirement, had taken on the duty of setting the table for breakfast and more than anything else, his life was duty. All his life, from when he was a boy, he had brought home the daily bread, first for his mother, then his wife. It meant he was taking care of us, that he was the provider. His responsibility had been on his mind and he had gotten up in the night to discharge it.

My mother and I had taken him by the arms and guided him down the hall to the kitchen. There I could see that he had, in fact, set the table — even the grapefruit halves were out on plates waiting for us. Tenderly, with gentleness and care, mother had wiped his bleeding nose. His face had bruises and welts all over and his nose was swollen.

I had been horrified and fascinated by what I saw — this ludicrous old man in his long johns, bleeding and battered, while my mother kept crooning soothingly, over and over, "What were you doing in the dark? Can't you turn on a light? Do you always have to save a penny?"

Maybe he was going back to his childhood when he grew up poor. I had watched with respect as mother took charge, grasping him firmly by the shoulder, wiping his face, and putting an ice-pack to his nose. I had avoided touching him but to do something, I got down and cleaned the blood from the kitchen floor. Why couldn't I have put my arms around him and steadied him? I, the dutiful true heir of his character, had simply become the menial Martha, mopping the floor so that I wouldn't have to deal with the person.

"I fell full force right on my hands," he had said childishly. "My wrist is full of pain." It was clear, instead, that he had fallen face first on the steps.

I had watched him, an obstinate man, who kept lowering his head even as my mother told him to keep it tilted back. Each time he looked down, blood spattered the floor. He remained silent at her accusation that he hadn't turned on the hall light, but went downstairs in the dark. "See how it is," she told me bitterly. "You see what I have to put up with! Sometimes I have say to him, It's like your head is made of concrete — how can I get through to you? That's his pride — he won't admit he didn't turn on the light. He never admits his mistakes."

She couldn't break into his lifetime of hardened habit anymore than I could converse with him. He is what he is, I had concluded. And we were the women of a house in which he had been the ruler. And now he had fallen.

Mother had given him a shot of whiskey and led him back to bed. After the lights were out his moaning had continued. "I can't sleep," he kept calling, "I'm in terrible pain." I had gone to my mother's room — "You should call a doctor because he might have a sprain or break in his wrist that should be treated, or else he has nothing wrong and should be told so that he'll stop moaning and go to sleep."

"I'll call the doctor in the morning," she had replied sleepily.

I dressed and said to him, "Come on, Pop, I'll take you to the emergency room at the hospital."

At the hospital he had fussed about whether I had locked the car doors. "It doesn't matter," I snapped.

In the cubicle where I had been told to take him and remove his clothing, I had been disgusted by his misshapen old hat, where, over the years, dust had collected in the brim, by his trousers soiled in the crotch. His undershirt had smelled of old-age, of his obstinate wearing it when it should have been washed. He had been docile, looking at me with his little-boy brown eyes and seeing my look of disgust. I had been overwhelmed with conflicting feelings as I thought of his obstinate goddam ways: compassion that he was caught in them, and anger at his having caused all this commotion either because he was so damn tight, or he was so damn sure of himself, that he didn't turn on the hall light when he went downstairs at night. My heart ached to see who he had become.

CHAPTER NINE

The last time I had seen Chessie was at a book presentation for one of Edith's authors. There, unexpectedly, in a room full of people I saw her. Our eyes joined across the room and she looked sheepish, faltering. I registered complete surprise — what was she doing in Boston? Why didn't I know she was in town? Still, I smiled and started toward her but Henry Levine stepped in my way to introduce someone. By the time I disengaged myself from Henry it was to catch a last glimpse of Chessie, coat in hand, hurriedly leaving.

"You look as if you've seen a ghost," Edith said.

"I have. The ghost of a daughter. Chessie was here and I had no idea she was even in Boston. She didn't greet me just now — she saw me and left."

"Your daughter Francesca? I've seen her book and it's brilliant. She gave a talk at Harvard, I hear. I wish she had stayed, I would have liked to talk to her."

"I, too," I said dryly. Chessie at Harvard and I hadn't known?

She was punishing me, as I wanted to punish her when, years before I had screamed, "I did not give all my efforts, my very bones and blood, to children who would turn on me and call me sick!" Chessie had screamed back, "That's the point! — how could you bring up healthy children!"

I had recoiled from the tremendous hurt, I had wanted to flay out and wound in return; take Chessie out of my will, drum her out of my life, curse her down through the generations.

Gradually it became understandable that blaming would not resolve my pain. But why were people always praising Chessie? They should know how she behaved.

Houston understood.

"Goddam it, Fran, you should sit her down and ask her what the hell is going on. How can she treat her mother like that? If she were my kid, I'd give her a piece of my mind."

"That's how she looked, Houston, like a kid who's been caught out. She looked scared shitless — a shrink caught in the act. I thought at least they knew how to be cooler than the rest of us."

"She could give you the time of day! I don't care how many degrees and accolades she has."

"So why is she afraid of seeing me?"

"Oh, hell, she wasn't afraid — she was probably just pissed that you showed up and could take the spotlight away from her."

When my mother called to tell me of Ethel Schotter's death it was no surprise, but it affected me more than I expected because I related it to Chessie's defection.

I also imagined how Ethel's death made my mother feel her own mortality. I could hear it in her weary voice as she told me the details. There was no estate and Yvonne had never been found; there was only the burial to be arranged and then her tenure as Ethel's keeper was over.

I listened with sympathy and foreboding, watching my right hand draw circles on a pad. My hand was no longer young. The back was showing thin lines, the knuckles were ridged and ravaged with deep furrows, the skin sprinkled with brown dots reminding me of the cinnamon-sugar I sprinkled on toast for my girls when we had played tea-party years ago. My hand said, your time will come, too, and you haven't completed anything: you're not home, your children are gone.

The minute my mother hung up, I dialed Chessie in New York. Breathless, over-anxious, my words came out too rushed, "Chessie?

Chessie, I'm feeling so bad. I never see you, I never hear from you. And now especially this news from my mother...."

"What news? What are you talking about?" Chessie's tone was cool, her interest clearly in the news, whatever that was, and not in my feelings.

"Chessie! Why don't you ever call? You know, people get sick, people die, and you don't stay in touch and suddenly they're gone and you haven't said the things that had to be said. Why have you been incommunicado?"

"Who died?" Chessie's voice was curious, cool.

"That's all you're interested in! But what about me? You don't answer when I write, you keep in touch with Adele or my mother, but not with me. What does that mean?"

"If you're going to go on like this, I'm going to hang up. I'm busy. Do you want to tell me who died or don't you?"

"First my cousin Vince, and now my mother's friend Ethel Schotter. My mother's very down — but it's not just Ethel, Chessie, the point is people die — I could die! — and then it's too late to make up for everything. I want to know why you're keeping me out of your life."

Her voice was clipped and controlled as she answered. "You'll have to ask yourself that. I have no wish to be in touch, or be in your life, until you change your attitude."

"What attitude? What the hell are you talking about?" My own voice rose, anguish and anger mixed, at the provocation of Chessie's coolness and her disregard of what I was feeling.

"I don't wish to discuss it, mom. Just start now with your having a new attitude if you want us to get together."

162

"Wait a minute! wait a minute!" Anger surged through me, I could feel its heat. "You've got it all wrong, Chessie — it's not *your* place to tell me what the conditions are!"

"Well, that's how it is."

Even as I was enraged, I was fascinated by the distancing and professionalism of Chessie's voice. This must be how one learned to be an analyst and keep emotions out of the workplace. But I was not dispassionate. "And you, Chessie, have to grow up, become less self-centered. I may die and it's all good riddance to you, but I'll tell you something — I'll never die in you and you have to come to grips with that. When you do, *you* get in touch!"

I hung up.

On Easter Sunday I was in Ferryville. Houston had gone to his mother's and Winnie was in Ohio with a classmate for spring break. I accompanied my parents to mass at St. John's which used to be known as the high Irish church and had been, until the late sixties, off limits to the Italians of lower Main Street. I am not a church go-er, no longer a Catholic, not even a sustainer of the Judeo-Christian apparatus which seems patriarchially obsolete to me, out of touch with life. When I do attend a service, of whatever kind, it's for the sake of the mythic ritual like the time Winnie and I had gone to Easter mass at a little Portuguese church made festively gay with guitar and tambourine music and a procession of children, dressed in Kate Greenaway outfits and straw hats, bearing colored eggs to the altar. That seemed like the right salute to spring. At home I had a basket for Winnie filled with chocolate bunnies and jelly beans, bright socks, and a kaleidoscope, and she had been happy, spending the day painting a composition of the flowering plant she had given me. This year I had Ferryville.

St. John's had come down in the world, reflecting the changes in the surrounding neighborhood. It looked shabby, paint peeling from the walls. It was the kind of Catholic interior I most dislike — a pseudo-gothic which is very cold and ornate, not a pure line anywhere. The altar was decked with white lilies. The elderly parishioners were dressed in Easter finery and many of the women wore hats as all of them had in my childhood.

The priest had on raiments of gold. Giving the sermon he said, the lines of the cross stand for the opposition of the mundane and the spiritual on which all are crucified. We must die, must know the end of hope, must know desolation before we can experience resurrection. Christ was dead and he came alive; this church seemed dead, and it is once again coming alive. There is light after darkness. Each of us bears some shadow of darkness, and in particular those who are abandoned and rejected.

I heard his words in a kind of swoon and they touched deep into my core of sadness.

But the Church is wise, said the priest, it does not permit despair. It tells us that the second birth, the one that is born from the darkness to be resurrection, is the one that counts. Rebirth. We all must connect to the resurrection, for that is the way of coming alive again.

I believed him.

A few pews ahead of me I saw a woman kneeling, her head bent over onto her folded arms which rested on the back of the pew in front of her. Next to her was a slim young man with a spiked up thatch of hair, thick as a girl's, who wore a leather jacket and stood in an indifferent stance with his weight on the foot away from the woman. On the other side of her an older man was soothingly rubbing the woman's back and looking protectively down at her.

She turned her head towards the young man and said a few words to him, then again lowered her head to her arms on the pew back.

I imagined her having an incurable sickness, cancer or heart disease, and trying to make peace with her estranged son. I was sucked into her despair at not reaching him. What ailed them, what was the pain between her and her son? Chessie was just as indifferent as the young punk in the pew ahead. I glanced at a prayer card my mother passed to me: St. Jude, help of the hopeless, aid me.

I recalled some lines from a poem of Marco's:

Infinite volte anch'io
sono caduto nella tristezza;
infinite volte sono risorto....

I knew exactly what he meant: infinite times, I have fallen into bottomless sadness; infinite times I have risen. I understood his sense of loss, the real pain of his life, beyond all the privilege, all the triumph. Once I felt Marco had everything, that I was the deprived one. But living is the great equalizer. Now I understood him.

There were times, anguished by the incomprehensible events of my life, I wanted to end everything and attain his peace. The feeling of dread went to bed with me at night, woke up with me in the morning. And yet, if I didn't give in to the sleeping pills or the exhaust from my car, it was because that beckoning was assuaged — by work, by Edith who had become my friend, by a call from Winnie or, once in a very blue moon, a note from Dee with a photo, perhaps, of her child Zeno. I learned that I did not have to die of despair, but the despair was in me nonetheless.

At the church service, the whole congregation, including the young man in the leather jacket but except myself and the woman in the pew with him, seemed to get up and file toward the altar rail for communion.

I watched the people taking communion in the new way: each drinking from the same chalice. And I thought of my blue and white Portuguese jug, a lovely thing I had bought in a Lisbon antique shop when I was there, years ago, with Marco. I keep it in my book case with long dried grasses in it. It has two handles, two spouts, and on its fat bulge is a Portuguese saying, *Ninguem diga desta agua nao beberei*: No one can say I will not drink this water.

It meant, for me, don't let me think that I will be exempt from what life exacts.

I thought of all the takers of communion drinking from the same chalice, all with the same wants, fears, pains, hopes. All drinking the same thing. For, in fact, we do all quench ourselves from the same source — one that, as in fairy tales, is replenished over and over again. We drink in joy and thanksgiving, or we drink in pain and defeat. But no one is exempt from the drinking, from draining down to the dregs the experience of life. No one can say, I will make my own life so safe and predicable, I will be so cautious and foresighted, that I will not have to drink from the same jug or chalice as others. Yes, jug, I drink from you, too; and that is my communion with everyone here.

After the communion service, people in the pews turned to each other and shook hands. I said, Peace be with you, to my mother. A woman, who was by herself in a pew, and too far to reach to others, nodded in my direction and I smiled and nodded back. Why was she alone? Had her husband died and her children left her? Everywhere I saw the derelicts of human ties. What a sad, spiteful and wasting warfare.... And now nothing. No. Not nothing. First we must die in order to live. That is the most we can believe, that we can connect to the truth of rebirth in our lifetime.

The recessional was being intoned and the priest's voice rang out: We rejoice in the life Christ has won for us/We believe that our lives have significance/Death and life have contended in that combat stupendous....

The service was over.

Adele and Meade joined us for Easter dinner at mother's. At the table Gussie said, "It's a shame Chessie and Jules aren't here. They never seem to come when you're here Fran. You think that means anything?" He laughed sarcastically.

Adele, sleek and fashionable, her hair now cut in bangs and set off by a satin turban that was gathered in the center by a jeweled clip, added, "Gussie may be right, Fran. I think your daughters fear you, you're so bossy. You're going to have to make the first move to get them to come round."

Both furious and anguished by their not understanding, I over-reacted: "I make all the moves — not just the first, the second, or the last. All the moves! They don't respond. They don't need me any longer and they don't want to know that I need them."

Adele beamed around the table and said, "I'd be lost without my friends, but I'm fine without children."

I had always thought that in her self-centeredness Adele was missing out by not having children. Now I said, "Children are like emotional warheads, always ready to go off."

"Face it, Fran," said Adele complacently, "you taught them to speak up and now you're getting the fruits of that teaching."

Years before, when she was a pestering child, I had been able to smack Adele when she annoyed me. Now I just had to sit there while she, grown to my size, smacked me back.

The last time I had tried to slap Winnie, Winnie had returned the slap and I, in my amazement, had started laughing at the absurdity and so had Winnie and we were both saved from the situation. I learned not to strike her again.

Pricer decided to send me to Bologna for the annual Children's Book Fair. "You're not a children's book editor," Edith acknowledged, "but the main thing is your experience of Italy and speaking the language, plus your husband's publishing contacts there. Italian publishers use Bologna not just for kid stuff, but to carry on business for all their lists. So, we get two for the price of one by sending you."

"And, I do, too," I agreed. "Bologna's not far from where my daughter Dee lives. I'll get to see her and my grandson."

I wrote to Dee:

Expect to see me soon, my company is sending me to the Bologna Book Fair. It will be so good to see you again! I feel my golden age is over – that magic time when we were all a family living in our house in Medwood – but there are some good new things, too. I am studying the Greeks at night, and I am writing poems whenever they hit me.

Here's a quote from Katherine Mansfield on Virginia Woolf that I copied in my diary: 'How I envy Virginia; no wonder she can write. There is always in her writing a calm freedom of expression as though she were at peace – her roof over her, her possessions round her, and her man somewhere within call.'

Isn't that the truth, Dee, isn't that it?

168

The Greeks, too, knew all about us, and it's never been expressed better than they did. Know thyself, said Socrates and I'm trying, harder than I ever wanted to before.

Why am I who I am, I ask myself. Who is my self? Where is home? And it seems to me I have first to know who I am before I can think of where home is. Or does the self keep changing according to where and how it's housed? Is it a chameleon, taking on some of its identity from interchange with other selves, from circumstances, experiences, and contexts? Do we keep on creating and choosing it, the truth being that it's never finished so there's no such thing as a completed person?

What was all that crazy eating, then dieting, as I was growing up but some wild effort to re-shape my self, make a better self – or, at least, package it better. If the package were attractive, maybe someone would be interested. Then, inside the package would be the real Self. But the damn thing doesn't stay still like a rock – it keeps changing its shape, like an amoeba, stretching this way and that, responding to nudges and pricks, recoiling inwards or flowing out depending on the outside stimulus.

My self is like an ongoing conversation in my head; a home movie of my experiences played over and over. That's what my poetry is – it's getting to know who I am, being both watcher and the watched. It's the struggle to come to terms of peace, to still the cluttering of all those disparate selves in my head.

It's difficult to build and know this Self, the way is filled with road-blocks – resistance to knowing, deliberate forgetting, denials, and not least growing up in an Italian tradition that put family over self. We were not supposed to be individuals, only part of the group. I've been taunted for being too much of a mother instead of myself.

I think that being tugged between two ways, the American and the Italian, will never let go of me. One can't just think oneself into one's whole Self! One can't just gather up the pieces and put them together with the soul's Silly Putty. *No one can do the job alone. I think we're meant to help each other integrate, and in the helping, help ourselves.*

Enough philosophizing. As I say, some good things are happening. I'll tell you more about Houston and our plan to move the house to the Cape when I see you after Bologna. Happy spring to you all and a bunch of kisses for my grandson. Love 'n kisses, Mom

Houston was miffed: "You're all over the place." He spoke in the mock gruff tone that, beneath the offhand manner he attempted, still meant to convey his annoyance.

"Sweetheart, it's only a week I'll be gone. What's that?"

Disingenuous, that's what I was. I knew as I mentioned the short time span that it wasn't about time, but about my moving around, being able to pick up and go, freedom.

"You're leaving me at a bad time, just when I probably need you the most — to talk out this manuscript I'm caught in. I don't know.... I'm in the bad mamma's grip ... what computer lingo calls the deadly embrace." He tried unconvincingly to laugh at his fears. "I've never been to a Book Fair, but I've read of them in Publishers Weekly — eighty miles of stands, all-night confabs, tons of shit. In a mother like that you've really got to get lost for good." He shook his head ruefully.

Houston sometimes affected what he thought was hip Black talk. I knew what he meant. It was when his writing wasn't going well and a great inertia came upon him, filling him with doubts; when, he said, his creative energy was low, practically at a standstill and he had great fear of being left on his own, without a good mother nearby to feed him and help him throw off the spell of the bad one. The bad one would keep him blocked, convince him he couldn't create, should give it up, just lay back and be a little boy again. He had described this state to me as we were going through a carwash: the giant rubber strips flapped about the windshield like the tentacles of some monster squid trying to get at us, while Houston exclaimed, "There she is! — it's all our worst fears or inadequacies piling up on us, beating at us on all sides, trying to make us give up and just keep on suckling at the breast of mother, not able to feed ourselves."

"That's good, Hous," I told him, "put it in your book."

"Honey," he said wryly, "you don't understand psychic monsters. You don't put them anywhere. They put you!"

I thought he protested too much. I remembered Marco, orderly and punctual as a banker, sitting down each day, no matter what might be churning in his gut, to write. Only by persistence, by Aristotelian habit (which became one's second nature), could one, he said, be a poet. Certainly not just by crying about the dark. I reconsidered my taunting of Marco as a professor with a regime. I suggested to Houston that he take an early morning walk and then go to his desk every day at a set time period and write whatever came out. Something would be usable and he would, at least, be revving up his psyche, getting it used to the idea that everyday it would be asked to produce something.

"That's what I love about you, you think everything's do-able, whatever you decide you can accomplish. Like the house. You want your old house? — so, just move the house!"

I knew I was not always so decided. For one thing, I was still ambivalent about him: *vorrei, e non vorrei/ mi trema un po' il cuore*; Zerlina's words and Mozart's music flooded my head like an anthem every time Houston appeared. I wasn't sure I could stick to him, nor, on the other hand, that I wanted to be completely without him. Gently, at first, I had tried to interest him in exercise to get his weight down, get the flab off him. I even thought he'd think better, be more creative when he came out of that moat of fat within which he immured the scared little boy.

"What is this? — a test for your approval?" he shot back.

"It's not for me — it's for your own good."

"Christ! where did I hear that before?"

"Well, where?"

"That's all my mother ever said — every goddam deprivation or humiliation she could think of for us was always for our own good, the build-up-the-character shit."

"Well, look at it this way, Hous, you think exercising to lose weight would be passing a test for me, but did it ever occur to you that it's the other way around — that you're testing me by wanting me to accept you at not your best. Why is that?"

It was stalemate, standstill. "Look, sweetheart, I love you, but you're not going to take me over. I am who I am."

Houston's mother lived in Albany. He'd say, every so often, "We should drive down and see the old girl — she'd love to meet you, she'd go to the piano and belt out her repertoire for you."

But his plans got mired in the passivity that came over him and kept him from following through on most things; or, sometimes, when he did undertake something, he'd do it so badly, in so bumbling a fashion, that it was clear that it was meant to fail. Then he'd laugh ruefully and say, "It's the monster ... bad mamma ... the three-headed bitch-dog who's standing guard." He wanted me to be decisive, tell him what to do, be the good mother. I couldn't wait, then, to get away from him.

Other times Houston was energized, practical, decisive, full of ideas and entirely forward looking. It was for the sake of those times, and their outcome, that I stuck with him and decided to be patient and wait it out. Wasn't that what any marriage was? Had Marco always been easy? No one was.

I set myself a mode of behavior, for when Houston was in a bad spell, to help us both get through it and I wrote my reminders on several cards — one for my purse, one to keep near my office telephone, one in my diary, one as a bookmark, so that I'd always be prepared:

Do not engage Hous in "dialogue," just listen

Consider alternatives

Don't proselytize

No criticism, only ask questions that elicit explanations

Do not be gullible

Count to ten

Do not condemn, shoot down, show contempt

PATIENCE IN THE ENDLESS RAIN!

I had told Houston about how great it would be to see Dee after Bologna.

"I've often wondered what she's doing in Italy," he said. "Why did she go there to get married?"

"Who knows? She keeps a lot to herself. She had a brief first marriage over here to someone I never met. She didn't tell me about it until it was over. Said it wasn't important, just a lark that happened one spring day when she didn't feel like studying for exams. Then she dropped out of college, went off to Italy. That's when she met Leone. She probably wanted to get as far away from her mistakes — or me — as possible. Not to mention Chessie, who was a hard act for her to follow."

"I'm still glad I had only one child."

"You bet. What do you want from Bologna, Hous?"

"Pasta bolognese from Il Papagallo."

"I have an idea! Do you know what I'll send back? — the corner-stone I found in Calabria years ago at a roadside flea market. I bought it because it was carved with a name and a date: Bartolomeo Chiarito, 1671. I left it with Dee. Now I'll have it shipped over here and we'll have it at the barn."

"See that," he said, "you can even turn pasta into stone! Medusa!"

I laughed self-consciously; he had hit on something. "Hous," I said, "I made reservations for us to go to the Cape for your birthday. How's that for consolation prize?"

I did arrange everything: the charming Bed & Breakfast place in Wellfleet and the arrangements for a birthday dinner at Peppino's. Houston loved it. "What do *you* want, what can I give you," Houston said later, gazing at me with his blue eyes like deep-set glass buttons in the soft mounds of his face. He puffed on his pipe and contemplated me benignly, contentment circling him. I gazed back calmly, wishing inwardly that he wouldn't phrase things as if I were the suppliant and he the bestower. I told him, if we were to be together it would be as equals, each giving each receiving. But he was what he was — a man whose attitude really hadn't much changed from that of being the provider for the woman who then owed him in kind. No matter how up-to-date Houston thought he was (and he had learned well to ape the language of liberation), he was still of the old persuasion. Deep down he believed what he always had: it's a man's world.

"I want your loyalty — 100%," I told him. "I want your word, and to believe your word always. No doubts."

"No doubts," he repeated solemnly.

174

"No more putting off about the house. No more excuses. If we have trust, and stay trusting, I want my house. I want us to have that house together. Then we can be a couple." Yes, that was what he could give me, something I couldn't do alone.

I smiled and reached for his hand, bending towards him until I was talking very close to his face and looking into his eyes. "You know, Houston, when the girls were little they had a picture book about nature's creatures. And there was a line in it that fascinated Dee, 'Where do butterflies go when it rains?' She'd ask me that, and I'd say home. That's what I want. To get out of whatever rain it's raining, and get home."

All my past dreams of witty guests in the great room, music in the walls, poetry, wise talk, gardens, hospitality, visiting grandchildren, pies baking in the kitchen — it all now was in the hands of Houston, a writer of mysteries.

Why not? Life was mystery.

Why can't one go home again? Who names the cars and why is it a Toyota Cressida rather than Troilus? Where *do* butterflies go when it rains? So many questions to be answered. Or maybe the only question was why did I think I could be safe when, instead, there was the dusk of ruin around us all with Vested Brands across the road from my once safe haven of Shady Brook Farm?

Where is home? Home is where you hang your hat. And even as Houston and I sat in Peppino's, comfortable on the Cape, Mrs. Harris was hanging her smart mink-ringed hat in a Bedford prison cell. The verdict had recently been given: Jean Harris was guilty of murdering her lover. She was every woman's nightmare of herself. It seemed that Mrs. Harris had her mistress and headmistress roles, but not her own self. It was as if her selfness had to be filled in by others, that her identity had got diffused, spread all over the place like thinning mist, shapeless effluvia. It became impossible for her to grab that vapor and shape herself back into her own being.

During the trial a woman reporter had wondered at Jean Harris' life as headmistress of a girls' school and the kind of sustained heartiness it must demand of an adult to endure boarding school life as a single person. How that struck home! Yes, I could understand Jean Harris, but not her refusal to see through the man who destroyed her. She defended him and imprisoned herself. And when the judge sentenced her to serve fifteen years in prison before becoming eligible for parole, Jean Harris said in court,

"It may not be so hard to be there. I don't have a home. I don't know where home is."

I shivered with knowledge. Jean Harris as Everywoman Abbandonata.

CHAPTER TEN

Bologna: thousands of people at the book fair and Fran managed to run into Henry Levine: "Hi, Henry," she said, "I see it's bow-tie day." He was wearing a green-blue polka dot bow-tie on a pale yellow shirt. Always sleek, he had an air of self-satisfaction that made him look new. Fran had heard from Edith that he was remarried.

"Fran, you here? How are you making out?" he boomed heartily, giving her pause. Did he mean with books, men? Fran played it straight.

"I've found there are Italian authors of children's books, after all — when I lived here I really doubted it. I've got some samples to take to my grandson."

"I have a grandchild, too!" Henry said, beaming. "Let's have an aperitif and I'll tell you about it."

Henry's step-daughter, acquired through his second wife, had borne a child from an in vitro fertilized egg. "*This* is what a miracle is all about," he exclaimed, jubilant, "not what the old-fashioned European shrines have always touted. Jennifer was one of those unfortunate young women damaged by an IUD in the seventies. It was thought that she would never bear a child. She and her husband finally adopted a baby when she was in her thirties, but all the time she never gave up hope of bearing her own. When she got a settlement from the IUD people, she enrolled in the fertilization program at Yale. Very expensive procedure, you know. She went through a couple of years of rounds with no viable implantation taking effect. She simply persisted."

"Must have been a terrible strain."

"Very stressful," said Henry proudly. His rationality was vindicated in the triumph of a step-daughter who reflected the qualities of her admirable mother, the wise woman Henry had chosen to marry. "Jenny drove to New Haven for each new round and it was timed so closely with her hormone intake schedule that it was practically split-second. Between that and her job she was all wound up. Then, to add to everything, on the last drive to New Haven she got a flat. Do you know, Fran, she got out and changed that tire in just ten minutes and got to the lab in time for her appointment? And that was the round that took!" Henry finished triumphantly, beaming and genial.

"Great, Henry, that's just wonderful!" Fran was genuinely pleased at his story. "I'm glad for her and for you. She's a real heroine of our times. A real mother!" Fran thought of Henry's past estimate of mothers — all changed since he had flung the word at her. "Imagine wanting a child that much and doing what she did to bring it into life."

Her own pregnancy with Chessie had also been one of mind over matter as she lay on her back for three months waiting for the iffy embryo to take hold. And when Chessie was born, she was perfect, as smooth as a plum, peachy beautiful. She had been deeply wanted, not let slip back into that chasm into which life returns, lived or not. *I made you to find me,* Anne Sexton wrote in a poem to her daughter. And too much, Fran had come to believe, had she wanted herself remade in her own daughter.

Henry confided with a self-conscious laugh, "We had some luck from the figa charm, too."

Her brows shot up. "Can that be what it sounds like?"

"Yes, a Brazilian fertility symbol — we weren't taking any chances."

So, Fran thought, when it comes to the important things, Yale high tech isn't enough, one needs the old-time charms, too. And that went for super-intellect Henry, even at the risk of his being one with the rustics all over the world who still wear phallic horns and carry figs to be fertile.

On the bus from Bologna to Pesaro Fran looked over her notes from the Fiera and went through the business cards she had been given. One was from a professor at the University of Bologna with whom Fran had chatted and to whom she mentioned her anthology of Italian American writers. He was deeply interested, he said, because he himself was working on a computer program for scanning the poetry written by Italian Americans in order to analyze the language for lost echoes of the homeland. That was an intriguing idea Fran told him, and Pricer might possibly be interested, so she took his card. Now she wondered about its commercial appeal. She put the card in her wallet next to a photo she was going to give Dee.

The photo was an old one, of Fran with Chessie and Dee on an Easter Sunday at Shady Brook Farm a year or so before Winnie was born. Fran was between the two girls holding Dee by the hand and with her arm around Chessie's waist. They're in Easter outfits in front of Fran's rock garden lavish with crocus, primula, snow-drops, and bluebells against a backdrop of yellow flowering forsythia bushes. Chessie smiles from beneath a wide-brimmed yellow straw hat; Dee is in a yellow coat; Fran wears a yellow checked suit. Chessie stands bolt upright, feet together, arms straight at her side, coat buttoned, socks up. And on the other side of Fran there's little Dee like a prankster, pointing one toe ironically in front of her, one sock down, her coat askew from being buttoned wrong. It happened over and over again in those childhood pictures — Dee lounging on a branch of her particular apple tree with ribbons wound fancifully around her legs, while Chessie is standing primly by her bicycle all put together in a biking outfit and looking like a child model. And yet, to this day, Dee couldn't seem to see, or believe in, her imaginative gift. Having decided not to compete with Chessie, she had simply relinquished everything including her gift for writing and gone far away.

Fran puzzled over Dee. Did she think she was disapproved of because she didn't stick to things as Chessie did? Is that why she had removed herself so far from all of them?

At the bus station in Senigallia where they stopped briefly, Fran stared out the window at a small, sandy haired man in a light jacket open over a striped shirt. It could have been John Cheever, Italian style, with a moustache. He had the same small-frame, lithe build and a boyish, grinning look on his face; he was smoking a cigarette. It made Fran think that everyone could be someone else, elsewhere — similar in looks, but different in outlook depending on where in the world one found oneself. As she had been different, when she and Marco lived in Italy, from what she was in Ferryville or Medwood. Now who was she? Fran asked herself. *In fieri,*(becoming) coming from the *fiera* (fair), she punned, amusing herself..

If she could have changed things Fran pictured Dee in a Vermont farmhouse filled with chintzy comfort and fireplaces, rocking chairs, ample beds, wooden floors, checkered curtains, and a warm, cozy kitchen. Fran saw her almost as another Ethel Schotter, beaming and motherly, benevolent and comforting, a jolly mother of a half-dozen kids she'd take to museums or swing on a hammock hung between leafy elm trees. She could see Dee, laughing and whimsical, married to a Yankee named Sam or Josh, being sociable with the neighbors and inviting the neighbors' children for hot chocolate and cookies after ice-skating; Dee would have an interest in local affairs, get involved in anti-nuclear protests, march for women's rights and legalized abortion; run for the school board and the library board; read her beloved childhood classics to her kiddies in front of a fireplace while they popped corn; climb the apple trees in her backyard to throw down the fruit for pie-making. Come on, babes, she'd call to them on a summer afternoon after letting them play under the sprinkler and then hosing them down, I'll make you a Black Cow or Purple Passion — which do you want? Those were the favorite drinks of her childhood, loved, Fran thought, more for their names than for the ginger ale or grape juice concoctions with ice cream that they were.

Fran hoped Dee was happy where she was, in her Italian countryside. She wasn't a regular correspondent, but when the mood struck her she occasionally wrote a gay note about some outing, or about being quarantined during little Zeno's bout with mumps and spending the time reading Trevelyan's history of England so that she was constantly thinking and dreaming of the Celts, the Picts and Jutes, the Angles and Vikings, and William the Conqueror crossing the channel. Or she'd send Fran a recipe she had just devised from the greens that she grew in her kitchen garden and she'd note that this year they couldn't pick wild asparagus in the woods because the hares and foxes had come down with the plague and might have infected the plants. But then, she'd ask rhetorically, what do we care about asparagus? How can we feel carefree enough to wander through fields picking wild asparagus or salad greens when we seem to be at the mercy of an ignorant, headstrong American president and a fanatic Arab leader in their silly battle of wills? whereas no individual, and certainly no nation could presume to hold the whole truth.

Dee still cared about the world and she criticized Chessie for being too out of it.

"Dee really idealized you, Mom," Winnie had reported to Fran in her ongoing story of all of them. "That's when she was a child — then when you didn't measure up, she went on her search for what would."

What a mystery mothering was. Aside from the blind procreative force, or what Marco called the generous impulse of giving life back to life, what was it that went beyond the physical birthing and made us lurch between being children, and then parents, somehow never in synch between the two, our footing clumsy in different steps to a different tempo, trying to reach forward and backward at the same time? Fran thought of Henry Levine's step-daughter Jennifer rushing to the petri dish at Yale.

She looked at Italy from the bus window, a different one from long ago with Marco. Now there were car dumps in the countryside, billboards advertising body control salons; on a TV commercial seen in her Bologna hotel room Fran had watched in disbelief a commercial in which a dignified older gentleman who looked like Toscanini put his lips sensually around a spoonful of mayonnaise from a Kraft jar and smile with delight.

On the bus, the woman passenger across from Fran chatted with the driver about food all the way from Bologna. It had cost 65,000 lire each for a complete Christmas dinner in a restaurant, with wines, spumante, and panettone — just what you'd expect, they agreed. My son paid, the woman said. But not everyone can allow themselves such prices and it now costs 35,000 lire to buy a capon in the market, she noted. The driver said he bought chicks for 1900 lire each to raise at home. But to have them slaughtered for market, after the expense of feeding them to a weight of three or four kilos, would then cost him 50,000 lire! Where was the profit in that? Where the justice? He'd have to ask 100,000 lire apiece for his

182

chickens at market. At some point the woman convinced the driver to make a stop on the road outside a town where she said they had the best *piadine* she had ever eaten, and she even got him to get out and make the purchase for her. "And after all that don't I get any?" he jested, back on the bus, as the woman unwrapped them and started eating. She made a big fuss, then, about sharing her breads with him, urging him to take more.

Fran divided her gaze between the unfolding landscape and the chattering woman who sounded like her mother, had the same broad peasant feet and stumpy legs, the same prominent nose and wide mouth. No matter how all-American Dolly Sturzo had made herself, she still harbored an Italian peasant who connected her in sisterhood to the chattering woman on the bus. They both had mastery of the minutiae of life with their continual commentary on food, the shopping know-how, the way they could get people to do things for them, could expect that sons would always take them out on a special occasion; their universe was the same.

Dee was always glad to see her when Fran arrived, hugging her excitedly and proudly thrusting little Zeno into her arms. Fran kissed and hugged them both, and then kissed Leone who was hanging back, shadowy and illusive, still timid, his shoulders curved over as if to hide himself. Once Dee had written Fran about Leone, How do you convince a person he is worth his beating heart?

Motherhood had widened and softened Dee's body, but her expression was that of always — a quizzical and teasing look on an unmade-up, girlish countenance. She had the same thick gorgeous hair that Marco had given to each of his daughters, but Dee's had the reddish glints of the Sicilian Sturzos. Dee's eyes were bluer than

Fran's, her cheeks rounder than those of the other two girls. Fran could see Dee examining her hungrily as if she were mentally making a list of what her mother wore and how much it must have cost; Fran could see in Dee's eyes that she looked smart, independent, good-looking. After each visit Fran left her some of her clothes.

Dee put her in the extra room they now had in their new place, the top flat of a two-family house outside the town walls. The room was filled with remembrances: poems and snapshots, rocks and sea-shells, pressed flower bookmarks, and a special box that Fran had decorated with collage for a past birthday. Fran was there, present, as she had not been in Chessie's place.

Dee worked at a glass covered table made from an ancient carved marble slab set in a wrought iron frame that was from Marco's family. The room was light-filled and clean and contained a huge pinewood wardrobe, book shelves filled with Dee's English library (Leone always said proudly that his wife worshiped the English writers, especially Virginia Woolf), and a cot bright with cushions and covered with a striped spread. The room was Dee's private study, everyone's storage space, and the guest room.

The apartment was filled with her simple, good taste. The upright piano shared the main room with a large green plant and some deck chairs. In Dee's bedroom the same Amish patchwork quilt was on the matrimonial bed. The child's room was filled with toys and drawings and Leone's paintings.

Each time Fran sat at the marble table to write up her notes from the Fair, or browsed through Dee's books, she thought of Dee not speaking English to her son. Was it out of loyalty to Leone, so that her son would not grow up with something his father didn't have and so diminish him?

Dee seemed content to have holed up in the hills of central Italy and let her other, American, life drift away from her. Beneath the window, Fran could hear her grandson call to his friend in the first floor flat: *"Deh! Gi-or-gio...o...o, vien fuori! Sono qua! Giorgio, vieni!"* Why, Dee challenged her, did she think he needed English? He was happy as he was. She was happy. Fran answered Dee with another question: Why do you tutor other parents' children in English and not give it to your own son? Is your English only for those who can pay for it? Dee had turned away.

The kitchen was the room they gathered in. Dee had made the room interesting with her ceramic plates and bowls and hand-woven baskets on open shelves. A bunch of wild flowers was stuck in a jug on the table. Their waste can was made from an outsize olive oil container. Leone's chair was in a corner beside a raised hearth that heated the room and was typical of that region. The television set was placed on top of their small refrigerator where, after dinner (but sometimes during), their eyes were raised to the screen as if to divine revelation.

Of Fran's three daughters Dee was the one who literally nourished her. She fed her food. She talked to her. Perhaps because she was a mother, she saw Fran as a human being, not just as her parent. Fran remembered Chessie's begrudging fridge in New Orleans; and how Winnie, at home, turned helpless, couldn't prepare anything, waited for her to get back and cook for her, snarling crossly if dinner took too long or wasn't what she liked.

But in her home, Dee was the giver and she refused to do things economically when Fran, looking at the expensive prosciutto, the beautifully arranged platter of roasted chicken and mushrooms set off by forms of pureed vegetables, felt regret and said, "Honey, don't fuss so — anything's all right for me."

185

"We never usually eat like this," Dee assured her solemnly.

She looked guileless, but that was her guile. In her childhood Fran called her The Wise Lady from Philadelphia after one of her favorite E. Nesbitt characters. Chessie, who blurted things out and then regretted it, was Mrs. Blabbermouth when she wasn't The Sun King. With Dee Fran knew the wheels were turning, the mechanisms operating, and yet something was always held back to disappoint later even as she seemed to assent and looked her full in the eye. Chessie, on the other hand would say NO! right out, remonstrate, but then usually come through to please her.

"I just didn't want you to take up so much of your time," Fran told Dee.

"But your visit is something special. I made the rice torta you used to make for Papà's birthday."

"That's right!" Fran made a mental note to leave Dee even more lira than first planned to make up for the extra food expenses. "You are certainly the remembering one of the family. I used to top the torta with a meringue. Did you save the egg whites?"

"Of course — I don't throw anything away that I can use."

"Well, give me an egg beater, sweetie, I'll beat them up for the meringue."

Dee frowned. "I don't have an egg beater."

"Not have an egg beater? Why not? How do you whip things?"

"I don't need gadgets. I use a fork."

"But Dee, an egg beater is not some luxury like Chessie's Cuisinart!"

"It's how I am. Why should I fill my life with contraptions just because you do? Here, give me those egg whites."

Dee took the bowl and started energetically beating them with a fork until they bubbled and turned a pale gray. The minutes passed.

Fran became uncomfortable, and looked out the window to the plowed hillside beyond the house. What was Dee trying to prove? — that she was purer? that she could live on principles and without conveniences? But why take a stand on an egg beater? Fran could understand her making a point about not having a V-B blender or electric mixer in order not to support a company that also supplied fixtures for nuclear arms. But on the other hand, why did Zeno have an electric train and an expensive tricycle and she didn't have an egg beater?

Now Fran saw there was a certain disheveled look about Dee that, at first, had simply seemed casual. Her hair needed shaping. Her skin needed attention. Her apron was shabby. She wore heavy socks and clogs. She had let herself go. Fran thought of Chessie's beautiful clothes and wondered if Dee would be offended if Chessie sent her some. But how could Fran get Chessie to do anything anymore? Dee was beating energetically and the whites were still only greyish foam.

"Here, let me take that over for a bit," Fran said. Dee handed her the bowl and fork. It was hard going. Fran tried to remember what her Fannie Farmer cook book advised when egg whites wouldn't rise.

"A pinch of cream of tartar would help," she told Dee.

"What's cream of tartar? I don't have any." Dee was getting testy and busily made a show of washing the piled up dishes in the sink. "I don't see the need for this meringue, either." Fran felt they could use a dish washer rather than pay rental on a separate studio for Leone. Dee was always having to heat water and the sink was always full of dishes from their last meal. Fran's arm ached from the beating even as she tried to think of it as an aerobic exercise testing her cardiovascular system and told herself to go one more lap. But the egg whites stayed froth and always would. It was disconcerting to stand there passing the bowl and fork between them as in a relay race. Fran wished Dee hadn't made it a mark of nobility and they could just laugh about the whole thing.

By asking for an egg beater, Fran seemed to have drawn attention to everything substandard in Dee's life — the tiny refrigerator that lacked a freezer top; the broken chair at the table; the mismatched tableware which was not silver, not even stainless steel. Suddenly the charm of Dee's kitchen faded and they were face to face with a gas stove which ran on canned gas and when it ran out, cooking shut down until they could get another. There was no telephone to make a call to the *gassista*; Leone had to drive to the crossroads bar to do so. Leone and Dee began to seem not so much stoic, as feckless: their money went for toys and things for the child, for gasoline in their drives back and forth to town for things they were always forgetting.

It was spring and outside the sun shone; inside there was permanent chill in the walls and on the cold terrazzo flooring because the flat was never adequately heated throughout the winter in order to save on oil. How could Fran give Dee everything that was missing?

"You're right!" she declared. "We don't need a meringue on the rice cake — that's just something extra I used to do because your father loved it. Actually, I like the torta better without it."

Fran put down the bowl and fork, renouncing the unequal battle.

Later, at the table Fran said, "It's a beautiful meal, Dee, just as is. I really appreciate it."

Fran admired this staunch daughter; she had made a pact and was sticking to it. There in the hills outside a walled medieval town, she was an English tutor, a cook, a wife and mother, a washerwoman, a gardener, a reader of Trevelyan and Virginia Woolf, and a born-again Catholic. And yet Fran felt something sad and forlorn about this middle child, the sly one who was always a bit different from the others. "You wrote me once about picking wild greens and making soup from nettles," Fran smiled encouragingly. "I thought, does she mean burdocks? — how can she eat burdocks?"

"No, no, Mom," said Dee smiling back, on sure ground once more, "it's *ortica*. Ophelia's fantastic garlands included nettles."

"...*out of this nettle danger, we pluck this flower safety*" — that's Shakespeare, too," Fran said.

Staying with Dee made Fran wonder how it would have been if Marco and she had always lived in Italy. Fran knew she would never have transplanted as radically as Dee had. She seemed to be a drifter, her home anyplace. Dee, instead, had grounded her life in one spot on earth and in beliefs as hard and stinging as her nettles.

Fran was a bum in spirit, always on the move, begging attention, worth, consideration, human exchange from the person at hand. Like a bag lady Fran carried the family belongings with her when she moved, curator of the family *Lares et Penates*, custodian of Marco's glory, and sometime cooker of meals if anyone came to visit.

Adele's terrible words echoed in her ears: "I'm glad that I didn't have children." For, Fran thought, Bums camping near their kids and asking for handouts, that's what mothers seemed to become.

189

They were in Dee's room while Fran packed to leave when Fran said, "Well, Dee, I really have to tell you how I feel," Fran said. . Dee's brows raised in alarm and her face took on a look of childish apprehension. "Don't worry, I'm not going to scold. But I have to say what I feel."

"Why?"

That was Dee, all right. She was the daughter who, aged four, when Fran said, you have to go bed, answered 'have-to's aren't nice.'

"Because I feel like it, I guess. I want to say that you seem to have turned your back on your family and your background. I guess I have never gotten over your not naming your son for your father. Zeno you call him! – where did that come from? Who in the family was ever a Zeno?"

Dee scowled. "I don't know why you think I'm in charge of naming around here. Don't you think Leone has something to say about it? And it certainly doesn't matter that no one in either family has that name. It's new, like Zeno is new."

"That's not the way it goes, and Leone knows it. If his father were dead, your little boy would have been named for him without any discussion about it. That's what Italian families do – they remember each other in the naming."

Dee's voice rose. "Why does that mean so much to you? I told you before – it's something we both wanted and it has nothing to do with not remembering a much beloved father. I loved papà!"

"But naming is important! All of you – Chessie, Winnie, you – you're all named for family. It carries us on, it's being part of each other! It's a linking of who we are to who we came from. Names signify, names are important! God gave Adam the power to name!"

Fran's voice was getting louder. Dee got up and closed the door, and said as she came back toward her, "You're so literal! The reason you want to believe in names and words being so important and meaning what they mean is that you don't believe it! You know, Mom," she said in a quieter tone, "it's really some kind of anxiety on your part."

"Forget about me! What you've done is let Leone take over. You've denied your father." Fran was surprised at her words. Did she really want to say this?

"I'm sorry you're reacting that way." Dee's look was forlorn, her face drawn. "I loved papà. And I wanted to please Leone."

Fran was unable to stop. "In a way you've denied me, too, to your son. You don't speak English to him and it's your mother tongue. *The mother tongue!* it's so obvious it's a joke! Why does Leone stop at his mother's every night after work, and then all of you are there every Sunday for the ritual dinner? *They* keep themselves together, but *you*, you've let our family fall apart!"

"Our family!" screamed Dee. "You can bet I wanted to get away from it! our family only knows criticism — you always undermined us with your words. Who do you think you are, some Generalissimo that we all owe you our lives and loyalty forever? Well, let me tell you, you're wrong!"

No one gets clear, Fran was learning, not as a child and not as parent to a child.

Her own parents had done their best as they saw it. But underneath it all ran the harsh rule, then, of their parents and on and on. They could be modernized only just so far: their children still had to be their children in the old way. And yet the real Italian sap — that sureness of custom, that confident knowledge of self, the dignified expression of verities — none of it had been theirs to bequeath.

"I didn't want this to happen, Dee," Fran said slowly, shaking her head. "I came because I love you and you are my family."

"Mom, I wrote it all down in my diary years ago — I wrote how I wanted to get far away and start clean. I wrote down how I hated all the criticizing, the emotional tantrums, how love was never expressed. What Leone has always called your stuff — *roba di quella gente.*"

Hurt, Fran said softly, "You left one family style to take on another — Leone's."

"I made my peace with that long ago. I have found safety and love here. The least of the distances between us is the Atlantic Ocean."

"Oh, Dee! Sweetheart, I hurt from our separateness. I can even understand why you may not have wanted to name Zeno for your father. I remember the time Marco sent you off to boarding school because he found you intractable and undisciplined, and how you suffered being away from your family, as if you were in exile, which, in a sense you were. I think you always thought I did that to you — but it was Marco. It was the one time I ever saw him act so decisively and quickly in a matter that had to do with you *children.* And then it dawned on me! — the same thing had been done to him as a child — he was nine when his father died and his uncle decided for his own good that he should go away to school. He hated that school, he hated being sent away from his mother and sisters, he said he suffered pains all his life from the chilblains in his hands and feet that he got in that miserable place. And yet I'm sure his past never occurred to him when he sent you away — it's just that we often — without knowing it! — do to our children what was done to us, and always from the best of motives. Sweetheart, I'm sorry I brought up the whole subject of naming Zeno. He's a beautiful child."

Fran took Dee's hand. "Zeno," Fran repeated. "Actually I like the name, it's different. Like the Greek philosopher."

Dee removed her hand, and nervously pulled it through her hair. "I hear you, Mom, and if I didn't care about anything, I'd let it all pass. If I thought everything were useless I would say nothing now. But some things have to be said. If you really love and care about me I should think you'd be happy and thankful for my life here. A few years ago where was I? I could have become a drug addict, died in squalor, been a whore. And all you could think about was that I dropped out of college! What happened, instead, is that I have a good marriage and a child and I'm happy. Why are you trying to undermine this? Is this Chessie's doing? She never writes, she comes to Europe and only once did she ever come to see us. Then she and Jules acted as if they were visiting the Third World. She wouldn't put her hand on my belly to feel the baby inside — acted as if I were indecent. Is she the one who's spread what a supposedly miserable life we have because we don't have the money she and Jules do? — That's what I guess from nonna when she sends me a Christmas check. And of course nonna worships Chessie — thinks everything she says is the absolute truth."

Dee's eyes were moist, her face was reddish and puffy.

"If you really love me, you would come and spend some time with us, not a day and a half — an overnight visit on your way back home."

"Oh, Dee, don't say that! I thought it was wonderful that I was being sent to Italy — it was a way to see you."

"The point is, when will you come for weeks, a month? To come for a visit with Zeno and be with him exclusively, not just because you have other business to do in Italy. Then you could talk to him and he might learn the English you're so anxious for him to have."

Fran knew as Dee spoke that she could not have her there for weeks, a month. A visit, yes, but not too long, not to annoy.

Dee went on. "And if you loved Winnie, would you really make her work to contribute to her college fees when she's got a hard enough time just trying to cope with her studies? Isn't there anything in your life which you could have given up so as to offer your last daughter the help she needs during this incredibly difficult period she's going through with you and your boyfriends?" How demanding my children are, Fran thought. More, they cry, more! more! Dee hasn't given the child English, so now it's supposed to be up to me. I'm supposed to work, but Winnie isn't, for her college education.

Fran flushed with anger thinking, Dee turns Catholic to sanctify her submissiveness to Leone, but storms and rages at me. She believes she loves her child as no other mother before her did, as if she is the only measure of it. What I gave her was love, but not so adhesive as that with which she will stick Zeno to her, just as Leone is stuck to his mother. Love, love, love, love! — that's all they talk about. Can't they get on with their lives?

Fran turned back to her suitcase.

"There's only one thing I'll say, Dee. I want and need your affection and loyalty. Maybe you're right that I'm all the bad things you say, that I made outrageous mistakes. But I wanted my daughters to be free and on their own because I had been brought up dumb and dependent. I suffered and am still suffering from that. My intentions were to give you what I didn't have. So, I am who I am, and this me is who you have for a mother. It may be poor stuff, but it's yours. It will always be."

Dee's rage subsided, she sat down on the bed, calm now and looked at Fran appraisingly. "Mom, I've decided to try to write," she said. "It means practically getting up at five before Zeno wakes up, and I think it will take awhile to produce anything. But I'll send you whatever comes out."

Fran smiled. She understood. This was reconciliation, this was a gift that Dee was giving her saying, Yes, I know you raised us to realize our gifts and I am going to try.

Fran hugged her. "That's wonderful, Dee. You have always been creative, your letters are full of wonderful things. You're wrong to think I only praised Chessie, and overlooked you — it's just that Chessie grabbed all the attention and made herself heard. But you have fantasy, more like Winnie. Like your father, too."

"And like you," said Dee.

"Time will tell," Fran smiled, repeating words she had heard from her own mother.

CHAPTER ELEVEN

In Rome, Fran found a telegram waiting for her at the hotel: *Dopo la pioggia, viene il sereno* — a little fast philosophy never hurts, Love, Dee.

It was true, after a storm does come the calm, and Fran was glad Dee knew it and could say so. Fran wondered who had first coined that expression. One of the Roman poets? Horace, no doubt. Or an epigrammist of the Enlightenment. It still made sense. Why couldn't Chessie send her such a message? She folded it and put it in her wallet.

As she left the hotel the Spanish Steps and Piazza di Spagna lay gorgeous before her and she thought of sending a postcard scene to Winnie but it seemed silly — she would be home the next day. New in the piazza, at the column of the Madonna, was a sign with golden arches advertising McDonald's. The barbarians were retaking Rome. Curious, Fran followed the sign's arrow and came to the site of a former caffè-bar she well remembered on Via Due Macelli. Never having been in a McDonald's at home, she decided to see one in Rome.

The old, familiar espresso bar was gone, its space turned into a forlorn ante-room. Fran had to go down a corridor, past a line of small, empty tables ranged against the wall that had enticed no sitters, and up a back stairway to the main area. Far from the light of day, a large interior room was thronged with people. Not just kids or tourists who'd go anywhere, eat anything, but also middle-aged citizens of Rome, businessmen, family groups. A salad bar held center floor in the dispiriting room. The Romans, as always, had adapted to outsiders. Their secret of holding on was to be chameleon-like, to change as circumstance dictated. Maybe they were right, maybe those middle-aged Roman noses sitting in a windowless room far from the street, each eating a big Mac (did they think it short for Machiavelli?) were in stride with the future.

But Fran had had enough. She headed for the Corso. Gone from the streets were the elegant women, the finely tailored men and the class distinctions of her earlier years in Rome with Marco. She was used to Americans having no sense of style and could see in her mind's eye the TV clip of the Secretary of State's wife getting off a plane in Moscow in a snowfall, hatless and dowdy, looking ridiculous while Mrs. Gorbochov, elegant in her fur toque, stepped forward in greeting. But for Italians to look bad was something new. Now, flaunting the new chic of shabbiness, they looked like everyone else.

Even the language seemed degenerate, newly punctuated with American slang or Anglicized constructions. Fran heard a young man with wispy hair around his bald spot shout *"Non poteva stare in linea?"* at someone in front of a bank cash machine. He shouted it twice and it sounded strange to her ear until she realized that he was transforming the Italian *in fila* to *in linea* to ape the English 'in line.' Small matter, no doubt, but it all added up in the end; American English was colonizing the country. Except, of course, in Dee's household. Always contrary, she was doing the reverse — Italianizing her English, her head, her life.

Everywhere things were mixed up. Back in the states frozen vegetables and Chinese water chestnuts were put on pasta to call it Primavera; cappuccino was served in a cup of styrofoam that added more non-biodegradable presence to the world. Above, the ozone layer was endangered by myriad sprays unleashed into the atmosphere: hairsprays, sprays for shaving, for killing bugs, for sweetening breaths, for unsticking slips that clung to skirts, for painting and rust-proofing, dusting. All superfluous, and all conceived to reduce human effort even as they poisoned the atmosphere. The bridges and roads of the Roman era were still intact while modern American ones were decayed and collapsing. AIDS and herpes and yeast infections were the new indices of social decline; people shot each other with the hand guns they bought because it was their right; Wall Street's white-collar Wasps modeled the way of total greed; teen-agers committed suicide. Child abuse and drugs were rampant in the states while the president and his wife spoke of great American values and refused support to Day Care for working women's children. Just stay home, said the rich woman to the poor. Fundamentalist religion was going strong — a sure sign of the country's decline — and was responsible for the slathering ooze of sanctimoniousness in religious men with bemusing names like Swaggart who got their sex in backstreets while they fleeced their followers up front. And the masses, non-thinking and empty, were hungry to be taken.

Via del Corso was now a pedestrian thoroughfare. Fran walked it in the direction of Piazza del Popolo. The street surged with people strolling up and down dressed in expensive rags and looking in store windows at other expensive rags. Those windows, which used to mesmerize her, halting her walk as she stood helplessly in front of them, glancing covetously at the beauty and boldness of their contents, no longer held her. Fran walked to Rosati's in Piazza del Popolo where she took a front outdoor table and studied the twin churches at the entrance to the piazza. No, not identical, but a subtle illusion. Opposite them, the group of buildings to the left of the great Porta caught her eye and Fran thought them splendid in their newly refurbished tones of pearly gray and peach. Previously, Fran remembered, they had huddled in beige blandness within the Aurelian wall where it met the great square. Piazza del Popolo, turned into a gigantic parking lot, was rimmed with police barriers in front of the two churches to keep traffic from gathering there. The square was loud and filled with the toxic fumes of motorcycles, taxis, buses. Pedestrians thronged, parading their tight crotches and punk hairdos, and exchanging obscenities. *Stronzo, cazzo* they greeted each other.

Fran ordered a Bitter Campari with soda and looked at the overhanging Pincio gardens, a sight which had always made her feel that she was about to see some wonderful drama staged among its shadows and cypress. Once, in the casino on the Pincio, there had been a party for Marco on the occasion of a new book and Fran had been notable, too, because she was his wife. Now she was someone else.

Dee had accused her of visiting them only on the way elsewhere. But why was Dee in that remote house, so secreted away, so hard to get to, in the first place? It was just like her. Dee liked things to be hard, her life a struggle. Yet she also yearned for the niceties of her youth and the enticements in store windows. She would have loved to travel, have vacations. She had learned to live in the cold because heating oil cost so much; she scorned egg beaters and shaving one's legs; she lived where her father-in-law had found them a place, not where she chose. Fran might have taken it as a defeat for Dee, but looking at the tawdry crowds in front of Rosati's she began to wonder if Dee and Leone were not better off where they were.

Fran shook her head at the piazza, at the beginning dusk; either it signified mightily, like Zeno's name, or it didn't at all and it was time for her to make peace with what was.

Sipping her Campari soda, Fran noticed an older woman waving in her direction and approaching across the square. She was handsome, supple in her stride, gray-haired, maybe seventy. She was dressed in classic American of a certain era: tailored off-white slacks, good silk shirt, a cashmere cardigan draped on her shoulders and, as a dash of exotica, an interesting Navajo onyx and silver necklace. Her face was tanned and healthy, her hair was pulled back by a scarf. She was smiling widely, her gaze directed amicably at Fran who wondered who she was.

"Hello!" the woman said spiritedly as she reached Fran's table. "Do you mind if I join you? I remember you from the Bologna fair — at the Pricer display."

"Of course," Fran said. "Come sit down. Who were you with?"

"I'm Gladys Gifford, a children's book artist. I've done so many and some have done so well, that my publisher decided to send me to the Fair." The woman extended her hand and shook Fran's with vigor.

"I know your name. Nice to meet you. Are you gathering ideas for your next book?"

"Yes indeed! But hardly the sort for a kiddy book. For years I've been interested in the Goddess figure, I've got sketch books full of the Goddess image from wherever I've been. But now I'm going back further to the primordial images of woman as force, as creative power...as the life image." Gladys Gifford's smile was sly and her light brown eyes lit with the energy of some inner sight. Fran felt her vitality and admired the kind of good looks, which were pre-served so well in older age without make-up or embellishment, the Katherine Hepburn good looks of character and good background. All-American.

"My dear!" Gladys went on. "The reason I was delighted to be at the Book Fair is that Bologna is so close to Modena. I got to Mode-na and it's just as I thought! I was so thrilled when I saw the sculpture on the cathedral. You see I'm studying the image of the vulva through the ages. And I've found this laughing granny woman called baubo-baubo, from the Greek, is a dildo — but anyway, she's a predecessor of Dionysius. I have drawings and photocopies of exemplars from museums and sites I've been to, starting with prehistoric scratches on rocks right down to the Potta of Modena."

Fran scanned the tanned, handsome face of Gladys Gifford with interest. Now here was a forthright woman, no effeminate mask on her. First things first, the vulva was her thing! Fran could see the point of being around people with vitality and bold ideas, for her spirits immediately rose. "The Potta of Modena?" Fran asked her. "Potta? she repeated, wrinkling her forehead. "Maybe it's a dialect form of *puttana* which means whore. That might connect with the vulva."

"The story," said Gladys, "is that there used to be among the statuary on the parapet of the duomo a particular figure of a woman raising her skirts to show her sex, an apotropaic gesture, you know, to ward off evil. Now, because of its age — it's datable to the late Roman era — and its poor condition (as you can imagine, the Christian zealots tried to destroy it), the figure's been taken down and put in the museum and a copy is in place outside on the duomo. This woman and her obscene gesture is known as "La Potta di Modena" and of course, a lot of legends grew up around her. Through the ages it became identified with a certain woman of Modena who was said to have borne forty-two children, most of them sons, and so she's pointing to her valiant vulva which gave so much man-power to her town. In 1494 the French king Charles VII invaded Italy and, well aware of the legend, when his troops got to Modena, they all tried to defame the statue by exposing themselves to her. There's been confusion over the centuries, but it certainly goes back to the

Roman era. The interesting thing is how it got incorporated into Christian icons on the cathedral!"

Gladys Gifford stopped for a moment to give her order of J&B scotch on the rocks to a waiter.

"Well, that's some story," Fran laughed.

"It's just what I needed to round out my theory. You see I have magnificent exemplars of the vulva from all cultures and civilizations from pre-history right through the classical period. But what I needed was something later — to show how the symbol of female power might have survived, somewhat disguised, from pre-history into later ages. Under Christianity, of course, it would have been interdicted, but as with all powerful ideas, it would not be totally eradicated, it had to pop up again someplace. And it did! In the Potta!"

"So, the vulva is a charm against evil, well that's good to know," Fran said. It could be a woman's counterpart to the Knight's sword which, grasped at the crossbar and held straight out, became a cross to keep evil at bay. The vulva was the *figa*, the female sex symbol which had helped Henry Levine's step-daughter conceive and bear a child.

"My sources say potta actually means vulva," Gladys continued animatedly. "But the curious thing is again how men take over any good thing connected with women and make it their own. They've actually tried to make potta a masculine word, as in *il potta*. The expression "to be *il Potta* of Modena," means to brag or boast, make oneself something important, and it's used with overbearing men."

So here, thought Fran, is Gladys Gifford, a charming woman, a trickster type, a conjurer, extolling the female part. She was the counter to the *malocchio* that depicted single women as demented demons — all those spinsters, widows, spurned fiancées, nuns, career

202

women, old maids and hags who did not have the protection and status of a man by their side and were believed to curse, by the force of the burning envy in their evil eyes, the women who did have a man. *Malocchio* was the vengeance of sexually frustrated women who were oddballs and outsiders by virtue of being single and unconnected — aberrations and freaks in a world of households. Paradoxically, that was also their strength — they were not dissipated into caretakers of others, they were unto themselves. If they had been Thoreau, they would have been honored as loners true to a vision; as females they were called witches.

What came to Fran's mind was the eeriness of having heard the old Italian women in Ferryville speak of those unfortunate people who became the bearers of the evil eye, those who had unwittingly committed some blasphemy or gone against custom. It had been whispered that Lella Grandi's child had been born not only handicapped, but also the bearer of bad luck, because Lella while pregnant had turned her head in church at the moment of the Elevation of the Host. All the old-timers believed in malevolence that could be unleashed in looks. Bad luck in one's life was due to an ever-present menace, the malignant power of another's envy. Thus, the caution against flaunting one's good fortune. Dolly Sturzo should beware — she was a ready mark in the grand Normandy house on the Hill. All discontents everywhere were capable of casting the evil eye, but mainly, the old concurred, it was discontented women who had the evil eye.

Fran was persuaded by the metaphorical truth in the old wives' tales and superstitions. Men feared intense women whose strength was not channeled into the family, but was used for themselves. It was the strength, Fran thought, of the great childless women authors; the focus was on themselves and their work. Was it Chessie's focus? she wondered.

In the old cultures from which her ancestors derived, one should never aim too far. Under the dominant fear of *malocchio* one understated one's condition in order not to excite envy and thus bring the evil eye upon you. To be an over-reacher was dangerous. You think you are better than we are, Fran's mother used to accuse her, burdening her with puzzled guilt for doing well in her studies.

Listening to free-wheeling Gladys Gifford, Fran felt the weight and clamps of thousands of generations of illiterate southern Italian witches on her shoulders. Perhaps it would take a few more generations of refining before anyone could emerge from those shadows and be free of them.

Gladys Gifford, a woman alone, had done it, turning the whole thing around for herself, making of Woman a power and protection, not a curse. Now she was waving again. "Oh, golly, there's Ezra Banks!" she said excitedly. "I guess if you sit here long enough you're bound to see everyone. Ezra! Ezra! — over here!"

Gladys summoned a tall, lean black man from the milling crowd in the piazza. Fran stared as he approached them. "Who is he?" Fran asked in an undertone before he got to their table. He had a moustache, he was smiling broadly, he was wearing a red shirt with a black tie and black pants held up by multi-colored suspenders. He was immediately and dazzlingly attractive.

"Oh, Ezra's my editor, dear. Such a good one! I just love him."

Yes, I could too, Fran told herself. Ezra Banks was dressed with a boldness that was just short of flamboyant, but confident enough to be elegant. He was a presence in the Rome dusk. His shirt, his tie, his black and white patent leather shoes — he had a style and stride no longer seen on the Corso. He had the look Fran no longer saw in Italian men. He was smiling, and Fran smiled back.

"How are you, darling," he said to Gladys as he bent over to kiss her.

"Ezra, darling! Meet this nice lady from Pricer. She's Fran Beniferro, she speaks Italian."

Ezra Banks bent over and kissed Fran's hand in greeting.

"You look like Garibaldi with that red shirt," she said.

"Think I could pass for him over here?" he asked with an ironic drawl.

"Maybe. If you had a beard."

Fran hoped he wouldn't spoil everything by being pompous. She had once sat next to a black author at a dinner party who had worn a careful mask of scorn and condescension during the whole time Fran tried conversing with him. He told and re-told his victories, his initiatives, his party-going. He sounded like any over-bearing writer. Then he began to talk of the future technological form of imparting what a writer wants to make known in some mass-marketing breakthrough. What form will it be, Fran asked him, not a book? Naturally, he answered her loftily, you can't conceive the future — no writer or intellectual can. And Fran had disagreed: the meaning of someone who uses the intellect and the scope of someone who writes is, precisely, to be aware of future things, not aligned to the past. But he had put her off and Fran thought of him as a stuffed shirt, an exceedingly unpleasant snob.

Ezra Banks was altogether different.

"How did you like the Fair?" she asked him.

"Pretty ho-hum. The only interesting gossip I overheard was that the author of Mme. Sadat's biography has been asked to do Nancy Reagan's."

"That's something! Why would that same person want to do a Reagan? And besides, why would Nancy want *her?*"

"That's not the point. It's all a question of packaging. What everyone wants these days is a scintilla of scandal. Just enough, not a dab deeper. Like a child's calculated book on a famous parent. A son's titillating revelation of his famous father's homosexual bent. That's what the public wants — the "balanced" revelation, the little shudder of shock à la *Mommie Dearest.*"

"What about truth?" Fran wrinkled her brow with distaste. "Is everything marketing strategies?"

"Before you joined us we were speaking of my book on vulvas, Ezra," Gladys said.

"Now *that* will be deep!" He laughed expansively with a rolling, hearty chortle.

"When you're both ready for marketing, you could connect it with the plate designs in Judy Chicago's Dinner Party project," Fran interjected. She was directly opposite Ezra, and leaning forward as she talked, looking at him intently. He lounged back in his chair, stretched out his legs under the table. The tips of his black and white patent shoes touched her sandals. Fran drew her feet back. He smiled ironically.

Into her mind's eye popped the sight from long ago of Winnie's black cat, Minou. Sleek, black, soft, silent, furry. It was as if, across the table, Ezra Banks was reading her mind for he chuckled softly and said, "How ya doing?"

Fran leaned back, stretched out her legs and mingled them with his under the table. Gladys was chatting on: "What a good idea, maybe some Judy Chicago illustrations would be fine in the book. Or, of course, Georgia O'Keeffe."

"Uh-huh." Ezra turned his head sideways to stare at the people moving in the piazza.

Feeling her heart beat more rapidly with what was for her a burst of unusual intrepidness, Fran said, "I used to confuse the vulva with the Volvo and would wonder why they'd name a car that. I thought they were both from the same Latin root."

"Not so far fetched," Ezra said lazily, relaxed in his slouch. "I guess you could say both Volvos and vulvas make the world go round."

Fran felt the sparks between them, their legs touching, rubbing — impressed that she could be so aroused. Marco had been so paternal. Max, such a wash-out after his extravagant overtures of love. Fran recalled Max's referring to Blacks as schwartzers; he had never hidden his fear and dislike of them. It was inconceivable to him that any of them could be like Ezra Banks, more educated, more cultivated, more attractive and more desirable than he. Once Max had told Fran a dream: that he and she were in a car that was stopped by four black young men who accosted Max and demanded his money. He turned over to them the $400 he had in his wallet and then pleaded with one of them to give him back something so he wouldn't be broke. One of the black youths gave him $10. All the time Max was afraid both of Fran's reaction because she had often told him not to carry so much cash with him, and also what would happen to them if the blacks "got crazy."

Chessie told her what his dream meant: the number four signified completeness of the integrated personality. The four Blacks stood for something instinctive in the personality that was repressed in Max. Primitiveness would be threatening to someone like Max who wanted everything under control. Rather than give himself up entirely to the Blacks, Max resisted and held onto part of himself thus losing the chance to become emotionally richer.

Howston, on the other hand, as an educated liberal, a writer, would certainly understand attraction to a black man. Howston, Fran repeated to herself, trying to remember him. Just before leaving for Italy she had stopped in Edith's office and asked Edith to tell her candidly what she thought of Howston. Edith, who described herself as someone who had happily divorced her one and only husband in order to get rid of an allergy, had met Howston several times.

"Well, Fran, he's very pleasant, I suppose. A nice chap, but hardly equal to Marco. You must have a touch of *schlusspanik*."

"What's that, Edith?" Fran frowned.

"Fear of the closing door. Maybe you think he's your last chance."

That exchange had dismayed Fran unreasonably. To hell with Edith and her ratings! The whole point of a relationship with Howston was to give her support, through his being there; to let her get on with herself and her life. Howston, in exchange, would have her as a companion. Fran had dashed out of her office saying I have a million things to do before going to Bologna.

At Rosati's, Gladys pulled out a notepad engraved with the arms of the Hassler Hotel and said, "I'll just make a note, Ezra, so I can show off my ritzy pad." She flourished the notepad with a mischievous look. "I stopped in the Hassler on top of the Spanish Steps to use their ladies room. It's much too grand and costly to stay there, but I picked up one of their note pads. I even asked the concierge to hold onto my shopping bag for awhile, and he did!" She was, Fran could see, an elegant prankster.

In the warm moments of dusk just before night fell, Ezra and Fran openly ransacked each other's faces over drinks, smiling, lurching forward over the table towards each other, leaning back, twisting and moving as if in some elaborate courtship ritual, saying sly things, coming to some unspoken agreement.

"Do you like licorice sticks," he asked lazily.

Fran knew what was coming. "Funny you should ask," she answered boldly, smiling and teasing, "all Calabrians have a taste for licorice. It goes with being who they are."

"Is that a fact? And that's what you are, Calabrian?"

"Well, I'm as American as you!" Fran laughed, "but way back — well, not so far, I guess — anyway, one pair of grandparents were from Calabria, the other pair from Sicily."

Just opposite them, a bunch of young men were lounging around the police barricades. Fran watched them scratching their crotches. Ezra followed her eyes. Meeting his look, Fran said, "It's for good luck."

"What's for good luck?"

"Scratching themselves there, it brings good luck, you know."

"Oh!" scoffed Gladys, "they just want to be sure their dicks are still there, that's why they're always touching themselves! They're scared they'll lose it."

Fran liked how Gladys wore her years so well, with such nonchalant gallantry. Aging was now something Fran began to think about each time she looked into the mirror, each time she searched for her glasses because she couldn't read a label, each time she heard the ominous creaking of her bones rattling inside her body like a loose skeleton detaching from its adhesive of strong, young skin.

Fran thought of looking into a mirror and seeing not herself but the recapitulation of the whole Sturzo tribe as if she personally summed them up. Scanning the remnant of the moon-face that she had loathed as a seventeen-year old for its mark of peasantry, Fran now saw it grown drawn. She used to think, if we were really descended from some English knight who had stopped in Sicily on his way to the Crusades, as Pop claimed, why don't we have the narrow chiseled faces and short noses of the Anglos?

She knew her face, her body. She saw the few crepey lines when she flexed her arm, but her breasts did not sag, were still firm and erect, her neck was long and not the support of multiple chins. And she felt, still, as if it were a distant whistle, prolonged and vibrant in the night, the desire to merge her body in love, to force it as she did jogging.

Fran was not satisfied with Howston. Their lovemaking was a performance Fran had learned to do proficiently enough. Just enough. Fran liked the closeness and the exchange of affection, but he did not move her sexually and if it hadn't been for the sensation of that sometime distant whistle in the night, Fran would have thought that desire was gone, that she had had what there was of it.

Fran wondered about having a woman lover and exploring that shore of love. It was fashionable, in the times, to be bi-sexual though Fran personally thought it pretentious when she heard certain women proclaim their dual sex lives as if they had achieved some prize: "Everybody's bi-sexual," Fran would scoff at the boasters, thinking back to Yvonne Schotter and their childhood exploits.

But her loyalty was to the male body which joined with and completed hers. And Fran saw that body before her now in the lounging, carefully posed casual attitude of Ezra Banks. He was beautiful and he was there.

They went to her hotel room where they undressed, and Fran stared at the beauty of Ezra's body. Clothed he was a dandy, the cock of the walk, a statement of style that made her happy just seeing him; but unclothed, his body straight and lean, rippling with the chiaroscuro of musculature, his abdomen taut, his legs long and finely articulated at the knee, his penis erect and facing her, he was aesthetically perfect.

"You're like the David," Fran said, standing back to look at him, resisting going to him and letting herself be enfolded and impaled. "You're the negative of the David photo. David in black. Negative capability."

"Come to David...."

They approached each other. His arms wrapped around her, pulling her breasts into his chest; his penis nuzzled at her crotch. Fran felt for it, undulating her hips, standing feet apart so that he could explore and probe. Fran raised up on her toes. He opened her lips with his mouth and they caressed each other's tongues, nibbling and kissing, until Fran leaned back, drawing in breath.

He backed her towards the bed, as if in a slow-motion dance, without losing his probing contact.

Fran felt she would come apart with longing and need and yet she held back, so that he would not enter too soon. Still holding him, gyrating her hips and moving her hands over his penis, caressing and directing it, Fran still stood, locked to his body.

He tilted her back over the edge of the bed, then went down between her knees and buried his head in the wide open, salivating cleft. Fran felt expanded to the horizons, great enough to engulf the world. Her head rested on the bed with her eyes set on the plaster rosette in the ceiling, her hands on his head feeling its motion. Fran visualized in terrific color a huge sign at a Mall with three-foot high

211

letters and decked with balloons: Grand Opening! it said. Fran felt his tongue dart and retreat in teasing overtures, his lips nibbling at the clitoris, then the steady rhythm as he went further and further in and Fran felt she would levitate, leave the room through the window and fly over Trinità dei Monti skimming the fountain in Piazza di Spagna and explode in a million flying pieces of cunt and guts.

"Oh my," Fran groaned, whimpered, gasped. "Oh my, oh my...."

He lifted up his head. "Yah, mamma, yah! — you come strong, like a girl."

Fran had drawn herself all the way onto the bed and pulled him down beside her. She kneeled next to him and began with lips and hands to cover his body. She kissed and licked the head of the penis and gradually took it into her mouth, circulating her tongue over it. Back and forth, in and out, caressing, licking, lapping, Fran kept the rhythm going until she heard his moan. Then she lay back and still holding him let the jissom jet over her stomach. They lay there, spent, dozing, her hand coddling him as if the thing between his legs was a small featherless chick and Fran, the brood hen, was keeping it safe and warm. And then it came to life again, expanded, filled her hand and started her own flow stirring again between the legs. And this time he entered her, filling her, it seemed, to the navel. Thrusting in, retreating almost fully out until Fran gasped with the terror of losing him, he kept up the strokes, crouched above her, and watching her closely. Heedless, Fran let her face crinkle into an ugly grimace of unbearable ecstasy, mouth open, eyes closed, her body, too, careless and undone, giving out little farts of excitement and pleasure. Fran had never let herself be so exposed, had never shown so openly what she felt. She didn't care. There was nothing to hide. This was as close to herself as Fran could come.

And come they did. As it all subsided and Fran held him close to her, their bodies plastered together with sweat and other effluvia, Fran saw their black and white limbs entwined in some graceful pattern, like the black and white Duomo of Siena. And lying there, Fran breathed out, "*Mamma mia!*"

Ezra laughed. "That's what Calabrians say when they fuck?"

Fran laughed, too, and said, "*Never*, and I mean never, have I *ever* said *that* before."

"Must be cause I called you mamma — put it in your mind. Anyone call you that before?"

"My children," Fran murmured, passing her hand up and down his hairless, David chest, imprinting the negative in her mind forever.

CHAPTER TWELVE

Back at Pricer, Fran stopped in Edith's office to give her a rundown of the Italian trip.

Edith lit up and smoked while Fran told her about Bologna and staying with Dee and her stopover in Rome. Edith's face crinkled with laughter and made her words come out with a snort: "So, you ran into Henry Levine. Well, let's just say the trip wasn't a complete loss if you ran into Ezra as well. Isn't he a dazzler? Good editor, too. I wish Pricer could pry Gladys Gifford away from him."

A warm feeling of pleasure recollected filled Fran at the mention of Ezra. Already he had become part of banked treasure.

The men Fran discussed with Edith were, in Edith's term, part of the "volume" Fran was acquiring as a single woman. After a long marriage, it was necessary, she said, that Fran scrutinize a variety of men and acquire a backlog — for how else could she know what would work? Then she added in her direct way, "Howston's been seen out with a young blonde."

Vicki, Fran told herself. To Edith she said, "It's not important. I understand Howston. He resented my going to Bologna; so he wanted to get even, have some short-range fun. But Vicki's definitely not long term. I am."

It had to be live and let live, no checks and controls between Howston and her. What else could she do? — hope that a Mr. Wonderful would turn up in the volume count?

Edith, in her enigmatic way, as she reached for her ringing telephone and waved Fran out, Edith tossed off parting words: "As the Sisyphists say, even as you both keep pushing it up, the rock keeps rolling down. *Ciao!*"

Howston had roses for Fran at her return. Over Bloody Marys at their favorite place for lunch he listened to her talk about Dee and Leone and Zeno. Howston was looking good. He wore a navy blazer over a light blue shirt and grey slacks and seemed fitter and trimmer than Fran remembered. She was glad to see him again, she felt good, confident.

"Howston," Fran said, reaching for his hand, "I found the cornerstone at Dee's and left her money to ship it over to you at your address. It should be here by the time the house is moved." "Super," he said, but his tone was not enthusiastic.

"What's wrong, Hows?"

"You don't give a guy much, Fran. You never make the overtures, you never even say I love you. What I need is to have some return feeling on your part, I need to know you adore me as I do you. Convince me, babe ... overwhelm me."

"Oh," she said, embarrassed. "I guess I just can't moon around — that's not my style, but you know there's no one I'm closer to, no one I'm planning to be with as I am with you." It was true. If not the gift to overwhelm, what Fran did have, and would give, was everything else: affection, help, companionship. "It's how we are together that counts. We're making plans for our house at the Cape. That's the commitment."

"Sometimes I wonder if it's just a dream, if I'll ever get to the Cape and live in a barn-house ... spend some time writing, some boating, or just hanging out on a deck with a beer watching the sunset."

"Of course, you will!" Fran said strongly. "I gave a lot of thought on the plane to the house and what we want to do and I have a great idea to get it moved. The thing is, I think it would work better if you wrote up my idea in your name and present it as yours. You've got a name as a writer — your name will carry more weight."

"I knew you'd get the weight in somehow," he said with a mock groan. "So, what's your idea?"

"Since the town owns the piece of land we saw at the Cape, write a proposal to the Town Planning Board that they sell you that piece at its assessed low price, below market, in return for your moving and relocating the former Charles Barr house there. What I am going to do is get Vested Brands to give me the structure for a token amount on the basis of moving it out and saving them the demolition costs. They'll be delighted!"

Howston began to look interested. As a writer of mysteries, Fran could see he was won over by the intricacy of the plan; he liked schemes and plots and clever maneuvers.

"Hmmm," he mused. "Not bad. But you'd have to have an understanding from V-B before I make a proposal to the Town Board. And why should the town want to sell the land below market?"

"Sweetheart, that's where your writing skills come in. You will convince them of what's true — that the town gets in return the prestige of having secured a landmark house. Even though it will be ours, we could agree to open it to visitors at certain times. The town can mention in their vacation brochures that the home of a famous American composer is preserved there and it will certainly draw people who will come for a look. And all that means business for the town."

Howston took a drink, cocked his head to one side and regarded Fran for a few seconds. "Not bad, kiddo." He took another drink. "Okay, let's do it."

"Fantastic, Hows!" Fran grabbed his hand again, elated. "We can work our way to the Cape gradually — we can start going up for week-ends, then summers, then eventually it will become our retirement place."

Fran was beaming, suffused with a confidence and hope that she hadn't experienced in years. The vision was compelling, and it began to be realizable. Please, let it happen! she said to herself. She could see her house overlooking the water; she could see herself there.

"We could put in a rental unit — get some income along with living there," Howston mused aloud.

Fran frowned. "Don't even think that way, Hows," she said evenly, "that would violate the intent of preserving the Barr house. That's asking for trouble. The planning board would never approve. The place has to be kept as it is — authentic." And that, Fran knew, was as much for her sake as for the Planning Board.

"Sweetheart, what a picture!" Howston, in high spirits, called her later at the office. "I can see us in that big room working on a book together." Fran sighed inaudibly; he was thinking of them as a Mom and Pop store. Just when things seemed to be smoothed out, he fished up the central dilemma of her life: her craving for freedom for herself versus her great desire to be attached to someone.

So began "the summer of the house." Without Winnie or Dee nearby to fill her time, Fran gave herself over to Howston and the house. As for Chessie, Fran felt the sadness of something having died between them; and as one does in grief Fran plunged into what could distract her the most to make up for the loss.

Howston and Fran spent several week-ends at the Cape, going to the land site where they paced off the dimensions of the Medwood barn-house, lengthily discussed its positioning, and planned the out-

217

side areas. They had both gotten tremendously interested in barn structures and brought along with them photos of other barn houses and ideas for the interior. Fran started making folders on landscape gardening, financing, house moving, names of specialists and architects. She made a list of other owners of barn houses whenever she came across one, thinking she could get in touch, or maybe visit, to get ideas. Fran advised Howston to look into veterans' mortgages that he could qualify for; and she got him interested in the Preservation League.

Over the summer Fran told Howston the history of the area known as Shady Brook Farm that she had put together from records found at the Medwood Historical Society. A very old settlement, Medwood was once a coach stop on the old Post Road. The land comprising Shady Brook Farm was, in pre-Revolutionary days, owned by a Loyalist named Abraham Hackett who had sympathies with the British crown. He fled during the War of Independence and his property was taken over by the Commissioners of Forfeitures who, at war's end, put it up for purchase. In 1797 Isaiah Buchard and his wife Jemima were on record as owners of the land. Their original homestead, much enlarged and embellished was, in Fran's day, the Buchard estate that was sold to the Vested Brands Management Institute.

The Beniferro property, had been a barn, one of several outbuildings on land across the road from the Buchard homestead. It had been made into a kind of theatre-playhouse by a contemporary Buchard descendant, and then into a residence on four acres. Originally farmers, the Buchards had, over time, become wealthy real estate developers and investment bankers; in their hey-day from mid-19th century until after World War II, they had used the Medwood property as their country place with their main residence in Boston. They were county gentry until they, too, fell into decline.

By the time Charles Barr came to Shady Brook Farm in the late forties, old Mr. Buchard, the last of the family, was selling acreage and buildings. Charles Barr bought the renovated barn-house and settled in, writing some of his most notable compositions while he lived there. "The barn," Fran used to tell Winnie on their long drives though the countryside, "is the one pure American architectural form. It's what really sprung up here and is suited to the landscape and temperament."

And Barr was the pre-eminent American composer. His name, synonymous with American music whose folk themes he made his own, was known everywhere. And at Shady Brook Farm he wrote his only opera, evoking the American landscape and ties to the land which must have flowed directly from the setting he lived in and was inspired by.

The wonder was that the land had never been fenced off into separate holdings, or broken up into developments. The natural look of orchard, wooded areas, open meadow, brooks and ponds, as in the original Buchard holding, had been preserved and the few residences that were created from the old structures in no way diminished the setting. In spring the hillsides were covered with daffodils naturalized from long-ago plantings. By fall orange bittersweet lit the low stone walls; and in winter all lay calm and secreted, guarded by the tall beeches, firs, and maples, the hills punctuated by russet spears of fox-grass rising from the drifts that blanketed all in quiet snow. It had changed when, one by one, the separate properties began to be bought up by V-B.

219

"You know, Fran," Howston said as they sat one evening over lobster at Rock Harbor on the Cape, paper bibs tied around their necks, their plates piled with wreckage, "Let me tell you something about T.S. Eliot — it wasn't literary achievement that finally brought him happiness. It wasn't the Nobel. It was marrying his secretary. It was human love — the very love he had once dismissed as the consolation of ordinary men. Love made him happy!"

"So what's the moral, Hows? That I should be a secretary to your Eliot? Then I could go over your manuscripts? I think I'd prefer your being Leonard Woolf to my Virginia."

And Fran recalled Marco's dictum of Life over Art; but studying the Greeks Fran learned from Aristotle that art is a higher type of knowledge than experience.

"Adele is getting her nose done," Fran's mother reported during her weekly call.

"That figures, after the hair-bleach and the tummy-tuck. What about Pop and his hearing-aid? — that's what should really be taken care of."

"Oh, he's driving us crazy! He keeps asking the same questions over and over because he can't hear the answer. He sits there like a blank. Gussie and Susan were here the other night and Susan says Pop can really hear and is just pretending not to."

"Where does Susan get her inside information?" Fran was annoyed. At the first sign of Pop's tottering, everyone seemed ready to tear him down.

"Oh I don't know! I don't know what to think. I called the hearing aid people and they told me he should have the kind that goes around the ear, but he refuses. Well then, they said, if he insists on the in-the-ear aid, he should learn to change the battery and keep the hearing aid clean — they gave us a demonstration. But no! He won't do anything for himself. Then he says to me, It's an awful thing not to be able to hear. And I find he's taken the battery out! So I say to him why didn't you put that new battery in yesterday when you were saying you couldn't hear? And he says, I had no confidence in it. That burned me up! I told him, how can you say you have no confidence in it when you didn't even try it! And you know him, he's so stubborn, he just went on saying he had no confidence."

"Mother, you're acting as if you expect a reasonable answer. Why is everyone so angry at him? He's not all there. If he can't manage the battery, then you have to do it for him."

"All my life I've been doing for him!"

"I know. That's what women do." Fran paused, then said, "Howston and I are making plans for the move of my old house."

Her mother's voice changed from exasperation to the special tone that predicts disaster. "Do you think that's right? giving the house where Marco lived and you brought up your children to someone else?"

There was so much misstatement in the remark that Fran didn't know what to address first. She blurted out, "That house was not just Marco's, it was also mine! For God's sake, what do you mean *giving*? This whole thing is *my* idea!"

"Are you sure about that man? Can you trust him?"

"I trust myself. I know what I want and since Howston wants me he gets the house, too."

"Well, I don't know."

"*You* don't have to. *I* do."

"You sound awfully sure of yourself, I hope you don't regret it."

But what Fran heard was, *You will regret it ... why should you be so sure of yourself when I've never been?*

"I just hope you won't be disappointed," her mother continued as Fran, the translator, translated: *You want too much, you reach too far – you will be disappointed and when you are, I will remind you of this conversation.*

"Don't worry," Fran said, "I know what I'm doing. What else is new?"

"Chessie says that you're exaggerating this thing about the house into a kind of make-believe that life was perfect there. She says you're such a revisionist, you never want to face reality."

"That's funny. She's always praised Jules' determination when he has some goal in mind. I remember her saying that Jules doesn't do leverage any better than any of us, but that he knows what he wants. Well, I know what I want. And what you should want, for your sake and Pop's, is to get out of your big house with all its stairways and pitfalls and move into a garden apartment all on one floor."

"Oh, I don't know!"

When would she ever know, Fran wondered. For as long as Fran could remember, that had been her mother's refrain.

When Fran had business in New York, she called Winnie and asked if they could get together – could she pay Winnie a visit in the sub-let she had taken in the Village?

"Sure, Mom," Winnie said cheerfully. "Come for supper."

When Fran called Howston to say goodbye, he gave a strained laugh and said in a light tone, "You'll never guess who called today."

"I'm busy Hows, I don't want to guess."

222

Briskly then he said, "Vicki called to tell me she was going into the hospital to have an operation. She thought I'd want to know."

Silence. Why was he telling her this? "What did you say, Hows?"

"I told her I'd pay her a visit."

"Oh? Did you think that's necessary?"

"Christ, Fran, I just wanted to be nice! She's all alone."

"So be nice, Hows," Fran said. She realized that the whole unaccountable conversation was a set-up in which she was supposed to blow up in anger so that he could, too. It seemed to happen every time she went someplace without him. "Let me know when I get back how Vicki's doing." So much, she told herself for the Vicki ploy and Howston wanting her to be jealous.

It was a fine summer day in New York. Weaving through Washington Square Park and the crowds of children, chess-players, roller-skaters, university students, pimps and pushers, Fran felt the tempo of the city and knew why Winnie wanted to move there and paint as soon as her school year ended rather than spend another summer waitressing on Cape Cod. She's a painter of people and human attitudes, Fran thought, not seascapes and sand dunes. The galleries of new work are here. Raw material is all around her — in the park, in the subway, in the crowds and in the people she sees on her messenger job. Fran admired Winnie's paintings, they were bold and colorful and full of her connectedness with people. Winnie had explained to her that an artist has a "registration" of color, form, and impact just as a writer has "voice." Hers was loud, Fran's quiet.

She also said, there's love and work, but the love shouldn't go to the work. Fran still hadn't figured that out.

The Village street where Winnie lived had a quiet run-down air that was reassuring. Except for a Korean greengrocer on the corner, it was still an Italian neighborhood where Fran knew Winnie would be protected and safe. The old men who sat out in the street kept their eyes open, they saw who came and went. They kept the peace. There was a school nearby where children played in the paved schoolyard. Winnie's place was between a laundry and a tarot card reader. Fran was buzzed into a narrow dingy entry where the small black and white floor tiles were familiar to her from a million Saturday afternoon movies in Ferryville. Fran walked up to the third floor on steps worn into craters with usage. Dark shadowed the halls. She saw no one.

Winnie stood in her open door, waiting. She wore her deadpan, aloof look. Beyond her a long narrow room ended in two high windows that looked out onto a fire escape where Fran saw a pot of basil, and a tiny backyard from which a tree shot up. There was a sink near the entrance, a stove and fridge; another door was half-closed on the bathroom. Winnie's easel stood in the center of the room near an opened sofa-bed littered with paint tubes and papers. The walls of the room were brick, lined with books and things and there was a cozy pleasant feeling to the space. "Hi, Win," Fran kissed her. "Well, you have a view, at least. This seems a good set-up."

Winnie looked unkempt, her hair long and straggly. "Hi, ma," she answered flatly. "I'm having trouble with the john." Her initial enthusiasm over the phone for the visit seemed to have gone. Since Fran's call, Winnie had moved into another mood.

"Have you been in touch with Chessie, lately," Fran asked.

"I can't stand Chessie! She calls and says things like why don't you and a boyfriend come up for dinner!"

"What's wrong with that?"

"You don't understand — she's into this whole other scene. Like some guy and I should go up to her apartment as if we're this other middle-class married couple and sit around with her and Jules and get bored to death."

"It's good for you to have someone to turn to in New York."

"I can take care of myself. Better than Chessie — she lets Jules take care of everything for her. What would she do without him? she wouldn't even be able to cross the street! She's as bad as nonna."

"Never mind that. What are we having for supper?"

Winnie's look turned blank. "Supper? What supper?" she said. "I've already eaten."

Fran looked surprised. "I thought we were going to eat together."

"Well there's nothing here," Winnie said belligerently, pointing to a fridge door which was covered with cartoons. One, showing a forlorn-looking guy caught by the neck in a hairy grip, was captioned Seized by the Imagination.

"Do you want an Oreo?" Winnie asked.

"No — let's go to Dean & DeLuca's and get some of their good bread and cheese, and whatever else you want. Come on, I'll buy you an ice cream."

Winnie had on green and white polka dot pants and a polo shirt open at the neck onto her white, smooth skin. Her waist nipped in and her hips rounded out, her stomach was enviably flat. She looked interesting. Standing on a corner at Broadway waiting for the light to change, they were approached by a young woman with a cloud of curly hair around her thin freckled face. "Are you the Brills?" she asked uncertainly.

"What's that?" Winnie laughed, "It sounds like birds."

"Oh," said the girl, "I'm sorry, I mistook you for some people."

"Do we look like Brills," Fran joked with Winnie as they crossed the street, "if anything, with our Italian noses, we could be Brillos."

"Hey, ma, that's cool — Brillo pads!" Winnie grinned and put her arm in Fran's as they walked.

Dean and DeLuca's superior food store on Prince Street was one of the chic places of Soho. "God, Winnie, what a place, it's like going to church!" Fran said as they entered and the strains of Mozart's Missa Solemnis were in the air. A display of beautiful fresh vegetables faced them like a high altar adorned with bouquets of radicchio and chard, upright stalks of asparagus like taper candles, bunches of verdant basil wafting the odor of incense. The faces of the shoppers were those of worshippers. Before the laden display cases, the communicants partook of bread, cheese, croissants, tarts, and mousses. Above them, like chapel decor, were the sacred wreaths of garlic, sweet Italian cherry peppers, and long pimentos.

Fran and Winnie ate in the park. Licking an ice cream cone, Winnie talked about her longing for a studio of her own, a place to settle into; but her fear, she told Fran, was that she would be as restless as her mother was. She told Fran of her panic attacks whenever one of her boyfriends tried to get close to her. Fran said, it's probably just nerves and growing pains, and told Winnie not to worry, that she'd grow out of it, told her of her father's internal centeredness despite his own losses and random moves; he had been ten years working in a bank, an underground partisan in the war, years a commuter to Harvard, but always centered in his art.

"I'm sorry you don't get along with Chessie," Fran said. "She and Jules could be company for you here in this city if you're feeling alone and panicky."

"You spoiled Chessie, Mom, and she treats you like shit. It gives me a panic attack just to see her. She invited me to lunch but all she really wanted was to ask me if you were getting the message."

"What's the message?"

"What she thinks of you and how you should apologize before she has anything to do with you."

"Don't pay attention, Winnie, she's all confused. Probably overworked. Your grandmother says Chessie's been sick."

"Maybe she's pregnant."

"Oh, I would have known...."

"Not necessarily, Mom, Chessie would never tell you."

Winnie's words were like punches in the stomach, but they fell on Fran with a truth she couldn't escape. Keeping calm she said, "Well, my mother will let me know. Anyway, I don't think Chessie's pregnant. It wouldn't fit in with her plans right now."

"I guess she thinks she should have children. It's like having a house, you've got to have a child, too."

"Dee's really mellowed with her child."

"I miss Dee."

Fran had never been close to her sister Adele and thought Winnie fortunate to have a close feeling for Dee. But Fran could never get used to the permutations of Winnie's alliances — or the switching alliances of any of them. Once Winnie had been captivated by Chessie's money, glamour, and independence and had written a stinging letter to Dee accusing her of being the family defector and having run off to Italy like a traitor. Then her allegiances had changed.

When Winnie discovered that bossiness and criticism came with Chessie's other qualities, she changed sides and reforged her bond with Dee. Dee, for her part, was offended by Chessie's disregard of her child. And in their different ways, both Chessie and Dee were strong defenders of Winnie whom they thought was being done in by Fran. How naive Fran had been to say, "Don't waste your anger and passion on me, save it for a big cause!" *She* was their big cause.

Winnie and Fran sat silently watching the people pass. A wrinkled old woman in a bright yellow wig came by. She wore black ballet slippers that were tied onto her feet with hot-pink yarn. She carried a bag that overflowed with odds and ends. She was followed by a black youth with a springy step who was eating a peach and reading a comic book called "Manual of Mayhem."

Winnie nudged Fran and said softly, "Listen to that kid," as she nodded to the park bench opposite where a good looking young man with ruffled hair, a beer can in his hand, an earring in one ear, was talking to two girls: "I'm going to Australia. My father says, make money. My mother says, get an education. My friends say, Be a porn star. So, I don't know, I'm confused. I'm nineteen, so I'm going to take time to think. I'll get the adventure out of my system, then I'll get some stupid money-making job. When I'm thirty I'll settle down, have a family. Well, that's it — first I'm going to sail to Australia."

"Hear him? Sounds just like me," Winnie said in an undertone. "That's what I'll be doing in the fall with my Junior Year Abroad in Italy — getting the adventure out of my system."

"And hopefully the panic," Fran answered. "I'll miss you, honey."

"You have Howston."

"It's not the same, even though things seem to be going well now that we have the house project to work on together."

"You're going to get hurt, Ma. It won't work." Winnie spoke those hard words mildly.

228

"Don't say that Winnie, it means a lot to me to get the house back and have a home again."

Winnie got incensed. "That's the trouble with you — always thinking you can go back and have things as they were. You can't! The old house and the old family that went with it are gone! Get it through your head. That's what I hate about Howston — he lets you think that your crazy idea is workable. And you trust him, and in the end you'll get hurt. Sometimes I think you're really stupid, like you're in this air bubble! Time to wake up, Mom!"

But Fran was thinking of her own mother's complaints. "I wish my mother were more like Meade's mother, more self-reliant," she said. She was thinking how Anne Meade McGraw was 100% Yankee self-sufficient. She could have built her own lean-to on Walden Pond if she set her mind to it, and gotten in her own provisions, too. Nowhere in McGraw's spare frame did the tribal turmoil smolder and stew as it did in Fran's family. But it was useless to think that her mother could be the same as Meade's. Still, Fran wanted to keep contact points with all of them, perilous or not; she wanted all of what they were to each other, booby traps and all.

CHAPTER THIRTEEN

The sight, fantastic, and like nothing Fran had ever seen before in Italy, gripped her. She was looking into a valley cupped and bordered by jagged mountaintops, and filled to the rim with a dense roiling cloud even as they — Winnie, Dee and her family, and she — stood in bright sunlight. It was like a Chinese scroll painting: mythical and illusionary, and, yes, as remote as China. Yet down there, under the curling fog, was Fossombrone, the town Leone had just driven them through, a place of gray, wretched people wringing red hands swollen with cold, huddling in porticos. Up where they were, instead, there was sun and no one around.

"Why did they build down there?" Fran asked Leone. "Just a bit further up and they'd be in the sun and light! How much depends on knowing the climate of where one is going to settle! Then you can plan right." She sounded to herself wise and judicious, a worthy grandparent for little Zeno.

"That's just like Mom," Winnie nudged Leone, as if sharing a secret with him. "She thinks things can be made to come out right. Like it's either all fog or all sun and you just decide where you want to be."

"*Mah, no,*" Leone protested, "In these parts we all get a little fog from time to time. The people of Fossombrone aren't always in fog or they'd be frogs by now. The fog shifts. When it's foggy in Fossombrone, it's sunny up here and vice versa."

"That's right," Dee concurred, "it happens all the time. I'll be hanging out the clothes in sunshine and Leone will come back and tell me how foggy it is in town."

So they say, Fran thought skeptically. Though the town was on the site of the ancient Forum Sempronii, its modern name seemed to translate into "shadowy ditch." There must be a reason, there's always a reason. Fran noticed how readily Dee seconded her husband.

It was Santo Stefano, the day after Christmas. That Fran was in Italy with Dee and Winnie for the holiday was a hasty decision made after Houston told her of his plans to be with Bick and his ex-wife for Christmas. "Just one of those things I can't get out of, love," he told her at the last minute. "I don't plan to make a habit of it, but Nadine thought it would be one last time for us all to be together before she moves to the coast."

Over the radio, a source of rapid enlightenment, Fran heard a woman speak for a group called Forgotten Mothers. She gave a hotline number one could call in distress. "Remember," she said, "you're not alone. But also remember not to have unrealistic expectations at Christmas and think your son or daughter will call. You have to send the card. Most of all, you have to live your own life."

Fran decided: Chessie had not called, so she would fly to Rome to meet Winnie who was there for her Junior Year Abroad and they'd go together to Dee's place for Christmas. They'd be a family. Fran wired Dee to ask if it were all right, and Dee called her from the bar down the road at 6 AM her time to say, "Wonderful, Mom! We want you to come!"

Leone had returned late from town that day after Christmas. Each day he drove off for his errands, or for seeing people, or to have a coffee and survey the piazza. Dee was left to take care of the child, the cooking, the housework and her lesson plans.

"Your husband and son make a lot of demands on you — you work so hard, you're so giving," Fran told her. "Think of yourself, too."

"As you always say, Mom, it takes two to tango. I like things this way, I like to be in control."

So be it. Fran knew it to be true, couples were the way they were because it suited them; they created their rhythm and either danced to it, or left the dance.

Still, Dee greeted Leone with sarcasm when he got back, saying, "I hope you were having a good time — we've been waiting for you so we can eat finally."

Leone shrugged, and gazed searchingly through his spectacles at Dee. He was a slight man, shoulders rounded and hunched forward, anxious looking even at the best of times. "It was a fine morning and I was enjoying it," he said, "I was here and there, I met Giovanni, I had some good ideas on my next project, and now you spoil everything!"

"Oh, good for you," Dee continued, perhaps to show how in control she was. "You had a nice morning while I've been here doing nothing, I suppose."

"Hey, you guys, don't bicker, it's still a nice day for everyone," Winnie called cheerfully from the table where she was sitting with Zeno while he ate a dish of pasta topped with cubes of fried potato. So much starch? Fran had asked and Dee told her it was a dish Leone had taught her; he liked it occasionally — called it a dish of the people, sound and appetizing. Since when has Leone liked things of the people? Fran wanted to ask, thinking of his scorn for the young couple, both factory workers, who lived below them on the first floor of the house. Leone called them beasts of burden, mindlessly driving themselves in endless work — no contemplative moments, no vacations. And yet Dee had said that the young couple were about to move out, having saved enough for a down payment on a house of their own after only a few years. Fran could hear the regret in her words that she and Leone had no savings for a similar move.

At the table Leone opened a bottle of wine with a flourish. "Try this, Fran," he said proudly as he poured into her glass a wine that was not a true red, but of a brownish rusty hue that seemed to hold little promise. "It's very special, a Sicilian wine." Fran took the bottle and read its label, *Ribera Rosso, Terra di Sicilia*. Fran sipped. It was a hard, graceless wine with a strong aftertaste, a stringent bite. She tried to visualize from what begrudging part of Sicily, land of the Sturzos, this bitter wine had been wrested.

"It has all the vein of Sicilian melancholy in it," Fran said.

Leone, pleased, took it for a compliment. He said the wine, seldom obtainable in their parts, was worth the price. Dee, who had understood her mother, was aghast: "You got a whole case of this? Why didn't you discuss it with me first, or just get one bottle so that we could try it?"

Leone looked startled, then crushed, and Fran felt sorry. She turned to Winnie and Zeno across from her who were oblivious of the discussion. "Are you really my nephew?" Winnie was teasing the little boy, who responded with peels of laughter.

"She's *zia* and I'm *nonna americana*," Fran joined in. Then she turned to Dee and said, "This rabbit is wonderful. You know, you have a real talent for concocting things. You could do a cookbook of your regional recipes. I recently drew up a contract with a $10,000 advance to a young woman who's doing Southwest American cooking."

"Ten thousand dollars!" Dee's eyes opened with wonder as if she had just come awake from a long doze. She looked at Leone and blurted out, "Why couldn't we do a cookbook together? — I'll do the recipes and you do the artwork. We'd have the down payment for a house if we made that much money." Her face flushed with excitement.

Now Leone was sarcastic. "Better for you to do your reading than recipes," he said curtly.

Dee's face fell. She got up from the table, taking dishes to the already filled sink. She was silent.

Fran was furious. For Dee to be able to read she needed free time as much as Leone did for his art — not be washing and cooking all day. Dee needed the means to hire someone to help her out. And what pays for that? A cookbook could make her the money.

Winnie read the expression on Fran's face and said in English, "Keep out of it Mom."

Leone got up and went to poke at the ashes in the hearth. Fran surmised she must have reopened a long-standing issue between Dee and Leone. She didn't care.

Rejoining them at the table Leone then said, "Let's go to the sea for Santo Stefano!" Fran smiled at his proposal. He was trying to create gaiety and a sense of adventure in an awkward situation.

"There's fog along the sea, I heard it on the news," Dee warned.

"Then let's go to Le Cesene above Fossombrone."

The cold in their flat had settled in her bones from the time Fran had arrived. She would be glad to get out and go anyplace. Messoni, the peasant landlord who lived across the road and was, Leone said, rich, *ricchissimo* and a veritable animal, had built the house where Dee and Leone occupied the second floor. It had the taste of a peasant newly moneyed but unused to middle-class comfort. He put in pretentious marble floors, but the windows were single-paned and badly fitted and did not keep out the drafts of cold wind. Living there you got up in the cold, went to bed in the cold. Even so, Zeno had never been sick; Dee said he was healthy as a fish. It was true. He was a beautiful child with eyes that shone with intelligence. He looked like Fran's father in photos she had seen of him as a child.

Before leaving Fran stood at the sink drying the dishes that Dee was finally washing with water that had been heating since the night before. Fran said, "You've got plenty to do with your tutoring and translation, you really should have a dish washer to help you out. Your mother-in-law has one for just the two of them."

"They're expensive, Mom, we don't have the money."

"You shouldn't be the only one earning while Leone concentrates on art that he doesn't even care about selling."

"Leone has other values. He's not interested in money."

"Of course he's interested in money! — enough to buy the most expensive Scotch there is, and a case of Sicilian wine just because someone told him it was rare. Of course he loves what money buys!"

"But he doesn't want a commercial life."

"Yes, I know the kind. They want the higher life while others — the beasts of burden — provide for them. What an attitude!" Fran was angry, but she didn't feel Leone was all to blame. He was floundering badly after giving up his teaching job, he needed some ballast of courage and confidence in life before he could give himself to art. All he had was someone like Dee who was willing to make sacrifices and even that was not enough.

"Your father was a poet," Fran told Dee, "but he never stopped working for a living; he always worked, during vacations, Saturdays and Sundays, night and day. He worked besides being a poet. Even Leone's revered Duke of Urbino was a workaholic! How do you think he'd have built his palace and glorified Urbino if he hadn't gone out and worked hard at war? What he was, really, was a hired gun as well as a patron of the arts."

Dee was silent while Fran considered the fifteenth century Duke Federigo: all that striving, and even his house eventually fell.

"Leone has his head in the clouds!" Fran went on. "It takes money to live. One doesn't live by sensitivity alone, and Leone's not exempt from this. What you have to do, Dee, is make more demands for yourself while you help him be what he wants to be but is afraid he can't."

Later Winnie told her mother that Dee had sighed and said to her, Mom's right about Leone.

The sun was shining when they set off. But by the time Leone had driven past the bar at the crossroads, it was visibly receding and a gray mist wrapped its tentacles around the car. They drove on, the greyness settling more and more on the flat countryside so that by the time they got to Fossombrone they were in thick fog.

"We'll stop for coffee," said Leone and he parked aside the portico in the town's old center. Fran shivered, her breath forming in front of her as the deep, penetrating, damp hit them.

The town looked deserted, and the few people in the bar Leone led them to were sullen and silent. They looked as grey as the scene outside. The usual Italian hill towns emanated the look and feel Fran had known on lower Main Street in Ferryville. The people she passed in Italian streets could have been those she had known in her childhood. There was the same sense of close-knit life. But Fossombrone was different. What a place, she thought, a real "shadowy ditch."

Leone drove up the town's steep streets to a high point where they emerged from fog and were back in full sunlight. He continued winding up a hill until he came to a pine preserve, empty of anyone, where he parked in a clearing. "*Ecco*, Fran," he said, "Le Cesene."

236

"*Bello*," Fran complimented him and he grinned. On his chin, where he had nicked himself shaving, were two little paper patches.

Fran stood in the sun, looking down at the thick cloud that squatted over Fossombrone blanking it out so that not even a tower or part of its walls came into sight. She could see tongues of fog flicking at the base of a Monastery, cypress-enclosed on a distant hill, for the moment seemingly impregnable and doused in sunshine, but inevitably to be submerged in rising fog. Soon the pine strand, so clear and sunny, would be enveloped. Then they would be enveloped.

"Spooky," said Winnie. "Look over there. Doesn't it look like someone walking out of the fog?"

"Yes," Fran said. "It looks like a great big black bear."

"*Nonna*," Zeno said to her in Italian, "are you afraid of the fog?"

"*Mah, no*," Fran said emphatically, shaking her head.

Dee said quietly in English, "That's our destiny, buried alive in fog."

Why so pessimistic, Fran wondered. Dee was the steadiest, the most fearlessly rooted in life of all of us. She had confided that on those starry summer nights at Shady Brook Farm when Chessie would beg their mother to let them sleep outdoors with a visiting friend, Dee would wait until the others were sleeping and then come in to her own bed. Just before dawn she'd go back outdoors where the other two, none the wiser, would find her when they awoke. Maybe Chessie didn't know that to this day. But Fran wondered if this were the same Dee as then. No. No one stays the same.

When Leone had driven over to Vico to pick up Winnie and Fran arriving on the train from Rome, Dee had been beaming and looking like a pudgy sixteen-year old. Driving to their place, Winnie sat up front talking art news with Leone. And Fran, dopey with jet lag, sitting in back with Dee and Zeno, had murmured that life had become vague for her, that she wasn't that attached to it anymore. All the time she was sitting next to Dee's child, the son she had never had, and she had thought, Dee lives in a family of men whom she mothers and loves. She lives in an Italian landscape, near a walled town of history. She has her niche and her place. She's home. But then Dee jolted Fran awake by responding, "Death doesn't bother me, either, I'm not all that attached to living. It's all pretty meaningless."

Now here at Le Cesene she was saying that their destiny was to be buried in fog.

As if she were feeling her mother's concern about her and wanted to be reassuring, Dee, who had been gazing intently into the cupped valley of fog, looked up and said, "I keep hoping a bird will fly out of there."

"Wouldn't that be a good sign!" Fran exclaimed.

But looking over the shifting fog, Fran was thinking she's not as rooted as I thought; just as Chessie is not as secure; nor Winnie as safe. None of us are what others think we are ... not even what *we* think we are.... All the more we should forgive each other....

Even Winnie had grown impatient with Dee. "Why does she do it?" she had asked Fran about Dee's decision to work so that Leone needn't.

"She takes sacrifice seriously — it literally means 'to make holy'."

"Oh, Mom," said Winnie, "I know you feel bad. I feel bad seeing Dee and what her life is, so I can imagine how a mother feels. But there's nothing you can do. It's her life."

"Let me tell you something about Dee," Fran answered hurriedly, glad to have this exchange with Winnie, "she always hated Pinocchio. Now I understand — it's really the story of personhood, of arriving at one's self rather than remaining the puppet who's maneuvered by everyone and bailed out by the Blue Fairy. Italian male intellectuals make a whole cause out of scorning Pinocchio when he becomes a real boy. They pretend that the wayward puppet was free and independent of society's demands. They mock the endeavor by which one becomes a full human being. Italian men would rather be mothered forever, forever be capricious, and forever forgiven by their adoring women who are always, for them, the indulgent Blue Fairy. That's Dee, a goddam Blue Fairy for a husband who won't grow up!"

"Mom, you take this too personally! Keep out of her life."

"She's my child, Winnie.

"Well, she's also a person! Let go, Mom."

Yes, let go — but not ever be able to hold out a hand to them? Fran thought. She grieved for the losses. And now there was what Winnie had told her on the train coming up.....

Mom, I have something to tell you.

What is it Win?

Oh shit. Fuck! I don't know....

Easy does it. Is it about your studies? How is the program going?

No, no — my work is great, I'm doing some good stuff. And the program's OK, even though it's got all these dopey Americans who don't understand shit about Italy.

So, what do you want to tell me?

Well, you see, I met this guy — Fabio. He's really cool. Not like American guys who are so repressed. Fabio's like papà, you know — his own person, not what someone thinks he should be. He's Italian and that's what I've always wanted in a man. He wants to come to the states to be with me when I go back.

Is that what you want to tell me?

It's so fucking hard to talk to you — it's like you're not really there!

I'm here, Winnie. Tell me if you want to — or, don't. But I'm here.

The only reason I'm going to tell you is that maybe Dee will let it slip about the money and so it's better if you hear it from me.

What money?

What I borrowed from her.

You borrowed money from Dee! Why would you do that? The program's paid for — if you needed more why didn't you let me know?

It has nothing to do with the damn program! It's cause I needed it, quick — for an emergency.

What happened?

I had an abortion.

Oh, Winnie! Where — in Rome? By yourself? Are you all right? And Fran had asked herself, why does she tell me this? It's over and done with, past history — I need never have known. It's not about the money. I don't think she really believes I'd have heard of the borrowed money from Dee — Dee isn't like that. It must be something else that matters to Winnie: Winnie is telling me this because it's a woman's thing, something that puts her on a level with me; it's part of being female and generative. It's her coming into power, her woman's state, her initiation. She's telling me she's my womanly equal. She's proud of who she now is.

Are you all right, Winnie?

Sure. I took care of it myself. It was Fabio who was all shaken up. He said it terrified him to see how cool I was. I think he thought I should fall apart and rely on him.

Did he help you?

He wanted to give me the money — I didn't want him to. I told Dee, and she gave it to me.

I'm surprised she had it to give. They don't have much.

Don't worry — she'll get it back.

So how do you feel? You used to get panic attacks at home just from going out on dates and yet here, all alone, you go through an abortion as if it's nothing.

I'm okay now. I just stayed in bed and slept for a couple of days.

Well, I'm just sorry you had to do it at all. Why weren't you and Fabio more careful?

It was just one of those things.

Putting her arm around Winnie, Fran felt her draw back. Fran squeezed her, skin to skin, blood of her blood. And yet the resistance stayed. Winnie has never been easy to hug. Fran felt her withdraw. It's as if the only touching they could do was at the sword's point of differences between them.

Fran stood watching the tumbling, shifting fog. Little Zeno, ran around the pathway excitedly picking up pine cones which tumbled from his grasp. *Bravo*, Dee called to him, get more, we'll throw them in the fireplace at home, they give off a good scent. Leone and Winnie were chatting. Fran was apart from them, her thoughts pressing in. She was recalling Winnie telling her that Chessie said her trying to get her house back with Houston was just like pissing in Versailles. Chessie said no matter how Mom thought she could recapture the past, her dream will crumble with reality because that dream is like the outward vision of Versailles where, behind the magnificent facade, lies the reality of courtiers pissing in its corridors.

At her lowest point Fran imagined how the barn-house would look with Houston there — will he want track lighting installed on the great beams; a jazzed up bar area? a sauna and Jacuzzi? a pool table and barbecue pit?

241

Fran noticed how he'd caught onto the plan, as if it were his to begin with. But he's so erratic! Something goes wrong in his work and suddenly he wants to give it all up. After being with him at those times, she feels the blessed peace of returning alone to her place where she can sink into the sofa, watch the television she wants, eat what she wants, read what she wants, undress when she wants, look how she wants, be silent, sleep alone.

Sometimes Fran feels as if she's in dialogue with herself aping Dr. Johnson telling Boswell to compile a Scots dictionary:

"What use what it would be, Sir?"

"No matter. Just do it."

So it is for her with Houston and the barn-house: no matter, just do it.

Yet Fran wavers back and forth, drifting like the mists and shreds of clammy greyness over Fossombrone. First she thinks, I'll cut out, not compromise myself with someone I don't love deeply just for the sake of the house and not being alone. Then she remembers the bond between them and how great things could be if everything went right..

Maybe her mother is right when she says give time to time. Let events take their course; don't make arrangements. Just hope a bird does fly out of the fog.

"You know, Leone, this was a good idea to come here," Fran said as they started back to the car. "I've learned something from the fog."

"*Vero!*" he exclaimed with a grin, pleased.

Fran took her grandson's hand and said in his language, "No, Zeno, *nonna* is not afraid of the fog."

Nor was Fran afraid any longer that she would always be an alien to the little boy, a stranger who came to visit every so often bringing him books he couldn't read, or sending cassette tapes he didn't understand. Fran had worried that he'd never know her, would laugh when she spoke his language with her American accent. He would think his real *nonna* was Leone's mother — Fran the foreign one, the gypsy nonna who showed up briefly, handed out gifts and then was gone. Fran was afraid it would be how it was when she was a child and couldn't speak to grandma Briciola because that grandmother was an old Italian immigrant dressed in black and Fran thought of her as a foreigner.

But Fran walked hand in hand with Dee's child, and he accepted her perfectly. He said to her, Nonna, do you have chickens in America? And Fran hugged him and laughed, and said, "Come see me, I'll show you." He chattered on, pointed out the plants and told her their names. Take a photo of me, he said, and Fran did.

Whether from the sight, the elevation, or all her thoughts, Fran felt a little giddy by the time they drove off. In the car she said, "You know what I heard once? That Isaac Newton, on his deathbed at age eighty-five, proclaimed his greatest triumph was having remained a virgin."

"And so?" Winnie asked.

Fran laughed. And so, she thought, I might once have gone to my deathbed, age whatever, and said that my greatest worth rested in being a mother. But not anymore. Motherhood was as mutant and circumstantial as the fog they were leaving behind, no more permanent than smoke-rings, mist.

"Honey, people think different things are important," she answered Winnie smiling. "And they are, at different times."

CHAPTER FOURTEEN

Edith was like Binaca: astringent and sharp, but ultimately bracing and good.

Fran learned about Binaca golden breath drops the first time she ever slept with Marco. The morning after he had reached over to the table on his side of the bed for a tiny bottle of amber colored liquid. He uncapped it and shook a drop onto his tongue. Then he had passed it to her saying it was indispensable. And so it had proved. From then on, through their married life, and back into her single life, every morning upon waking Fran performed the Binaca ritual — a drop on her tongue and instantly her head, breath, attitude, and reluctance to rise, cleared. She was ready for the day. Sometimes Fran thought of Marco along with the Binaca, mostly she did not.

Edith's advice came with that same kind of Binaca awakening. Edith was good on losses; possibly because for years she had been composing and reading eulogies for her family members and friends as, one after another, they died and left her to mourn and await the next passing. One evening Fran was at her place, and they were having sherry in front of the lit fireplace. Edith's apartment was carved from one of the stately residences in the Bay Back area and had not only a fireplace but an entrance onto a garden area, twelve-foot high rooms with ceiling moldings and arched passageways. It was extremely tasteful, spacious enough for a piano and walls of books, and made comfortable with armchairs and a large sofa. Fran considered that Edith was the sort of woman she could share a home with — the conversation would be so good.

"I don't think I can do it, Edith," Fran said as Edith stoked the fire, rearranging a log to expose it more to the flames. Edith had a tall, full figure and she was dressed in a long robe, so that she seemed in the glow from the fireplace a kind of oracle. "I just can't go through with this house plan with Howston. I don't trust him! First he worries about the payments on a $200,000 mortgage, then he'll call me as if money's no object and say what about putting in a tennis court, what about a boat mooring? He's so impractical — we still don't have any facts and figures. It's as if he's stalling, is doing everything to undermine my confidence so that I'll pull out. Then it will look as if I walked away from the plan and he's in the clear."

Edith, her expression unperturbed, sank back into a wing chair facing Fran's; they were on either side of the fireplace. She settled in, then raised her feet to the needlepoint covered stool in front of her. She was deliberate in everything.

"I always thought it would come to that, Fran," she said. "It's his answer to powerlessness. I hoped you would come to your senses before he did this to you."

"Actually, Edith, I've been too much in my senses! What I need is to be more rational. But I'm stuck in this ambivalence — you know my theme song, *Vorrei e non vorrei* – yes, I would like my house and no, I can't see myself there with him."

"Try to focus, Fran," Edith said slowly, petting the sleek black cat that had jumped into her lap. "All the energy you're pouring into keeping a poor relationship going, and trying to move a house of your past into your future, could, instead, go into yourself. You keep trying to please people out there rather than honing in on yourself."

"I suppose that's because I don't want to be alone. And I wanted the house. And Howston seemed to be the way to get it."

"But you're beginning to see, don't you, that it won't be a dream house, only a nightmare if the wrong person is there with you?"

"Yes, I suppose.... Winnie, too, has seen it that way. She says, *Ma, you've got this sick dichotomy with Howston that goes like this, you*

245

play *'You can't really get the real me because that me is too good for you.'* Then he plays, *'Yes, I can, I may not be a classy gent like Marco but I can give you what you want here and now.'*

"I think Howston is confused, Fran. He's not sure of you because you're not sure of yourself. You've got to declare yourself, you can't sit on the fence looking both ways."

"That figures, Edith."

"Some people make a whole lifetime of being in the middle."

"That's my mother!"

"It usually is."

"What happened is that with my own family gone I felt deserted. It's something I could never stand, as far back as I can remember I always wanted to be part of things. Howston made me part of many things. It's just that now, when I've ditched my values, they haven't ditched me. That's the conflict! The truth is I never could believe Howston. It was just that I wanted what I wanted no matter the cost."

"You wanted someone to hang onto. And there is no one. Never has been. Once you accept that you can be in charge."

"I used to be in charge when I had young children. But the incredible paradox is that they grew into just what I had hoped for — independent, out-spoken, self-sufficient young women. And I was left behind still in the old way. I'm like my father, my version of love is to be dependable, providing, bossy. But without his money I never got the respect he got. He was boss in a man's world where it's OK for him to be how he was. Look at how my children look up to him. It's *me* they call a fascist."

"Yes. Your father not only had money and male authority, but he was also probably consistent in his power. You waver."

"That's it! I'm democratic as well as bossy! I'm a literal middle-of-the-road driver. Winnie's always screaming at me, Mom, choose a lane!"

"You scold yourself too much. You're not the only one who's wanted it both ways. Think of how Americans love franchises — and what do they represent but the yearning for one's own business coupled with the dread of independence."

Edith shook a cigarette out of the open pack on the table next to her and lit up. She took a deep drag, inhaled, and blew out the smoke.

Dejectedly, Fran watched her brilliant friend who so many times had tried to give up smoking, was briefly successful, and then relapsed. Habits were hard to change, and not only for her.

Howston came over to Fran's the next evening. He arrived with a bottle of French wine which he handed to Fran saying, "*Voilà, jolie Madame.*" He always brought something, arriving with a bountiful air. But this time he looked uneasy, almost truculent.

Fran had prepared a dish he loved, seafood risotto, and as they sat at the inlaid fruitwood table that was part of Marco's family things and on which she had put a bowl of fresh flowers, she thought once more how nice, how civilized, how comforting it was to sit down to dine with one's partner; to exchange conversation, to listen to someone else, to have someone with whom to share food.

"What's wrong, Hows?" Fran reached over and patted his hand. He hadn't commented on the risotto.

"Oh, I don't know. You're all over the place — going off to Italy for Christmas dinner, for God's sake! I can't get my bearings. Jesus, Fran, I'm in this house thing for you and I can't feel you! There's no commitment."

"That's what I say. I've been feeling the strain for months. I've been spending time calling people, getting estimates, consulting on the work to be done. And what have you done? Do you know how many times I've asked you about the title search and survey? You simply keep putting me off. Why?"

"Come on, Fran, don't play games!" He pushed back in his chair with an angry movement. "You know what I mean. I mean a commitment to us. I'm tired of these prolusions."

She wanted to say, that's an interesting word, but said only, "It takes two to tango, Hows." The important thing Fran had to decide was whether she should go forward on the moment's impetus to say what she had to, and ruin the rest of the meal, or postpone it and let Howston eat in peace. Fran raised her wine glass and took a sip. A new white Bordeaux. Not one they had had together. She thought, he's changed his wine.

Fran took a deep breath, looked Howston in the eye and said, "There's no use pretending. You've discouraged me by delaying decisions on the house. And you never want to stay over anymore. Something's wrong. How can I believe you want a life with me when you act the opposite? I can tell you that as things are, I can't see any basis for us to go on with the house plan."

"What does that mean? Are you backing out?"

"I think you backed out but didn't have the nerve to tell me. And what's to tell? Your behavior speaks for you. Why would we move the house in order to live together when you no longer even sleep with me?"

He jumped up as if stung. "That's not true! You know I'm under incredible pressures. I've got this book I'm trying to wind up and now this house thing. The reason we haven't had any sex is because I can't be sure of you.... "

"As you are of Vicki?"

"What do you mean by that?"

"Just asking. You never had any trouble writing books and having a sex life with her, by your own account."

"She has nothing to do with this. You know I love you. But you're the one who backs away mentally, and then I do physically. I've wasted my time with you!"

Fran looked ruefully down at her plate. She had ruined his meal and wasted her own time preparing it.

"It won't work, Hows. I will not go on with the house idea. All I want is for you to sign the release form taking your name off the joint account, the one where I put up the money to pay V-B for the house."

"Send it to me. I'll sign. No problem. I'll be well out of it. Let V-B demolish your house. I'm not saving it! I was doing it for you. I was getting involved over my head to give you what you wanted. Because I thought that what lay in store for us would have guided the last part of our lives into an exciting, beautiful, and secure period. I know that's what you want for yourself — but evidently not with me. You've led me on. And it wasn't worth it, it was all a waste. My work suffered, I suffered. I'm leaving."

"Without finishing?"

He glared at her. His final look was of rage. He left, slamming the door. Her bravado collapsed. They had equally not trusted each other, equally deceived.

Of course her mother exploded. "Fran, I can't believe it! First you give up that Jewish man, and now another! You'd think, at your age, men could be picked off trees!"

249

"Mother, there was no use. We couldn't get along in the long run."

"Listen, don't you think your father and I have been incompatible for sixty years? Look at me. I didn't give up on him!"

The simplicity and loyalty of her statement touched Fran. Look at me, she said as if Fran should emulate her. And sometimes Fran did. Even though she could pinpoint accurately, precisely, what it was in her parents that she refuted, Fran could not always act on what she knew. Knowledge was not stronger than blood. She was also who they were.

Dolly Sturzo went on, "You should have stuck with that man now that your children have left you. If you didn't always act as if you could do everything on your own, you might get your daughters and everyone else to do things for you. Instead you're so damn independent!"

Oh God, make it be true! Fran prayed.

"There was no use, mother. He had no word I could rely on."

"There's a lot of things women have to put up with. Why would they if it wasn't worthwhile in the long run?"

Fran didn't know. Was it fear? the survival of the species instinct? social conditioning? or, once in awhile, real love? Winnie had auditioned for and been accepted in the drama program at a college of her choice. Then she had decided she wanted neither that college, nor drama as a major. "The important thing," Winnie explained, "was knowing I was accepted." And so, Fran, too, after having been accepted, was giving it all up.

"Well," her mother sighed, "do you have anything else to tell me?"

She always concluded by sounding like the priest at confession..

For the next few weeks, Fran busied herself more than usual with her work. She wrote at length to Winnie who was still in her Italy semester, and sent Dee suggestions on how to draw up a proposal for a cook book which could be submitted to an agent. She started a new evening course and added an exercise program at the gym. She tried to see women friends whom she had neglected. She was filling time, filling herself, building existentialist muscle, making a central core.

Fran had reasoned things out and knew she couldn't carry on the house plan alone. Giving that up created a vacuum in her; she felt depleted. She would go to a concert or the movies and catch herself nodding, her eyes forcibly closing. Once at a lunch counter a man sat next to her and looking over at the moussaka she was eating said, That looks great! Fran felt totally exposed, and so embarrassed she couldn't answer, only nod. She walked along the streets, looking into store windows and not really seeing anything. She was absent from everything, yet straining for something. Something shadowy had to be retrieved and she kept searching her mind for whatever it was.

Then it came to her with a shock: Howston had her Italian cornerstone. With that realization, the blood started coursing again and she came out of her stupor. She had to get her stone back. Howston must not have that piece of Magna Graecia that was her ancestry and history, not his. For the first time in weeks Fran called him. She told him she wanted to have her stone returned. He sounded in good humor, and jovially proposed that they meet for lunch; he'd have the stone in his car. Fran felt uncertain about lunch, but agreed. She wanted her stone.

"What are you going to do with the cornerstone," Howston asked directly over drinks at the place they used to frequent. His

251

manner was relaxed but assured. He was always attractive when he felt in charge, had something to bestow. He wore the cashmere argyle sweater Fran had given him for his birthday and she thought of how much better he dressed since they had been together.

"Winnie was with me when I got it on our trip to Calabria," Fran told him. "She can have it for her own someday. Why do you ask? The real question is, what has it to do with you?"

He laughed, "Prickly as ever, aren't you, Fran! It has to do with me as much as the barn does — I like those things, and you seem to walk away from them. You know, I've had time to think things over since we last met. Things have changed in my life. I'm on an even keel again, writing well, feeling good." He paused for this to sink in, watched her for a reaction, and then went on. "I've been in touch with Vested Brands and I've decided I'm going to go ahead with the house move."

Fran moved not a muscle, showed nothing in her face though it was as if a blow had hit her in the stomach. She studied him. A good looking guy even if hefty. His expression was contained: man of the world. She hadn't given him enough credit for craftiness. She should have calculated his skill in devising plots, his characters in and out of threatening predicaments.

Or, was he bluffing? When they were supposedly involved in the house together, he had been nervous and defensive and endlessly procrastinating. He said he was too old for pipe-dreams, he had to make a living. He couldn't manage to talk to an architect or find out who did house-moving; he kept forgetting, making excuses. He had worried about the costs and kept hammering at her about how much she would come up with. Now, suddenly, Howston had the cash and the balls to do it alone? Fran didn't believe him. Perhaps he was only saying that because, beneath the veneer of sociability, he was a bully and he wanted to make her feel bad, see her react to the news that would hurt her the most. Fran looked at his bland face and could see nothing there to read. He wasn't looking spiteful, revengeful, angry, disturbed or even self-congratulatory. He was expressing nothing except matter-of-factness. Could he be telling the truth? Fran was at a loss while he was completely at ease.

"My house, you want to live in *my* house," Fran said sarcastically. "What changed your mind?"

"Well, I've always liked the idea of having a place on the Cape. And I've always wanted to live in a barn.... "

"You also always said you'd never live alone in a house."

"I won't be alone — I always told you that, too."

It was true. He had always said that he wanted her, he loved her, but if she weren't available, someone else would be.

"The disposable society," Fran said scathingly. "Nothing's supposed to last. One's true love wears thin, just get another — no sweat, no pain, a replacement always at hand." Fran pushed back her chair. "Let's call this lunch off. Just get the stone from your car to mine."

It was surely true that Howston already had another woman — Vicki or another; and that bothered Fran not at all. A pair of his pajamas had been left on a hook in her closet. Fran thought of them as "the comfort pajamas" left there as a visible pledge that someday he'd be back, functioning, just as it was said that absentee workers on the Cape left a comfort ladder leaning against the house they were supposed to be working on so that the owner wouldn't despair and would know that someday the work would get done.

But Edith, waxing Biblical, said it all: "Who plays with pitch defileth himself." Fran had known for some time who Howston was — now she knew who she had become.

As Fran drove away, the cornerstone in the rear of her hatchback Honda, she switched on the radio and heard, from one of those execrable talk shows that fill the air of the times, an excitable woman exclaiming, "For God's sake, schizophrenia is better than living alone!"

The next day Fran went into Edith's office with coffee for both of them and told her about Howston. "Can you figure the fucker out? I don't believe he's going ahead with the house, he never completes what he sets out to do. But why would he tell me that and set me up for the satisfaction of seeing him flop? Or, do you think he means it?"

"Why shouldn't he mean it, Fran? He's completed books, hasn't he? He completed a marriage. And if he really loves the idea of living in a barn and has got the person to live with, you've handed him a plan on how to get a piece of land at the Cape at a bargain. Why wouldn't he go through with it? Even if he decided not to live there himself, he'd make a pile of money selling it. He'd be a fool if he didn't go through with it."

"God, Edith, he'd be a monster to take over my idea and pretend it's his own!"

"He's angry, Fran. He wants to get back at you and hurt you in the worst possible way. He probably realizes that you can't be jealous of anyone like Vicki. He must know that you wouldn't be jealous of *any* woman he took up with because you don't care that much for him. So how can he hurt you? — by taking your house. That, for sure, he knows will devastate you."

Edith's words pummeled Fran. She could hardly breathe. Was she going to lose her dream to him? She stared wildly at Edith until she could catch her breath and speak. "God, Edith, you're right. But how could anyone who thinks of himself as a kind and considerate person do this to someone he says he loves?"

"It's not what he says, it's what he does. What he's doing is a symbolic rape. He's doing violence to your idea and your hopes, your very house and all it stands for — your past happiness, the meaning of your family life, your closeness to your husband and children — everything that means the most to you. He's pissed, Fran. Don't let that bland, outward demeanor fool you. Underneath he's a raging bull. He's angry at you and at all women. From what you've said his mother is a dominant factor in his life. He hates her, but he can't admit such a heinous thing."

"I don't think he's impotent with Vicki."

"Probably not — she doesn't threaten him. But he has no use for her otherwise."

"That's right. But why did he pretend he loved me?"

"You're like his mother: cold, regal, disapproving. You were always apportioning the time you had to spend with him as if you resented it. You really only let him into your life when your daughters were gone. He was probably brought up to think he deserved no better, that he should be treated badly and punished."

"Poor guy!" Fran said sarcastically.

"He's a loser, Fran, because he wants to be. It fulfills what his mother thinks of him. You're lucky you got out."

"I think you're right about his hating women, Edith, he told me he hadn't slept with his wife for years before they divorced."

"Just the same, he's given you fair warning about his intentions with the house. If I were you, Fran, I'd believe that he's going to go through with it."

"It's so depressing. Not just Howston. I mean, what is it about our times? no one's word counts anymore."

255

But Fran left the office knowing that Edith's words did count and would force her to act.

Driving to Medwood Fran pondered why she had let the old house have such a hold over her. Because it embodied the period of her life when she was in a beautiful place, protected and loved. And now, in the present, there was even more to it. She had created an idea, an ideal. She was rescuing the Charles Barr house, which had been her home, in order to see it preserved with all the associations of the artists who had lived and worked there. That was the worthy and noble thing to do.

Driving into Shady Brook Farm Road, which V-B kept plowed and accessible, Fran took the left fork and went up the road past the helicopter pad to the main building. She parked near the shining, copper-roofed showplace and thought how fungible all plans were — hers, Howston's, and even those of the Buchard descendant who had sold the estate to V-B. The last Mr. Buchard had been a consultant and author, known as "the father of scientific business management." He had lived and worked in the expanded homestead of his ancestors where he kept a considerable multi-lingual library of books on management and business. He had stipulated in the purchase agreement with V-B that his library be kept intact and always housed in the original structure which would then be known as the Buchard Memorial Library. And while Fran lived at Shady Brook Farm, the house and library were still here. After her house had been sold and Fran went back to visit the site with Winnie, all traces of the original old buildings on the Buchard estate including his Memorial Library had vanished, confirming all Fran had ever imagined of corporate perfidy.

At Vested Brands headquarters, Fran went to the Director's suite where the receptionist asked her to be seated. Fran could hear herself being announced to Mr. Stratton. He came out of his office, a very tall young man with a thatch of thick tawny hair, extending his hand, and saying, "Mrs. Beniferro? I'm delighted. I understand you once lived in the Barr house."

"Yes, I did. That's what I've come to see you about."

"Please come in."

He was affable, he was young and her hopes lifted for Fran saw that the meeting would not be as cold and businesslike as she had dreaded. She had never met and dealt with Mr. Stratton directly before, for she had always had Howston carry out the negotiations.

"Mr. Stratton, you are aware of the plan I devised with Mr. Kelly to move my former house. The token price of $2000 had been agreed upon with V-B and I was to pay this with my check. I have reasons, now, for withdrawing from this plan and I am wondering about the status of the house."

Jeremy Stratton appraised Fran, cocking his head to one side. Behind him, through the expanse of window, the ground lay covered with snow, the huge brick wings of the Institute's ugly new building engulfing the grounds where the old Buchard house was.

"I knew your name was somehow associated with Mr. Kelly's proposal to move the Barr house, but you seemed to be mentioned only as a former owner, not as a party to Mr. Kelly's plan. My dealings have only been with him, Mrs. Beniferro, and he has just recently once again stated his intentions of moving the house."

"He said that?" Fran looked searchingly at Stratton. "Mr. Kelly's plan? Oh, no. The idea was mine, just as the house was. He assured me he would never go ahead with the move on his own. Nor should he!" Her voice began to quaver and rise with the strength of her feeling. Looking straight at Jeremy Stratton, Fran blurted implausibly, "What has he to do with my house?"

"What you're telling me is interesting." Stratton sat back in his executive chair, nodding his head and smiling as if to placate her. "Mr. Kelly first introduced himself to me as a writer who was acquainted with the former owner of the Barr house — you — and upon hearing that it was to be torn down, conceived the idea to remove and relocate it for his own use. Just recently he spoke to me of his alternate plan — to make it over into rental studios for creative people, like a kind of artist's colony with possibly an attached conference center. He's very keen on the idea. He's talking of a dedication ceremony with a lot of coverage and some of Charles Barr's descendants present."

Fran was stunned. Stratton's words knotted her stomach, making her feel sick. She formed a response with effort.

"Mr. Stratton," she said, leaning forward towards him, her body tense, her look direct, "what Howston Kelly says and what the truth of the situation is are two different things. How would Howston Kelly have known of the house's existence if I hadn't taken him there? It was I who proposed to him that we acquire the house jointly from Vested Brands and move it to the Cape. The idea was always mine. What I want to know now is how I can gain control of my former home."

Stratton the businessman turned cautious, obviously unwilling to be drawn into something messy. Fran could see him mentally weighing her against Howston. And she told herself, he's one of those who promised Mr. Buchard his library would always remain intact, and then shredded it in the name of progress. What do any of them care about honor or pledges?

When Stratton spoke, he said with some sympathy, "There's no way, I'm afraid. Mr. Kelly has signed a contract with us to remove the house by September 30th and he's given us payment. It's my impression that he intends to move the house quite soon. At least that's what he said in my presence to the woman who was with him."

Vicki? or was the woman with Howston another whim of the moment? But the house, if he got it, would be his for keeps. Fran gazed out the window, feeling helpless, hoping for inspiration.

This was the worst that Howston could do to her. This was to nullify and humiliate her. Was that putting it too strongly? No, Fran felt his treachery touch her very sense of herself. She saw in a flash how he envisioned himself: Lord of the Manor. He will glory in everything I once had — fires on the hearth of the great room, genial people to entertain, sunsets to watch. Or he'll make himself a studio there and rent out the rest for income. If all he wanted was to live in a barn, he could go find any barn. But it was mine that he wanted, not only to demolish me, but because only with my house, the former Barr House, and with my idea could he secure the land on the Cape at a bargain. I am banished from my own plan and Howston would get the glory of having saved a landmark.

This minor mystery writer, this thief of ideas abetted by a callous corporation — Fran would not let it happen without a fight. And though she dreaded the idea of having to confront Howston, or challenge V-B, she knew she would. She would not walk away from this. She had walked away from too much in her past. She would not let them do this to her.

Incredibly, and involuntarily, Fran heard herself murmur aloud in Jeremy Stratton's office, "I feel like an orphan." And as she said it, so wishy-washy, so spineless, Fran understood how her daughters could think badly of her. What pushed those abject words from her? It must have been the last giving up of the ghost of who she once was. Fran quickly laughed ironically to convey that her words were sarcastic.

"Mr. Stratton," she went on in a clear, firm voice, "it was not my intention, when I conceived the idea to preserve my former home as the Barr Landmark House, that it would become a personal real estate bonanza for Howston Kelly! How far has this gone? Did he take title to the house?"

Now it was Jeremy Stratton who looked uncomfortable. Was he thinking of adverse publicity for Vested Brands? Would V-B be put in the philistine position of insensitivity to America's cultural heritage? Fran could imagine his apprehensions. What had seemed a convenient deal for getting the old house off V-B property and saving them demolition costs, had deteriorated into a show-down between vengeful lovers.

"Well, there's no title per se, just a signed contract. And we have Mr. Kelly's check."

"His check! I can show you the receipt for *my* check which was put into a joint account with both our names on it with the understanding that I would pay for the house."

"Mrs. Beniferro, I have no problem in accepting that you were part of the original plan — after all, you did live in the house."

"My plan has been stolen! Can't the check Howston sent you be refunded? As long as there's no title.... "

"It's a legal matter and it depends on how the contract reads. I can ask our contract department to look into it. I would think, however, that time is on your side."

Fran wondered what that meant. How could time take sides? But suddenly she felt that if Jeremy Stratton could take sides, it would be hers. For the moment that was all she had.

At the office, fortunately, Fran had Edith.

"Edith, what shall I do? He's actually bought my house — he is going to move it. Either he'll live in it or he'll use it as rental property or he'll do both. Whatever he does, I'm sunk."

"Blacken his name up there on the Cape. Get to the Town Selectmen and plant the seeds, let them know of Howston's exploitation. Get to the Barr descendants and let them guard against being exploited, too. Work up the feeling against him."

"Is that enough?"

"Nothing's enough when the barn door's been opened and the horse has been let out. But it's better to try than not to."

At 5 AM Boston time Fran telephoned Dee's mother-in-law in Italy and left a message with her for Dee to call her mother collect from the bar.

With Dee, Fran began apologetically. "I feel like the Ancient Mariner — I'm compelled to tell my story to everyone. You can pass it on to Winnie when you see her. Imagine, Dee, Howston is going to move our house after all and use my idea to re-locate it on the Cape." With each telling Fran's feelings got fanned into outrage. Her voice crackled over the Atlantic: "The crook! The cheap crook. But he won't get away with it!"

Finally, Dee asked quietly, "Why are you up so early, Mom?"

"I have so much work, so much on my mind!"

"Well, go easy. Is Chessie in touch with you? Did she call for the holidays?"

"No."

"It's a shame she doesn't participate."

261

"I agree, honey. When will Chessie realize that blood is thicker than water? Well, anyway, you keep well. Kiss Zeno for me. *Ciao!*"

Fran relayed the story of the house to everyone she could get to listen. With each telling the excitement in her voice grew. She called Adele and Meade, Henry Levine, her mother, former neighbors in Medwood, Marco's colleagues, her lawyer. Fran kept Dee and Winnie updated by letters. And of course, there was Edith, her best listener. Compulsively, heatedly Fran went over everything with all of them, asking advice, confirming her strategy, telling her story. Now everyone heard her.

It was hard for Fran to fall asleep at night. She played over in her mind, like a late night movie, what she had accomplished that day to advance her cause and stop Howston. Fran thought of every angle, tried to anticipate his moves and deduce what he would do next. She kept in touch with Mr. Stratton at V-B's headquarters. At times she would wake in the night, and make lists of people she thought she should call: the National Preservation League in Washington, state preservationists, musicians and composers who might be sympathetic to preserving the integrity of the Barr home, people at the Cape, environmentalists, social activists against V-B, her representatives in Congress. She took on a complete new authority, no longer reserved and quiet, Fran became a warrior against Howston.

Sometimes her courage rose to an exhilarating pitch: she would show him! he would learn who she was! Other times, in the dark, as she could not sleep but tossed with the force of her anguish, she fell into the pit of her own despondency. How could she possibly stop him when he had a contract and V-B only too willing to stand by him as long as he removed the structure for them and got this mess over with?

Again and again Fran had to gird against the temptation of letting it all pass, just quietly accepting it and letting herself be persuaded that thus she would be wise, mature, philosophically sound. But passion and her anger at betrayal energized her. She hadn't known she was capable of it. It was as if, in this difficult and impossible enterprise, the core of a true self had begun accruing, building up, layer by layer, like a pearl around an irritation.

Without responding badly to her mother, Fran simply let it pass when Dolly called and advised her, "Are you sure you can't get back together with that man instead of fighting him?"

Always the appeaser, her mother counseled Fran that she would catch more flies with honey than vinegar. Fran didn't reply to her words, so irrelevant were they. Fran was in charge and wherever it would lead, even to defeat, it would be through struggle not surrender.

CHAPTER FIFTEEN

Each Sunday Fran got her mother's call with news of Fran's father as he got worse. Pop had become incontinent. Dolly would find him in a soiled bed and have to change him and the bedclothes. She couldn't get him to shower — would have to propel him into the bathroom with the help of Eloysia, the black woman she finally hired as live-in help, to get him washed. Or, during the day, she would smell the odor on him and know he had to be changed again.

The end came when his legs gave out. He fell, dead weight, and both women together could not raise him. Dolly called the ambulance service, and they charged her, she told Fran bitterly, $70 to get Pop off the floor. Still she resisted what she called "putting him away." She had to justify his being taken from his home by first running herself down, losing weight and sleep and getting so gaunt that Gussie and Susan finally put the law down to her, as she said, and told her Pop had to go, thus relieving her of the decision.

Then she would talk as if he would be away only until physical therapy rehabilitated him enough to get him to walk again. But therapy was a euphemism; a way of not admitting the truth which was that Gus Sturzo would never walk again, not because of some physical impediment, but because whatever impulse from his will to his brain which controlled his locomotion was not working — he did not will himself to walk.

Fran could understand her mother's reluctance to see him at the St. Tarcisius nursing home, and also her unwillingness to admit that he was there for good. When she said, "It's very lonely here at home, and I wonder why your father should be up there in that nursing home and I should be here alone," Fran could feel for her.

Now her mother was faced with knowing that if they had been in a garden apartment, as Fran had urged her for years, he might have been kept at home in a wheelchair with a nursing attendant. Even though she had eagerly accepted it when everyone reassured her that his continual refrain of "Let's go home ... come on, it's time to go home" was the same whether he were at St. Tarcisius, at Gussie's house, or even in his own house, Dolly knew that he felt the difference. She knew in her bones that he should be home, in his own bed, with her nearby. And now it was too late.

Once when his grandson Freddy had gone to visit him, Pop had grabbed him with his still strong grip and said, perfectly lucidly, "Wait til the nurses go, then pretend you're going to take me for a walk and we'll get out of here." Freddy had, in fact, pushed him in his wheel-chair out onto the grounds, but before they had gone too far an aide had come out to summon them back.

It was a time, for Fran, of sharp swings from determination to despondency as she plotted her strategy against Howston. Her desk was laden with scraps of paper napkins, envelopes, torn pages from magazines, as, wherever she was, she thought of something and wrote notes to herself. Her planning was incessant. She scribbled in the form of royal decrees: *Let Howston move the house and spend his money, then attack!.... Have Selectmen put in covenants and restrictions against the possibility of Howston's speculating on the property.... Get to Ralph Nader!* She wrote to Charles Barr's biographer in the wild attempt to enlist his aid in her struggle to keep the composer's home from falling into the hands of the philistine Howston, but received no reply.

Revenge thrummed and buzzed around her like an insistent gnat always near and arousing. Still at times, she faltered and it could be heard in her voice: "Edith, I can't let this thing take over my head and use all my energy. I could be writing, visiting Winnie, I could be doing a dozen things. I don't want to give my all to this or it will be just as if Howston is in charge of my life!"

But Edith would not let her off. "This *is* your life right now, Fran. Accept it."

"To the last drop," she answered dejectedly.

"Yup. You've still got to come to terms with the fact that he didn't steal the house — you gave it away."

By summer Winnie had returned from Italy, dressed in Italian clothes, ready for her last year in college and looking forward to Fabio's promised visit to the states. Winnie was with Fran when the call came from the town clerk on the Cape with whom Fran had struck up an acquaintance, explaining her interest in the Barr house project as a former owner. Fran had asked the clerk to alert her when the plans for its relocation were submitted and open for inspection, and had in turn learned of the planning board requirements: Howston had to submit an architectural plan to the board for approval before he would be permitted to move the house on site. His deadline with V-B was September 30th; it was the end of August when the town clerk called Fran to say that Howston's architect had submitted a plan.

Fran took a day off and asked Winnie to drive to the Cape with her. Winnie was dressed in a tight mini-skirt and a bright t-shirt. Her hair was long and loose, she was thinned out and shapely, and striking in a totally new way. She had become an attractive young woman. Fabio, she told her mother, said he made her bloom — before she was nothing. Fran hooted skeptically and said, Come on, Winnie, you're too smart to fall for that! You were already something all on your own, without any guy taking credit. And Winnie's answer — I knew you'd say that, you're so negative — left Fran again to sort out the contradictions.

In the car she said, "I'm glad you're here to make this trip with me, Win."

"It just happens to work out, Mom. I'll go to the ocean. It's worth it."

"OK, honey, while I'm at the town offices, you take the car and go where you want. But come back for me, I may want to go to the ocean, too — to drown myself!"

Winnie, who was driving, gave a snort. "Ma, why do you say such stupid things? Be glad you're not with Howston. You can't live with anyone ... you're the wrong type. You're a lone wolf. You're not a giving person like Aunt Susan."

"Susan! She and President Reagan! — neither can admit a mess that's right in front of their eyes. She's Candide in Ferryville, for God's sake."

"See! You're so critical. Just what Aunt Susan isn't. You're not at all good at give and take with people. And to tell the truth, mom, I'm sick of all that shit about the house. I don't want to hear about it because there's absolutely nothing I can do."

Fran sighed deeply. "Winnie," she said patiently, "You're very intolerant with me — and let me tell you, if you picked that up from me, just stop. It doesn't work! You tell me I criticize, and there you are sounding like a harpy. I'm not asking you for anything, I wouldn't put that on you.... I'm just batting ideas around."

"Bat them with your friends. Edith's a good sort for you — she's used to listening. If I wanted a close friend I'd definitely choose her, she tells you where she stands and even if she disagrees with you, it's not all over between you. She's not judgmental like Chessie or floozy stuff like your sister Adele. But you say such stupid things, you really have to think before you speak, Mom."

"Right," Fran said and then, after a bit, added, "You remember, Winnie, when you told me about how the cashier at Walmark's thought you were being derogatory when you asked her something and she became defensive and told you she was going as fast as she could, but you hadn't intended any criticism. She had misunderstood you completely and it bothered you because you weren't trying to make her feel bad. That's how I feel, too, when you take what I say the wrong way. Observations aren't criticism. It's an exchange. We'd turn mute if everyone were so touchy."

"All right, Ma," Winnie sighed, "is that the lecture?"

Fran shook her head. She looked out at the passing scenery. "It's so difficult. I could never imagine my life this way. I could never imagine my family not holding together. I put everything into it, and still it falls apart."

"You never should have counted on holding us all to you. That's perverse."

"No one is meant to be *nudo e crudo* in the world, all alone. I think you'd feel lost if you thought I weren't there for you. Time will tell."

"Yah. It's ok, Mom, it will work out. Maybe you just haven't had your life's orgasm yet."

"Now what does that mean?"

"It means you still have to have your prime experience."

Fran shook her head, put on her glasses, and rummaged in the fine-grained leather briefcase Howston had once given her. She had stuffed it with all the papers that documented the background of the house, including her own research on its importance in the Barr career and canon, and an article she had written about him at Shady

268

Brook Farm for a historical review. She had a print-out of chronological events which showed her part in the house plan from its inception as her idea. Also among her papers were photos of the house, the floor plan and survey, and the old deed in which it showed that Marco and Frances Beniferro had taken title to the property from the estate of Charles Barr.

Not among her papers, but limned into her consciousness were the words of her former lawyer, a man of conservative principles and an over-fussy legalistic mind who had heard her out and then replied, "Fran, emotions are a red herring. I wouldn't get into this if I were you — it looks like the revenge of a woman scorned. And legally, there is nothing you can do if you have nothing in writing. It's only your word that you gave him the idea. The proposal is signed with his name. He has a contract with Vested Brands. I advise you to forget it."

It was Edith who then recommended Persis Williams, a lawyer who had made her name by championing women. Fran had a moment of doubt when she learned that Persis was an ex-nun, but went to see her anyway. She was a small, wiry, alert, neatly dressed woman with salt and pepper short hair and Fran said when she met her, "I hear you're good at fighting for women."

Persis impressed Fran with her quiet acceptance of the story, her indignation at Howston's deception, and her determination to see what could be done: it would be an uphill battle at best, she said, the law did not protect moral visions nor provide for "trust" relationships between people. That's why everything should be in writing. She would start on the basis that Fran's creative idea had been usurped and that Howston had gone back on his word that he would not proceed with the house on his own.

"Frankly," Persis said, "there's not much you can do except get some allies up there at the Cape who will keep you informed of his moves." She asked Fran to call Howston and get his clear statement, in his words, of what his intentions were with the house. Tape the phone conversation, she said.

"Do I have to?"

"Yes. Keep talking to him. Learn all you can, express your interest in what he's doing with the move, even your admiration. Your mistake was to let months go by without keeping in touch with him, as if you had written the whole thing off. Learn what you can, then we'll put on the screws."

Fran had a lot of respect for Persis; she was a woman who had liberated herself from her past and started her life again. Fran would do whatever she asked.

When she called Howston, he sounded like a talk show host at the other end of the line: "How *are* you, Fran?" he crooned. "Great to hear your voice!"

The minute Fran heard him, all the control and cunning that Persis had counseled her dissolved. "You're so rotten!" she exploded. "How can you do this to me? That's my house! my idea! All my feelings are connected with it! And you'd give it to a Vicki?"

"Easy, easy ... you *know* what you were for me! But you walked away. I was hoping lightning would strike, that you'd eat or drink a magic potion, that you'd change. I wanted you to be part of this."

"How can you say that? — you never called, you never kept in touch."

"I was afraid, Fran. I was afraid to call you."

She heard the voice of the man with whom she had been close and with whom she had had great plans, and despite herself she was touched. "Was that it, Hows? you went to Vicki for consolation?"

270

"I am a human being, Fran. You psyched me out." Mellifluously, smoothly his voice began its job of beguiling her back into belief. "I always wanted to share my life with you. I still do."

"How can you say that when you're with Vicki again? What about her?"

"That's a temporary situation."

"Temporary? You mean like an office temp?" Outraged again, Fran's voice rose in pitch. "And then what? You put her out again like the garbage and think I'll be ready to step in?"

"Easy, easy!" He spoke soothingly. "I'm not doing anything about Vicki until I know I can have what I really want. Vicki has nothing to do with the house."

"Christ, Howston! I can't believe what I'm hearing! You're lying, you've gone too far. She *is* in on the house, Stratton told me. Now you want to string us both along. But I'll tell you something, you're not taking over my idea."

"So what's the story? Do I owe you some money?"

"You would put it in those terms! As if all you have to do is pay up and the betrayal goes away!"

"Well, what's your solution?"

"Back off, Howston. You can't have the house. If I don't get it, you certainly won't. I'd rather see it razed to the ground."

"It's a do-able project, Fran. I'm going through with it. If I can't do it with you, I'll do it on my own and enjoy it."

Steely and skillful, Persis Williams was ready for him,. "Frame him," she said coolly. "Get him to put the frame around himself as a public benefactor through his publicly declaring his intention to preserve the Barr house. Call the Globe and get them to publicize

271

the story. Let him be shown as a public spirited patron of the arts who will be saving a structure of artistic associations. That way, he indeed uses your creative idea and we get him on that. Or, he doesn't fulfill your idea, which was the only basis by which the town voted him the sale of the land at below market price, and then he'll forfeit the land, and so the house. But make it public. Frame him. He'll hang himself."

Fran reviewed the framing to herself: I'm in the house with a young woman reporter from the Globe. It's a frigid, grey day and we are waiting for the photographer who's coming to take shots to accompany the story about Shady Brook Farm. We shiver and shake with the cold and speak in clouds of our frozen breath inside the vast empty space of the great room. We chat companionably and I tell her stories of the parties there, the well known visitors from all over who came to see Marco. I am both exalted and troubled. I exalt in having the reporter there, but wonder if I can make it work ... if I can, as Persis counseled, frame Howston. I have to establish him on record as the person who took over my plan to move and preserve the Barr house. As we talk, I see with dismay the discoloration way up on the ceiling that shows water seepage; it looks like a giant, ugly spreading mold, a mark of decay, corruption. I take it as a sign. The house is dead and mouldering; even as I look, the wood-paneled walls are a dreary dark, out- side is bleak. The sounds of the piano or Marco typing or children playing are gone. Why am I here with this young reporter trying to stake my claim? Why don't I flee? Then I toughen against the cold and the rot. I will enlist the reporter in documenting the place spiritually as mine, always mine, nev- er Howston's. Here came the best Italian writers of our time to see Marco; here came our artist and writer friends. Here the rafters rang with our talk and laughter, while upstairs off the balcony the children slept sweet, protect- ed dreams. Now I stand in its emptiness for the photo opportunity that will help frame Houston.

I don't quite see the preservation angle, the reporter says. I want to shake her. See? What does she have to see? She has only to listen to me, write down my words and get them printed in the Globe. I will have to contact Mr. Kelly and get his confirmation, she says. I sense that she is uncomfortable about something – is she wondering why the story is coming from me and not Howston? I try to allay her investigative scruples; I invite her to stop at my place where I will show her the books Marco wrote while we lived at Shady Brook Farm, where I will pull out my photo albums and the research I did on the house, where I will make her a present of some Pricer books.

The photographer arrives and takes shots inside and out as I continue the commentary and the reporter writes it all down. She is now on my side – she understands my emotional tie to the place and how much of me is invested in it. She will write her story around the premise that the house is to be preserved by purchaser Howston Kelly, based on my idea, to commemorate both composer Charles Barr and poet Marco Beniferro who once lived there.

When she calls Howston to get his confirmation, he bullies her and says she's asking for trouble. She calls me back, saying he won't confirm everything I said. What's up between you two? she asks, am I being used in some personal thing between you? I get angry. I tell her Howston is a master liar and relies on bluff to make people back off. What can he do? The truth is the truth, I tell her, and whether she writes the story or someone else does, the story will be told. She does write the story and it appears in the Globe with Howston Kelly cast as the buyer and mover of the Barr house which he is determined to preserve. He is framed.

In the town offices on the Cape an obliging clerk retrieved the rolled up plan and spread it out for Fran. She had a bad moment as she read: *Plans drawn for Mr. Howston Kelly, owner of the Barr House.* Her eyes filled as she studied the rendering; yet as she focused she saw that what was drawn there was not the outline of the barn-house, but a new configuration altogether. Three wings had been added, decks, more windows. Fran sucked in her breath and exhaled deeply. Now she would win.

Howston must have directed his architect to alter the simple rectangular barn into something grander. What Fran saw in the architectural rendering was no longer recognizable as the Barr house. Either it was Howston's attempt at a mansion, or it had been redesigned to accommodate rental units. He would ransack the old place for the beams and barn doors as elements of his structure and dare to call it, as he did on the plan, the "Barr House." Conspicuously drawn in were the spurious patios and decks on which he probably pictured himself, beer in hand, watching the sunsets with Vicki. His arrogance was colossal! He must have been confident that no one on the Cape would have known the difference; that the plans would automatically be okayed as long as frontage and zoning laws were observed. He had overlooked her intervention. Persis was right; and Jeremy Stratton was right, time had been on Fran's side.

Joy and relief coursed through her flushing her face. But mostly she was thankful for her luck that, with all the people she had obsessively contacted about the house, the one she hadn't called was Howston's architect. She had heard who he was and had sometimes thought of calling to tell him he shouldn't have anything to do with Howston. But if she had, she now realized, she would have tipped him off as to the original preservation concept on which the land sale was premised, and he would have alerted Howston. They could then have submitted a fake plan with the authentic Barr House dimensions and configuration, while later, after approval, constructing what Howston wished on the site. She would have been done in by her own zeal. "You're lucky ... you always land on your feet," her mother used to say. So it seemed.

"This is not the Barr House!" Fran told the town clerk. She drew from her briefcase the photos and floor-plan of her old home showing the clear discrepancies with the architect's drawing. Then she showed the clerk the Boston Globe article with Howston's own words about his intention to preserve the house as it was when Barr lived there. Persis' plan was working.

Setting out, Fran had counseled herself that the trip was a point of honor for her; that she shouldn't expect anything; that all that might be left for her to do was to appear at the Planning Board meeting and identify herself publicly as the initiator of the plan that Howston Kelly was using. And then what? Who would have cared? She would have felt like a public nuisance who was spouting ad nauseam, like the Ancient Mariner, a private grievance that was irrelevant to the Board; she would have been seen as a woman spurned and bent on revenge. And Howston would have come off the hero who was saving a structure and improving the town. Then she would have slunk out, defeated. Even if that were the cost, Fran was prepared to be heard for the record.

"Well!" said the Town Clerk, showing her indignation, "the Planning Board meeting will have to be canceled. No use wasting their time with this plan! I'll make a copy of your documents on the Barr House to send to the Chairman. I can tell you, the Selectmen will take a dim view of this — they won't like being misled. They've already seen the copies you sent of the piece in the Boston Globe, and they've fully believed Mr. Kelly's stated intent to preserve the house. This will really upset them."

"What is his deadline with the town?" Fran asked, savoring each moment. "He has to have the house removed from Vested Brands property by the last day of September."

"The deed with the town says that work has to be begun on a foundation by the first of next June, otherwise the land reverts to the town. But he can't start work until his architectural plan is approved. A lot of people here are unhappy that he got that land in the first place. And now, if he's not living up to the proposal ... well, the Board may rescind the whole thing."

Fran had won for the moment. Now it depended on Jeremy Stratton not extending the V-B deadline and giving Howston time to re-submit his plan.

The following week Fran drove over to see Stratton. At her former property she was aghast to see signs of ground-breaking around the house and posts staked out in the area. Alarmed, she asked Jeremy Stratton if Howston were preparing to dismantle the structure. No, he told her, the posts were V-B's own markings. Then he disclosed something else: the contract with Howston had been drawn up with an incorrect date, somebody had typed the deadline date as the 31st of September rather than the correct one of September 30th.

"Don't your people know 'Thirty Days Hath September'," she asked caustically, wildly wondering if such an error would now give Howston unlimited time to correct his plan. As she deliberated on Howston's probable next step, her short-lived victory was tempered by reality. Houston would surely rebound. It was all the worse because she was so tantalizingly close to stopping him.

Jeremy Stratton, who once told Fran that time was on her side, now deftly switched it to V-B's side. He was a businessman, he had to be practical. It was to V-B's advantage not to be a stickler on the contract's dating, he said, but to give Howston time past the deadline so that he would move the house and save them demolition costs. As Fran listened to him, realizing how little weight compliance with a contract (and, even less, compliance with her vision) carried in the material view of things, she thought of the imprisoned anti-fascist Italian leader Antonio Gramsci: Pessimism of the mind, and optimism of the will, he counseled, knowing well that one must never give up, even as one saw the probable reasons for defeat.

Edith once said, "There's something odd about you, Fran. You can relate to your feelings and describe them and even, in your poetry, state intricacies with understanding. But you are moved by impulse. You are like a blade of grass that bends not only in a storm, but with every infinitesimal whisper of air. And it is time you knew better."

Now she told Fran, "You're doing a good thing, you're restoring yourself. You had given too much of yourself away. This fight is good for you — I can already see it. You're thinking things out, you're not acting only on impulse or reacting to events, you're plotting your own strategy. It's a huge difference."

"Thank God for you, Edith, my family sees this as my obsession, my sickness. But I don't feel sick! Given that I made the initial mistake of letting the proposal be in Howston's name, and then, when I got out, trusting his word when he said he wouldn't go on — given that, I've made a comeback."

"You're damn right!"

"It's even exhilarating!"

"You better believe it!"

"You know, Edith, this small-scale matter between Howston and me has bigger implications. It's a useful exercise in civic and political action. I talk to the people who govern, I find out about planning boards, I arrange to get heard in the Boston Globe. I've become persuasive, not victimized."

"Because you're acting, not just being acted on. Just keep reminding yourself!"

"Even if the house is demolished, it doesn't matter. It's become an empty shell of my past. It's a mirage, like the old Building in Ferryville where I grew up. I'm not interested anymore in mirages."

To Persis, Fran said, "Now there's the winter and spring to get through before I know for sure that Howston doesn't come up with another architectural drawing and still get the house. How will I get through this time while I'm waiting it out to see if he does, or doesn't re-submit?"

"You won't think about it," Persis said brusquely. "Get on with your work."

"He's made work impossible, my head is filled with this house stuff."

"So we'll add that to the complaint — the mental anguish he's caused you, and what it's cost you in not being able to work. And, we will let his lawyer know that should he move the house, you will be suing for recompensation of your creative idea and for a percentage of what he stands to gain if he should ever sell the property. That may give him second thoughts."

Fran thought to herself, for a woman who had once taken vows of poverty, Persis certainly knew the value of money. And although she admired Persis Williams, her diffidence about the legal profession stuck. The law was indeed a double-edged sword; it could smite as well as protect. Her stand on the house might come down to a matter of monetary compensation, and that was not what had mattered to her.

That spring Fran got a call from Persis. "Congratulations, Fran," she said, "you won."

"Tell me, Persis."

"I've just had a call from Mr. Stratton of Vested Brands. This past week-end, they demolished the Barr house. Howston Kelly never came up with alternate plans, never contacted anyone. Stratton couldn't reach him — but he heard that at the Town Board meeting Howston tried to blame the architect for submitting a faulty plan. So the architect pulled out of the project. Stratton thinks Howston just got fed up with the whole thing. He may also have had second thoughts when we entered suit against him. He seems to be out of the country. He didn't meet the extension V-B gave him, and Stratton was under pressure from his bosses to get rid of the house and not let it drag on. So Howston Kelly can't get your house because there is no more house."

"So that's the end. And without the house he won't get the land at the Cape, either."

"That's right," Persis said in her clipped way. "He gets nothing but a bunch of bills. It's over."

"Thank you, thank you Persis!" Fran exclaimed. She had won. And what kind of adversary had Howston been? Just a vindictive schemer who had ventured too far. He had been sucked into a pipe-dream and Fran could even feel sorry for him.

And now she was without a house to fight for, alone again with her thoughts.

Men can abstract about not being able to go home again, about loss of innocence, paradise lost, the existentialist predicament. Men engage in the long pursuit of the white whale, the white elephant, the abominable snow-man, the Loch Ness Monster. They philosophize, theorize, build rockets to breech space, head for the South Pole, and assuage their loneliness.

But women pine. Women feel the lost bond, the severed connection deep inside and pine.

And we try by every means to keep the children, keep the house, keep the garden, keep life intact. But nothing stays: centers do not hold, children grow up, love dissolves, and life – the germ of it – is a brief visit that cannot be repaid.

That night of Persis' call, Fran heard on public television a group of learned men and one woman, all scholars, celebrating the great quest of Herman Melville. The theme of *Moby Dick* was a weighty, abstract, man-centered search into the secret of existence. They spoke of good and evil, and many lofty abstractions. They spoke of strenuous, masculine adventure in the search for man's soul. No one mentioned woman's soul. Perhaps, like the ancients, they still did not believe women had souls.

So, Fran thought, man's search was conceptual – for the meaning of existence, the knowledge of good and evil. And Melville had embodied it in Ahab's manic search for the whale. And woman's quest? It's reality-based: daily bread and human exchange. Their Moby Dick is the whitewashed illusion of the enduring family. Now Fran's illusion was sunk and gone with her house.

Adele and Meade, smartly dressed and coordinated in shades of yellow like two daffodils, came to Winnie's graduation. Chessie and Jules were away at a professional conference, and had sent a con-gratulatory telegram and an artist's portfolio carrier as a gift to Winnie. Some of the Ferryville family were there, but Gussie and

Susan were with Dolly at the St. Tarsicius home where Pop's condition had worsened.

"Well, Fran, I must say I thought you were crazy, weird, to have taken that whole house thing so seriously — to have spent so much time and energy on an old barn!" Adele said.

Fran studied her sister, taking in the successful nose shortening which made Adele even more unrelated to her than she had always been. With each alteration, the sister who had never been close, receded all the more into a person Fran cared little about knowing.

"It's easy to be crazy in this family, Adele," Fran remarked drily. "All you have to do is grow up with mother, the Artful Dodger, to get your head screwed up for good."

"There you go, always blaming mother! Isn't it time you took charge of yourself?""

There was a poem in the anthology Fran had edited called, "Naturally Mother" with the lines: *Freud aside, all our fathers/ do not matter/ A woman bleeds through her mother.* No use quoting that to Adele, Fran thought. Not only did Adele never hear her, but it didn't matter.

And Fran's poetry was being published. She was occasionally asked to give readings and people listened. Some readers wrote to her and told her how much she had touched them. Fran always answered. They heard her, she heard them.

Thirty years after Fran's own college graduation, in a scene light years away, Winnie was getting her diploma in a flapper-style black charmeuse dress bought at Saks Fifth Avenue in an after-Christmas sale. No cap and gown for her, and some others of her classmates. She looked lovely, Meade said and Fran agreed, and she was pleased that he presented Winnie with a bouquet of spring flowers.

Winnie's Fabio never did arrive from Italy. All through the winter and into the spring, through an occasional letter and phone call, he had kept her hope up. The last promise was that he'd arrive for her graduation. When he didn't, Winnie made light of it: "All the men in my life disappear, starting with papà." That seemed to be at the bottom of her panic attacks — she froze when she was attracted to a man, tried to ward him off, then got won over, until, whoosh!, he disappeared and she, sick with the shame of a loss that was somehow her fault, vomited her humiliation, trying to rid herself of what was wrong.

Before her graduation, Fran turned over to Winnie the small inheritance which Marco had left her when she came of age; Fran had taken care of it and increased it tenfold by careful investments and told Winnie that it was now hers. As she did so, she supposed that Winnie would take her nest-egg and disappear into Italy as Dee had, squandering it all in a year. Winnie surprised Fran: she would, she said, spend the summer working at the Cape and then use her inheritance money to give herself a year or so in New York working at her painting. The money would support her while she tried herself out.

The graduation ceremony was held on campus under a gay yellow and white striped tent.

They heard the college writer-in-residence say that every life has a theme...." That's the root discovery of narrative literature. You are in charge of your life. The education you learned here, the small stack of books you take with you, are the icons of the humanist ideal. Your enlightened minds must be enlisted in the struggle for the future.... It's not you who'll have the commitment, it's the commitment that will get you. And if you're doing the right thing with yourself, you won't have a job, you'll have work.... Real individualism means a tough, embattled life...." He told an anecdote about the American penchant to probe and analyze a thing to shreds without ever finding the heart of it: in Japan, on funded research jaunts, an American scholar of world religions kept questioning a Shinto monk to explain his theology, his ideology. Finally the monk replied, I don't think we have a theology, I don't think we have ideology. We dance.

Fran was conscious of Meade McGraw, the eternal prep school debater, next to her as a kind of American prober who didn't know about dancing. Meade derived his identity from the schools he had attended, and they were all establishment grounded. He was sure to scoff at the commencement address they had heard. He'd mimic the speaker for months to come. For his sake Fran hoped the food at the collation, at least, would be worth his while.

The college president, a formidable woman in a cap and gown rich with insignia and honors, got up after the speaker and partially covered his wilder tracks, endorsing, carefully, those who would go on to be lawyers or doctors, not dancers.

And so it went. And then Lavinia Beniferro's name was called, and Winnie received her diploma that, beaming, she presented to Fran who hugged her. They spread out onto the lawn for the barbecued chicken wings, platters of veggies with dip, and champagne and Winnie took her mother's arm affably and said, "Well, Mom, it's the end of an era." She was radiant, hopeful, happy. "Just keep evolving, Mom. Now you won't have to deal with me anymore, and I won't have to deal with you, we can visit each other as friends. I'll be going to New York after the Cape. So what can I say?"

Fran was happy for her. "Say *ciao, arrivederci*, to your old ma," she said. "And I'll say *buona fortuna* to you." Patting her daughter's full, young cheek, she seconded Winnie's emancipation proclamation. "You remember your painting of Lucky Life, Winnie? You seem ready for it."

"I'm ready," Winnie grinned. "It's exciting these days — just look at what women are doing. Just think of the poets and artists."

"I'm glad to be Mother of the Artist," Fran smiled.

And yet, she considered, it couldn't be easy for Winnie or any other young woman of her times. Women's lives were like crosswinds in a canyon. Conflicting currents, uncertainty of choices. There was no permanency anywhere; marriage had long ceased to be a haven. Winnie would struggle with being a woman; would be torn between work and family, her independence and relationships. She would come to know the struggle between the conflicting impulses, how hard it would be for her yearnings to be fulfilled. Would Winnie be smarter than she had been? Yes, Fran told herself, I've helped her to be.

CHAPTER SIXTEEN

Picking up Winnie on the way Fran drove them to Ferryville for Stella's wedding. She was the first of Gussie's children to marry and it would be, of course, an expensive country club affair. It was an evening wedding, giving Stella a chance to sunbathe at a pool party in the afternoon, and time for Fran to visit her father, with Winnie, at the nursing home.

Fran had a horror of places like St. Tarsicius, the more so that, as in this case, it was noted for being top of the line, as if such shelters could be ranked in desirability, could be camouflaged from what they were — warehouses for the helpless aged.

She was affronted by the overheated, hothouse atmosphere of forced life; of life being held not in bloom, but in suspended decay, the inmates like those over-mature, soft melons that Dolly Scalzo bought at bargain prices in the supermarket. The warmth emphasized the pervasive smells of the place; the long, bland, unadorned and synthetic-floored corridors made present and visible the long tunnel to nowhere that was the reality for the inmates. Why were they there? Because they were the new commodity, new sources of jobs and income in a competitive market. People drew salaries and benefits dependent on keeping these aged ones propped into some semblance of life in their wheelchair containers. Gus Sturzo, in his right mind, would have understood that where there's demand, there'll be supply. He would have understood it as progress that people no longer died at home.

"He's lucky to have gotten in," Gussie told Fran who, instead, saw it as the beginning of a sad end. The king was dead and they shipped the remains off to St. Tarsicius. Gussie had started the procedure and then Fran's mother had elaborated on it. "You know,"

Dolly now said, "I don't think Pop was so intelligent after all. He had a lot of luck in the beginning starting his business — there were no income taxes then — and he's worked hard. But you can't say it was intelligence."

As they walked through the nursing home, Fran whispered to Winnie, "Don't do this to me. I'd rather die than be put in such a place." It was hard enough for her while healthy to be among people. At camp, or with a roommate in college, or in groups of any kind she had always been shy, uneasy; so to be in her father's condition with a long yellow catheter of urine always trailing from a wheelchair, and having to eat and sleep and waste away in a strange place, overheated and sick smelling, among so many other staring relics would be the real hell. And it cost four thousand a month.

Eagerly dispensing greetings to the inmates like a Good Cheer matron of ceremonies, Dolly Sturzo led them down the corridor. She was again in her element as she had been with Ethel Schotter. She was the ambulant one among the grounded; they made her look good. Fran spotted her father slumped over in his wheelchair, a big white terry cloth bib on him, in the corner of a mean little windowless space between two corridors nonsensically called the recreation room because it housed a television set that was always on, day and night. Tossed on a table were a couple of cheap magazines with headlines like parodies: "MOM, 51, HASN'T AGED SINCE 18" ... "300 LB NUN IS ROLLER DERBY QUEEN."

"Hey, Pop," said Winnie. He was near the television, eating a quarter wedge of tuna-fish on whole wheat, a glass of milk with a straw in it on his tray. "Wouldn't you think they'd know better than give him tuna fish," Dolly stormed, "I told them he doesn't like it!" Hearing her, he looked up and stopped eating. Fran shook her head disapprovingly at this interference. She wondered what he was doing with a glass of milk. She had never, in her whole life, seen her father drink milk.

Dolly was still going on. "I told them no sandwiches, and no Italian food. And what do they give him one night — baked macaroni and cheese!"

"That's not Italian," Fran said, "that's institutional. And besides, he eats everything until he hears you say he doesn't like it, and then he stops."

"It's not right, with what it costs," Dolly said. "I'll threaten to take him out of here if they don't take better care."

"And then what? Have him at home?"

That shut her up.

Fran thought her father didn't look too bad, even though his face showed the white stubble of not having been shaved that day. She stared at his hands on the tray; they were thin, but the nails were pink and healthy looking, and his fingers elegantly long and tapered, like an El Greco grandee. When his white bib was removed, she could see that, shrunken into his clothes and slumped lopsided into the wheelchair, he was dressed in a blue sport shirt and plaid trousers. His expression was of a child, a baffled child.

He didn't seem to be hurting or to have any awareness of where he was. And yet Aunt Josie had said that at times when she visited him, he refused to speak because he did know where he was and he didn't want to be there. That made Dolly furious, as if she were being criticized.

"It's good to see you, Pop," Fran said, bending over to kiss him.

He grabbed her hand in a surprisingly still strong grip. "Good to see you, too," he answered. But she couldn't tell for sure if he knew her. He was always polite to strangers. Then he said, "You know, I don't have my wallet. How I am going to pay for my lunch?"

"Don't worry," Fran said, "it's all paid for."

But that was exactly what did worry him; he was used to paying, it did not relieve him to hear he didn't have to pay. "What do you mean," he said, his irritability flowing back. "I told you I've got to pay!" He started to tap his fingers impatiently on the metal tray.

"I mean, it's charged, Pop, it's on the bill, you can pay at the end of the month."

He looked at Fran in his old way, as if she were presenting an obstacle to him and this he would not tolerate. "What are you talking about, pay at the end of the month?" His words were biting and angry. She thought then that he must for sure have recognized her and that the connection brought him back to life because it gave him the illusion of his old power over them. "Are they sending this bill to the office?"

"That's right," she told him. And since he had mentioned his office, a place he hadn't seen in a quarter of a century, she went along with it. "How's business, Pop?" she asked.

"Oh, I can't complain," he said. "But what I want to know now is how I'm going to pay this bill."

Fran understood. Since he was a boy and had given his paper-route money to his mother, and then promised her when she was dying that he would not go to California and lead the life he wanted to, but would stay there, tied to Ferryville, and carry out the duties she gave him — since way back then, he had always been responsible and he would certainly not end his days not paying for his tuna fish sandwich.

Gussie and Adele had been saying for months that he was goofy, that it was a big relief to Mom that he was out of the house and she could have a life of her own. But Fran knew they were wrong; their mother was now eighty-three and she had no life apart from Pop's and though she might occasionally go out to lunch with a woman friend, her life revolved around visiting him. She was still completely tied to him and to her feeling that, in the end, after he had taken care of all of them, she had let him down.

Abruptly her father addressed Fran: "Do you see much of Marco anymore?"

She was startled. Should she pretend? She said, "Marco's dead Pop."

"Dead?" He looked bewildered. "When did that happen?"

"Oh, some years ago."

"Well, I didn't know that. Were you with him?"

"Oh, yes."

"Well I'm sorry to hear that. He was a nice man."

"Yes he was, very nice."

"Very nice, Pop," Winnie echoed. She was holding his hand.

Marco was someone Pop had been able talk to as he never was able to talk to his own children. He had esteemed Marco, maybe even loved him.

He turned and called mother. She said, "I'm not your mother, I'm your wife. Do you know what my name is?"

"Of course," he said, "Agostina."

"No, that's your mother. She's dead. I'm Dolly. Let's get him back to his room, honey," she said to Winnie.

Fran felt like *pius Aeneas* with old Anchises on her metaphorical shoulders as they made a slow cortege up the hallway. Her poor old father's search for his mother would now be hers. As he quested for his mother, so did she for hers, and her daughters for theirs. They would never find perfect, true Mother, and they would never get out of trying. Everybody searching. No end in sight. That's how it was.

In front of Pop's room they stopped while Dolly offered the candies Fran had brought her father to the Greek man who was parked outside the next room, sobbing. She started rearranging some of the people in their wheelchairs until one cross looking old man said to her, "Just leave me alone, let me be."

Rejoining them, Dolly said, "That Archie is such a grump."

"They can't stop you, can they?" Pop said, making total sense.

The Greek man's daughter-in-law came over to hug Dolly and to say to Fran, "She's always so nice, every time I come here she's doing something nice."

Dolly basked in the tribute. In Pop's room she signed the guest book that was on his bedside table with her name, and then, in parentheses, added "wife."

Gus Sturzo was living in an ongoing golf game. Most of his remarks were about playing the game. He asked Fran about her handicap, how many holes she played. Over his lifetime, what had remained most impressed in his consciousness was the fact that he had played golf and had been able to join a golf club. It was his crowning achievement, and though it seemed sad to her, it made sense, too. From hard work he had gotten money; from marriage, a family; but from golf he had gotten his own measure of self-esteem because he had been accepted into what was, in his youth, an exclusive American world. Golf had made him a member of the club. He sat in his wheelchair, waiting to tee off, mechanically eating what Dolly jabbed into his mouth. She had brought a bag of food from home and started her force feeding, which was her own life's game. She fed him cutup watermelon pieces, a package of M&M's, and a few macaroon cookies; as he chewed, she poked a half-pint carton of milk with a straw in it at his mouth.

All the time he ate he compulsively folded and refolded the towel on his tray. He folded it, turned it, folded it again, smoothed the edges, made it neat. Fran watched as he kept patting, folding, shaping and turning the towel. Even with all that ordering, he was blind to what didn't concern him. Fascinated, Fran watched him edging off his tray the plastic bowl of watermelon bits, not caring that he was pushing it to the edge because he was only intent on what he had put his mind to — neatening the towel.

It reminded her of how, with them, he ran roughshod over everything that he didn't want to know about. If ordering the towel was all to him, why should he care about a dish of watermelon about to fall to the floor? He hadn't measured the consequences of his single-minded will to do what he wanted, and that's how he had been in all their lives.

Fran did nothing to prevent the dish from falling. "Oh, Pop," said Dolly, her glance drawn to the fruit splattered on the floor "now look what you've done!" He paid no attention. Nor did Fran as her mother and Winnie got paper towels to wipe up the mess.

Returning to her mother's home, Fran asked her, "Do you believe in the afterlife?"

Dolly shook her head. "It's a relief to think there's maybe just nothing, just a sleep. When I was younger I used to be terrified to think I'd wake up in my coffin and be helpless to get out."

"What about your mother?"

"Oh, she believed in going to heaven."

"Do you think she's there?"

And again Fran's mother, the faithful churchgoer and believer in St. Jude granter of the impossible, surprised her. Shaking her head, Dolly said, "No. She was too hard-boiled."

After almost a century Dolly had finally consigned her mother to hell.

It was a very hot summer night for a wedding and the church was not air-conditioned. Stella was not married in the Italian church, familiar to Fran from childhood, but in St. John's, lavishly decorated with floral arrangements by Susan who was, everyone agreed, great at creating an ambiance.

All the females of the bridal party, including the two mothers, were dressed in white, virginal white no longer reserved for the bride alone. Just as well, Fran thought, as far as the facts went, but there might still have been symbolic significance in setting off the bride from the others. Stella, in fact, in white looked splendid — her bare shoulders tanned, her hair drawn back under a tiara that gave her a regal bearing. Simple bouquets of Queen Anne's lace and fern decked each pew entrance. They contrasted with the sophistication of Stella's embroidered gown and headpiece and the formal procession of attendants and ushers. The bridesmaids wore white gowns baring one shoulder and no headdress. They were all young and beautiful and tanned.

The bride's grandmother, Dolly Scalzo, sat alone in a front pew, conspicuously dabbing at her eyes, until she was joined by Freddy, the chief usher.

The priest who officiated wore a stole embroidered with two large shamrocks and said he wanted everyone to have a good time, that a wedding was a joyous occasion and he wanted people to feel good. "I'll skip the homily, OK?" he said, and then, "By way of loosening things up and getting you all acquainted, I'll just mention where you're all from." He called out the names of those who had come from New Jersey, Boston, Detroit, Canada, and California and there was a round of applause for each place name. There was greater applause when he said, "And let's hear it for Susan who made these beautiful bridesmaids' gowns." Then again when he announced that everyone present was excused from Sunday mass the next morning because the wedding mass would count for tomorrow, too. More applause.

The church was uncommonly hot. The best part of the wedding was the bride who was stately and composed in contrast to the quipping Irish priest. Stella and her groom, a good-looking young man whom Fran had never met, faced the congregation during the ceremony. That surprised Fran and she imagined it had to do with the overall reform of how mass was said since she was a long ago churchgoer. After the ceremony, Gus Sturzo's insurance agent added more fun to the occasion by recounting his visit to Pop at the nursing home: "Gus said, Oh, are you here, too, Ed? The food's not bad, but I can't find the way to the first tee." Everyone laughed.

The reception was held at Gussie's country club. Sitting with Aunt Josie and young Josie at an outside table, near the pool, to get the evening breeze, Fran was pleased when Chessie and Jules came over to them. They had arrived by themselves, unperturbed and looking coolly above the fray of a wedding reception. Chessie was stunning in an off-one-shoulder navy silk dress and a strand of long pearls. Coming or going, Jules never greeted. He'd walk into a room, look around, and stand there waiting for someone else to greet him first.

Chessie greeted everyone and sat next to Fran as if nothing were amiss, as if they'd been in constant contact all this time.

"How's your work, Chessie," Fran asked.

"Oh, fine."

And how's your life, Fran wanted to ask; the life she knew nothing about. She had to admit, Chessie and Jules were a handsome couple, but they did not dance, they did not mingle, they did not revel. Why had they come? Certain familial duties are required, they must have reasoned.

Then, in a tone that indicated her attitude had softened Chessie said to Fran, "Are you sorry your house is gone, Mom?"

"I could have had it, Chessie. All I had to do was pick up the phone and call Houston. All I had to say was, Houston let's have dinner and talk things out. I could have had him back and with him the house — he would have dumped Vicki."

"That's really having power over someone," Chessie said. Fran heard in her tone that she was impressed. This surprised Fran for surely in her profession Chessie wielded an even greater power. Or was it, Fran wondered, that what Chessie attained professionally she paid for by what she then surrendered in her personal life.

"No, Chessie," Fran replied, "the real power was to let the house go."

Winnie was slumped on the opposite side of the table, noticeably estranged from the occasion. She had told Fran in church that she felt out of place with everyone eyeing each other's clothes critically. She was in too organic an outfit, she said, which meant that this was not the crowd where she could be wearing an embroidered Mexican peasant dress. Chessie said that Stella was wearing a smidgen too much make-up. Jules, monolithic, silent and handsome in his beige linen suit, looked as if he were light years away from all of them, safe in his own realm of higher thought. After a few drinks, Chessie said contentedly, "This is a wonderful moment! We're all together — just let me enjoy this evening!"

Fran was pleased at Chessie's newfound equanimity; so, what made her say, looking at the sky, "There are no stars — and it's so humid."

"Oh don't be so literal!" said Chessie, "Just enjoy."

"Aren't you and Jules going to dance?"

"He doesn't dance."

"But you always loved to — get Freddy to dance with you."

"Would you mind leaving me alone!"

Winnie got up from the table and left, walking towards the golf course. She had little tolerance for Chessie and her mother being together, especially now that Chessie was affecting a show of reconciliation. Winnie was edgy; she had changed from a confident, sociable girl to becoming reclusive. Fran frowned as Winnie went off. She worried about her; did she feel odd and alone among all the dancing couples, odd and alone in New York and in her solitary pursuit of painting? Then Fran knew exactly how she felt. Even in Winnie's art work, the joy that had once flowed into her forms and colors seemed to have soured, the colors muddied, the faces and postures grim. There was one painting, a self-portrait of an ashen-faced and white-haired, grimacing Winnie astride a chair, that Fran had silently termed The Crucified Crotch.

After awhile, Fran went off to look for Winnie and found her sitting on the ground, against a tree, shivering. "What's wrong, Winnie?"

"Can we go home? I can't stand these things."

"We came with Meade and Adele and they're dancing up a storm. They're not about to leave. Maybe you could ask Jules, he always looks bored and ready to leave. What's wrong?"

"Oh, mother, I can't stand it! You saw how Pop was today — he didn't have his teeth and no one was paying attention when he said he had to go to the bathroom. That nurse said he could go when they make their rounds. Can you imagine that he can't even go to the bathroom until it's convenient for them! And here we all are as if it didn't matter."

"I know what you mean. But Stella's wedding was planned long before Pop got put in the nursing home. You can't connect one with the other." Looking more closely at Winnie's tense face, Fran said "Are you sick?"

"I had a panic attack. I've just thrown up and crapped out."

"Oh my God, Winnie! Can't you hold yourself together for one evening?"

"Am I embarrassing you? You're so self-centered all you can think of is you!"

It was the usual displacement Fran heard from her daughters. It was meaningless. Just words. And Winnie knew it, too.

"Come back and sit with us," Fran said, giving Winnie a hand, and she did.

Gussie, drink in hand, was making the rounds as Father of the Bride to greet everyone. "There's nothing so important as family," said he tipsily, as if he were bestowing a benediction at their table. He, the boating fellow, who for years had gone off with his fishing and boating pals and left Susan with the care of five kids, was playing family man. And Fran wondered if those old-time, devout Catholics, Gussie and Susan, knew from the St. Matthew gospel what Jesus himself had said about family, words that had exploded from the Pasolini film: *"Think not that I am come to send peace on earth: I come not to send peace, but a sword. For I am come to set a man at variance against his father, and the daughter against her mother, and the daughter-in-law against her mother-in-law, and a man's foes shall be they of his own household."*

Verily, Fran echoed. She had always wondered why family as such never lived up to the ads for it. No one, except Jesus, really told the truth. And who paid attention to him? His was not a message Gussie and Susan would consider Catholic enough for them. It was Greek tragedy.

After the wedding and before going their separate ways, Winnie and Fran stopped at the nursing home to say good-bye to Pop. Over the loud speaker system came the strains of The Poet and Peasant Overture, something Fran remembered her father used to whistle since he had once played it on the clarinet in a school band.

In the room her grandfather shared with a fifty-four year old cerebral-palsied man whose mother was there tending him, Winnie said, "How's everything, Pop?"

"Things change," he said, "you've got to be prepared for them, too. Now the community's smaller, one can get along and get around quicker and easier."

"Good-bye, Pop."

"Yes, it's time to go home," he answered. The woman tending her son looked up and said, "You can tell where his heart is."

"Where's mother?" he asked Fran. His expression was meek now, like a baby, his brown eyes liquid. "Is mother coming?"

And Fran thought how, in a unique moment of confidentiality, her mother had told her what had never been known: how, each night, without fail, no matter what the day had been, Pop would kiss her good night and say, "You know I love you." Fran had wished she had known, years ago, that in that household which seemed subject only to fear and tyranny, there had also been this affection and tenderness, hidden though it was. Her life would have been different. She had witnessed the fights and sarcasm between her parents. How could she have ever known there was also love?

"Yes," Fran told her father, "mother will be here soon."

Fran invited her mother to Cape Cod with Winnie for Labor Day weekend. "Well, I might," Dolly said in a tentative way. "I would like to see Cape Cod. It's terrible being alone."

"Yes, it is, mother." Fran could sympathize with how drastically life had changed for her. Not so long ago, all over America, women like her were playing cards, making each other tea sandwiches, and eating bridge mix. Now they couldn't find each other.

"That's right," she said, "you don't have anyone, either."

Fran felt as if she had finally been seen.

At the Cape, Fran and Winnie were protective of Dolly: she seemed so old, almost bewildered. Fran saw the dazed and almost crazed look in her face that said, What happened? What was it all for? What now? And she knew her mother wouldn't know what to make of her own answer — that life is only a force we pass on to others. She would have thought it was to have a good time and be happy. In the American formula of success and happiness, the measure of one's net worth was in money. And Pop had made it! But it hadn't been enough to buy a good time right up to the end.

Fran took her mother to buy her a belated birthday present, her first pair of long pants. Contrarily, Dolly resisted anything Fran showed her in the nice shops. Finally, in the Army and Navy store, Fran picked up from the sale counter what seemed a youth's pair of cotton-knit pants and had her mother try them on. They fit perfectly and at the sight of Dolly, like a skinny scarecrow in bright blue clown pants, Winnie smiled, delighted, and said, "Cool, Nonna!"

Dolly Sturzo's birthday had coincided with Madonna's, with the anniversary of Elvis Presley's death, and with the harmonic convergence of the planets: Fran read in the Sunday paper of crowds gathering in New York's Central Park to refocus psychic energy and to meditate. Then Winnie suggested they take her grandmother whale watching. On the boat, looking out to sea, Fran thought about things. No one could be blamed, no one was blameless. She thought of the tough old peasant woman who had been her own mother's mother: Grandma Briciola had been Mom's first boss, had ground her down then given her a trousseau, all for her own good; and so Dolly, too, had acted on her children for their own good; and so Fran with hers. They all had to believe that their own parents were benevolent and loving, and to be copied. Otherwise the world would end.

Fran acknowledged that she was not the kind of daughter her mother had wished for, one that was, say, like Adele or Susan. She could also acknowledge that she herself didn't always enjoy being with her daughters. ("So strange, Edith," she had said once, "I would never have imagined it. I mean, being uncomfortable with my own kids. When they're all together, or even with just two of them, there's this aggression in the air. I can feel it. Or Chessie walks in a room and doesn't meet my eyes and it becomes passive aggression against me; or Dee always saying yes, she'll do something, like write to me and then never doing it; and even Winnie, and all her terrible language against me.")

Finally Fran took her mother to see the piece of land that had reverted to the town and had almost been the site for the relocated

299

Barr house. It was still unbuilt upon and it was probable that after all the controversy with Houston and his fraudulent plan, the town would keep it as a conservation area since it abutted the marshlands. The beauty of the place still affected Fran. The marsh was a vivid green and blue where the undulating channels of water flowed through the tall, swaying grasses. Beyond, the gold sandbars of the Bay at low tide. The sun was sinking in jagged stripes of pink and orange and purple.

"Here you were going to put your house?" her mother was asking, looking around with a skeptical expression. "It's just as well nothing came of it."

CHAPTER SEVENTEEN

Fran's book of poetry was published and she was invited to give a reading at a writers' conference in Denver. She was both exalted and humbled to be there, among poets she had long admired, and she was most moved by a stunning young woman of the Creek tribe. As the woman read her poetry Fran felt deeply the lines:

What do I know?
Only the prayers I send up on cedar smoke, on sage.
Only the children who are bone-deep echoes of a similar life.
Only the woman who sleeps generations in my bed.
A continuum flows like births...

The Creek poet was tall and commanding, a superb presence who moved with supple grace. She had a magnificent cascade of black hair — a black that was not the soft Mediterranean black of Chessie's hair, but another black that was luminous, sleek, deep black, utter black — no blues or reds in it. She wore a many-colored jacket adorned with symbolic figures that might have been part of tribal patterns; her waist was cinched with a heavy silver and turquoise belt and her wrist weighted by a thick turquoise bracelet. She could have been a tribal queen. She could have been a new world version of Fran's Sicilian grandmother Agostina. There was that air of secrecy and knowledge of ancient things about them both.

The poet looked to be Chessie's age. And as she read, she prefaced each poem with a bit of her life history to explain where the poem had come from in her experience. So young, she had a son of sixteen and a daughter a bit younger. Her eyes, shadowed and dark and filled with a woman's knowledge, were keener than Chessie's sea-grey eyes. Both young women had full breasts and curving fig-ures, both were beautiful. Strong and clear in her reading was the passion of vision and an intense linkage to heritage. She knew and honored female strength; she was her own world.

Following the reading Fran approached her and said, "That was so fine! I'm with Pricer Books and I'd love to have your new work with us. Here's my card."

The Creek poet was pleased, and as Fran looked closer at her, at the well defined nose and set lips, she felt even more the affinity in the poet's countenance with that of her Sicilian forebears. The poet said, "That's great. I'll be in touch after I get back from Arizona where I'm going to a sweat with some other women."

"A sweat?"

"A retreat. Six women meet and stay for some days in a trailer on the desert. We seclude ourselves and tell stories. It's wonderful. After the last one, when we emerged from the trailer, an eagle was flying overhead and he dipped and passed four times over our heads."

"Beautiful!" Fran said, imagining how from the women's stories would come the signs of who they were and what they were about and where they should go. Fran thought of her own long ago re-treats at Concordia Convent School where, however, no beautiful sign had ever emerged, or if it had, Fran hadn't been able to see it. Or could it have been, Fran wondered, the bread of the angels? On-ly now, emerging from the past, could she be fully receptive to fu-ture-pointing signs. She felt a bond with the striking young Creek woman just as she did with Black women writers, and with the His-panic women who told their stories. Fran was connecting to their womanliness, to their expression of themselves. Fran felt a part of all women's stories.

The poet said, "If you ever come to Tucson let me know, we probably have stories to tell each other."

"Yes, I will, and yes, we do," Fran smiled. Leaving the reading, Fran thought, she sees me, she knows I have things to tell; when will my daughters know the same?

Fran no longer dreamed of her old home: neither the golden-hued, serene dream, nor the disturbing nightmare of shrieking demons. With the house's demolition went the image of life it had held for her. Trying to get back again to a home whose occupants were gone had been a romanticized, extreme longing. Where is everyone? Fran used to call frantically as, one by one, they left, until she found that no matter where in life or death they were, they were still part of who she was. What Fran could now fashion, through visits, was continuance. She had hoped for miracles, but faced instead with reality, she had become clever: it was she who had to create the rituals and affections to see them all through.

Truth is various. Fran was right in her happy memories of Shady Brook Farm; but so, too, was Chessie in saying that she had invested it with much untruth. With both the house and Howston gone, Fran was at a turn-around. The least worthy part of her might yet become the best. By luck, Fran had stumbled upon a path after having bumbled in the dark for years. She told this to Edith who agreed. "Stumbling and bumbling is not for the young," Edith said, "it's for us who are past our prime. It's our being Dante lost in the deep forest. It requires a sense of our stupidity and failure for which the young haven't yet accumulated enough experience. We're ready to let our fool out."

Edith. Fran thought there would always be Edith. But the summer of Stella's wedding, her friend was diagnosed with cancer. Fran was more overwhelmed than Edith who seemed imperturbable and continued to work even as she underwent chemotherapy treatments. After some months she was thought to be out of danger. But who ever knows? By winter when Edith decided to anticipate her retirement and plan a trip to the South Pacific, a party was given for her. Not long after, she had a seizure and collapsed. The tumor had passed to her brain. There was no question now of the trip, of her planned retirement projects, of books to write, of further life. Edith's days were numbered and it so deeply shook Fran that at first she could hardly bear seeing her. She sorrowed not only for Edith, but for herself. *All love reverts to self-love as its cause*: St. Thomas Aquinas. It was true. Fran was seeing her own mortality. She frequently checked her hands: they would soon be her father's, fragile and useless.

Only her work went well. *Only!* Fran rebuked herself, knowing that the qualifier had been added as her mother's daughter, never satisfied, wanting more. The work, both at the office and on her own, gave her a center she knew would hold. It was a new beginning and Fran went into it intensely, with total surrender, and in the knowledge that aiming high she might never see it perfectly realized. And that, someone had said, is the secret of all art.

On a visit to Edith Fran told her about a book on ecumenism by an African woman that she was editing. "It's intriguing." she told Edith. "Since schism is perennial and the Church is becoming divided against itself, this woman is proposing the African family as a possible model against division."

"How does she do that," Edith asked, interested still in books and new ideas.

"She mentions specifically the example of her people, a mother-centered clan who trace their lineage matrilineally. What holds them together is a common language, a community of symbols and

304

a shared spiritual interpretation of the universe. Households are of three or four generations, plus wards and other adoptees. You're nobody if you're not connected. Even in travels, one seeks out the clan. It's the ultimate haven — you cannot be excommunicated from it, nor can you resign or defect. In other words, you cannot get out of belonging. The worst fate of all is not death but getting lost from one's clan."

"How does she make the analogy to the Church?"

"She makes the point that we delude ourselves with the notion that we have the freedom to "relate" or not to relate to others. We *must* relate. For without that, one ceases to be human. Without your clan you are nobody and so, too, without the Church. You cannot be an "individual" Christian, she says; wholeness comes from community."

"Yes," said Edith. "I've always thought western Individualism too extreme — it lets us drop out of anything at the blink of an eye."

Fran was also thinking of the modern affliction, anomie — a kind of rootless lack of purpose and lawlessness, but literally from the Greek meaning without pasture (the antecedent *a* meaning without and *nomia* meaning green); to be without one's home pasture was a dangerous state for anyone, and ultimately for the surrounding society. Anomie, said Fran's strongly worded dictionary, is a social vacuum, "as in the case of a rooming-house area for single people in a large city." What a statement! Was her apartment building, full of other apartments for singles, another such vacuum? Was singleness the new lawlessness and all unattached people outlaws of the social order?

"Still," Fran said, "the Church, as with any family or clan, must be prepared to accept the diversity of its members. The goal is for the community to be cohesive without crushing the individual."

"We live by negotiating," said Edith.

And Fran lowered her eyes, not able to look at Edith as she spoke the word "live" — as if it were now too delicate to be uttered in her presence.

Chessie had studied Greek in college. Fran always maintained that giving her children the excellent education she herself hadn't had was one of the fine things she had done for them. Fran had insisted on good schools even when Marco contended what she eventually came to accept: that it really doesn't matter so much what school you go to as it does that you continue to educate yourself.

Fran was covetous, of Chessie's Greek. Marco and Fran had often talked of their going to Greece together. After Marco's death, when Chessie was putting herself through graduate school, and had no money to spend on gifts, she gave Fran for Christmas an elaborately decorated I.O.U. note on which was written GOOD FOR GREEK LESSONS. Fran had tried now and then to claim her gift but Chessie was never ready; first she was doing her dissertation; then she was in Dallas; finally she was busy with her training and practice. She was really fed up, she said, with her mother's always trying to recapture the past.

Fran explained her attraction by saying that she always felt she must be Greek: on her mother's side the Briciolas came from what, in ancient times, had been Magna Graecia; and Eastern Sicily, where the Sturzos came from, had also been Greek territory. No matter that Magna Graecia had turned into lowly Calabria; no matter that hordes of its people, with no language and no education, had left the depleted mountains and burnt out plains for America. The glory of its past was still there.

Fran had once explained to Edith that her basic uneasiness with Max probably had as much to do with his Talmudic certainty about truth and a heavy, archaic dogmatism which brooked no doubts, as with his drinking problem. Fran was for classical inquiry as she probed for answers. Can't you relax? he'd say.

When everything else failed, Fran went back to the Greeks, to the essential dramas of stark human relationships. The Old Testament had given Abraham the right to slay his son Isaac before his hand was stayed, thus endorsing the law and order code of that society, male over female, and parents' rights over their progeny. Where in the Old or New Testament did the child slay the parent?. Fran searched the concordat to the Bible for references to matricide or patricide, and found none. There were none because it is so beyond law, so unthinkable: parents are authority, the great moral calm of the universe to whom respect is owed, because if that is touched all becomes darkness and anarchy. Judeo-Christian belief relied on a strict moral code to keep out the unthinkable.

"If I were to paint that flower — simply that flower the size it is, no one would ever look at it," said Georgia O'Keeffe explaining her outsized forms. And so, Fran thought, if the Greeks had depicted life only life-size, who would still read them? They painted it large and with all that was unthinkable showing.

The Greeks dared broach the dark side — because evil was — and is — humanly thinkable and everything human had to be examined, the dark as well as the light. Greek drama stung with the wildness of passion: not only Medea slaying her children, and Agamemnon sacrificing Iphigenia, but Orestes and Electra then killing their mother because she had murdered their father. Long, dark trails of retribution. What Freud called "the family romance." The Greeks took the

307

most taboo of human secrets — parent-child rage — and played it out to the end.

Fran must have been the last of the old-time mothers who believed children owed parents something, as she had been brought up to believe. Once she had rejected her father's saying to her, I only want you to be happy. She dismissed his imagining that he knew what her happiness could be, without, however, having had the grace to discuss it with him.

But now, when Fran finds Aristotle urging happiness, she is ready. Life is habit, and good ones lead to the greatest good. Fran finds it beautiful to think of Aristotle creating reason out of the blue, creating the vocabulary to conceptualize, and reaching the verities with his naked mind. His business was thinking. No printed books or concordances, thesauri for him — he simply watched the cuttlefish and the stars and observed his way through all of nature and human nature. That is beauty, far more moving than the movies she used to love, Fran decided.

Around her, life in the Reagan era was regressive and hard. When Fran got her groceries at the supermarket, the big brown bag reminded her SAY NO TO DRUGS. The wispy words of the anorexic First Lady were thrust on them like some enormous, cynical joke; she was the symbol of the times: elegantly starved and thin-dimensioned, stinting, detached, bug-eyed. Her husband's administration preferred the Central American drug lords and murderers to commies. What a mess. Did Nancy read the papers? Could she really believe in him?

Better the Greeks who saw the Cosmos whole, with both order and chaos, and so could account for the darkness with no pretense about perpetual bliss.

Fran had gone to Persis and made her last will and testament. She accompanied the formal document with a personal note to each of her daughters. She told them she loved them; she said not all poets are Catullus, and that living with a poet is no better or worse than living with a broker or plumber as far as the mechanics of life go, but life is not all mechanics and that with their father she had lived, indeed, moments of true bliss. Marco's handmade booklet of his poems to her, unique in the world, Fran left to Chessie; also unique, his delicious watercolor paintings of their home and children in snowsuits which were for Dee; and also precious the drawing of him as a young man, looking down at an open book, for Winnie. His letters, the sweet messages, and even the little love notes with his drawings which he had fastened to the fridge for her, Fran still kept until the day she would send it all to the collection named for Marco in Italy.) Fran told her daughters not to give her a religious burial, that she was not one for formal prayers, but she had always said, "Give us this day our daily bread...." for that is prayer based in reality and the reminder that it is communion to break our bread with others. Fran asked her daughters to remember their father and mother and to speak of them to their own children. And she wondered, when she finished her note, why Chessie had none yet while Dee was expecting again.

When Fran returned from Denver and the West Coast and went to visit Edith, she saw a great difference in her friend. Before Fran left, Edith had been walking, able to go out to lunch with her Hospice visitor. That had given Fran a chill: going to lunch with the preparer for death? Edith had been cheerful though her voice was clouded, and had introduced Fran to her companion. And Fran was remembering one perfect afternoon in the country when she and Edith had gone antiquing. They stopped in a small town and lunched outdoors at an umbrella-table in the oblique sunlight. It was marvelous to be in Edith's company, and there was a glow of peace and restfulness to their time together, so that the antiquing and the sunlight, the food and the talk left them in a cloud of well-being.

Now Edith no longer left her apartment. Change seemed to come daily. The day of Fran's visit Edith was sitting in her chair, the blue velvet one near the coffee table that faced the door to her garden. Nearby was her wheelchair and walker. Open on a stand, as if the world were her oyster, all to be enjoyed, was the large Times Atlas which had been given to her at the retirement party. The stand bore a brass plaque, which recorded the date of the event. Like a memorial.

Edith looked good; she was dressed neatly in one of her shirt-waists with a bead necklace that picked up the colors of the stripes, and she gave still the impression of fastidiousness that Fran always associated with the nuns at Concordia. Way back then admirable women had been (as the nuns were) impeccable, unruffled, sexless beings who were both dainty and strong; wise and innocent. Edith was like a nun of the spirit.

Edith's face was placid and unlined. She wore a platinum-blond wig that reconstituted the familiar lines and dips of Edith's own lost hair with, at the base of her neck a light stubble, like a parched field that has been mowed, that showed the remains of her natural hair. Her blue eyes were clear and her glance open and peaceful. On her engagement finger, Edith wore a dinner ring set with an opal. (After hearing that opal is an unlucky gem, Fran has never worn the opal pendant her father long ago brought her from a business trip.) Only

Edith's legs appeared out of order — they were mottled and the ankles swollen, perhaps from medication. In Fran's presence she had never complained of anything. The only emotion that transpired would be a sudden flushing of her face and neck to a bright pink when something in the conversation alluded to her state.

Speaking had become difficult for Edith. At times Fran could barely make out her words as Edith bobbed and gyrated, her head searching to launch them in Fran's direction. She spoke slowly, waiting for the articulated word to force itself out of her invaded brain. Staunchly she groped within herself to bring out her words. She was brave and still in possession of herself, and Fran marveled that she could be so.

Finally the particles of speech made a whole: Edith was asking, "Will you have some tea?" She had a mug of tea lightened with milk in front of her on the coffee table. Fran said no and watched, fascinated, as Edith, like a schema of slow motion, started the action to bring the mug to her lips without a spill. She swayed, she bent, she focused utterly on the mug before her; She grasped it with both hands, and slowly, precariously, she got it to her mouth for a sip. Then began the long journey back to replace the mug on the coffee table. It seemed endless to Fran, The quickness and verve of Edith's life had been slowed to the successful grasping hold of, and sipping, a mug of tea.

Edith understood everything Fran said. Fran was aware of her still functioning intelligence as she asked about Winnie, of whom she was very fond, and made apt responses. She laughed wryly at some of the office gossip and stories with which Fran tried to amuse her. Fran was there about an hour and then Edith said, Don't let me keep you.

Leaving, Fran asked the woman who was Edith's live-in attendant, "When did her talking get difficult?"

"It's the new medication. The situation is steadily getting worse."

The next weekend, Fran returned bringing fresh strawberries. Edith seemed miraculously better, her speech was clearer, she did not bob and weave so strenuously as before to get her words out. "Wonderful," she exclaimed. "I'll have them with ice cream."

"I didn't think you liked ice cream, Edith, or I would have brought some. In fact, I've never seen you eat any desserts."

"That's my dirty secret. I really love them. I just never allowed myself to eat them. I smoked instead. I was a fat little girl once and I guess I never got over that horrid feeling of being encased in fat and hating the jokes about me. I never wanted to be fat again so I started smoking. What we really want always catches up with us. I was so frugal and saving — now I long for shopping and spending, buying three Gucci bags at a time."

"Oh, Edith, I'll bake you a cake! — name your kind."

"Amaretto cheesecake," she laughed. "Or isn't that classic?"

"Whatever it is, it's yours. Anyway, classic is a word reserved for the Greeks, not cheesecakes. I'm still studying the Greeks. I got to the dramatists after Aristotle. It's a balance to the American self-reliance myth."

"Oh, I agree," Edith nodded. "I don't know what I would do without friends like you and family. My niece comes by everyday and one nephew flew in from Baltimore Friday evening with a soft shell crab dinner which he served us by candlelight. He even brought the flowers for the centerpiece. They've all been extraordinary. The answer is to find and use our own individuality while staying connected."

"An ideal, and I'm for it. Oh, Edith, how I wish I had had a son! All the competitive emotions of daughters is so grueling!"

"They see you as strong. You seem to survive everything — Marco's death, Max, the House. You've done what they haven't yet. In simple terms, they have to live."

But when were terms simple? "I never felt strong, vulnerable is more like it," Fran replied.

"Don't forget, your early strength, Fran, when you turned away from Ferryville and found a new life in Marco and Italy."

"Yes," Fran mused, "I did change. Then I changed again when everyone left and I got afraid of being alone." At that, considering that soon she would not have Edith either, Fran said angrily and bitterly, "I still hate the losses!"

"Accept, Fran. Accept the grief. That is true feeling."

Fran was humbled by Edith's equanimity.

"You can miss your daughters, but you'll acquire others. Think of the young Native American poet you told me about. Go see her, learn her way. They know about not possessing the earth, nor anything on it. You cannot be possessive of your natural daughters. But there will be daughters of the spirit for you. There are the young women who look up to you because your work has brought them some dignity and understanding of themselves. Try to understand your own daughters — they must separate, as you did."

"I was so foolish. I thought it would not happen to me because I was different from my mother."

"There is love between you all. I can tell from the energy all of you put forth towards each other. Just accept."

As Edith spoke, Fran felt as if the long dry reservoir of her spirit were slowly beginning to fill with something refreshing and new. Tears gathered behind her eyes and she strained to hold them back in Edith's presence. Then she forced herself to say in a self-mocking voice of put-on ruefulness, "You know, now that I'm so into the Greeks, I'm reminded of Chessie when she was ten or eleven, coming home from school one day and saying to me in this tone of infinite condescension, Mom, I bet you don't know who Sappho is."

Edith laughed. "What a wonderful mind she has, Fran, you should be so proud."

"Madame Butterfly!" Fran answered, both proudly and sarcastically, thinking of the butterfly symbol of the psyche which she had once given Chessie. "Madame Butterfly of the soul."

"She's at the age when she esteems authority and doing it by the book, being the good girl who's head of her class. She'll grow into the bumblers and stumblers we are. But enjoy her now as she is. You can wait for her to make her journey back."

That evening, before going to bed, Fran got down the volume of Sappho with the Massimo Campigli lithographs that Marco had published in a limited edition from his long-ago small press in Italy. When he courted Fran, he had given her a copy of the precious edition. Now Fran slowly turned the elegant handset pages, reading each of the twelve fragments.

The last was: "The moon has set, and the Pleiades/ it is the middle of the night and time passes/ time passes/and I lie alone."

CHAPTER EIGHTEEN

Fran was in New York for a meeting at Pricer's mid-Manhattan office after which she was to meet Chessie for lunch. Before leaving the office Fran stopped at a mirror near the door to check her hair. It was thinning on top, frizzed and lightened from a recent permanent. She imagined how she would look to Chessie who, the last time they met, had already noted change when she told Fran she'd taken a great spurt forward.

"Spurt?" Fran repeated.

"It's just that you looked so young in your forties." Chessie meant, you have aged

Fran herself could not see much alteration from how she had looked when she was about to marry Max five years earlier. But what she did begin to see in her face was the look of her father and all the Sturzo family. It didn't matter. What mattered was the eagerness in Chessie's voice as she agreed to meet for lunch. They had reached a plateau of civility.

As with the shrinks Fran knew, Chessie, who now had a practice, was also a virtual recluse, circumscribed by work on a new book and her need to be alone and recoup herself after the intense focus of meetings with her patients. She and Jules were so much to themselves. Thanksgiving by themselves, Christmas by themselves, New Year's Eve at a neighborhood movie. Where did Chessie wear all her expensive clothes? Why did she subscribe to Vogue? When she did dress up, she still wore her hair long and loose. Jules liked it that way. And so, it must be, did the men in her profession for they doted on her as if she were a child prodigy. Chessie played by their rules; not for her the feminist role of tipping the scales of their comfortable male universe to balance them more towards her own sex.

She was exceptional; let other women be, too, if they wanted to get ahead in a man's world. Men's laws fit her temperament; she liked a bounded world, and things in their place; she liked precision, close analysis, steel-trap minds and textbook rules; and she upheld the conventions. Chessie's drive was based on a conviction of being able to master (that give-away, gender-weighted word!) knowledge, people, career techniques, social advancement and the politics of ambition. Fran thought how different they were: Chessie needed and wanted admiration more than freedom.

"Nonna said you've never been happy," Chessie had once challenged her, her eyes flashing, "not even as a child!" Fran thought it certain that her mother could have said that to Chessie. But it reflected no accurate measurement, only her mother's puzzlement over how Fran could be so different from the rest of them. Difference to her had meant unhappiness.

So Fran laughed it away saying to Chessie, "Oh, that's because I didn't play golf like the rest of them and I wasn't popular the way Adele was. My mother used to say I always had my nose in a book, and she thought I should have my nose shortened instead of hiding it in a book."

Over the years Chessie seemed to have become wary towards her mother and her sisters. Perhaps she begrudged what they had that she did not — Dee a son, Winnie her art, her mother her freedom. Winnie said Chessie knocked on wood and hoped she wouldn't have a daughter. Was it because of the way the world was now? women freeing themselves from the old time pater familias pattern? Was it the fear of retribution? It was an intricate dance to be a woman, and a mother of daughters, so Chessie knocked on wood and hoped not to beget her own affliction.

Friday lunch was convenient for them both. Fran had finished her work and had no other appointments for the rest of the day. They would meet at the professional women's club Chessie belonged to, an elegant place just off Park Avenue. Leaving the Pricer office, Fran entered an elevator where two women were speaking of Handel's Messiah.

"Did they stand for the Alleluia?" asked the younger woman.

"Oh, yes, they stood — but after that most of them left!"

"I'll never forget hearing the Messiah at Saratoga Springs," the younger woman recounted. "The audience was full of upstate provincials. I was with Edgar and he's an incredible opera goer and everything. And at the Alleluia, of course he sprang up and I was so glad I knew what to do because everyone else kept sitting. And he just about freaked out — he kept saying, Look at these people, don't they know they're supposed to stand?"

Fran was attentive to the elevator conversation and smiled as she listened for she had recently heard it verified that King George II, at the debut of the Messiah had not been moved to rise to his feet as legend has it. The whole rite of standing during the Alleluia was a silly snobbery with no basis in fact and Edgar was the real provincial. Fran exited the elevator almost laughing.

Out on the street, in the midday bustle, Fran noticed a nun in a long blue habit topped by a black veil who, lifting her skirt to ascend the steps of St. Patrick's, disclosed a pair of worn running shoes. Stopped at a corner by the traffic light, Fran heard one young man say to another, "She's got cable TV now and watches the sex movies, so she calls me the other night about three in the morning and says, Why don't you come over?" Nearby a young black street vendor of watches was trying to coax a hesitant customer: "Time's going to close the door on you," he chuckled in warning to the buyer who couldn't decide.

At the club, Fran waited in the foyer watching Chessie turn heads as she approached. She was dressed in a turquoise and violet print dress and wore a beribboned wide-brimmed straw hat with streamers down the back. She came over to Fran and gave her a quick kiss on the cheek. "What did you do with your hair?" she asked giving her mother an appraising look from head to toe. Fran raised her hand to the side of her head and felt her hair. "What do you mean? Does it look dry? Too curly?"

"It's different," Chessie said.

They moved into the airy dining room where tables were filled with chattering women and stood in line at the buffet table. "It looks a little bleached out," Chessie continued, still scrutinizing her mother's hair and then said, as she turned her gaze to Fran's feet, "Are those sandals leather?"

"Well, actually not," Fran laughed self-consciously and thought, What is it about Chessie that makes her inspect me so? "They're what's called man-made uppers, but I only wear them one season. I should have gotten rid of these by now, but the weather's been so warm...." Her voice drifted off. Fran was forever explaining to Chessie because she forever wanted to know and it gave Fran a feeling of tenderness towards her daughter that she wanted to know these things about her.

They selected the same luncheon: stuffed Cornish game hen. At the table Chessie ordered wine for them. She took off her hat and put it on an empty chair. Fran noticed a single white strand in her dark and luxuriant wavy hair and re-heard the street vendor saying, Time's going to close the door on you. She wondered what she'd never put into words: were Chessie and Jules ever intending to have

318

a child? Once, Chessie had breezily repeated Jules' saying that they shouldn't even think about having children until they agreed on everything. Fran had been struck silent by that; life on earth would have long since stopped if every couple had such rules.

They talked about Winnie and her art projects and Chessie said she hoped Winnie would take her life seriously and get it on track. The food was good and they were enjoying their conversation. Then it changed. Fran couldn't remember what led up to it, but Chessie mentioned some assumption Jules had made that turned out wrong.

"You and Jules made a lot of false assumptions," Fran said, "and that's dangerous because it's prejudging without the facts. Mistakes are made that way."

Suddenly, Chessie became confiding. It must have been the wine. She said, "I always assumed Jules was a monolith of strength and control. He was like a Rock of Gibraltar, utterly rational and unperturbed by emotions. I felt I could tell him everything. And I did. But somehow he took everything more seriously and personally than I intended. He had a drastic reaction."

"You mean against me," Fran surmised.

Chessie nodded, her eyes down. "I felt I had to make a decision — detach from the past so I could have a future with Jules. At the time detachment from you seemed a good idea. We were too close, all of us, Mom. After papà died we were like Little Women all stuck together! So it was good for both of us to have some distance. It's just that it went too far."

How easily, Fran thought, the years of her deep pain could be gotten past with the help of a little wine. She marveled at the ease with which Chessie smoothed out estrangement: Jules had willed it! Chessie had complied.

Fran felt wearied and saddened. "I'm glad you've told me, Chessie. Does that mean you and Jules have come to a better understanding about yourselves?"

Then Chessie's eyes filled with tears and she reached for Fran's hand. "Mom, I have something to tell you — I'm leaving Jules. I've told him I want a divorce."

"Oh, my God!" Fran exclaimed, echoing her mother at each report Fran had given her about leaving a man. But Chessie's news was more riveting — Chessie had been so much more committed, so sure of herself. "What happened?" Fran gasped.

"I revered Jules, you know that — I felt he was totally loyal to me as a person as well as loving me as his wife. When he suggested I leave teaching and prepare as an analyst I did so even though I loved teaching and the contact with my students because I thought he understood me so deeply. And I thought when I finished analytic training, that would be the time we could start a family. But he was always putting it off."

Fran listened incredulously to what Chessie was telling her. So she, too, had been mislead by someone who kept saying he loved her! "My God, Chessie, this is terrible for you!"

"I know! And for how long I wanted to call you and talk it over with you and ask you what to do!"

"Did you talk it over with anyone?"

"With my own analyst. And I finally came to the conclusion that I had become Jules' creature — how he wanted me to be and look. And I'd never have a creature — a child — of my own because that would take my full attention away from him."

"Oh, dear Chessie! I'm so sorry for you — how hard this must be for you!"

"Yes, Mom. But I'll get through it. I already feel better having made a decision. And I've left Jules. I'm staying with Aunt Adele. I asked her not to tell anyone until I saw you."

Fran thought, finally Adele has served some good purpose. "You haven't told Winnie or your grandmother?"

"Not yet. I will. Then I will do this divorce quickly."

"You mean Jules agrees?"

"He has to — I had it out with him and then I left. I could even have an annulment because of his not wanting children. But I've decided to go to Reno and get it done quickly."

"And then?"

"I'd love to go back to teaching literature — that's what I've always wanted."

Fran held Chessie's hand — no use going over the wasted years between them. What mattered was now. Here was Chessie vulnerable and needing her. It was recovering her as she was in graduate school, years earlier, when they had been close and confident together.

"Chessie, if all this is so, if you've made your decision and are going to act on it, then I'm glad for you to be out of what's bad and looking forward to something better. You'll have a whole new future and that's a precious thing. You'll teach again and in time you'll remarry and have children. Jules was a step in your life, but not the final one. It will work out."

"Do you think so, Mom?"

"I *know* so!" Fran knew that Chessie liked her to be decisive, oracular; not a waverer. She would do anything for this beautiful and brilliant daughter. Now she attempted solidarity. "Did you ever notice, Chessie, how much men need us? We think — and they want us to think — they're the strong ones, they're secure and can make us secure, but most of them are little boys bluffing. There's my father looking in the dark for his mother. Howston, whom I thought so solid, falling apart, unseamed. And your Jules! You thought he was the Rock of Gibraltar. They pretend to be strong, but when we get close enough we see their feet of clay."

Fran scanned the room, looking away from Cheesie, and her thoughts seethed in that pleasant room filled with chattering, accomplished women. How hard it had been to try to build contact with Chessie. Either she brushed aside everything with her superior silence as if it weren't worth responding to, or she hung on every word, giving undue weight to utterances that should have been considered only of the moment. For years she had let them be judged by overheated words that should have been let evaporate, dissipate into the air.

"It's not too late, Chessie ... not too late," Fran said, patting her hand, "but why didn't we talk sooner?"

"I felt you never understood me." Chessie dabbed at her eyes. "Do you know the sense of insecurity it gave me to be threatened by the loss of your love, and then to have a father who, though his love felt secure and absolute, was himself a dim and detached figure — remote, unreal, so that, in the end, his love was frustrating for all his children. Probably for you, too, and that's the only reason I can forgive you. But I want you in my life, Mom!"

Fran heard her in silence, her heart beating great thumps against her ribcage.

Chessie continued, "Do you know how I felt when I was a child and broke your tree-of-life bowl?"

Yes, Fran remembered. They were vacationing at Cape Cod, at a place where there had been horses to ride, and a pond to swim in and they had a cottage for the four of them: she and Marco, Chessie and little Dee. Antiquing in Sandwich, she had found a rare tree-of-life bowl of a brilliant canary yellow, the glass a pattern of interweaving branches. She prized it because she had three others at home and had never found a match for them. She brought it back to the cottage, elated, still wrapped in its paper and told the children she was putting it on the top bookshelf because it was so rare and precious and they mustn't touch.

But Chessie, for whom mysteries were invitations, had wanted to see what was so rare and precious. And now, a quarter century later, Fran knew that the child had been right. Why shouldn't she see something that sounded so enticing? Why had Fran put away the bowl without showing it? Why had she relied on commanding that they mustn't disturb the package? Now, late for everyone, Fran realized how wrong she had been to tempt the child, and then to punish her. For Chessie had, of course, gone to the shelf, and trying to reach the package, had caused it to drop to the floor where the bowl smashed.

"Do you remember what a rage you went into," Chessie was saying, "and how you stormed and cried and went off to your room and wouldn't speak to me? I felt like the world's worst criminal! I hadn't just broken the bowl, I had broken your love for me. Nothing papà said could make it right. I thought I could never make it up."

"Oh, Chessie!" Fran, too, with her father, had once been that frightened child. Sweetheart," she said, leaning over to pat Chessie's cheek, "it's past. You've never lost my love!"

"Did you put a curse on me?" Chessie asked, her look wary.

"What an idea!" Fran retorted dismissively, but knowing what she meant. Chessie who had once told her she was not the good goddess she supposed, might well have seen her then as a vindictive one.

Instead it was Chessie who had put a spell on herself. It was as if, striving and straining in a man's world, trying so hard to be as valued as a man, to gain male admiration by mirroring their own qualities at the expense of womanliness, she had un-sexed herself. She, with those rounded Mediterranean hips made for frequent child-bearing, and those ample breasts meant to suckle babes, was meant to be a mother. To think of Chessie not bearing children was profoundly contrary and unthinkable. "Chessie, you were loyal to Jules and that was a noble quality. Now you'll be loyal to yourself — we'll all help you through this hard time. Your work will flourish. So will the family you will have someday. Keep your spirits up and your feelings open. Be confident." Fran said this boldly, the counter-incantation Chessie needed.

Openly relieved, Chessie blew her nose and took out a pocket mirror to scan her eyes. She renewed her lipstick. Once again self-possessed, she said in a crisp manner, "Lunch is on me, Mom. This is my turf."

"Delighted," said Fran. "Come to Boston sometime and I'll re-pay the favor."

"Maybe I will — Winnie and I could go up together. Be kind to her, Mom. I mean give her support, uncritically, unreservedly. Show her your love." Chessie signed the check and dispatched it to the waiter with a smile, then turned to Fran and said, "You know, Mom, you must have been made awfully afraid at some time in your life."

"Yes," Fran smiled back, trying to make light of it. "But, as the song goes, *Who knows where or when?*"

Fran had felt and responded to Chessie's needs; and maybe now Chessie understood hers. The image of Gertrude Stein, powerful, a Mater Matuta seated with knees apart, came back to Fran: *There is not all of any visit*, she had signed off in the guest book as she left her hostess' villa outside Florence.

"Chessie," Fran said, as she kissed her goodbye, "We can talk anytime, if you want."

"Yes, I'll keep in touch. I mean it, I want you in my life. I'll let you know what's happening as I make my plans."

Chessie was still wary. But she would learn. Chessie made idols of her beloved people — then they crashed. It was her failing not to see them all as troubled people, caught in their times. Always in the process of becoming.

Fran felt both sad and filled with hope when they parted. What had Heraclitus said? Without hope it is impossible to find the unhoped for.

Leaving Chessie Fran walked towards Fifth Avenue, distracted from the life around her until her eye caught a window display full of appealing gifts. She spotted a box with a little spoon in it. A hand-lettered card said Runcible Spoon — Sterling Silver. Fran went in and purchased it to put away for Chessie's baby to come.

Then, her head filled with the echoes of her meeting with Chessie, her eyes moist with the newly-filling reservoir of the spirit, and her conviction that they were all acting from being acted on — Chessie, Jules, Meade, Gus and Dolly Sturzo, Winnie, Howston, all of them — Fran walked down Fifth Avenue until at 42nd Street, the grey bulk of the New York Public Library came into sight.

Fran thought of the Library Director, immigrant Vartan Gregorian, pumping lifeblood and vision into the place that the old guard
Wasps had let fall into shabby decline, even closing it on Thursdays.
Gregorian was today's hero; the old befuddled Anglos had lost their
sap, were even losing the New York Historical Society, it was time
for new blood and ideas everyplace. Fran decided to visit the restored library. She entered from the 42nd Street side, rather than
climb the main steps between the lions Patience and Fortitude. By
doing so Fran came upon an exhibit called "Jews in Germany under
Prussian Rule." But it was more than the Jews and Prussia for it began with the diaspora under Titus, ended with the holocaust.

Fran slowly progressed through a room filled with illustrative
panels, reading and seeing the story of the Jews. What a dreadful
irony is history, Fran thought: first the Jews were needed — not only
as money lenders and brokers and financiers of wars, but as the
convenient scapegoats of natural catastrophes and humanly con-
nived disasters. St. Augustine counseled the Christians that Jews
should be preserved, "as models of what you should not be." Fran
saw them begin to be slaughtered, to be identified with the invading
Mongols, and to have their "Jewish look" taken for the evil eye.

In 1763, to increase the profits of the Berlin porcelain works,
Frederick II decreed that every Prussian Jew be made to buy porcelain on the occasions of marriage, birth, death, business openings,
purchase of a home, and so on. "In this manner," stated the legend
under a photograph, "Moses Mendelssohn in due course acquired a
collection of twenty life-sized porcelain monkeys." Moses Mendel-
sohn, who had married a Guggenheim and was a literary critic,
translator of the Bible into German, philosopher and factory owner,
died in 1786, the same year as Frederick II, and a year before the
porcelain requirement was finally dropped. Or who knows how

many monkeys, accompanied by what mordantly humorous comments, Moses might have had to go on acquiring.

Fran observed with fascination as the Jews of modern Germany, documented in photos and words, attempted to become more German than the Germans. There was the Jewish maiden, Helene Mayer, Nordic blonde hair braided and caught under a white headband, her tall lithe body erect, her right arm plunged straight ahead in the Nazi salute as she stood on the 1936 Olympic podium, the second of three Jewish women who won all the medals in the fencing competition. Surely she represented, in looks and deeds, the acme of the Aryan race! And all the while assimilation, conversion even, was a terrible illusion: the illusion of being home.

By the time of the Nazi persecutions and the camps, the American Labor Unions did not want refugee Jews coming into this country. Nor did President Roosevelt nor the Prime Minister of England nor the Pope want to address the problem. Finally there was the infamous arch at the end of the train line and the cruel jibe under which they passed to extermination: Work Makes One Free.

Fran stood, caught, in front of the blown up familiar photo of the little boy in the Jackie Coogan cap with his hands raised in the air, his coat lifting above his thin little legs in knee-socks. At his side is a bare-headed young woman in black glancing over at him. His mother? It is a photo seen round the world over and over through post-war years, a photo that has passed into the world's consciousness. His is as famous a face as the Duke of Urbino, as Botticelli's Venus. And with a profound sadness Fran recognized him as her own son. The little boy with the wistful, wondering, shocked (how can this be?) look on his face as he raises his hands in surrender to those big, tall men in boots aiming guns at him — he was in fact her own. "Turn your eyes to the hill of corpses, students of history...."

read a legend. And there was the hill of corpses entwined in a tangled mass. A middle-aged man standing before the photo shook his head and said aloud, to no one, "It's a sad commentary on the human race."

At home, Fran wrote in her diary: *I think of the irony of Aristotle's pupil, Alexander, putting an end to the Aristotelian world. Just as all children put an end to their parents. Aging makes us wise — we see, hear, grasp the particulars that are the stuff of life and that we used to rush past. Now they lead to wisdom. Following wisdom is to be as divine as we can, to participate in life. I am ready for Greece.*

Last night, as if passing someone and only afterwards recognizing who it was, I glimpsed my reflection in a mirror. My face has pared down from a full moon-face into something leaner, more lived out, more worn, classic. ("You have a nice face," an old man, standing close to me in the elevator of our apartment building and smiling up at me, once said to me.) I see not only my father, Aunt Josie, Feeney, the whole tribe of Sicilians pass in review in my face, but I also see some attitude of attentiveness which says, all is not settled; all is not wonderful; but a start can be made.

Didn't the Hellenes know? didn't they just know that passions and emotions cause turbulence and troubles in the world? Of course they knew. Of course they cultivated the mind. But passion over-rules the good resolutions — just ask Medea. Just ask Aristotle Onassis or Stavros Niarchos, or the tragic sisters, Christina and Eugenia, doomed brides of those men. Ask the Kennedys. Look at all those tragedies: essentially the story of the Fall of Houses.

At her mother's weekly call, Fran said, "I'm thinking of taking a trip to Greece, mother, I feel very drawn to it. I've always loved Greece since I was a child reading the mythologies. And where the Briciolas came from in Italy was all Greek in ancient times."

"You could have been really Greek if I'd married the Greek lawyer instead of your father," she said.

"Poor pop. I guess you thought you were taking the easy way out."

"Maybe. The lawyer had sweaty hands and he wanted me to read the Harvard Classics."

Poor mom.

Fran thought of the bizarre title of a book, *Acres of Diamonds*, that her father often mentioned when she was a child. It was something about searching the world over for treasure when, instead, acres of diamonds were lying undiscovered in one's own backyard. Pop liked these easy morals. My philosophy, he called it. After years of belittling his moralities and the collection of diner mats with their homespun messages of "Words to Live By," Fran was ready to accept that they were as true as anything else, and available right there at home. You don't have to seek far, go on world searches, marry exotically, dig and delve, visit shrinks, travel to far peaks, retire to monasteries, sweat in jungles or freeze at the poles — unless you want to, which is all right, too. Of course, there's a catch to simplicity: you have to be ready to know it. It doesn't come with a bullhorn, blaring, *here I am!* You have to know when you're home safe.

More fortunate perhaps, are the Wasps like her brother-in-law Meade who were taught to be on their own early, who were sent off to school to learn independence and Emersonian virtues and became accustomed, thus, to endure stoically their abiding loneliness in the world. More drive of their anguish to propel them; and, will it, nil it, a faith that marked them and made them know who they were.

No matter, Fran thought. I am who I will be.

She and Chessie had refound each other and she would see Chessie through the hard time; she has heard from Dee that the due date for her second child is soon and as for her garden, she said, she is the gardener and the garden is herself; Winnie had found a small gallery to show her work and Fran was still in her turbulent affection. Fran would wait for them to come visit and they will, when they are ready. When they do, she will be whimsical and quote Dr. Johnson about a down-on-his-luck acquaintance who could afford to wash only occasionally: "On clean-shirt day he went abroad, and paid visits."

She would be herself, understand from whom she came, and understand her daughters. On her middle finger, left hand, Fran wore a turquoise ring she had bought when she was nineteen and had told herself, yes, I will write poetry. Her wedding band had gone to the grave with Marco, tossed into his coffin before it closed. What she would have from now on, for as long as there was, would be the ring she gave herself.

In daily life, there were the little gains, the momentary pleasures, as well as the long cool pain which Fran now knew is also a presence to accommodate. She might see a good film, sunsets were frequent enough, she had found an excellent Italian bakery where she bought bread, thinking of her father; she would practice yoga and play tennis, read about Greece, visit Edith. She walked among trees, she felt herself changing, she felt her age, she planned to visit Dee's new child. I write poetry, she told herself; I work at my work. I live alone.

It was both joyful and hard. Like giving birth.

ABOUT THE AUTHOR

Helen Barolini's fiction and non-fiction has created a bridge between the United States, her homeland, and Italy, the ancestral land. Awarded a writing grant from the National Endowment for the Arts for her first novel, *Umbertina*, Barolini is the author of twelve books and many short stories and essays that have been cited in annual editions of BEST AMERICAN ESSAYS. She has received an American Book Award and other honors, has been a Resident fellow at the Rockefeller Foundation's Bellagio Center on Lake Como, and a visiting artist at the American Academy in Rome, an invited writer at Yaddo and the MacDowell colony, a writer in residence at the Mark Twain Quarry Center of Elmira College. Three of her books have appeared in translation in Italy where she has lectured as an invited American author. In 2007 she spoke on her late husband, Antonio Barolini, at a conference in Padua, Italy.

Helen Barolini was born and raised in Syracuse, NY and attended local schools. She attended Wells College, graduated *magna cum laude* from Syracuse University and received a Master's degree from Columbia University. She was an exchange student at the University of London where she studied contemporary English literature, and then traveled in Europe writing "Letters from Abroad" for the Syracuse Herald Journal. Following studies in Italy, she married the late Italian author and journalist Antonio Barolini. In their married life of several moves between Italy and the United States, Helen Barolini became the English translator of Antonio's writings that were published in *The New Yorker*, *Reporter*, and other American publications.

Given the intercultural themes of her work linking her American birth and education with her ancestral Italy, Helen Barolini has participated in international conferences and her work has been the subject of many student theses both here and abroad. She has been honored by MELUS, the Hudson Valley Writers Center, and other organizations for her literary work.

VIA FOLIOS
A refereed book series dedicated to the culture of Italians and Italian Americans.

ERNESTO LIVORNI. *The Fathers' America.* Vol 112 Poetry. $14
MARIO B. MIGNONE. *The Story of My People.* Vol 111 Non-fiction. $17
GEORGE GUIDA. *The Sleeping Gulf.* Vol 110 Poetry. $14
JOEY NICOLETTI. *Reverse Graffiti.* Vol 109 Poetry. $14
GIOSE RIMANELLI. *Il mestiere del furbo.* Vol 108 Criticism. $20
LEWIS TURCO. *The Hero Enkido.* Vol 107 Poetry. $14
AL TACCONELLI. *Perhaps Fly.* Vol 106 Poetry. $14
RACHEL GUIDO DEVRIES. *A Woman Unknown in her Bones.* Vol 105 Poetry. $11
BERNARD BRUNO. *A Tear and a Tear in My Heart.* Vol 104 Non-fiction. $20
FELIX STEFANILE. *Songs of the Sparrow.* Vol 103 Poetry. $30
FRANK POLIZZI. *A New Life with Bianca.* Vol 102 Poetry. $10
GIL FAGIANI. *Stone Walls.* Vol 101 Poetry. $14
LOUISE DESALVO. *Casting Off.* Vol 100 Fiction. $22
MARY JO BONA. *I stop waiting for You.* Vol 99 Poetry. $12
RACHEL GUIDO DEVRIES. *Stati zitt, Josie.* Vol 98 Children's Literature. $8
GRACE CAVALIERI. *The Mandate of Heaven.* Vol 97 Poetry. $14
MARISA FRASCA. *Via incanto.* Vol 96 Poetry. $12
DOUGLAS GLADSTONE. *Carving a Niche for Himself.* Vol 95 History. $12
MARIA TERRONE. *Eye to Eye.* Vol 94 Poetry. $14
CONSTANCE SANCETTA. *Here in Cerchio* Vol 93 Local History. $15
MARIA MAZZIOTTI GILLAN. *Ancestors' Song* Vol 92 Poetry. $14
DARRELL FUSARO. *What if Godzilla Just Wanted a Hug?* Vol ? Essays. $TBA
MICHAEL PARENTI. *Waiting for Yesterday: Pages from a Street Kid's Life.* Vol 90 Memoir. $15
ANNIE LANZILOTTO, *Schistsong*, Vol. 89. Poetry, $15
EMANUEL DI PASQUALE, *Love Lines*, Vol. 88. Poetry, $10
CAROSONE & LOGIUDICE. *Our Naked Lives.* Vol 87 Essays. $15
JAMES PERICONI. *Strangers in a Strange Land: A Survey of Italian-Language American Books.*
    Vol. 86. Book History. $24
DANIELA GIOSEFFI, *Escaping La Vita Della Cucina*, Vol. 85. Essays & Creative Writing. $22
MARIA FAMÀ, *Mystics in the Family*, Vol. 84. Poetry, $10
ROSSANA DEL ZIO, *From Bread and Tomatoes to Zuppa di Pesce "Ciambotto"*, Vol. 83. $15
LORENZO DELBOCA, *Polentoni*, Vol. 82. Italian Studies, $15
SAMUEL GHELLI, *A Reference Grammar*, Vol. 81. Italian Language. $36
ROSS TALARICO, *Sled Run*, Vol. 80. Fiction. $15
FRED MISURELLA, *Only Sons*, Vol. 79. Fiction. $14
FRANK LENTRICCHIA, *The Portable Lentricchia*, Vol. 78. Fiction. $16
RICHARD VETERE, *The Other Colors in a Snow Storm*, Vol. 77. Poetry. $10
GARIBALDI LAPOLLA, *Fire in the Flesh*, Vol. 76 Fiction & Criticism. $25
GEORGE GUIDA, *The Pope Stories*, Vol. 75 Prose. $15
ROBERT VISCUSI, *Ellis Island*, Vol. 74. Poetry. $28
ELENA GIANINI BELOTTI, *The Bitter Taste of Strangers Bread*, Vol. 73, Fiction, $24
PINO APRILE, *Terroni*, Vol. 72, Italian Studies, $20
EMANUEL DI PASQUALE, *Harvest*, Vol. 71, Poetry, $10
ROBERT ZWEIG, *Return to Naples*, Vol. 70, Memoir, $16

Bordighera Press is an imprint of Bordighera, Incorporated, an independently owned not-for-profit scholarly organization that has no legal affiliation with the University of Central Florida or with The John D. Calandra Italian American Institute, Queens College/CUNY.

AIROS & CAPPELLI, *Guido*, Vol. 69, Italian/American Studies, $12
FRED GARDAPHÉ, *Moustache Pete is Dead! Long Live Moustache Pete!*, Vol. 67, Literature/Oral
 History, $12
PAOLO RUFFILLI, *Dark Room/Camera oscura*, Vol. 66, Poetry, $11
HELEN BAROLINI, *Crossing the Alps*, Vol. 65, Fiction, $14
COSMO FERRARA, *Profiles of Italian Americans*, Vol. 64, Italian Americana, $16
GIL FAGIANI, *Chianti in Connecticut*, Vol. 63, Poetry, $10
BASSETTI & D'ACQUINO, *Italic Lessons*, Vol. 62, Italian/American Studies, $10
CAVALIERI & PASCARELLI, Eds., *The Poet's Cookbook*, Vol. 61, Poetry/Recipes, $12
EMANUEL DI PASQUALE, *Siciliana*, Vol. 60, Poetry, $8
NATALIA COSTA, Ed., *Bufalini*, Vol. 59, Poetry. $18.
RICHARD VETERE, *Baroque*, Vol. 58, Fiction. $18.
LEWIS TURCO, *La Famiglia/The Family*, Vol. 57, Memoir, $15
NICK JAMES MILETI, *The Unscrupulous*, Vol. 56, Humanities, $20
·BASSETTI, ACCOLLA, D'AQUINO, *Italici: An Encounter with Piero Bassetti*, Vol. 55, Italian
 Studies, $8
GIOSE RIMANELLI, *The Three-legged One*, Vol. 54, Fiction, $15
CHARLES KLOPP, *Bele Antiche Stòrie*, Vol. 53, Criticism, $25
JOSEPH RICAPITO, *Second Wave*, Vol. 52, Poetry, $12
GARY MORMINO, *Italians in Florida*, Vol. 51, History, $15
GIANFRANCO ANGELUCCI, *Federico F.*, Vol. 50, Fiction, $15
ANTHONY VALERIO, *The Little Sailor*, Vol. 49, Memoir, $9
ROSS TALARICO, *The Reptilian Interludes*, Vol. 48, Poetry, $15
RACHEL GUIDO DE VRIES, *Teeny Tiny Tino's Fishing Story*, Vol. 47, Children's Literature, $6
EMANUEL DI PASQUALE, *Writing Anew*, Vol. 46, Poetry, $15
MARIA FAMÀ, *Looking For Cover*, Vol. 45, Poetry, $12
ANTHONY VALERIO, *Toni Cade Bambara's One Sicilian Night*, Vol. 44, Poetry, $10
EMANUEL CARNEVALI, Dennis Barone, Ed., *Furnished Rooms*, Vol. 43, Poetry, $14
BRENT ADKINS, et al., Ed., *Shifting Borders, Negotiating Places*, Vol. 42, Proceedings, $18
GEORGE GUIDA, *Low Italian*, Vol. 41, Poetry, $11
GARDAPHÈ, GIORDANO, TAMBURRI, *Introducing Italian Americana*, Vol. 40, Italian/American
 Studies, $10
DANIELA GIOSEFFI, *Blood Autumn/Autunno di sangue*, Vol. 39, Poetry, $15/$25
FRED MISURELLA, *Lies to Live by*, Vol. 38, Stories, $15
STEVEN BELLUSCIO, *Constructing a Bibliography*, Vol. 37, Italian Americana, $15
ANTHONY JULIAN TAMBURRI, Ed., *Italian Cultural Studies 2002*, Vol. 36, Essays, $18
BEA TUSIANI, *con amore*, Vol. 35, Memoir, $19
FLAVIA BRIZIO-SKOV, Ed., *Reconstructing Societies in the Aftermath of War*, Vol. 34, History, $30
TAMBURRI, et al., Eds., *Italian Cultural Studies 2001*, Vol. 33, Essays, $18
ELIZABETH G. MESSINA, Ed., *In Our Own Voices*, Vol. 32, Italian/American Studies, $25
STANISLAO G. PUGLIESE, *Desperate Inscriptions*, Vol. 31, History, $12
HOSTERT & TAMBURRI, Eds., *Screening Ethnicity*, Vol. 30, Italian/American Culture, $25
G. PARATI & B. LAWTON, Eds., *Italian Cultural Studies*, Vol. 29, Essays, $18
HELEN BAROLINI, *More Italian Hours*, Vol. 28, Fiction, $16
FRANCO NASI, Ed., *Intorno alla Via Emilia*, Vol. 27, Culture, $16
ARTHUR L. CLEMENTS, *The Book of Madness & Love*, Vol. 26, Poetry, $10
JOHN CASEY, et al., *Imagining Humanity*, Vol. 25, Interdisciplinary Studies, $18
ROBERT LIMA, *Sardinia/Sardegna*, Vol. 24, Poetry, $10
DANIELA GIOSEFFI, *Going On*, Vol. 23, Poetry, $10
ROSS TALARICO, *The Journey Home*, Vol. 22, Poetry, $12

EMANUEL DI PASQUALE, *The Silver Lake Love Poems*, Vol. 21, Poetry, $7

JOSEPH TUSIANI, *Ethnicity*, Vol. 20, Poetry, $12

JENNIFER LAGIER, *Second Class Citizen*, Vol. 19, Poetry, $8

FELIX STEFANILE, *The Country of Absence*, Vol. 18, Poetry, $9

PHILIP CANNISTRARO, *Blackshirts*, Vol. 17, History, $12

LUIGI RUSTICHELLI, Ed., *Seminario sul racconto*, Vol. 16, Narrative, $10

LEWIS TURCO, *Shaking the Family Tree*, Vol. 15, Memoirs, $9

LUIGI RUSTICHELLI, Ed., *Seminario sulla drammaturgia*, Vol. 14, Theater/Essays, $10

FRED GARDAPHÈ, *Moustache Pete is Dead! Long Live Moustache Pete!*, Vol. 13, Oral Literature, $10

JONE GAILLARD CORSI, *Il libretto d'autore*, 1860–1930, Vol. 12, Criticism, $17

HELEN BAROLINI, *Chiaroscuro: Essays of Identity*, Vol. 11, Essays, $15

PICARAZZI & FEINSTEIN, Eds., *An African Harlequin in Milan*, Vol. 10, Theater/Essays, $15

JOSEPH RICAPITO, *Florentine Streets & Other Poems*, Vol. 9, Poetry, $9

FRED MISURELLA, *Short Time*, Vol. 8, Novella, $7

NED CONDINI, *Quartettsatz*, Vol. 7, Poetry, $7

ANTHONY JULIAN TAMBURRI, Ed., *Fuori: Essays by Italian/American Lesbians and Gays*, Vol. 6, Essays, $10

ANTONIO GRAMSCI, P. Verdicchio, Trans. & Intro. , *The Southern Question*, Vol. 5, Social Criticism, $5

DANIELA GIOSEFFI, *Word Wounds & Water Flowers*, Vol. 4, Poetry, $8

WILEY FEINSTEIN, *Humility's Deceit: Calvino Reading Ariosto Reading Calvino*, Vol. 3, Criticism, $10

PAOLO A. GIORDANO, Ed., *Joseph Tusiani: Poet, Translator, Humanist*, Vol. 2, Criticism, $25

ROBERT VISCUSI, *Oration Upon the Most Recent Death of Christopher Columbus*, Vol. 1, Poetry, $3

www.ingramcontent.com/pod-product-compliance
Lightning Source LLC
Chambersburg PA
CBHW072317020726
47501CB00002B/546